"Hold on now. You okay?"

Maybe it was the heat of the day, or the rush of adrenaline. When Griff looked at Juliet, to assure himself that she was all right, his gaze was drawn to her mouth. Such a fascinating mouth. The lips slightly open, round with surprise. Perfectly formed lips just made for kissing.

For the space of a heartbeat he saw her eyes widen, as though she was reading his thoughts. And though he hadn't planned it, and for the life of him he didn't know how it happened, his mouth was on hers.

At first it seemed an innocent mistake. But the moment his lips touched hers, everything changed. He was engulfed in heat. The simple kiss was no longer simple. It had fireworks going off in his brain. A brain that had gone completely blank, except for a wild surge of hot, shocking arousal.

His arms tightened around her as she returned the kiss, and then he could feel himself sinking into her, into the heat...

Raves for R. C. Ryan's Novels

THE MAVERICK OF COPPER CREEK

"Ryan's storytelling is tinged with warmth and down-to-earth grit. Her authentic, distinctive characters will get to the heart of any reader. With a sweet plot infused with family love, a fiery romance, and a bit of mystery, Ryan does not disappoint."

—RT Book Reviews

JAKE

"A must-read...cozy enough to make you want to venture into the wild west and find yourself a cowboy...And if you haven't read a western romance before, R. C. Ryan is where you should start."

—ReviewsbyMolly.com

"Wonderful characters who quickly find a way into your heart...a glorious picture of the west from one of my favorite authors."

—FreshFiction.com

"A heartwarming tale about love, loss, and forgiveness...The characters seemed to spring to life from between the pages."

—SeducedbyaBook.com

JOSH

"There's plenty of hot cowboys, action, and romance in this heady mix of a series that will leave you breathless."
—*Parkersburg (WV) News and Sentinel*

"A powerfully emotional tale that will connect with readers...Love a feel-good cowboy romance with a touch of suspense? Then pick up *Josh*."
—**RomRevToday.com**

"This story is action-packed and fast-moving...A good solid story with fantastic characters and an interesting story line."
—**NightOwlReviews.com**

QUINN

"Ryan takes readers to Big Sky country in a big way with her vivid visual dialogue as she gives us a touching love story with a mystery subplot. The characters, some good and one evil, will stay with you long after the book is closed."
—*RT Book Reviews*

"*Quinn* is a satisfying read. R. C. Ryan is an accomplished and experienced storyteller. And if you enjoy contemporary cowboys in a similar vein to Linda Lael Miller, you'll enjoy this."
—**GoodReads.com**

MONTANA LEGACY

ALSO BY R. C. RYAN

Montana Legacy
Montana Destiny
Montana Glory

Quinn
Josh
Jake

The Maverick of Copper Creek

THE REBEL OF COPPER CREEK

R. C. RYAN

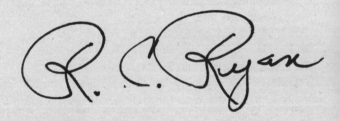

FOREVER

NEW YORK   BOSTON

Copyright © 2015 by Ruth Ryan Langan
Excerpt from *The Legacy of Copper Creek* copyright © 2015 by Ruth Ryan Langan

Forever
Hachette Book Group
1290 Avenue of the Americas
New York, NY 10104

www.HachetteBookGroup.com

Printed in the United States of America

First Edition: January 2015
10 9 8 7 6 5 4 3 2 1

OPM

Forever is an imprint of Grand Central Publishing.
The Forever name and logo are trademarks of Hachette Book Group, Inc.

The Hachette Speakers Bureau provides a wide range of authors for speaking events. To find out more, go to www.hachettespeakersbureau.com or call (866) 376-6591.

The publisher is not responsible for websites (or their content) that are not owned by the publisher.

ATTENTION CORPORATIONS AND ORGANIZATIONS:

Most Hachette Book Group books are available at quantity discounts with bulk purchase for educational, business, or sales promotional use. For information, please call or write:

Special Markets Department, Hachette Book Group
1290 Avenue of the Americas, New York, NY 10104
Telephone: 1-800-222-6747 Fax: 1-800-477-5925

*To my beautiful and talented
daughter-in-law, Randi,
Who uses her skills to teach very
special students.*

And to Tom, my forever love.

THE REBEL OF
COPPER CREEK

PROLOGUE

Billings, Montana—1997

He's trouble."

Twelve-year-old Griff Warren sat hunched in the principal's office, his split lip swollen and bloody, scowling as his mother and Principal Marcone discussed his latest run-in with a classmate.

"Griff gave Jeremy Thornton a bloody nose and a black eye." The principal's voice frosted over. "Jeremy's parents will be sending you the medical bills, Ms. Warren."

Griff's mother held tightly to her handbag as she turned to her son. "Why did you do it?"

"He called me a name."

"What name?"

The boy shook his head, unwilling to say *bastard* in front of his mother. It always hurt her more than him.

She turned to the principal. "Perhaps we could speak more openly if my son could leave your office."

The principal nodded. "Griff. Go to the gym. Maybe

you can work off some of that aggression while I speak with your mother."

Griff rose awkwardly to his feet.

As he crossed to the door, he heard his mother say, in a voice barely above a whisper, "Griff is a good boy."

"Good boys don't react with violence whenever someone angers them." The principal waited a beat before adding, "I really think you ought to consider military school next year, Ms. Warren. Your son needs more discipline than we can offer him."

"Griff is all I have..." His mother turned. Seeing him still in the doorway she frowned. "Go on now, Griff."

He stalked to the gym and tossed aside his backpack before picking up a basketball and hurling it toward the hoop. It dropped cleanly through the net, and he raced up to catch it. In one reflexive movement he hurled it all the way across the floor toward the opposite hoop, where it circled the rim before dropping through the net.

A deep voice from the locker room startled him. "Pretty impressive. Think you can do that again?"

He turned and glared at Mr. Wood, the new coach hired at midseason when old Mr. Harris was forced to take a sick leave. "What do you care?"

The young coach shrugged. "Since you didn't try out for the team, I guess you're not interested in basketball. But I just figured, with all that anger, it might be interesting to see if you can repeat that performance."

"Who says I'm angry?"

"Aren't you?"

Griff tossed the ball as hard as he could, and had the satisfaction of seeing it drop through the net. Working up a full head of steam, he raced to retrieve it before tossing it to the opposite net where, once again, it circled and dropped.

When he retrieved the ball yet again, the young coach walked up beside him. "A dollar says you can't do a repeat of that."

"Make it five bucks."

The coach shook his head. "Two."

Griff heaved the ball and turned away, not even bothering to watch as it swished through the net. With a frown he held out his hand and Mr. Wood dropped two bills in it.

"Can you do it anytime? Or only when you're mad?"

Griff shrugged. "I don't know."

"What's that supposed to mean?"

The boy picked up the ball. "I only play when I'm mad."

"I see. Tell you what." The young coach gave him a long, assessing look. "You come back tomorrow after school and play with the team."

"Why should I?"

"I could say because it's a great stress reliever." The coach grinned. "The truth? Jeremy Thornton wants to be captain. That honor goes to the best player on the team. You know what I've learned?" His voice lowered. "A good, old-fashioned fight may be good for the soul, but there are better ways to exact revenge."

Startled, Griff looked up and saw the glint of unspoken humor in the coach's eyes.

Seeing his mother waiting in the hall, he dropped the ball and picked up his backpack.

As he started away Mr. Wood said, "I heard what Jeremy called you, son. That's some shiner you gave him.

Just remember—there are other ways of winning without resorting to your fists. Sometimes, success can be the sweetest revenge of all."

Something in the quiet way the man spoke to him had Griff's mind working overtime as he followed his mother to the car. He had a whole lot to think about.

Maybe there *was* a better way. Maybe he'd even think about military school for next year. For now, he'd just decided to give basketball a try. Not because he loved the game. But Jeremy did, and he expected to be captain.

For the first time in hours Griff smiled.

It caused his lip to start bleeding again.

He never even noticed the pain.

The Hills of Afghanistan—Winter

Thirty-year-old Capt. Griff Warren tucked the envelope into his back pocket and filled a foam cup with coffee. Spotting a vacant corner of Tango Company Compound, he ambled over, juggling his rifle in one hand, coffee in the other. For Griff, now in his third tour of serving with the marines in Afghanistan, it was second nature to grab these quiet moments when he could, knowing that at any time the stillness of the night could be shattered by a blast of incoming fire.

Dropping into the dirt, he settled his back against the low stone wall and tore open the envelope bearing the name and address of a Montana law firm. After a long drink of steaming coffee, he unfolded a letter from his mother, which, according to the date, would have been written shortly before her death. Her musings, handwritten and often several pages long, were always filled with news of the fickle weather in Montana, drought, range fires, and occasionally the misbehavior of local politicians. Seeing the date at the top of the page, tears sprang to his eyes, and he felt a band tighten around his heart as he realized this would have been her last letter to him. He blinked, expecting more of the same sort of mundane news.

His attention sharpened as he began to read her stunning words.

My dearest Griff,

Please understand that this is the hardest thing I've ever had to write. I know that you gave up asking about your father when you were no more than five or six, after learning that your questions would send me into fits of tears. I saw the way you backed off, keeping your questions to yourself, rather than hurt me. I knew that my silence was driving a wedge between us, but I simply could never bring myself to speak of the man I'd foolishly loved and lost. Now, however, since my doctor has told me to get my affairs in order, my only affair of any importance, my only concern, is you, Griff. You deserve to know the truth.

When I was very young, and enjoying my first teaching assignment in a tiny Montana town called Copper Creek, I met a handsome young rancher who took my breath away. For several weeks we enjoyed a torrid romance, which I foolishly assumed would last a lifetime. Within weeks I heard that his former fiancée had returned from a modeling as-

signment in the South Seas and had agreed to give up her career to become his wife. Shortly after that, I learned I was expecting a baby. Instead of confronting him with what I knew would be unwelcome news at such a time in his life, I chose to remain silent. Instead of renewing my teaching contract, I quietly moved to Billings and made a life for myself and you. Over the years I had many opportunities to marry, but somehow, after that one blazing romance, the prospect of a life with anyone else seemed dull and bland. I decided that my wonderful son and the many students whose lives were touched briefly by me would have to be enough to fill my life.

Though it shamed me to contact your father after all these years, my first duty must be to you. Therefore, my darling Griff, I have sent him the necessary documents to prove the legality of my claim. If you are reading this letter, it means that he and his lawyers are convinced that you are, indeed, his son and heir, and they have included my letter to you in their formal documents as I requested.

Please accept my heartfelt apology for withholding such vital information from you for a lifetime. I have always loved you, Griff. And now, with death at my doorstep, my greatest hope is that you will forgive me and understand that I was doing what I thought best for both of us.

Your loving mother

Shocked to his core, Griff unfolded a second lengthy document, signed, witnessed, and duly registered with the state of Montana, declaring him the legal son and heir of Murdoch "Bear" MacKenzie.

At long last his father had a name. After a lifetime of questions and doubts. After a lifetime of searching the faces of strangers, wondering if the man passing him on the street could be the one. At long last, Griff had his answer:

Murdoch MacKenzie.

The name meant nothing to him. The truth meant everything to him. There really was a man out there somewhere who had learned of a son he'd never met. But he would, by God. As soon as this tour was up, Murdoch MacKenzie would meet the result of a careless, reckless love affair of thirty years ago.

Griff's hand fisted. And then he would do what he'd wanted to do for all these endless, painful years. His blood ran hot with the thought of a knock-down, drag-out bloody fight ending with MacKenzie flat on his back and regretting the day he'd walked away from Melinda Warren without a second thought.

Melinda. The thought of his very private, stoic mother had Griff going still. How she must have suffered for her foolishness. And how she must have loved this man, to walk away with her secret intact rather than intrude on his life.

Griff had never questioned her love for him. But he'd spent an entire childhood wondering about the man who had fathered him. Had he abandoned her because she was pregnant? Had she been the one to flee rather than spend the rest of her life with someone she deemed unworthy?

Now Griff knew otherwise. Though this letter gave a name, there were still too many gaps in his information.

How had Murdoch MacKenzie received this sudden, shocking news? Was he angry? Dismissive?

The fact that his lawyer had forwarded Melinda's last letter, along with legal documents declaring him the son of Murdoch MacKenzie, proved that the man was at least trying to do the honorable thing.

Everything else remained a mystery.

But, Griff vowed, he would have his answers.

After a lifetime, he deserved the truth. All of it, no matter who was hurt by the questions.

"Hey, Captain."

The shout from his buddy Jimmy Gable had him looking over with a blank stare.

"I said, you just got mail, Captain. Me, too."

"Yeah." Griff tucked the letter in his pocket and got to his feet, his mind awhirl with so many jumbled thoughts, he could barely speak.

He'd been home to bury his mother less than a month ago. And now this letter was proof of just what had occupied her mind as she lay dying. Instead of worrying about herself, she'd been more concerned with connecting him with his father. A man he'd never known. A name he'd never heard until now.

Serving in this godforsaken outpost, he'd already learned how crazy life could be. Now he'd just been given proof that life as he knew it had gone completely mad.

CHAPTER ONE

Copper Creek, Montana—Present Day

G et 'im in that chute, Griff."

The cowboy's shrill voice had Griff Warren singling out the next calf from the portable corral and urging it into the narrow passageway toward a branding cradle. At least that was what the wranglers called it. Griff thought it was more like a torture chamber.

Once in there, the headgate slammed shut, the walls of the chute closed in, and the entire cage tipped to hold the calf on its side while Griff's newly discovered half brother Whit MacKenzie pressed a sizzling branding iron to the calf's right hip area.

The entire operation took only a few seconds, and the bawling calf was righted, released, and sent racing toward its mother in a second holding pen, while Griff, amid shouts and catcalls, was forced to prod the next calf toward the same fate.

The process was repeated over and over, for five hot,

sweaty, endless days, until every calf born this spring on the MacKenzie Ranch had been branded with the unique MK on its right rump. Then they were herded by a team of wranglers, or in some cases trucked to the highlands in cattle haulers for a summer-long eating frenzy on the lush grasses that grew in the hills around Copper Creek.

When the last of the calves had met its fate, Whit dropped an arm around Griff's shoulders. "Great job, cowboy. You just had your baptism of fire. And look at you. Still standing."

"Barely." Griff, his shirt so wet it stuck to his skin, eyes red from the dust of frantic cattle, managed a weak grin.

Brady Storm, foreman of the MacKenzie Ranch, offered a handshake. "Welcome to Ranching 101, son. It's hard, dirty work. And not one of us would trade this job for a suit and tie in the city."

Griff shook his head. "Don't tempt me, Brady." He tempered his comments with a sly grin. "At the moment, that almost sounds like heaven."

"Another fine supper, Mad." Griff sat back, sipping coffee. Fresh from the longest shower of his life, he was feeling almost human again.

He'd been living with the MacKenzie family on their ranch since mustering out of the Marine Corps. He'd arrived in time to bury the stranger who had been his father. But though he'd been acknowledged as the son of Bear MacKenzie, he resisted accepting the MacKenzie name, choosing instead to continue using his single mother's last name as it had been recorded on his birth certificate.

"From what Brady told me, son, you deserve a good

meal." Seventy-year-old Maddock MacKenzie, Bear's father and therefore Griff's biological grandfather, was called Mad by all who knew him. The nickname suited him, since his temper was legend in this part of Montana. He seemed especially furious at being confined to a wheelchair since a ranch accident fifteen years earlier. And though he worked hard to hide his frustration for the sake of his family, it showed in the way he often slammed a hand down on the arm of the hated chair. Mad MacKenzie did everything he could to pretend that his life was the same as before, including his absolute refusal to have ramps built in and around the house, which he felt would shout to the world that he was a cripple, a word he detested.

The cantankerous old man winked at Brady Storm. "Brady tells me you've been jumping into ranch chores with both feet. But branding's another thing altogether. For a novice, branding can be pretty grueling, even for those of us who cut our teeth on ranch chores."

"Tell me about it." Whit, twenty-five and the youngest of Bear MacKenzie's three sons, shot a grin at his brother, Ash, who was seated across the table. "The first time Pa took me with him to help with the branding, I was five or six. The wranglers were still branding the old-fashioned way. Wrestling calves to the dirt, holding them down, and driving that hot iron into their rumps. I've never forgotten the smell of burning flesh and the bawling of those calves. I was sick for a week."

"I guess to a kid it's pretty barbaric." Mad polished off the last of his garlic mashed potatoes, one of his favorite side dishes, which he prepared at least once a week.

"Not just to a kid." Willow MacKenzie, mother to Ash

and Whit, turned to her father-in-law. "I may have grown up on a ranch, but I'm still troubled every spring during branding."

"Can't be helped." Mad shared a knowing look with the foreman. "We can tag a cow's ear or implant a chip, but the process our ancestors came up with is still the most efficient. The state of Montana is open range. We've got thousands of acres of rangeland. Those critters can hide in canyons, wander into forests. But the state demands that we register our brand with the state brand office. Not only the brand, but the exact location on each calf. That's why we've got that MK on the right rump of every one of our cattle. It's pretty hard for a thief to explain what he's doing with your property."

Griff shook his head. "All I know is, I'm glad that particular chore is finished for the year. Now I can get back to learning the easy stuff."

"You think tending herds in the high country in blizzards or summer storms is easy? You like mending fences and mucking stalls?" Ash shared a look with the others. "I guess that's what happens when you survive three tours with the marines in Afghanistan. Everything after that is gravy."

The others around the table joined in the laughter.

Myrna Hill, plump housekeeper for the MacKenzie family, set a tray of brownies on the table before passing around hot fudge sundaes. "You have Brenna to thank for the dessert. She drove all the way into Copper Creek, to that cute little shop I's Cream, for Ivy's special chocolate marshmallow walnut ice cream."

Ash nudged his bride, Brenna, seated beside him. "Is this a special occasion?" He put a hand to his heart.

"Don't tell me I've forgotten an anniversary or something already."

"Now you've done it, lad." Mad's Scottish burr thickened along with his laughter. "Don't you know that the first rule of a new husband is to never admit that you've forgotten a special day? You're supposed to just smile and remain silent, and your bride will think you've known about it all along."

"Now you tell me." Ash put his arm around Brenna's shoulders and nuzzled her cheek. "Whatever the occasion, you know I'm happy to be celebrating it with you."

"Uh-huh." With an impish grin Brenna smiled at Myrna, whose cap of white curls bounced with every step she took. "I suppose, if you're feeling guilty enough, I could get a new washer out of this. Or maybe something really big, like a new truck at Orin Tamer's dealership. But the truth is, babe, you haven't forgotten a thing. I just thought you'd want some comfort food after dealing with all that branding for the past week."

"Whew." Across the table, Whit made a big production of wiping imaginary sweat from his brow. "You really ducked a trap this time, bro."

"Yeah." Ash lifted Brenna's hand to his mouth and planted a wet kiss in her palm. "See how she pampers me?"

"Don't be fooled, bro." Whit dug into his sundae. "Our Brenna's smart. That means she'll figure a way to get what she wants even without playing on your guilt."

Brenna dimpled. "Better eat that dessert as fast as you can, or you may find it dumped over your very adorable head, my sweet brother-in-law."

"That's 'bro-in-law' to you, Bren." He held up his now-empty bowl. "And you're too late."

Around the table, the others enjoyed the banter while they finished their desserts.

Afterward, they lounged comfortably, drinking coffee and discussing the week's activities on the thousand-plus acres that made up the mighty MacKenzie ranch.

With the sudden, shocking murder of Bear MacKenzie, the operation of the ranch had fallen to his three sons and his widow, Willow. Since Maddock's accident, he'd merged his ranch with that of his son and had commandeered the kitchen chores, much to Myrna's dismay. Though the two shared some cooking skills, Mad's overbearing personality often drove Myrna to hide out in other parts of the house. But when she did work in the kitchen, she was more than ready to stand up to the old curmudgeon. And though they enjoyed spirited arguments, there was an underlying affection that was obvious to everyone.

Ash turned to his mother. "Any news from Chief Pettigrew on the investigation into Dad's ... death?" As always, the very mention of Bear MacKenzie's murder at the hands of an unknown coward who had shot him with a long-range rifle caused a chilling silence around the table.

Willow shook her head. "As a matter of fact, Ira called this morning just to touch base and let me know he was doing all he could. The state police crime lab has concluded the estimated distance the bullets traveled. That's an important step in the investigation. Once they determine the exact location where the shooter was concealed, they can begin going over the area with a fine-tooth comb. Ira assured me that if even a single thread of evidence exists, they'll find and identify it."

Mad patted his daughter-in-law's hand. "Keep the faith, lass. They'll get the coward who shot Bear."

She nodded. "I know, Mad. But every time I go into town, I can't help thinking that someone smiling at me, talking to me, could be Bear's killer." She shuddered. "I can't bear the thought that such a monster is still walking around, enjoying his life, while Bear is..." She couldn't bring herself to say the word.

Brady Storm, always sensitive to Willow's emotions, quickly changed the subject. "I saw Lance McMillan fly in that sleek new plane. What did he want?"

At the mention of their longtime lawyer's son, who had recently taken over his father's practice, Willow sighed. "I told him his father knew better than to interrupt a rancher at branding time. And without even the courtesy of a phone call. But he said he was on his way up to join his father on a fishing trip in Canada, and it was Mason who'd wanted me to sign some papers."

Mad looked over. "What kind of papers?"

Willow shrugged. "Lance said they were just routine documents needed after the death of a spouse. I told him to leave them for me in the office and I'd read them later, when I have my wits about me."

"Good." Mad nodded his approval. "Mason would have never brought documents for a signature without taking the time to explain them thoroughly."

Willow gave a short laugh. "That's what I said, though in truth I didn't want to give him any more of my time. The irony is, after I took my shower I went to Bear's office to read them, and they weren't there. When I phoned Lance, he said he'd spotted some typos and taken them back to be corrected. He has them with him in Canada.

Now he'll have to bring them to me when he gets back from his fishing trip with Mason."

"So his visit was a waste of time."

"I don't know about Lance's time, but it was certainly a waste of mine."

Willow looked up as Whit clapped a hand on the foreman's back. "How about a beer at Wylie's?"

Brady nodded. "I'm in." He turned to Griff. "You joining us?"

Griff smiled. "Good idea. Willow? Mad? Ready for a night in town?"

Both Willow and Mad shook their heads.

Whit turned to the newlyweds. "Ash and Brenna?"

The two turned to one another, smiled, and shook their heads in unison. Ash spoke for both of them. "Thanks, but we'll pass tonight."

Whit waved a hand toward the others. "What did I tell you? The way those two are looking, I'm betting that before the night's over my big brother will be promising his lady love that new truck she's been mooning over."

"Nobody deserves it more," Ash said, stonefaced.

"Oh, man." Whit turned away with a mock shudder. "Now I really need a beer at Wylie's to wash away the taste of all that sugar."

At that, everyone burst into gales of laughter. Even Myrna joined in as the men made ready to leave for town.

As the others headed outside, Mad snagged Brady's arm.

The foreman turned back with an arched brow. "Something wrong, Mad?"

"I want your take on Griff. How's he working out?"

"Even better than I expected. Oh, he's green. No doubt

about it. But he's a quick study. You show him what to do, he gets it done."

"So he's not just coasting on the fact that he's Bear's other son?"

Brady chuckled. "You know how gossip spreads like a range fire on a ranch of this size. Let one person know something, all of Montana knows it the next day. So the fact that he's Bear's son is no secret around here. But I've never once seen him use it as leverage. He's tough. This is a marine who's seen his share of war. Now, with that life behind him, he's ready for the next stage of his life."

"How about Ash and Whit?" The old man's eyes narrowed. "You see any power plays between them and this newcomer?"

"Not one bit. Even though it's been a bitter pill for them to swallow, finding out their father had another son, they've stepped up to it like men. I haven't seen a trace of jealousy or animosity between them and Griff." The foreman paused. "Bear would be proud of them, Mad. And so should you. Every time I look at Griff I see Bear."

As he walked away, the old man blinked hard against the sudden tears. Damned dust motes. He pulled out his handkerchief and blew his nose before turning his wheelchair toward his suite of rooms down the hallway.

Copper Creek, more than an hour's drive from the ranch, was little more than a main street, with rows of shops and stores, a church, a school, a medical center, and a town hall connected with a jail and a courthouse. The Boxcar Inn was a real boxcar turned into the town's favorite restaurant, and owned by a retired railroad conductor and his wife. It was no competition for Wylie's Saloon, the official watering hole for the surrounding ranchers, who had been drinking with the owner for thirty-plus years. But the food at the Boxcar was a hundred times better than the greasy burgers at Wylie's.

"Hey, Whit. Griff." Nonie Claxton, a waitress at Wylie's Saloon since it first opened, paused while juggling a tray holding half a dozen longnecks. She wiped stringy orange bangs from her eyes as she gave Brady Storm a long, admiring look. "How lucky can a girl get? Three sexy cowboys. Park somewhere, boys, and I'll take your order in a minute."

Seeing no seats left at the bar, they grabbed a table in the middle of the smoky room. Within minutes Nonie returned and set three frosty longnecks in front of them.

Griff nodded toward a noisy table in the corner. "Who're the guys in uniform?"

Nonie glanced toward the assortment of men in wheelchairs, others balancing crutches or canes across their laps. Several wore faded military fatigues. "They call themselves Romeos."

At Griff's arched brow she laughed. "They're all part of the band of veterans who spend time at the Grayson Ranch. It's a take on the owner's name. The widow Grayson. Her name's Juliet. Get it? Romeos? Juliet?" She nodded toward Whit. "Your brother here could probably tell you about the place."

Whit shrugged. "I'm afraid I don't know that much about it, except that when Buddy Grayson's widow came back to Montana to take over the ranch, she offered to turn it into some kind of therapy place for wounded vets."

"How can a ranch be a therapy place?" Brady asked.

Again that shrug as Whit said, "I don't have a clue. I'm thinking it's like a dude ranch. All phony, and not a working wrangler in sight." He turned. "Maybe we ought to ask the Romeos about their Juliet."

Just saying those names had him grinning, and Griff and Brady chuckled at the joke.

A short time later Griff felt a hand on his shoulder and looked up to see a bearded man in a faded denim shirt and torn jeans, seated in a wheelchair and grinning from ear to ear.

"I thought that was you, Captain. What in hell are you doing in Copper Creek?"

It took Griff a moment to place the face, but the gravelly voice was unmistakable. "Jimmy? Jimmy Gable?" He was up and leaning over to grab the bearded man in a bear hug.

When the two had stopping punching one another's shoulders, Griff stood back. "I thought your home was somewhere back East. What are you doing way out here in Montana?"

"Wanted to see how the other half lived." The man chuckled at the look on his old marine buddy's face. "Okay. Truth. After my little...accident..."

He looked down at his empty pants legs before smiling. Griff was forced to fight back a rush of sudden emotion, seeing the young marine who'd always been a whirlwind of activity now confined to a wheelchair.

"...a guy I met at the VA hospital invited me to join a group called the Romeos," Jimmy continued. "They spend a lot of time at some ranch."

"Playing cowboy?" Griff asked drily.

Jimmy shrugged. "Something like that, I guess. And

since that was just about the best excuse I could think of to get away from my doting family, I jumped at the chance."

With a grin, Griff turned to introduce Jimmy to Whit and Brady. After a round of handshakes, Griff took a seat beside the younger man. "I thought you were leaving the Corps when I did."

"I planned on it. I had only another month when my luck ran out."

"How bad is it?"

Jimmy's voice lowered. "I won't be running any marathons." He brightened. "But then, I was never much of a runner anyway. The doctors think I'm a good candidate for prostheses."

"That's great. How long will you have to wait?"

The younger man shrugged. "I'm working with a doctor who is hooking me up with a guy he calls a genius at these things. But it all takes time. And while I'm waiting, I thought I'd take a break from my family. Ever since I got home, they've been all over me. Won't let me do a thing. Running ahead to open doors, picking up anything I drop before I even know I dropped it."

Griff chuckled. "Don't fault them, Jimmy. You know they love you."

"Yeah. And they're smothering me with all that love."

He studied Griff, whose already muscled body was now honed to perfection, his skin tanned from weeks in the hills with the herd, and nodded at his wide-brimmed hat hanging on the back of his chair. "Something tells me you've turned into the real deal. A cowboy."

Griff couldn't stop the grin that spread across his features. "Guilty."

Jimmy nodded toward Whit, seated across the table. "Did I hear you call him your brother?"

Griff chuckled. "You did. And yeah, before you ask, I'm as new at this family thing as I am at being a rancher."

Jimmy looked at Brady, whose handsome, tanned face and white hair, along with a perfectly toned body, made him look like a poster boy for the State of Montana. "And is this your long-lost father?"

That had all of them chuckling.

"Brady is the foreman of my father's ranch."

"Okay." Jimmy rubbed his hands together. "Now tell me about your mysterious father."

With a glance at Whit, Griff was quick to say, "Maybe some other time. Right now, tell me about those Romeos."

"Better than me telling you, why don't you join us?"

Griff shrugged. "Join you for what?"

"A military reunion. We're heading over to the Grayson Ranch tomorrow. Want to join us?"

Griff was already shaking his head. "Maybe, after chores—"

Brady interrupted. "After the week you put in, I think you deserve a day off. Grab it while you have the chance."

Griff looked pleased. "You're sure?"

When Brady gave a quick nod, Griff didn't take any time to consider. "Why not? If it's got something to do with veterans, I'm intrigued. Just tell me where and when."

"We'll be heading over around noon. I'm told it's somewhere out in that vast expanse of wilderness folks around here call a hop, skip, and a jump from town."

Whit was smiling as he added, "I know where it's at.

I'll give you directions before you head out tomorrow, bro."

Jimmy drained his beer. "I'd better get back to my buddies. Nice to meet you fellas. I'll see you tomorrow, Captain. We'll reminisce about the good times we had in the hills of Afghanistan." He turned to Whit and Brady. "That's where the captain got that pretty scar."

The others glanced at the thin white scar that ran from below Griff's ear to disappear below the collar of his shirt.

"An insurgent breached our security while we were all sleeping, and slit the captain's throat. He'd planned on wiping out our entire company with the explosives he was wearing. Though he nearly bled to death, the captain saved our entire company. A grateful military awarded him a Purple Heart. So I have him to thank for still being around."

With a twinkle in his eye Jimmy turned his wheelchair and returned to the table in the corner, where the voices grew louder with each round of longnecks.

Whit narrowed his gaze on Griff. "'Purple Heart'? 'Captain'?"

Griff tipped up his longneck. "Not anymore. Now I'm just a ranch hand learning how to shovel manure."

"And doing a damned fine job," Whit exchanged a look with Brady, who gave a quick shake of his head, discouraging any further questions. It was obvious that Griff was reluctant to talk about himself.

Whit then caught Nonie's eye and lifted his empty bottle. Within minutes she'd brought them another round of drinks, and the talk turned, as always, to the daily grind of running a ranch the size of Rhode Island.

CHAPTER TWO

Summer had settled in to Montana, bringing with it hot, sunny days and warm nights perfumed with bitterroot. The pale pink blossoms covered the hills around the MacKenzie Ranch.

Griff leaned against the sill and stared at the scene outside his window. Everything on this vast ranch seemed more. More space to roam. More cattle than any one man could count.

An eagle soared high above the herds that darkened the landscape. For as far as he could see, this land belonged to the MacKenzie family. His family now. The thought had him frowning. It didn't seem possible. After growing up dreaming about the father he never knew, he'd now acquired a grandfather, two half brothers, and a stepmother who still looked more like the model she'd once been than the rancher's widow she was now.

What was even more impossible to process was the

fact that before his death, Bear MacKenzie had not only accepted the truth that Griff was his son but had included him in his will, leaving a portion of all of this to him if he decided to stay and become a rancher. If Griff chose instead to walk away, he would relinquish his share but would find himself a very rich man.

He shook his head at the absurdity of it all. How could anyone starved for family turn his back on all this for mere money? What Bear had offered, and what Willow MacKenzie had agreed to when she'd learned of her husband's will, was worth so much more than wealth. She and her family had accepted him as one of them.

He'd arrived here an angry, bitter man, war-weary from three tours of duty, expecting to resent the sons who had been privileged to grow up alongside their powerful rancher father. Instead he'd been made welcome, and was learning, by trial and error, to become worthy to be called Bear MacKenzie's other son.

It was proving to be a difficult transition. He'd been a loner all his life. Tough, angry, and always fighting against the rules. Now he'd acquired a big, noisy family that worked together like a well-oiled machine. He found himself working overtime just to keep up, and wondering if he'd ever fit in.

"Hey, bro."

Outside in the hallway, Whit pounded a fist on the closed door as he headed for the stairs. "If you're late for breakfast, I get your steak."

Griff was still buttoning his shirt and tucking it into his jeans as he made a wild dash to the kitchen. "If Mad's making steak and eggs, you'll lose your hand if you even think about touching mine."

The old man looked up from his wheelchair positioned in front of the stove, where he was flipping steaks onto a platter. "Any fighting at the table, the two of you will be shoveling manure for the rest of the day."

"Yes, sir. Thank you, sir." Whit grinned at Griff as the two shared a laugh behind Mad's back.

The old man turned to give them a hairy eyeball. "Don't think I don't know what you're doing. Even grown men can misbehave, given the opportunity. But I do like the way Griff's military attitude is rubbing off on you, lad."

Whit shot his grandfather one of his famous grins. "Now if only my charm with the ladies would rub off on Griff."

At Willow's raised brow, Whit chuckled. "There were half a dozen hot chicks at Wylie's last night, all giving big bro here that 'let's hook up' look, and he spent all his time ignoring them and talking to a bunch of military guys over in the corner."

"Military guys here in Copper Creek?" Intrigued, Willow set down her coffee cup and turned to Griff. "There's no military base for hundreds of miles. What were they doing here?"

He shrugged. "They call themselves Romeos, because they're involved in some kind of therapy at the Grayson Ranch."

"Ah." Willow nodded. "I heard rumors that Buddy's widow was living there, but I hadn't heard any details. What kind of therapy are they involved in?"

Griff shook his head. "I don't have a clue."

Whit chuckled. "Since you're going over there later today, Mom will expect you to have some gossip ready when you get home."

"You're going to the Grayson Ranch?" Willow flushed, knowing she sounded a bit too eager. "It's not gossip. But like everyone around town, I'm curious to know what's going on there."

"We all are." Mad wheeled closer to the table and began filling his plate as Myrna Hill passed around platters of steak and eggs, cinnamon toast, and little pots of jam.

"What's that supposed to mean?" Griff turned to Willow. "Isn't it a working ranch like all the others around here?"

"It was." She tasted her steak and smiled at her father-in-law. "Perfect, Mad. How do you always manage to get my steak exactly the way I like it?"

"I'm a genius in the kitchen." He winked at his youngest grandson. "And don't you ever forget it, laddie."

"As if you'd let me," Whit deadpanned.

Willow turned to Griff and picked up the thread of their conversation. "The Grayson Ranch is fairly small by Montana standards, but it used to be one of the finest around. Buddy Grayson was the last remaining member of his family. When he died, we expected the place to go up for auction. Instead we heard rumors that his widow had shown up to take over the operation."

"Good for her." Griff took his time, savoring every bite of his breakfast. There'd been a time when he had only dreamed of meals like this. Now that it was a reality, he was determined to enjoy every moment. "So Buddy Grayson married a rancher. Did she grow up around here?"

Willow shook her head. "I'm not sure, but I heard she comes from the Midwest."

Griff turned to Whit. "Not exactly ranching country.

But then, I grew up right here in Montana, and the closest I ever came to a working ranch was on a field trip in third grade. We all got to feed some hogs and milk a cow."

"What?" Mad grinned at him over the rim of his cup. "Those teachers didn't have you shoveling manure?"

"They knew better. With a bunch of city kids like us, we'd have been holding our noses and climbing back onto the school bus, ready to hit the road at the first smell."

That had everyone around the table laughing.

Griff returned the conversation to the Grayson Ranch. "So if this guy's widow doesn't know a thing about ranching, how does she expect to keep it going?"

"That's the million-dollar question around these parts." Willow shrugged and turned to Brady Storm. "Have you heard how she's doing?"

He shook his head. "Word is, Jackie Turner, the ranch foreman since old Frank Grayson was running things, retired right after he heard about Buddy's death. His heart was broken, and so was his spirit. Without somebody to ride herd on the few wranglers that are still there, the place is looking pretty shabby these days."

Willow pinned Griff with a look. "As long as you're going there today, I expect a full report."

"Yes, ma'am." He shot her a grin. "Maybe you'd like pictures?"

"Words will be enough. At least for now," she added with a smile. "Your father was a good friend to Frank Grayson. I think he'd be appalled at the thought of all that rich grazing land going to seed."

Mad nodded. "While some outsider turns the place into a spa."

Griff was quick to defend, even though he knew it was useless. "I don't think it's a spa. It's a place for some kind of therapy."

"Massages. Therapy." Mad scowled. "Same thing in my book. It's probably some fancy dude ranch and spa."

Brady pushed away from the table. "I'm heading up to the highlands today. Whit, you coming with me?"

"Yeah." Whit turned to Griff. "I wrote directions to the Grayson Ranch. The far end of their ranch butts up to our north ridge. Take the interstate and you'll be there in an hour. If you use the back roads, it'll take closer to an hour and a half. But if you'd like to take the Cessna, you could be there in no time. I don't know if their airstrip is still in good repair, but I know that Buddy used to keep a single-engine plane in one of the barns."

Mad's head came up sharply. "You licensed to fly in Montana, lad?"

Griff nodded. "After flying with Brady for the past month, I went to the county offices a couple of weeks ago and took the test. The formal documents came in the mail the other day."

The old man gave him a long look. "You're just full of surprises, aren't you?"

Before Griff could respond, Mad's mouth curved into a wide smile. "I see you play your cards close to the vest. Just like your pa."

Griff had no words.

It was, he realized, the highest compliment Maddock MacKenzie could have paid him.

It was a perfect day for flying. The sky was a clear, cloudless blue. A gentle breeze was blowing in from the west.

Griff had thoroughly enjoyed being tutored by Brady, who had regaled him with hair-raising stories of the early years working with Bear MacKenzie. During those long airborne hours, Griff and Brady had formed a bond, discovering that they both preferred reading biographies to fiction, watching suspense movies over outrageous comedies, and both had grown up without a male role model in their lives.

Griff could see, through Brady's eyes, the sort of man Bear MacKenzie had been. Blunt, hardworking, driven to succeed. A tough, demanding taskmaster who saved his harshest criticism for his own sons, believing it was the only way to assure that they would be able to survive in this unforgiving land.

Maybe, Griff thought, he was lucky to have been spared that part of his education. Military school had been bad enough. He'd been forced to fight his way through the first couple of years. Growing up under the thumb of Bear MacKenzie would have been a lot tougher. Which explained why Bear's son, Ash, had left in a rage after a particularly unjustly earned tirade, returning only after his father was dead.

Griff adjusted his sunglasses before peering at the land below. Just as Whit had promised, it was easy to discern where MacKenzie land ended and Grayson land began. The undulating hills of MacKenzie land were black with cattle, with dozens of capable wranglers to tend the herds. The sparsely populated hills to the north were nearly barren, with only the occasional small herd grazing. Griff saw no sign of horsemen below.

As the plane drew near the Grayson house and barns, the distinction was even clearer. There were gaps in large portions of the fences. The roofs of the buildings appeared worn and shabby, the barns were in need of paint, the sprawling house sported a sagging porch, and shingles were missing from the peaked roof.

A couple of trucks and a shiny new bus were parked near one of the barns. After circling the barn and concluding that the asphalt strip looked safe enough, Griff brought the little Cessna in for a smooth landing.

He was smiling as he opened the door and stepped down.

"I hope you have a good explanation for making me wait a whole week."

The feminine voice was low, the words spoken in a tone that left no doubt that the one speaking was furious.

Griff turned to see a slender girl in torn denims and a skinny T-shirt standing just inside the doorway of the barn, hands on her hips, dark eyes barely visible beneath a faded baseball cap, spitting daggers at him.

His own eyes, hidden behind the mirrored sunglasses, widened in surprise.

He stepped closer, his tone lowering to a growl to reveal his annoyance at this unexpected greeting. "I beg your pardon."

"You'd better beg my pardon. You were supposed to be here last Monday. You know how critical your equipment is to my operation. I can't believe I haven't heard a single word from you. And after you promised to repair that lift as soon as possible."

"Look." Griff reached out a hand. "I don't know who you think I am, but—"

She was too busy chastising him to hear a word he said. "Just take a look at the mess I've been dealing with."

She turned away and stalked into the barn, expecting him to follow.

He did, reluctantly, and was forced to remove his glasses in order to let his eyes adjust to the gloomy interior. As he did, he became aware of a cluster of men in wheelchairs, all watching him in sullen silence.

A movement to one side of the barn had him looking over at two little boys, cowering in the corner, staring wide-eyed at him.

Sensing their alarm, he immediately tamped down on the angry words he'd been about to unleash. At least now, having met his new family, he understood why he'd spent a lifetime fighting that hair-trigger temper. It was a legacy from his father and grandfather, and he was determined to curb it before it took control of him.

The girl snapped on a series of lights before pointing to the ceiling. "I hope you've brought all the right parts. I don't want to hear that after keeping me waiting all this time, you can't get this lift up and running properly without another holdup."

Using these moments to cool off, Griff studied the track that had been mounted to the ceiling, forming a circle around the midsection of the barn.

Though his tone was still gruff, the words were muted. "I'm sorry about the missing parts, but you've made a mistake. I'm not the person you were expecting."

She spun around to face him. "Don't tell me..." Her look went from fury to bewilderment. "You're not here from Endicott Medical Supply?"

"I'm here because a marine buddy of mine invited me to stop by and see the Romeos in action today."

For just an instant Griff thought she might break into

tears. Then she composed herself. "Sorry. It's just that I've been waiting…" She turned away and stuck her hands in the pockets of her torn jeans before shaking her head and kicking at a clump of dirt. "It doesn't matter…"

"Captain?" said a voice from the group of men.

Griff turned. "Jimmy."

He watched as one wheelchair separated itself from the others, and Jimmy Gable rolled forward, his face wreathed in smiles.

"Hey. You came to see us. I was engaged in a serious poker hand with my pal Hank when you came in. Since I figured it was the medical supply guy, I wasn't paying attention. Sorry."

"I said I'd come, so here I am." Griff reached down to clap a hand on his friend's back.

Jimmy turned to the young woman. "This is Griff Warren. He and I served in Afghanistan together. He left shortly before me. Who'd have believed we'd run into each other here in the middle of nowhere?"

Griff smiled at the young woman. "I'm from the MacKenzie Ranch just over those hills. I guess I'm looking for your mother."

Her head came up sharply. "My mother?"

"Jimmy said this place belongs to Juliet Grayson."

"I'm Juliet."

At her words he couldn't hide his surprise. "But I thought…" He swallowed and decided to try again. "Sorry. I was expecting someone—"

"—older?" She nodded. Though she was trying for sarcasm, her voice betrayed a deep pain. "I guess 'the widow Grayson' confuses some people." She turned away. "You've come all this way for nothing. I was just telling the Romeos that today's therapy session is cancelled. In fact, it remains cancelled until I get this lift repaired."

Now that Griff had time to study the lift, he understood. "So this device is used to lift the men from their wheelchairs—"

"—into the saddle. Exactly. Until this machine is repaired, everything grinds to a halt."

"And the repairs aren't handled locally?"

She shook her head. "The company is supposed to be flying the parts in from Helena. At least that's what they've been telling me for the past week. But every day they come up with another excuse to put me off. When we spotted your plane, we thought we'd finally had some good luck."

"I'm sorry to get your hopes up and then dash them. How about your wranglers? Any of them know a little about electronics?"

She gave an expressive lift of her shoulders. "I didn't think to ask. The few wranglers left are so overworked, they can barely keep up with the day's chores as it is." She turned to him hopefully. "I don't suppose you...?"

"Sorry. I'm pretty good with my hands. But my specialty is woodworking." He glanced at the ceiling, considering. "Besides, this isn't something that can be done on a ladder. In order to take a look at that track, the company will need to send along a bucket lift for the repairs."

She nodded. "I suppose you're right."

He turned to the two little boys, who hadn't moved. "Yours?"

She beckoned them closer, and when they hurried over

to stand on either side of her, she gathered them close and hugged them.

Getting down on her knees, she said, "This is Ethan and this is Casey."

Griff followed her lead and knelt down so that his eyes were level with theirs. He turned to the older one. "Hey Ethan. How old are you?"

The boy buried his face in his mother's arm.

Jimmy Gable said in an aside, "The kid doesn't speak."

"Efan's six." The younger one held up six fingers. Then he held up three fingers. "And I'm free."

Griff's smile grew at the little boy's attempt to speak clearly. "Three? And your brother is six? I bet you two are a big help to your mom."

The younger one nodded. "Efan can pour the milk on our cereal. Mom won't let me 'cause I spill it." He looked down for a moment while he considered his own skills. "Sometimes I feed the chickens, don't I, Mama?"

"Yes, you do. And you both do a fine job of helping."

When she got to her feet, Griff noticed that Ethan clung tightly to her leg and refused to look up. Little Casey, on the other hand, was content to stand beside her while he studied Griff with a look of open curiosity.

Casey tipped his head back to peer up at him. "Are you a giant?"

That had Griff laughing. "No. Sorry. I'm just a man."

The little boy pointed to the Cessna. "Is that yours?"

"It belongs to my...family." The word still caused him such a jolt, he had to give himself a mental shake.

"My daddy flied planes," Casey said proudly.

"Flew," Juliet corrected.

The little boy nodded. "My daddy flew planes."

"Did you ever get to fly with him?"

The little boy's eyes grew round with surprise. "I wasn't borned yet. But Efan got to watch, didn't you, Efan?"

The older boy buried his face in his mother's frayed denims.

Juliet turned to the group of men, who'd been watching and listening in silence. "I guess you all know what this means. No lift, no riding. I'm sorry. Whenever Endicott gets this up and running, I'll contact Heywood Sperry, and he'll let the rest of you know. But at least we got in a little talk about exercise and nutrition."

As the men began moving toward the bus parked outside, they paused beside Jimmy to introduce themselves to Griff.

"Hank Wheeler." The heavily tattooed man gave a smart salute. "Any friend of Jimmy's is welcome here."

"Stan Novak." Rail-thin, head shaved, the man maneuvered his wheelchair close. "Did four tours of Afghanistan. One too many," he added as he passed with a wave of his hand.

"Billy Joe Harris" came a Southern twang. The young, bearded man had a face so round it resembled a basketball. His stomach protruded over the waist of his tattered shorts. "I saw you with Jimmy last night at Wylie's."

"Yeah. Hey, Billy Joe." Griff shook the man's hand.

A big man in a muscle shirt in red, white, and blue stripes started past Griff in his electric scooter until Jimmy Gable stopped him with a hand to his arm. "Hey, Sperry. Take a minute to say hi to my friend Griff Warren."

From the waist up, the man looked like a bodybuilder,

with bulging muscles in his arms, and a lean, chiseled face that might have been handsome if it weren't for his dark, glaring frown. He looked Griff up and down before dismissing him completely. "What's he doing here, Gable? He doesn't look to me like he needs therapy."

"The captain and I served together in Afghanistan. I invited him to come here and meet my..."

The scooter rolled away before Jimmy had finished talking.

The young veteran shot an embarrassed look at Griff. "Sorry. As you can imagine, there are a lot of angry hotheads in the group."

"No need to explain that to me. I served with guys like that. Remember?"

Jimmy chuckled. "Yeah. I'm just glad you were the one who had to deal with them and not me." Hearing the sound of an engine roaring to life, he turned his wheelchair away and headed out of the barn. "Gotta go. It's Sperry's bus, so he gets to call the shots."

"That's some vehicle. Had to cost a few bucks to install that hydraulic lift."

"Not to mention the custom interior. It's like a rock star's." Jimmy chuckled. "Rumor is that Heywood Sperry's family has millions."

"Nothing like flaunting his wealth."

"Hank Wheeler says Sperry should have painted some rust on the outside as a joke, so folks would feel sorry for us poor old vets." Hearing the roar of an engine, Jimmy started rolling toward the bus. "No time to chat, Captain. Sperry's made it clear that when he says he's leaving, we'd better be aboard or we're left behind."

Griff frowned. "That's not the way of a marine."

"Yeah. But it's Sperry's way. I hope you'll come back another time and watch us in action, Captain."

"I'll try, Jimmy."

Griff stood in the barn watching as Jimmy's wheelchair was boarded onto the bus by way of the hydraulic lift. When all their wheelchairs were secured, the vehicle left in a cloud of dust.

"Can he stay for lunch, Mama?" Casey asked.

Griff turned in time to see the annoyed look on Juliet's face. "I'm sure Griff isn't interested in peanut butter and jelly."

"Is that what we're having?" The little boy brightened. "I like peanut butter and jelly, don't you, Griff?"

Griff thought about the wonderful ranch meals he'd been enjoying since arriving at his father's home. He hadn't once had anything so simple.

If he hurried, he could join Whit and Brady Storm up in the hills for a close-up lesson on wrangling thousands of cattle on the range in the highlands.

Still, the pull of this angry young woman and her two sons was surprisingly strong. And something perverse in his nature had him enjoying the fact that he could annoy her even more.

"That's one of my favorites, Casey." He looked at Juliet. "I'd be happy to stay and have lunch with you."

"Well then. I guess, since you're not my repairman, I have no reason to stay here. We may as well head on up to the house." Looking about as happy as a fox caught in a trap, she turned away and steered her sons from the barn.

CHAPTER THREE

Juliet led the way to the house, with Ethan clinging tightly to her hand and Casey dancing along behind them.

Griff climbed the steps, noting the sagging porch, the dangerous gaps between some of the boards.

Inside, he felt as though he'd stepped back in time. The makeshift mudroom appeared to have been an open breezeway at one time, but it was now closed in by the addition of walls. There were a few hooks along one wall for hats and parkas; a big, stained, cast-iron sink sat in one corner, with a towel slung over the edge.

Juliet pulled off her baseball cap and shook out her damp hair.

Griff was unprepared for the spill of thick auburn tangles that tumbled halfway down her back. It changed her look from waif to woman in the blink of an eye.

She stepped to the sink and scrubbed her hands, while calling over her shoulder, "Boys, you need to wash up while I make your lunch."

When she walked away the two boys scrambled to stand on a wooden step stool and vigorously scrub their hands. Griff followed suit. Both boys looked up as he rolled up his sleeves and began to wash and dry.

"I bet our daddy had hair on his arms like that." Casey turned to Ethan. "Didn't he?"

Ethan shrugged and turned away. But not before taking a long, hard look at Griff's tanned, muscled arms.

Griff toweled dry and followed the boys into the kitchen. The floor was well-worn linoleum. The wooden cabinets wore many layers of peeling paint. In the middle of the big room stood a scarred wooden table and chairs. Though ancient, they appeared sturdy enough.

The two boys took their places at the table.

Griff watched Juliet lay out bread before slathering it with peanut butter and grape jelly. "I'd like to do something to help."

Her voice betrayed her weariness. "Do you know how to make coffee?"

"Sure."

"Coffeemaker is over there." She pointed with her knife. "A package of coffee beans and a grinder are up in that cupboard."

He filled the coffeemaker with water and measured freshly ground coffee into a filter. Soon the kitchen was filled with the most wonderful aroma.

He turned to the two little boys. "Milk?"

"Yes, please." Casey answered for both of them.

He located glasses and poured before setting them down. Both boys had drained them before he could return the milk to the refrigerator.

With a grin he filled them again. "Looks like you two little wranglers are thirsty."

"Mama, he called us wranglers," Casey laughed, while Ethan stared hard at the table.

"Well," Griff said with a wink, "you're living on a ranch. Isn't that what you'll be when you grow up?"

"I want to be a pilot like my daddy," Casey announced.

"What about you, Ethan?"

At Griff's question, the little boy kept his gaze averted.

"He'll be anything 'cept a doctor." Casey turned to his brother. "Isn't that right, Efan?"

The boy nodded and, crossing his arms on the table, buried his face in them.

"Here we are." Juliet set a big plate of sandwiches, cut into quarters, in the middle of the table.

Griff waited until both boys had chosen one before he reached over and helped himself. While he ate he remarked, "This is just the way my mom made these."

Casey's eyes went wide. "You had a mom?"

Griff chuckled. "Everyone has a mom."

The little boy looked at his mother, who took her place at the table beside Griff. "How come he has a mama and you don't?"

"Because my mother died when I was in third grade," she said matter-of-factly.

"I'm sorry to hear that. I guess I was luckier. My mom was around while I was growing up. She died this past year." Hearing the ping of the coffeemaker, indicating it was ready, Griff pushed away from the table and filled two cups. "Cream or sugar?"

Juliet shook her head. "Black, please."

He carried the two cups to the table before sitting. "How about your father?"

Juliet sighed. "He died my first year in college. That's when I dropped out and started working for a cosmetic firm in a department store."

"And my daddy bought perfume, just so he could meet her." Casey was beaming over a story he'd apparently heard often enough to repeat.

"I don't blame your daddy." Griff helped himself to another sandwich.

"Did you buy perfume from the lady you married?"

Griff laughed out loud. "I would, if I was married. And I definitely would if she was as pretty as your mama."

"You think Mama's pretty?"

Ethan glared at his little brother before staring down at the table again.

Griff decided to steer the conversation in a different direction. He turned to Juliet. "Where did you grow up?"

"Chicago." The very word had her smiling.

"You miss it."

She shrugged. "I haven't been back in years."

"I guess with both of your folks gone, there'd be nothing to go back to."

"Oh, I wouldn't say that. There's still the pull of the big city." She sat back and sipped her coffee.

"Any relatives still there?"

She shook her head. "There's just me and my boys." She gave them each an affectionate smile.

"How do you like living on a ranch?"

She thought about it for several seconds before sighing. "I haven't really given it enough time to make a judgment. The last three years have been pretty chaotic.

Buddy's accident, and all the therapy, and then relocating here after..." Her words trailed off.

Griff saw the way the two boys were listening to every word, and decided to keep the conversation light. "So I guess we're all in the same boat. You're new to ranching, and so am I."

"Is your daddy a rancher?" Casey helped himself to another sandwich.

"He was."

"Why didn't you learn from him?"

"I didn't grow up on his ranch. I just came here a few months ago, after he died."

"You don't have a daddy, either?"

"That's right." He sat back and sipped his coffee.

"But it's different for you. 'Cause you're big. Isn't that right, Mama?"

Juliet nodded. "Big people can take care of themselves."

"We're just little." Casey slurped his milk. "We still need help with stuff. Like buttons and zippers and pouring milk."

"Especially pouring milk," Juliet said with a gentle smile.

"But I'm getting better. I only spilled two times this morning." He glanced at his older brother, who was scowling at him, and said quickly, "Well, maybe free times."

"I think you'll get the hang of it," Griff said with another wink. "Besides, with enough cows, you can always get a refill."

That had the little boy giggling.

Juliet set a plate of strawberries and sliced melon in the middle of the table and the boys helped themselves.

When they'd eaten their fill, they pushed away from the table. "Can we go play with our trucks?"

Juliet nodded. "For a little while. When I've finished cleaning up here we'll head upstairs to get you both ready for your naps."

Casey glanced at Griff. "Want to see our trucks?"

"I'd love to. But first I'll help your mom with the dishes."

"There's no need..."

He waved aside her objection. "It'll take half the time if we both work. Besides, you fed me." He popped another strawberry in his mouth before stacking the plates and carrying them to the kitchen counter. "After that excellent PB and J, it's the least I can do."

She nodded. "All right."

While the two little boys raced from the room, Juliet filled the sink with hot, sudsy water and began to wash. "There are towels in that drawer."

He followed her direction and began to dry, afterward returning the dishes to their proper cupboards.

She raised a brow. "How did you know where to store them?"

"I saw you remove them before we ate."

"You're pretty observant."

He shrugged. "I had no choice. Besides the fact that my mother was a stern teacher, I was a marine. You pay attention. You adapt if you want to survive."

"Good life lessons." Juliet sighed. "I hope I can instill some of that in my boys."

"Give them time. They're little."

"Yeah. I'm trying to learn patience."

Griff laughed. "I'd bet good money that every mother says that. But especially mothers of little boys."

"They do try my patience."

"You strike me as a patient woman."

He was standing so close, she could feel the heat of his body. He had a way of staring at her so directly, it was unnerving. "You mean after that scene in the barn, when I practically attacked you?"

His smile was quick and easy. And sexy as hell. "Okay. We'll forget about that. It was a natural mistake. I was talking about the fact that you want to work with a bunch of wounded vets. I'd say that takes patience."

Another sigh, before she moved a little away, hoping to catch her breath. This man made it hard to breathe. "More than you can imagine." She drained the water. "Want to see their trucks?"

"Sure." He followed her through the doorway and down a hallway to a big room. Like the kitchen, the floor and furnishings looked old and worn. But with sunlight streaming in the windows, and the two little boys kneeling on the floor and moving an array of toy trucks and farm implements around the chair legs, it had a cozy feeling to it.

"Look, Griff," Casey called. "I'm hauling cattle." He opened the back end of a cattle-hauling truck to reveal a dozen or more metal cows. "Mama said these belonged to my daddy."

Griff examined one of the metal trucks. "And probably his daddy before him. These are really old."

"And solid, thank heaven," Juliet added. "They'd have to be, to survive several generations of little boys."

"Want to play?" Casey asked.

Before Griff could respond, Juliet shook her head. "Maybe another time. Right now, you and Ethan are heading upstairs for a much-needed nap."

"Aw, Mom."

Even though Casey was rubbing his eyes, practically asleep on the floor, he made a weak protest before following his mother to the doorway. There he turned to Griff. "Will you stay 'til I wake up, so I can watch you fly away?"

Griff glanced at Juliet, standing behind her two sons. She gave a quick shake of her head.

He managed a smile. "Sorry, little wrangler. Not today. But maybe I'll fly over again another time and let you sit in the cockpit."

"Oh boy. Tomorrow?"

Griff was about to say no, but when he saw the pleading look in the little boy's eyes, he didn't have the heart. "Okay. Tomorrow."

At his words, Casey made a fist pump before racing up the stairs behind his mother and brother.

Halfway up, Juliet turned. "I'll be right back. Ethan and Casey, say good-bye."

"Bye, Griff," Casey called for both of them. Ethan merely paused and shot a quick look at Griff before hurrying away.

Alone in the old parlor, Griff picked up one of the metal toys, an ancient tractor, and turned it over and over in his hands. Still holding it, he crossed to the fireplace to study the framed photographs on the mantel. Judging by the hair and clothing, some of them dated back a hundred years or more. Several generations of Graysons, he imagined. His interest was caught by a wedding picture of a handsome, dark-haired groom in navy dress whites, and Juliet in a lacey white gown and veil. Despite the stiff, formal pose, there was a hint of laughter dancing in their eyes.

He lifted the picture from its resting place and turned toward the window for a closer look.

"Weren't we a pair?"

The voice from the doorway had him looking up in surprise before he started toward the mantel. "Sorry. I didn't mean to—"

"It's all right. I stare at it sometimes, late at night, just to remind myself that I was ever that young and innocent." She walked over to take it from his hand. "That was when I was silly enough to believe in happily-ever-after." She pointed to a second picture of a beaming couple. The man's arm was around the shoulder of a very young Juliet, holding Ethan with a look of such love, it seemed to fill the entire frame. "Buddy and I had just celebrated the fact that we were having another baby. Buddy was sure it would be a girl. I told him I was just as positive it was a boy. And then..."

She returned the photograph to its place on the mantel.

"How did he die?"

She kept her back to him. "An engine malfunction on a routine training mission. He made certain that his crew was clear. When he realized that the plane was too close to a playground full of children, he opted to stay with it and do his best to minimize the damage on the ground."

"So he died a hero."

"He didn't die." She turned. "Though he lost both legs and sustained severe burns over half his body, he survived. Barely. For another seven months."

Griff knew, by the pain in her voice, in her eyes, what that survival had cost them both. He could only imagine the pain, the turmoil, and the feeling of hopelessness and despair as she watched the man she loved suffer and die a slow, agonizing death.

Though he knew his words were inadequate, he was quick to say, "I'm sorry."

She lowered her head, avoiding his eyes. "I don't mean to be rude, but I really need to take advantage of their nap time to get some household chores done. Then I can take them with me while I tackle the outside chores."

"I understand." He followed her to the door. "I hope it's okay if I fly back tomorrow and let Casey sit in the cockpit."

"You don't have to do that."

"I gave him my word." And Griff knew from a lifetime of experience how much a promise to a fatherless little boy could mean. Whether it was made by a compassionate teacher or a comrade-in-arms, a promise was an unbroken bond.

There was a weariness in her tone. "You're under no obligation. You won't be the first to disappoint him. Nor the last."

"I said I would, and I intend to do it, as long as it's all right with you. Maybe I'll get here in time to see you get those parts from Endicott Medical Supply."

"Endicott." The very name had her temper returning. "All right. Suit yourself." She was frowning as he offered his handshake.

When his big palm closed around hers, he absorbed a sudden rush of heat. His eyes met hers, and he saw the way they widened for one brief moment before she lowered her lashes.

He cleared his throat. "Thanks again for lunch. It's

been too long since I've had peanut butter and jelly. It brought back a lot of memories."

"You're welcome." The look in her eyes didn't match her words as she jerked her hand away. It was obvious that she didn't like being touched as she took a quick step back, eager to break contact.

At the sudden movement, her foot encountered something hard and slippery. Before she knew what was happening, she lost her balance and was stumbling backward.

In the blink of an eye Griff's big hands were at her shoulders, keeping her from falling. "Hold on now. You okay?" Instinctively he gathered her close. So close, her breasts were flattened against his chest and her thighs were pressed firmly to his.

Maybe it was the heat of the day, or the rush of adrenaline. Whatever the reason, sweat pooled between his shoulder blades and trickled down his back. When he looked at her, to assure himself that she was all right, his gaze was drawn to her mouth. Such a fascinating mouth. The lips slightly open, round with surprise. Perfectly formed lips just made for kissing.

For the space of a heartbeat he saw her eyes widen, as though she was reading his thoughts. And though he hadn't planned it, and for the life of him he didn't know how it happened, his mouth was on hers.

At first it seemed an innocent mistake. But the moment his lips touched hers, everything changed. He was engulfed in heat. The simple kiss was no longer simple. It had fireworks going off in his brain. A brain that had gone completely blank, except for a wild surge of hot, shocking arousal.

His arms tightened around her as she returned the kiss,

and then he could feel himself sinking into her, into the heat...

"How dare you!" Her words were followed by a sharp, stinging slap across his face as she pushed free of his arms and jerked backward.

Once again her foot encountered whatever had caused her to stumble the first time, and she was forced to grab hold of his arm before staring down at the floor.

Beneath her foot was one of the metal trucks.

Though his mind was still fogged, Griff managed to bend and retrieve it. When he glanced at her, he realized that she was close to tears.

Sadness?

Anger? Or something else entirely?

"Look. I'm sorry..."

"You should be. I didn't invite that kiss."

"No, ma'am. You didn't."

"I know what men think. They think, because I'm alone now, that I'm some kind of love-starved, easy mark. Poor little widow Juliet Grayson. She'll be so grateful for some crumbs of affection."

"I wouldn't...I didn't..." He stopped himself in mid-sentence. He really had no defense for his action, and anything he said now would only make things worse, since her temper was beginning to grow into a full-blown rage.

Carefully banking the fire raging inside, he softened his tone. "I don't know what came over me. But you're right. I was out of line."

He handed her the metal toy before turning away. Even that brief contact sent a sizzle of heat along his arm.

Though it took all his willpower, he walked the entire distance to the Cessna without once looking back.

CHAPTER FOUR

Griff made a careful preflight check before climbing into the Cessna and flipping on the instruments.

He allowed himself a glance at the old ranch house and saw, framed in the upper window, the figure of Casey. The little boy lifted a hand and Griff returned his wave before moving the throttle forward, sending the plane surging along the little strip of asphalt.

As always, Griff felt a quick rush of excitement as the plane lifted free of the earth. But there was something else lifting his spirits. The sight of that little guy framed in the window. Despite all that had gone wrong in his young life, he was so innocent. So trusting.

Once in the air Griff circled the house and, seeing Casey still at the window, dipped his wings and waved a hand before heading toward home.

When he'd reached a comfortable altitude, he allowed his thoughts to drift back to Juliet Grayson.

What the hell had happened back there?

One minute he was just being gallant, and keeping her safe from a nasty fall. The next instant his mouth was on hers. It wasn't even much of a kiss. Hell, he'd kissed dozens of women with a lot more passion. But never, never had he felt that kind of reaction from a simple contact.

One kiss and his blood had been so hot, he'd been on fire. One kiss and his mind had been wiped clean of everything except her. Her taste. Her body, pressed to his. Such a slender body. No wonder he'd mistaken her for a girl. But once in his arms she'd been all woman.

Even now he was achingly aware of the way those small, soft curves had fit so perfectly against him.

She'd tasted of peanut butter and desire. And right now, he couldn't think of a more potent combination.

He knew he'd crossed a line from that first moment. But though dozens of alarm bells had gone off, the blood had already left his brain and rushed to his loins, creating a fire that had him trembling.

She'd had every right to be upset. A woman alone, with two little boys depending on her, had to take extra care to insure her safety. Still, her reaction seemed over the top. Judging from the fire in her words, there was more going on here than mere resentment from his kiss.

It had seemed to him that she hadn't so much resented it as feared it. But why? What would make a grown woman afraid of a mere kiss?

Maybe she'd had to fend off unwanted advances in the past. Or maybe she was feeling guilty for kissing him back. But why?

Not his business, he reminded himself. If he hadn't

made a rash promise to fly back and allow Casey to sit in the plane, he wouldn't ever have to see Juliet Grayson again.

He'd given his word to a lonely little boy. A boy who had touched his heart. Maybe, he thought, because he'd once been that boy.

Then he thought about Ethan. Looking back at his childhood, he'd been much more like the angry, silent older brother than happy, outgoing little Casey.

He'd grown up resenting all the classmates who'd had their fathers at their games to cheer them on and celebrate their wins. And he'd resented his mother for not understanding when he'd resorted to his fists, believing that a father would have known exactly what to say to an angry, confused boy.

Ethan and Casey had a lifetime of moving forward without the solid comfort of a man to lean on.

There was no doubt about it. Those two fatherless little boys had found his weakness and had shot an arrow straight through his heart.

So, too, had their mother.

Juliet tossed and turned in her bed, frustrated at the way her mind refused to shut down for the night. Though she was exhausted beyond belief after a day of never-ending chores, she couldn't find escape in sleep.

Not that she'd expected to. Not after that little scene with Griff Warren.

It was only a kiss. Hadn't she told herself that a hundred times or more? What was the harm of a simple kiss between a man and a woman?

She slid out of bed and drew on a robe before padding

down the stairs to the kitchen. Turning on the light, she went through the motions of grinding coffee beans and filling the coffeemaker with water. A short time later she poured a steaming cup and sat at the old table.

She crossed her arms over her chest, thinking about lunch. It had been such a long time since peanut butter and jelly sandwiches with her boys had been anything other than routine. But Casey had become absolutely animated in Griff's presence. And though Ethan had remained silent and distant, she'd seen him watching Griff when he thought no one was looking.

She supposed, for two little boys starved for the company of a man, this had been a feast. In truth, it had been pleasant for her, too. She couldn't recall the last time a man had offered to make coffee or help with the cleanup. Such little things, but they made her feel... special.

Why did he have to spoil it by kissing her?

Now she had all these emotions churning inside.

She pushed away from the table and walked to the window. The midnight sky was black velvet. The stars were so big, so bright here in Montana, they looked more like theatre props. Everything here was so big, so vast, so... overwhelming.

That was how she was feeling now. Overwhelmed. This huge ranch, needing more than she could possibly give. This strange new life, alone with two little boys, needing more from her than she felt capable of giving. And her promise to Buddy, to do something for his pals who'd survived.

How was she supposed to do all this when she felt absolutely drained? Running on empty.

She was giving serious thought to going back to

Chicago with her boys. At least there she wouldn't be a fish out of water. She could get a job. Enroll the boys in day care. But the thought of raising Buddy's boys anywhere but here, on the land four generations of Graysons had called home, seemed a betrayal to his memory.

Betrayal.

She shivered and turned away from the window, pacing the length of the kitchen and back. That was what it all came down to. She was trapped here by a promise to a man who was gone now, a man she'd loved more than her own life. And because of that love, she was furious with Griff for kissing her. How could she claim to love Buddy and still feel what she'd felt when Griff's mouth had touched hers?

She'd been shaken to her very soul. And still was, if truth be told. All she had to do was think about the way his lips felt on hers, and she was aroused all over again.

When she'd slapped his face and looked into his eyes, she'd seen something so rare, it had left her trembling.

Not lust, as she'd expected. But rather, simple honesty.

Looking back, it seemed to be just as he'd tried to explain. It had simply happened. And if she hadn't reacted with all that drama, that would have been the end of it.

It shamed her to admit that her anger had been a cover for her true emotion. In truth, she'd been so caught up in his kiss she'd wanted it to go on and on.

There had been such strength in him. His arm, when she'd reached for it to steady herself, had rippled with muscles. His chest, when she'd been nearly crushed against it, had been a wall of muscle. But it was more than physical strength. There was a strength of character, a goodness in him, as well. A tenderness that had touched something in her soul. And that she couldn't allow.

She didn't want him coming back here to keep a promise to Casey. She didn't want him anywhere near her sons or near her. Especially near her.

She didn't want to get to know Griff Warren. She didn't want to like him, or care for him, or, worse, kiss him ever again.

Because she knew in her heart that though she'd evaded all men since losing Buddy, this man wasn't like the others.

This man, with his soulful eyes and simple goodness, could get to her. And that could lead only to heartbreak.

"Hey, Griff." Ash and Brenna, who seemed constantly joined at the hip since their marriage, walked into the kitchen arm in arm. Ash helped himself to a biscuit cooling atop the counter, ignoring the hairy eyeball from his grandfather, who was busy flipping eggs in a sizzling skillet.

"I see your wife didn't feed you again this morning," the old man barked.

"Why bother, when we can finish our chores and still make it here in time for chow?"

That had Griff grinning from ear to ear. "Why don't you two just move back into your old rooms? Then you can enjoy Mad's great cooking for every meal."

Ash winked at his wife. "I love my family. And I'd love to ease our workload. But there's something to be said for having some privacy."

Brenna kissed Ash's cheek and stole a piece of his biscuit out of his hand.

Whit and Brady, just back from the hills, strolled into

the mudroom and washed before taking their places at the table.

Willow, following behind, kissed her sons and Brenna before helping herself to a cup of coffee. Ash held out chairs for his mother and Brenna, then settled himself between them. He glanced across the table at Griff. "Why weren't you up in the hills with Whit and Brady?"

"I took the day off yesterday to fly over to the Grayson Ranch."

Willow set aside her cup. "I expect a full report on what's going on over there."

"The rumor in town is the widow Grayson is in over her head." Ash accepted a platter of eggs and sausage from Myrna. He held it while his wife and mother filled their plates before helping himself.

"I'm not interested in rumors." Willow looked at Griff. "You saw for yourself. What's going on?"

Griff took his time filling his plate and holding it for Mad before passing it to Whit and Brady. "The ranch is in pretty bad shape. I didn't see any wranglers around, although Mrs. Grayson said there were a few who were overworked."

"And underpaid, I'm guessing." Mad dug into his breakfast, and the others did the same.

"How about the Romeos?" Whit asked around a mouthful of biscuit.

"She had to send them home. Equipment failure." Griff accepted another cup of coffee from Myrna, who circled the table filling cups before taking her place beside Mad.

"So you missed the chance to see your buddies," Whit remarked. "Looks like you flew all the way over there for nothing."

"The Romeos were there when I got there. Apparently she does some lectures about exercise and nutrition, but that's about it when the equipment is down. I couldn't blame them for being disappointed. One of them, a guy named Sperry who is the apparent leader, was steamed."

"So the whole day was a waste."

Griff shook his head. "It wasn't a total washout. I had lunch with two great guys."

"Military?"

"More like junior grade. Extremely junior. Ethan and Casey. One is six, the other three. Or as Casey said, 'free.'" The very word had Griff chuckling.

"Buddy's sons?" Willow exchanged a glance with her father-in-law. "I'd heard there were two boys, but I didn't realize they were so young. Buddy Grayson's only been dead for—"

"—three years, I guess." Griff met her look. "Casey was born after his father died. Ethan would have been three."

"Oh, that poor woman." Willow set aside her coffee. "I can't imagine being left all alone to raise two little boys. How do you think she's getting along, Griff?"

He took his time setting aside his fork and picking up his cup. "I think she's having a rough time of it. Imagine inheriting a ranch when you've never even been on one before. And doing it without any help."

Mad shook his head. "She ought to just put it up for auction and walk away."

"Where would she go?" Griff met his grandfather's look. "She has no family left in Chicago. She wants her sons to grow up on their father's ranch. And from the looks of it, it's falling into more disrepair with every day they stay there."

Brady Storm broke the silence. "When old Jackie Turner was running things over there, he kept his wranglers hopping. He used to brag that every man in his employ could do the work of five men."

Griff turned to Brady. "Know where I could find him?"

"I heard he went to live with his daughter. She has a little spread a couple of miles past town. I could give you directions to her place."

Before Griff could respond, Mad made a sound of annoyance. "Jackie Turner has to be older than me. How can you expect him to up and leave his own kin to clean up a mess somewhere else?"

Griff said softly, "I'll take those directions. No harm in asking. All he can say is no."

Around the table the others fell silent. Griff could sense that they all felt he was being foolish or stubborn for even considering the idea of following up on an old man who had once been the Grayson Ranch foreman.

But he didn't see any other course of action. And as he looked around at his new family, he realized he came by both his foolishness and his stubborn streak naturally.

The thought had him actually smiling as he thanked Mad and Myrna for the great meal. "I'll be flying to the Grayson Ranch later today."

Mad looked up. "Again? What for?"

"I promised a 'free-year-old tenderfoot' I'd be back to let him sit at the controls of the plane." He got up and started toward the back door.

"Where're you headed now?" the old man called.

"Time to meet Jackie Turner. If I'm going to face defeat, I'd rather it be sooner than later."

CHAPTER FIVE

Griff followed Brady's directions and left the main highway to turn onto a gravel road. It seemed to stretch for a mile or more before coming up over a rise to reveal a modest ranch house and several barns and outbuildings. Everything sparkled under a fresh coat of paint, including the fence around the horse barn, where several mares and their young looked as if they'd been posed for pictures in a catalog.

As soon as Griff's truck came to a halt outside the main barn, a figure stepped out to peer at him.

The man was thin and wiry, standing no more than five and a half feet tall. His legs were so bowed, he could easily fit a giant beach ball between them with room to spare. He wore faded denims, a plaid shirt with the sleeves rolled above his elbows, and a wide-brimmed hat. Beneath the hat was a weathered face and blackbird eyes that widened as Griff stepped out of his vehicle.

"Creepers! You've got to be..." The old man swallowed. "Bear MacKenzie's other son. You're the spitting image of him."

Since arriving in Copper Creek, Griff had become accustomed to this reaction. People stared at him as if seeing a ghost. And then, as recognition dawned, they would call him "Bear's other son." Never "bastard" or "illegitimate." They were too polite for that.

The sting of those words had long ago been erased. Now, they were as acceptable as any other greeting.

"Yes, sir. My name is Griff Warren."

"Your mama's name?"

"That's right. I came looking for Jackie Turner. I guess that'd be you."

"It is."

The two shook hands.

"What can I do for you, son?"

"I paid a call on the Grayson Ranch yesterday. I know you used to be foreman there, and I wondered if you'd consider lending a hand to it again."

That black, penetrating stare was like a laser. "The young widow send you?"

"No, sir. She doesn't know I'm here. But the place needs a steady hand."

"What's that to you?"

What indeed? The old man's question had him searching his mind for something that could possibly explain his sudden interest. "I don't know the Grayson family. I never met Buddy. But I served in the Marine Corps, and I'd like to do something to help a military family in need."

Jackie Turner seemed to mull that for some time before saying, "Come on up to the house. We'll have some coffee and talk."

Griff studied the ground below, enjoying the sight of vast hillsides dotted with cattle.

The same question returned to his mind time and again. What kind of man had his father been, to turn this forbidding land into his own little kingdom? If even half the stories about Bear MacKenzie were true, he'd been larger than life, tough, demanding, arrogant, and driven. A man determined to take the legacy of his own father, Mad, and grow it into the stuff of legend.

Griff pondered how much of those qualities he'd inherited from his father and grandfather. Was he driven to succeed? Was that what had kept him alive while under enemy fire? And what of the famous MacKenzie temper? As a boy, he'd always been fighting, much to his mild-mannered mother's despair. In military school he'd learned to channel that anger into a useful tool to become a platoon leader as well as place at the top of his class by the time he'd graduated. Later, facing combat, the combination of quick temper and quick thinking had held him in good stead during the most deadly operations.

Today, knowing what to watch for as the plane's shadow crossed from MacKenzie land to Grayson land, the change in the landscape wasn't nearly as sudden and shocking. Instead of herds, there were small clusters of cattle spread out over barren hillsides. Instead of the occasional bunkhouse, there were a few deserted, windowless range shacks that appeared to offer shelter only to wild creatures.

As the plane circled the Grayson ranch house and

barns, the neglect became even more obvious. A rusted truck was parked behind the horse barn, where several nervous mares began circling the corral at the drone of the plane's engines.

Juliet and her two sons stepped out of the larger cow barn to watch as the little Cessna began its descent. After a smooth landing, it rolled along the asphalt strip.

By the time Griff stepped from the plane, little Casey was racing toward him. "You came back," he cried.

"I promised, didn't I?"

"Yeah." He turned to call to his mother, "Look, Mama. It's Griff. He came back."

"I see him." She approached more slowly, holding on to Ethan's hand.

Griff smiled. "'Afternoon, Juliet. Hey, Ethan." He glanced around, for the first time seeing the cluster of men in wheelchairs and on crutches inside the dimly lit barn.

He strode across the distance separating them and clapped a hand on Jimmy Gable's back, grinning at the look of his old military buddy. Now, with that shaggy beard and faded denims, he looked nothing like the buttoned-down kid Griff had known in Afghanistan. "I take it your equipment hasn't been repaired yet?"

Before Jimmy could shake his head, Juliet's quick frown was answer enough. She turned to the veterans. "I guess it was too much to hope this plane was from Endicott."

"Told you." Stan Novak, his skinny body looking frail in an oversized sweatshirt with the sleeves cut off, nodded toward the others. "Looks like another wasted day."

Heywood Sperry spun his scooter around to give the

man a withering look. "You shut that mouth. Even without riding a horse, you're on a ranch. We did stretching
exercises." He shot a sly smile at Juliet. "But it would
have been a hell of a lot better if we'd get back and arm
massages."

Juliet's tone was controlled. "I've told you, Heywood,
I'm not licensed as a physical therapist yet. I never completed all the classes. And I did caution you to check with
me before driving the men all this way."

His voice was a low growl of fury. "What else do we
have to do but sit around all day waiting for you to call?"

"Having a pity party, Sperry?" Happy as a puppy at the
sight of his old friend, Jimmy Gable was grinning as he
pointed toward their bus. "I know what I want to do. Let's
get back to town. I heard there was a hot gin rummy tournament going on all day at Wylie's."

Sperry glared at him. "You'd rather play cards than be
on a ranch?"

"And do what?" Jimmy demanded. "If we're not going
to ride horses and make like cowboys, what's the point?"

Spurred on by his comments, the others began nodding
and murmuring among themselves.

"Come on, Sperry," one of the men called. "You
dragged us out here for nothing. Now it's time to get
moving."

As they began filing out of the barn and using the hydraulic lift to enter the bus, Heywood Sperry remained
behind, staring from Juliet to Griff and back again. "What
about him?" He jerked a shoulder in Griff's direction.

Before Juliet could say a word, Griff nodded toward
the pitchfork in her hand. "I guess I'm in time to help
with some chores."

She started to protest. "There's no need. The boys and I have it under control."

"That's right." Casey stood in front of Griff. "Mama's shoveling and we're spreading clean straw." He pointed toward the bus. "And those men said they were our..." He turned to his mother for help with the word.

"...our audience," she said.

"That's a lot of work. Maybe, instead of watching, I could lend a hand, and we can have it done in half the time."

Sperry crossed his arms over his chest. "I don't care who does the ranch chores. What I'd like to know is when I can count on having that lift repaired so we can get on with the therapy we're paying for. Why don't you ask the cowboy here to fix the lift first?"

"That's not fair, Heywood," Juliet said, quick to defend Griff. "Repairing the equipment isn't his job."

"Neither is this ranch. Why is he sticking his nose in our business?"

Juliet looked shocked. "It's my business, not yours. Why are you being so rude?"

He scowled at Griff. "Maybe because you're so freaking determined to defend this guy."

Before she could respond, little Casey began dancing up and down, staring hungrily at the Cessna, gleaming in the sunlight. "What about your airplane? You said I could sit in it."

The muscled veteran fixed Griff with a look of fury. "Using the kid to get to his mother?"

Ignoring Sperry, Juliet pointed to her son's dung-covered boots. "Casey Grayson, you're not going anywhere near that plane until you've had a chance to clean up after your chores."

The little boy looked so sad that Griff knelt in front of him. "How about finishing chores first? Then a tour of my plane will be our reward later. Okay, little wrangler?"

"Okay." Casey sounded subdued.

When the men on board the bus began honking the horn and shouting for Sperry to join them, he swore and huffed out a breath before turning his scooter toward the door. Without a word he left.

Griff watched him leave before turning to Juliet. "How did you happen to hook up with them?"

She gave a quick shake of her head. "I started studying therapy when Buddy was in the hospital. When I came here, I hoped to put what I'd learned to good use. Heywood Sperry contacted me out of the blue and said he'd heard that I was offering veterans an alternate form of therapy. I have to say I was surprised, since very few people had heard about me, but when he told me he had a group of veterans willing to pay a great deal of money to visit a working ranch on a regular basis, I couldn't refuse. Especially since I remember how desperate Buddy was to get away from a hospital setting and back to his ranch. He would have given anything to be able to get therapy at a ranch, surrounded by the sights and sounds and smells he'd always known. These veterans have already given so much. They deserve whatever comfort they can get."

He gave her an admiring look. "I guess that explains how you manage to cope with more than just their physical wounds. You're one of them."

"My troubles are nothing compared to theirs. They have a right to be angry. Their lives as they once knew them are gone."

Searching on a shelf, Griff located a pair of men's rubber boots, which he swapped for his leather boots. He helped himself to a pair of well-worn leather gloves and reached for a pitchfork hanging on a hook by the door.

By the time he was ready to work, the bus had left, with Heywood Sperry in the driver's seat.

While Griff began cleaning a stall, Casey climbed up on the wood railing to watch. "Wow. You do that a lot faster than Mama."

"That's because I'm bigger."

"When I get big as you, Mama won't ever have to work again."

Though he didn't say a word, Ethan climbed up beside his little brother and watched in silence.

"That's a nice thought, Casey. And generous. But there's nothing wrong with hard work. Everybody does it." Griff tossed a load of dung-filled straw into a wagon.

"But Mama never stops. Isn't that right, Efan?"

The older boy ignored him and studied Griff as he bent to his chore.

Griff finished cleaning the stall and moved on to the next, aware that the two boys had hopped down from their perch and were now spreading straw over the floor of the freshly cleaned stall.

As soon as he finished, little Casey climbed another rail and leaned his chin on his hands, watching every move Griff made.

"Did you and Mama fight yesterday?"

Griff saw Juliet's head come up sharply in the other stall.

"No." He bent to his work. "Why?"

The little boy shrugged. "Mama didn't sleep last night."

"And how would you know that?"

"I smelled coffee 'fore I fell back asleep. Whenever Mama can't sleep, she goes downstairs and makes coffee."

"Well, if she's done this before, how can you think it's my fault?"

"'Cause Mama was sad when we got up from our nap. Isn't that right, Efan?"

His brother kicked at some straw.

"Maybe your mama was sad because the parts for her ceiling lift didn't come. And without them, she can't help all those vets."

"Is that why you were sad, Mama?"

Juliet tossed a load of dung-filled straw into the wagon and frowned. "That's as good a reason as any."

"And you're not mad at Griff?"

She gritted her teeth before snapping, "No."

Griff couldn't hold back the grin. "Well, that's a relief, isn't it, little wrangler?"

"Yeah." Casey returned his smile. "Mama, can Griff stay for lunch?"

"He just got here. I'm sure he's not hungry."

The little boy swiveled his head. "Are you, Griff?"

"Not yet. But maybe by the time I've finished these chores, I'll manage to work up an appetite."

"Mama's making grilled cheese. Is that okay?"

"That's better than okay. I love grilled cheese almost as much as I do peanut butter and jelly."

"Hear that, Mama? Griff loves grilled cheese sandwiches."

Juliet held her tongue, though Griff could tell it cost her. That only had his smile widening as he moved on to another stall. It gave him a measure of satisfaction to know, thanks to Casey's remarks, that Juliet had been as unnerved by yesterday's scene as he'd been.

An hour later Juliet announced abruptly, "As long as you three have this under control, I'll head up to the house and get lunch started."

Griff and the two boys were so engrossed in their work, they didn't answer.

Just as Juliet set aside her pitchfork, a voice from the doorway of the barn had her pausing.

"Well, well. Mrs. Grayson. You're looking mighty hot and sweaty. Care to cool off down at the creek with me?"

Her voice was pure ice. "What are you doing here, Mitch?"

"Cooper sent me to pick up the stake truck and drive it up to the herd."

She planted her hands on her hips. "Funny. I don't see any truck in here."

His voice lowered to a seductive purr. "I figured I'd check and see how you're doing." He started toward her. "Hell, Cooper can wait. I've always got time for a damsel in distress. Especially one who's all alone and in need of my special brand of...comfort."

She grabbed up her pitchfork. "You take another step and it'll be the last you ever take."

He threw back his head and laughed. "I hope you've got an army to back you up."

Griff stepped from his stall, his own pitchfork held loosely in his hand, to face a lanky, muscled cowboy in a sweat-stained shirt and faded denims. "How about a marine?"

The wrangler's eyes went wide as he looked from Juliet to Griff.

Stuffing his hands in his pockets, he backed away. "Guess I'll get that truck." He shot her a parting sneer. "I'll let you get back to your—" he paused and glowered at Griff for emphasis before swiveling his head toward Juliet "—chores, Mrs. Grayson, if that's what they're called these days."

Griff crossed the distance to stand beside Juliet. Together they watched as the man climbed into a rusted stake truck and drove it across the hills.

Knowing two little boys were watching and listening, he said softly, "You okay?"

"I'm fine. Thanks." She set aside the pitchfork and sucked in a deep breath before starting away. "Lunch in half an hour."

Ethan raced to catch up with her. When he caught her hand she paused to look down at him before the two of them crossed the distance from the barn to the house.

Griff returned to his work. Casey sat on the top rail of the stall.

"You know who that wrangler was, son?"

The little boy frowned. "His name is Mitch."

"One of your mama's wranglers?"

The boy nodded. "Uh-huh." A moment later he added, "He has mean eyes."

Griff stored that thought away. He hadn't had time to see Mitch's eyes, but his sarcastic words to Juliet left no doubt as to his intentions.

When the last stall had been cleaned, Griff hung the pitchfork on a hook and exchanged the work boots for his own. With Casey dancing along beside him, keeping up a steady stream of chatter, he made his way to the house.

They paused at the big sink in the mudroom to roll their sleeves and wash before stepping into the kitchen. The table was set with glasses of milk and a platter of sliced tomatoes and cucumbers in the center.

Juliet called over her shoulder, "Your sense of timing is amazing. Lunch is ready."

Casey climbed up beside his brother. "Griff said he didn't even have to look at his watch. He could smell the grilled cheese all the way to the barn." He turned to the man, who was busy filling two mugs with coffee. "Could you really? Or were you just teasing?"

"Now what do you think, little wrangler?"

The boy's smile lit up the room. "I think I smelled grilled cheese, too."

"There you are." Griff set down the two mugs and turned to Juliet. "Can I help with anything?"

"Let's see." She set down a plate of sandwiches cut into triangles and watched as her boys helped themselves. "Where to begin? There's the equipment, of course, which Endicott will probably never repair. Then there's the truck in the other barn that won't start. A tractor that's down. A group of wranglers who've been up in the hills for weeks with the herd, and will be here in the next few days expecting to be paid so they can go into town and drink away their paychecks. Is that enough?"

Griff heard the frustration in her tone and decided to keep things light. Though his heart went out to her, he knew her sons were listening to every word between them.

"More than. But I was talking about helping you with lunch." He reached for a sandwich and bit into it before giving a sigh of satisfaction. "Looks like you didn't need my help with these. Could there be anything better than a perfectly melted grilled cheese sandwich?"

"Did your mama make them just like this?" Casey wiped a milk mustache on his sleeve.

"She did. She knew that next to peanut butter and jelly, these were my favorites."

Casey took another bite of his sandwich and turned to Ethan. "Griff went to army school."

"Military school," Griff corrected.

Juliet looked over. "Why military school?"

"Like you, my mom was a single mom. By the time I was eleven or twelve, I was a handful. The principal at my middle school didn't give her much choice. He suggested I might need more discipline than regular school could offer. I think what he was really saying was they didn't want me back."

Juliet said in a matter-of-fact tone, "So you were trouble."

"Yeah. You could say that."

She eyed him over the rim of her cup. "I think maybe you're still trouble. So, how did you take to the sudden change in your life in a tough military school?"

He shrugged. "I sorted things out. And one day I realized I could adapt, or I'd be out of options."

"What are options?" Casey asked.

"Choices. In life we make choices." To prove his point, Griff nibbled his sandwich. "I can eat or go hungry." He winked and speared a slice of tomato. "I can eat my veggies, or somebody else will eat them all and I'll have to do without."

The little boy imitated him, helping himself to a tomato slice and several cucumber slices. "Me, too." He turned to his mother with a look of surprise. "Hey, these are good."

"That's what I've been trying to tell you for weeks."

The boy polished off his vegetables and helped himself to more.

As he did, Griff winked at Juliet. "Options, Casey. Now you're sorting them out for yourself."

"I am?" The little boy looked pleased before turning to his brother. "You should eat these. They're really good."

Ethan continued nibbling on his sandwich.

Casey fidgeted with energy. "You said after lunch Griff could let me sit in his airplane." He nudged Ethan. "Want to come with us?"

The boy looked away.

To Griff, Casey said, "Efan's afraid of airplanes, 'cause our daddy's crashed. Isn't that right, Mama?"

"Yes." The single word was said softly.

"But your airplane can't crash 'cause it's on the ground."

"That's right. And that's where it's going to stay until you get tired of being in it."

"I'm never getting tired."

The little boy was so earnest, Griff had to fight to hold back the smile that tugged at his lips.

Casey looked over at his mother. "Can me and Griff go now?"

"It's 'Griff and I,'" she corrected.

"You're coming, too?" His eyes went wide. "Oh boy."

Juliet couldn't hold back her explosion of laughter. With a shake of her head she muttered, "I give up. Yes, I'm coming along. And I think maybe even Ethan will want to sit inside for a moment, as long as the plane isn't leaving the ground."

CHAPTER SIX

"Can we go to the airplane now, Mama? Pleeeease?" Casey drew out the word until Griff had to turn away to keep from laughing.

"All right." She pushed away from the table. "You go along, and I'll join you when I've cleaned up here."

"That's not the military way. First rule. Never leave anyone behind." Griff winked at the two little boys. "We'll all clean up the kitchen. Then we'll all go together to the plane."

Though Casey's little frown revealed his disappointment, he was too excited to refuse. "Okay. I'll carry the plates to the sink."

"Maybe you'd better let Ethan carry them," Juliet said. "And you can handle the napkins."

"Okay."

While the boys cleared the table, Juliet filled the sink with hot water and began to wash. Griff stepped up beside her, drying the dishes and setting them in the cupboards. Each time he reached above her head, she seemed to get very still and watchful.

It was impossible not to notice his body, so close to hers. The ripple of muscles with each movement he made had her throat going dry. She could still feel the power, the strength in him, when he'd held her and kissed her. But despite his strength, there had been such control. It was something she admired in a man. But it wasn't admiration she was feeling at the moment. Right now, with him reaching above her head to deposit a platter, it was something far different. She could almost feel the heat. The fire. The hot, burning rush she'd experienced in his arms.

She drained the water and turned away, annoyed at the direction of her thoughts. She was here in Buddy's family home, sharing chores with his sons, and it seemed somehow disloyal to be thinking about another man.

Within minutes Griff draped the damp towel over the edge of the clean sink.

"Okay, little wranglers. Let's go take a look at the plane."

Casey flew out the door ahead of everyone. Griff moved along at a leisurely pace. Ethan walked beside his mother, looking more like he was going to a trial than a treat.

Juliet studied the way Griff moved. Smooth, sleek, like a panther. He had a quiet way about him. Like a man trained to watch and listen. A marine, who'd seen plenty of combat. It had showed in the way he'd stepped quietly out of that stall to face down Mitch.

Mitch. She would have to tell Cooper to fire him. At

first it had been merely snide insinuations. But he was growing bolder. She liked to think she could handle him, but it had been extremely satisfying to watch the way he'd run when he realized Griff had her back.

Griff. What was she going to do about him?

She found herself admiring the view of those broad shoulders. Those strong arms. That trim, fit body.

She'd actually felt a little thrill shoot through her when he'd raised his arms above her head to stow some dishes. She'd found herself thinking about those arms gathering her close, holding her against that hard, muscled chest.

She must be a glutton for punishment. Why else would she tempt herself with such thoughts?

When they reached the little Cessna, Griff opened the door before lifting Casey up and into the small space.

He turned to Ethan. "Want to look around inside, or would you rather stay on the ground?"

The little boy shrugged before lifting his arms.

Griff easily lifted him up and settled him beside Casey in the pilot's seat before turning to Juliet. "It's a tight fit, but there's room."

She accepted his hand. Such a big, work-worn hand. He settled her in the copilot seat before crouching behind them, between the seats.

"What's this?" Casey already had his chubby little fingers poking at the controls and dials.

Griff took his time giving a name to every dial and button and control, and explaining what it did. Though Casey did all the asking, Ethan gradually reached out to tentatively touch some of the controls.

Within a short time Casey was making little engine

noises in his throat, and it was obvious that he was mentally high in the air, flying the plane.

When Juliet glanced at Griff, he winked and smiled. The sight of it did strange things to her insides. It was impossible for her to keep from returning that smile. But even as she smiled, she felt a quick stab of pain at the thought that Buddy should have been the one showing his sons the inside of a plane.

They stayed for nearly an hour while Casey asked a million questions. Each time, Griff patiently answered, even when the same question had been repeated a dozen times or more.

"How do you know when you're high enough?"

"That dial there. It tells you."

"How do you know how fast you're going?"

"This dial."

"What if you go too high?"

"This sounds an alarm."

"What if your motor stops?"

"You get it started."

"What if it won't start?"

Griff chuckled. "You'd better be wearing a parachute."

"Have you ever jumped from an airplane?"

Griff shook his head. "I got ready to jump a time or two, but I never had to."

Finally, Casey seemed to have run out of questions and energy.

As the silence grew, Juliet touched a hand to his arm. "I think it's time for a nap now."

"Not yet, Mama." Even as he said it, his eyes looked heavy.

"Come on, little wrangler." Griff stepped down from

the plane and assisted Juliet, then Ethan, and finally Casey.

As the little boy was lifted down, he wrapped his arms around Griff's neck and held on.

Seeing it, Juliet felt a swift stab of pain. It broke her heart to know that her youngest son had never been held by his own father.

She lifted her arms. "I'll take him."

"That's all right." Griff nodded toward Ethan. "You take your big guy and I'll take your little one."

With Juliet holding Ethan's hand, Griff followed, with Casey in his arms.

Once in the house Juliet turned, expecting Griff to relinquish his hold on the little boy. Instead he shook his head. "I'm not sure, but I think he's asleep."

He turned, giving Juliet a chance to see Casey's face, tucked into the hollow of his shoulder.

Juliet nodded. "Sound asleep."

"You lead the way, and I'll carry him to his bed."

Upstairs, Juliet turned down the covers and Griff deposited the sleeping boy on the bed. Juliet removed his shoes and tucked the blanket around him before turning to Ethan, who had climbed in on the other side.

Juliet bent to him. With a few whispered words and kisses, she covered him before turning away. At the door, both Griff and Juliet gave a last look at the two boys before she pulled the door closed.

Once downstairs, she turned. "Thank you. This has been quite a day for both of..."

She looked up sharply at a knock on the door. Seeing a stranger on the porch, she kept a firm grasp on the door as she opened it just a little. "Yes? Can I help you?"

"Juliet Grayson?"

"Yes."

"I'm Jackie Turner."

"Turner? The former foreman here?"

"That's right, ma'am." Jackie whipped off his hat in a courtly gesture. Seeing Griff behind her he said, "Hey, Griff. After our little talk, I decided to drive out here and see for myself. Ma'am, I wonder if you might be interested in having me take a look at how things are going."

"You talked with...Griff?" She swallowed her surprise. "I'm sorry, Mr. Turner. I can't afford to pay for any more help."

"I haven't said anything about pay, ma'am. Maybe you could think of me as an old family friend who'd like to look out for your interest here."

"But I..." She bit her lip before saying, "Why don't you come in?"

"Thank you." He stepped inside the kitchen and glanced around with a smile. "Creepers. I've been in this room a hundred times or more. I'm glad to see it hasn't changed."

"I know it's old..."

"I'm not talking about the way it looks, ma'am. I'm talking about the way it feels. This place has always had a feeling of home. A feeling of family and love. I'm glad to see that's still here."

"Thank you, Mr. Turner."

"I answer to Jackie, ma'am. Just Jackie."

"And I'm Juliet." She turned toward the stove. "There's coffee. Would you like some?"

"I've never refused a cup of coffee, Juliet."

She turned to Griff and he nodded.

She filled three mugs and carried them to the table. "Cream or sugar?"

"None for me." Jackie sat and took a long drink before setting the mug down and meeting Juliet's look. "How many wranglers do you have right now?"

She shrugged. "Six. I had five, but Randy Cooper said it wasn't enough."

"Cooper's a good worker. Is he in charge now?"

She nodded.

"Is he out in the barns?"

"The entire crew is up in the hills with the herd."

The old man cleared his throat. "I've known most of the wranglers around these parts for years. I know the steady ones, and those I wouldn't put much faith in. If you don't mind, I'd like to take a ride up there, just to see for myself how they're doing."

"It's a long way to the highlands."

He smiled. "I'd know a thing or two about that. Been riding these hills since I was a pup. Since your crew isn't expecting me, I'll get a pretty good idea of how things are being run." He pushed away from the table. "I'll stop back to report to you tomorrow."

She gave a long, deep sigh as she followed him to the door. "I can't tell you how much I appreciate what you're doing, Mr....Jackie."

"Don't thank me yet, Juliet. You may not like what I have to say when I get back."

"At least I'll have the advice of an expert."

He shook her hand before looking past her to Griff and giving a nod of his head. "Good seeing you, son."

Juliet waited until he drove away before turning. Her voice turned frosty. "Was there some reason why you didn't bother to mention the fact that you'd paid a call on Jackie Turner?"

"The opportunity just didn't come up. But I'd have gotten around to it sooner or later."

"Sooner would have been nice. Why are you making my business your business?"

He picked up his empty cup and deposited it in the sink, along with Jackie's. When he turned, there was a look in his eyes that had her throat going dry.

"I've been asking myself that same question."

When he took a step toward her, she thought about backing up. Then she thought better of it and held her ground.

He caught a strand of her hair that had fallen over one eye and tucked it behind her ear. It was a strangely intimate gesture that had her chin coming up even as color flooded her face.

He stared down into her eyes and she felt the heat of his touch all the way to her toes.

His gaze burned over her mouth and she knew, in that instant, that he wanted to kiss her.

Even more, she wanted him to.

Instead, he very deliberately lowered his hand to his side before turning away.

He walked to the back door and opened it. With his hand on the door he said, "I know I overstepped my bounds. And I don't have any good reason why." His tone hardened as he turned to her. "Now that Jackie's on board, you'll be in good hands. I won't be bothering you again."

"I didn't mean—" She saw the way his brow shot up.

She forced herself to meet his stern look. "Could we start over?" Before he could say a word she went on in a rush. "Let me just say this and get it over with. Thank you for standing by me today when Mitch got out of hand."

"About Mitch." His tone lowered. "Do you feel safe with him around?"

She gripped her hands together. "Not really. But I keep Buddy's rifle in a locked cabinet in the den."

"That may give you some peace of mind, but that cow boy didn't look like the type to wait around while you unlock some doors and load a weapon."

She flushed. "It's the best I can do. I have my sons to think about. I can't keep loaded weapons around for them to find."

"True. But you don't want them witnessing another scene like the one Mitch created today in the barn."

"I know."

When he said nothing more she added, "And though I don't care much for surprises, I want to thank you for talking to Jackie Turner. I never would have had the courage to call him, even though Buddy thought the world of him. I have no idea how I'll pay him, but I'm grateful for anything he can do to help me."

When he remained silent she added, "And I'm sorry for the way I behaved yesterday when you—" she sighed and plowed ahead "—when you kissed me. I wasn't so much mad at you as mad at myself."

"What's that supposed to mean?"

"I haven't felt like a woman in a long time now. I guess, between raising two sons alone and trying to salvage a dying ranch, I've forgotten what it feels like to be..." she shrugged "...kissable."

His smile was quick and unexpected. "Oh, no doubt about it. You're kissable."

She gave a self-conscious laugh. "I wasn't fishing for compliments." She chewed her lower lip. "I'm not doing this well, but what I'm trying to say is, I have deliberately cultivated a reputation for being an ice maiden. I may have lost my husband, but in my heart, I still love him. There isn't room in my life for a man." She exhaled. "There. Now that I've said it, I hope you understand."

"Got it." He gave her a long look before opening the door and stepping out onto the porch. "If you need anything, call me."

"How will I reach you?"

He arched a brow. "Got a cell phone?"

She lifted one out of her shirt pocket.

He gave her his number and watched as she added it to her directory.

"If there's ever trouble. If you're worried about anything at all, you call me any time of the day or night and I'll be here."

She had no doubt he meant it. "Thank you, Griff."

She remained in the doorway and watched as he made his way toward the plane parked on the strip of asphalt. Though she felt a pang of regret, she knew she'd done the right thing by telling Griff exactly how she felt. Buddy might be gone, but he was still alive in her heart. And there was no room for any other man in her life.

She stayed where she was until the little Cessna was airborne.

Then, with a thoughtful look, she squared her shoulders and began moving through another round of endless chores.

CHAPTER SEVEN

W ell, look who's here." Nonie Claxton sidled up beside Griff and winked at Whit and Brady, who trailed behind him. "You sexy things have just lifted this tired old soul considerably." She pointed to an empty table near the back of the room. "Park it and I'll be right over to take your order."

"Just a round of longnecks," Whit called. "Cold and frosty."

"You got 'em."

She walked away to see to another table and returned a short time later with a full tray of longnecks.

When she left, Griff nodded toward a table of rowdy cowboys across the room. "Either of you know that wrangler called Mitch?"

Brady took a long pull of beer. "Mitch Cord. I think he's been fired from every ranch from here to Wyoming."

"Fired? Why?"

"For one thing, he's got more mouth than muscle. For another, he just can't be trusted."

Griff's eyes narrowed. "He's working at the Grayson Ranch now."

"I'm sorry to hear that." Brady shot a glance at the others drinking with Mitch. "Maybe they all work there. Recognize any of them?"

Griff shook his head. "I've never met any of the wranglers. Except Mitch. He showed up at the barn today and made some pretty crude comments to his boss."

"I'm not surprised." Brady took another drink. "But I am surprised that the widow Grayson would keep him on."

"Not for long, I'm thinking." Griff watched as the table of cowboys ordered another round.

An hour later, the roar of voices in Wylie's had reached a fever pitch.

Brady sat back. "I'm ready to head on home." He glanced at Whit and Griff, who had met him in town. "You two coming?"

The three shoved away from the table. Griff reached into the pocket of his jeans and dropped a tip on Nonie's tray.

As he turned, he heard a familiar voice saying, "…take that bet. Twenty says I'll have her purring like a kitten."

"Not a chance." Several of the cowboys seated at Mitch's table shared a laugh. "They don't call her the ice queen for nothing."

"That's just 'cause she hasn't been lucky enough to taste my magic potion. I'm telling you. By this time tomorrow night, that frigid widow will be putty in my hands."

Griff continued on past the table, aware that the boastful cowboy hadn't even noticed him.

Outside, as Whit started to climb into the passenger side of their ranch truck, Griff put a hand on Brady's arm. "Would you mind driving Whit back?"

"Sure thing." Brady gave him a long look. "Where are you going?"

Griff glanced skyward, at the full moon, and then over at the truckload of rowdy cowboys climbing into a convoy of trucks and heading toward the highway. "It looks like a good night for a long drive in the country."

Whit circled around the truck. "Look. I heard what that loudmouth said. But it's just the liquor talking. Halfway home, he'll be sleeping it off."

"And if he's not?" Griff's voice was soft enough, but both Brady and Whit heard the edge of steel.

Whit glanced at Brady before turning to Griff. "I'll come with you."

Griff shook his head. "After the day you put in, you need to sleep. I'll handle this."

Brady reached into his truck and removed a rifle. "Take this along. It's a good companion on a long drive."

Griff weighed it in his hand before stowing it on a rack behind the seat. "Thanks."

Whit scrolled through his cell phone until he came to the number he was searching for. "Put this on speed dial."

Griff copied the number. When he looked up with a questioning frown, Whit grinned. "Police Chief Ira Pettigrew. A good guy to know."

As he stepped into the truck, Whit slapped his arm. "Just remember, bro. If you need me, I've got your back."

"I'll remember."

Griff pulled away. In his rearview mirror he watched as Brady and Whit headed away from the interstate and turned toward home.

Home. He had already begun thinking of the MacKenzie Ranch as home.

He switched on the radio and listened to Carrie Underwood sing about dealing with a guy who did her wrong. It had him smiling as he thought about the way Juliet had stood up to Mitch in the barn.

Yeah, he thought with a grin. She'd scratch a cheater's car. Or scratch his eyes out. And she probably wouldn't need any help doing it. But he had to make the long drive anyway. He knew there'd be no sleep for him until he had satisfied himself that she was safe.

Griff drove along the gravel road. Up ahead, the big ranch house was in darkness. A good sign, he thought. If all the lights had been blazing, he'd have speeded up. But now, seeing the curtain of darkness, he felt relief pour through him.

He cut the lights, so he wouldn't wake Juliet or the boys. There was no sense causing them alarm.

It was probably just as Whit had predicted. The drunken cowboys were already sleeping it off, and Mitch along with them.

He glanced toward the barn, expecting to see the trucks. Rolling down his window, he heard the faint hum of engines, and he could see headlights moving along a hillside toward the highlands. Two rusted trucks remained. One was idling.

Parking his truck alongside the others, he peered inside the truck with its engine idling, expecting to see someone asleep. Finding it empty, he felt the hair at the back of his neck prickling. He took up the rifle and made his way under cover of darkness toward the house. He wouldn't wake Juliet. He would just walk the perimeter of the house to assure himself that Mitch wasn't hanging around.

He was halfway there when he realized the back door was standing wide open.

Drawing near he heard Juliet's voice: "...kind of trouble?"

"An accident." Mitch's voice sounded extremely agitated. "Cooper said I should come and get you."

Griff stood in the shadows. By the glare of the overhead light in the mudroom he could see Juliet clearly, her hair disheveled, wearing a baggy T-shirt that fell to her knees.

"But what can I do? Why didn't Cooper phone the police?"

"You'll have to ask Cooper. Come on. Let's get moving."

"I can't just leave with you. I have two little boys asleep upstairs."

"You said yourself they're sleeping. I'll have you back before morning."

"How do you know that? What if we have to haul the accident victims all the way to town?"

"We'll stop here and pick up the kids. Come on. You're wasting time."

Juliet dug in her heels. "You go ahead. I'll put my boys in the back of the truck and drive myself to the hills."

"You won't know where to find us."

Her voice turned to ice. "I'll call Cooper and have him

direct me to the camp. But right now, I need you to leave so I can go upstairs and deal with my boys."

Mitch made a sound that could have been a laugh or a groan of frustration as he kicked the door shut. "You're not going to make this easy for me, are you? You're just too damned smart for your own good."

Her head came up sharply. Her eyes narrowed on him. "What are you—?"

He snaked out a hand and caught her by the wrist. "You look mighty fetching in that getup, ma'am." He dragged her close. "You'll look even better in nothing at all."

Before he could say more, the back door was kicked open and Griff"'s voice, deadly soft, was the only sound. "Step away from the lady, or you're a dead man. You have five seconds to live."

"Who do you think—?" Mitch spun around.

He took in the sight of Griff standing in the open doorway, eyes hard as granite, rifle aimed directly at Mitch's head.

The wrangler shot a look at Juliet. "So. It's like that, is it? I can't wait to spread the word around town that the MacKenzie bastard's a new boarder at the widow Grayson's ranch."

Griff never raised his voice. It was still little more than a whisper. But every word cut razor-sharp. "You had to the count of five. Now you're down to four. Want to try for three?"

Mitch's furious reaction was to press one beefy arm around Juliet's throat and twist around to face Griff, holding her firmly against him as a shield. "You wouldn't want to shoot the wrong one now, would you?"

Griff's words remained deadly soft. "When I take aim I never hit the wrong target, whether it's an enemy in combat or an ordinary scumbag. Now you have two seconds left."

Juliet dug her elbow into Mitch's midsection at the same moment that she planted her heel in his groin with as much force as she could muster.

Stunned, he released his hold on her.

Griff used that moment to haul her behind him before taking careful aim.

Mitch lifted his hands in a gesture of defeat. "Hold on. You can't kill an unarmed man."

"I can and will if you're still here in one second. It'd be justice for what you planned on doing to the lady."

At Griff's words, Mitch raced past him and dashed out into the darkness.

In that same instant Griff saw all the color drain from Juliet's face as she sagged against the edge of the table.

Instead of giving chase as he'd planned, he gathered her into his arms. When she went limp, he scooped her up and cradled her to his chest.

The sound of a truck's engine broke the stillness.

Headlights drifted across the walls and ceiling before fading from view.

Griff touched a hand to her cheek. "You all right?"

She couldn't speak. Instead she buried her face in the hollow between his neck and shoulder and struggled to keep from weeping.

His voice was a whisper. "It's okay to cry."

"I'm not crying. I never cry." Even as she said it, his collar grew damp from her silent tears.

All he could do was stand there, holding her as the aftershocks rolled through her. A trembling began in her legs and moved up all the way to the tips of her fingers, which were wrapped firmly around his neck. She held on to him as if he were a lifeline. Gradually, as the tears and the shaking passed, he carried her toward a chair and eased her down.

He crossed the room and locked the back door before setting aside his rifle and dropping to his knees in front of her. Then he handed her his clean handkerchief. "Better now?"

"A little." She blew her nose before taking in deep drafts of air.

He pulled his cell phone from his shirt pocket. "I need to call Chief Pettigrew."

She nodded.

He felt a wave of gratitude to Whit as he touched the number programmed into his phone and waited as it rang several times. Then he heard the voice, gruff from sleep.

"Ira Pettigrew here."

Griff handed the phone to Juliet, who said softly, "Chief, this is Juliet Grayson. One of my wranglers talked his way into my home and threatened to . . . hurt me."

"Give me a name."

"Mitchell Cord."

"I know him. Is he armed?"

"I don't know. I didn't see a weapon."

"Do you know where he is now?"

"He left in one of my ranch trucks. He could be any-where."

"Are you alone, Mrs. Grayson?"

She hesitated for a moment before saying, "No. My two sons are here, and so is Griff Warren."

"Bear MacKenzie's other son?"

"Yes."

"I'd like to talk to him."

Juliet held out the phone to Griff.

"Griff Warren, Chief."

"You witnessed this attempted assault?"

"I did."

"I'd like you to accompany Mrs. Grayson when she comes into town tomorrow to swear out a warrant."

"I'll be there."

"Thanks, Griff." The chief cleared his throat. "Do you think Mitch might return and try again?"

"If he does, he'll face my rifle again."

"Again?"

Griff turned away and kept his tone low. "I threatened him with my rifle. I intend to keep it handy in case he wants to try his luck one more time."

"Thanks, Griff. That's all I need to know. I'll see both of you in the morning. Until then, I'll have my deputies keep an eye out in town for a Grayson Ranch truck."

Griff rang off and deposited his phone in his pocket. To give Juliet some time to compose herself, he said, "I'll make some coffee."

Quickly, efficiently, he moved about the room, plugging in the coffeemaker, filling it with coffee and water, taking cups and saucers from a cupboard. When it was ready he filled two cups and brought them to the table.

Juliet blew her nose and stared down into the cup, avoiding his eyes. "How did you know what Mitch was planning?"

"He was at Wylie's. Drunk and bragging."

She shook her head. "I can't believe I let him in the

door. But he said there'd been an accident in the highlands, and..." Her lips trembled. "I let down my guard.
What would have happened if Casey or Ethan had come
down those stairs?"

Griff reached across the table to lay a hand over hers.
"They didn't. No sense borrowing trouble."

She let out a shuddering breath. "Heaven only knows
what lies he's spreading about me to the others."

"What do you care?"

"I know. I shouldn't." She tried a sip of coffee, but her
hand was shaking and she was forced to set the cup down
with a clatter. "But I do care. I hate that he can lie and
boast about his 'conquests' and people will believe him."

"Only a fool would believe a scumbag like Mitch."

He watched as she steadied her hand and took a drink
of coffee before looking over at him. "I don't know how
to thank you."

"No thanks necessary. I'm just glad I followed my instincts."

"Your military training?"

He shrugged. "I don't know if it's military, or just plain
common sense. If something doesn't seem right, it probably isn't."

"That's going to become my mantra." She paused. "Except that ever since coming here, nothing seems right."

He gave her a gentle smile. "Give it time, Juliet.
You've got a lot going on in your life. But most of it is
good. You've got two great boys. A ranch that holds a
wealth of history for them. A chance to build a good life
here for them and for yourself."

She let out a long, slow sigh. "You make it sound so
easy."

"Maybe not easy. But possible."

She managed a weak smile. "Why is it that when you say it like that, I believe you?"

Again he reached across the table to cover her hand with his. "Keep on believing. That's all we can really do in this life. Believe things can be better."

He noted the color that had returned to her cheeks. "Why don't you go up to bed?"

She looked startled. "I couldn't possibly sleep. What if he comes back?"

Griff stood. "If he does, he'll deal with me."

She made a feeble attempt to protest. "You can't just stay here all night."

"I'm not leaving you alone." He smiled. "I think I saw a sofa in that other room."

"It's old and lumpy."

"Sounds perfect." He turned away. "Go upstairs now. Get some sleep."

She paused. "Oh, Griff. How can I thank you?"

"I'll let you make me breakfast."

He watched as she started up the stairs. Halfway up she turned and mouthed *Thank you.*

He winked before picking up the rifle and heading down the hallway toward the old parlor.

The sofa was lumpy, as Juliet had said. Not that it mattered. He was so wired, he knew he wouldn't be able to sleep.

It wasn't just the thought of Mitch that had the adrenaline pumping through his veins. It was knowing he was just steps away from where Juliet Grayson, in that clingy T-shirt, was lying.

He'd had plenty of time to feel that slender, perfect

body, so clearly visible through the thin fabric of her nightshirt, pressed to him as he'd held her.

The thought of holding her again was enough to have him up and pacing in the darkness.

And the thought of Mitch Cord harming someone so wounded, so vulnerable, had all his protective instincts on high alert.

CHAPTER EIGHT

Juliet lay in bed, shivering despite the blanket.

The thought of that braggart Mitch had her balling her hands into fists. He'd been making insulting comments ever since he'd started working here. But she'd never dreamed that his talk would turn to dangerous actions.

How could she have been so careless?

One minute she'd been sound asleep. The next she'd woke to the sound of someone pounding on her door. She'd taken every precaution, standing inside the locked door to ask what he wanted. But when he'd told her there'd been an accident in the hills and Cooper had sent him to fetch her, she'd been so startled, she'd forgotten all the rules she'd set for herself.

What would have happened if Griff hadn't arrived on the scene?

She couldn't put aside her fear. She knew, without a doubt, how this would have ended.

She rolled to her side and drew the blanket over her head. She hated the fear that was now firmly planted in her heart. She'd been through so much. After dealing with the pain of Buddy's accident, and watching him slowly lose the battle he'd fought so bravely to win, she'd honestly believed that there was nothing that could ever again have her trembling like a coward. But right now, right this moment, the only thing that kept her from curling into a fetal position was Griff Warren's presence downstairs.

Her fierce, avenging angel.

He'd looked so calm, so in control. But she'd seen a flash of something feral and dangerous in his eyes that told her that beneath the air of cool command there had been a warrior poised to attack.

She would be forever grateful for the way he'd taken over when she'd fallen apart.

She hoped and prayed that police chief Ira Pettigrew would have Mitch in custody by morning, when she went to town to sign the documents needed to keep him safely away from her and her ranch. Otherwise, she would have to spend every day and night looking over her shoulder.

That thought had her sighing as she fell into a deeply troubled sleep.

Griff heard the sounds coming from the upper floor, indicating that Juliet and her sons were awake and moving. The occasional creaking of a floorboard. The sound of a shower running. Voices. Laughter.

By the time they trooped down the stairs, he had bacon and eggs sizzling in a skillet, and was busy feeding bread into a toaster.

He looked over to see the two little boys, eyes as round as saucers, peering at him in surprise.

"Mama, look." Casey was grinning. "Griff's here." He turned to the man standing at the stove. "I didn't hear your plane. When did you fly in?"

"I didn't fly. I drove. Good morning." Griff glanced beyond the two boys to their mother, who paused uncertainly on the bottom step. "I thought, since I was here early, I'd make breakfast. I hope you all like your eggs sunny-side up."

"What's sunny-side up?"

"This." Griff lifted down the skillet to show both boys the eggs. "See? Their yellow sides are called sunny sides."

"That's how our mama makes them," Casey said.

Griff caught Ethan studying the colorful place mats of red and yellow and green, set with bright yellow plates and green paper napkins, all of which he'd found in one of the cupboards.

"Look, Mama," Casey called. "Griff used all the stuff you said was too good for us to use."

"Too good to use?" Griff winked at the little boys. "I think we should always use the good stuff. And do you know why?"

"Why?" Casey asked.

"Because we're worth it." He turned to include Juliet. "Why don't the three of you sit down and I'll serve your breakfast."

He carried a tray of glasses, some filled with orange juice and some with milk, and deposited them around the table before handing Juliet a cup of steaming coffee.

After popping up the toast, he carried over a platter of

toast and jelly and another of bacon and eggs, which he set in the middle of the table so they could help themselves.

Finally he filled a cup of coffee for himself and took a seat at the table.

"Well." He took a moment to taste the coffee before looking around at the other three. "How did everyone sleep last night?"

Casey answered for all of them. "I sleeped all night. And now I'm glad, 'cause this is the best breakfast ever. Isn't it, Mama?"

She was grateful for the easy banter between Griff and Casey. It gave her time to compose her crazy heart, which was beating a wild tattoo in her chest.

She smiled and nodded. "You're right, Casey. This is the best ever. And do you know why?"

"Why?" Casey's eyes were big and round.

She shot Griff a blazing smile. "Because I didn't have to cook it."

Griff winked. "Maybe you'd better wait until you've had a taste before celebrating."

Juliet dipped the edge of her toast in the yolk and closed her eyes on a sigh. "Perfect. Just the way I like it."

Her two boys followed suit, dipping their toast in egg, breaking off bites of bacon, and washing it all down with milk.

They were still eating when they heard the approach of a vehicle. A minute later a knock on the door had Griff peering out the window before throwing the lock and holding the door for Jackie Turner.

"'Morning, Griff. Is Juliet here?"

"She is. Come on in."

The old man hung his hat on a hook by the door of the mudroom before stepping into the kitchen.

"Good morning, Jackie." Juliet indicated a seat at the table. "Will you join us for some breakfast? There's plenty."

"No, thank you, ma'am. I had breakfast with my daughter. But I'll have some of that coffee, son."

Griff filled a mug and handed it to him.

While the boys finished their meal, Jackie made small talk, mentioning the perfect summer weather, the herds growing fat on grass in the hills, and the fact that ranchers in these parts were saying it was one of the best seasons ever for growing wheat and corn.

Griff bit back a smile, knowing the old man was biding his time until he had Juliet alone to give her a report of her wranglers.

Taking pity on him, Griff glanced at Juliet. "Since Casey and Ethan are finished eating, do you think they might like to go play with their trucks in the other room?"

"Oh yes." Juliet nodded to her sons. "Put your plates in the sink and you can be excused."

The two little boys jumped up eagerly, gathering their dishes and dropping them in the sink with a clatter before running from the room, eager to escape grown-up conversation.

Griff circled the table, filling their cups with fresh coffee.

Jackie drank before meeting Juliet's eyes. "Randy Cooper's a good man, but he can't be everywhere at once. So I guess I'm not surprised at what I found up in the highlands yesterday." He set aside his cup, taking a moment to choose his words carefully. "Most of the wranglers who work these parts do it for the freedom it offers. They go from ranch to ranch until they find a place that suits them. Sometimes they'll stay on for a lifetime. But there are always a few who just never fit in. Maybe it's because they're lazy, or they have some bad habits, usually liquor or women. I suggested to Cooper that he ought to consider letting Mitch Cord go."

Juliet glanced at Griff. "Why?"

"He was drinking while he was supposed to be tending a herd on the north hill. It wasn't even noon, and I could smell the liquor on his breath. I guess he figured an old man like me wouldn't notice." He drained his coffee. "Cooper agreed with me. Said Mitch slipped away every chance he could, probably to drink, or maybe gamble with some of the other wranglers. So Cooper gave him his marching orders while I was there."

"Are you saying that Mitch Cord was fired yesterday?"

"Yes, ma'am. It was my recommendation, but it was Cooper's order. I hope you don't mind."

"Mind? Of course not. From the beginning, I've let Cooper know that the hiring and firing of wranglers is his job. And since the suggestion came from you, I feel even more confident of his decision. You're the expert on running this ranch."

"Thanks for that vote of confidence." Jackie got to his feet. "If it's all right with you, I'd like to check out your barns today. See the condition of your equipment. Then I'll give you another report tomorrow, if you don't mind."

"Yes. Of course. And Jackie, thank you." Juliet rounded the table to shake his hand. "I have to go into town this morning, but I'll be back by afternoon."

"You take your time, Juliet. Creepers. I certainly don't need anyone with me. I'll leave when I've finished my walk-around."

"I'm grateful for your help, Jackie."

The old man turned and shook Griff's hand before taking his leave.

When they were alone, Juliet seemed distracted as she filled the sink with hot water and began washing the dishes. Griff cleared the table before picking up a towel and drying. All the while he remained silent, allowing her time to mull the old man's words.

Finally she looked over at him. "Do you think that scene last night was retaliation for being fired?"

Griff raised a brow. "Do you?"

She sighed. "Maybe. I guess that could have been the trigger. But I think there was more than just getting even. Mitch has shown so much contempt for me since he started here, and I don't know why. I haven't given him any reason for his behavior."

She pulled the plug and drained the soapy water before drying her hands.

Griff draped the damp towel over the edge of the sink before looking into her troubled eyes. "Guys like Mitch don't need a reason to do what they do, Juliet. It isn't just contempt for you. I think he has contempt for all women. You just happened to be a convenient target. You're young. You're inexperienced at being a rancher, and he saw that as a weakness. But you're not weak. You're not helpless. And you're not a victim. And when he's arrested and facing charges of home invasion and attempted rape, he'll be stopped before he can hurt another woman."

She lifted her chin and gave him a weak smile. "I guess that answers my next question. Whether or not I ought to follow through on swearing out a warrant for his arrest."

Griff touched a hand to her cheek. "You don't need my advice. You already know you're going to do the right thing."

She sighed. "Yeah. I know. I just wish I could feel the confidence you seem to feel in me."

He winked. In his best imitation of the old cowboy he said, "Come on, boss lady. Let's round up those sons of yours and head on out to town."

She actually managed a laugh as she followed him to the parlor, where the boys were busy moving their trucks around the furniture.

Half an hour later they were in Griff's truck and headed to town.

"Chief Pettigrew."

The police chief looked up as Juliet and Griff stepped into his office.

Her two sons sat in the outer office, playing with the trucks their mother had brought along to amuse them while she dealt with the unpleasant business that had brought her here.

Ira motioned for them to sit in the chairs that faced his desk.

"Did you catch Mitch Cord?" Juliet's hands were clutched firmly in her lap.

"No sign of him, Mrs. Grayson. But I've faxed his description and the license number of your truck to the authorities in neighboring counties. I expect he'll turn up in the next day or so." He reached into a drawer and handed her some documents. "Read these and sign them. That'll make it official."

Juliet did as he asked and when they were signed, handed them across the desk. "You don't think Mitch would stick around and try to...follow through on his threats to me?"

The chief met her concerned look. "I wish I could ease your fears, ma'am. But there's no way of knowing the mind of a guy like Mitch. I've fielded complaints about him from ranchers in the past. Mostly petty things. Drunk on the job. Leaving his duties to drive into town to carouse with other cowboys. And he once threatened a rancher with a rifle, when the rancher refused to pay him at the end of the season because he'd been derelict in his duties. But that was resolved without any violence, and the rancher and Mitch ended up settling their differences without prosecution." He glanced at the documents she'd signed. "This time it's more serious. An attack on a woman and the theft of her truck. He'll probably do jail time, and that won't sit well with a freedom-loving cowboy like Mitch Cord."

Juliet hugged her arms about herself and glanced toward the outer office, where her two little boys were seated.

The chief followed her look before adding, "You ought to be aware that he may very well show up, mad as a hornet. If he does, he could be armed and dangerous."

"Thank you, Chief." She stood and offered her hand.

Ira shot a meaningful look at Griff before saying, "I wish I could spare a deputy to watch over your place, but I just can't. You might not want to be alone until Mitch is caught, ma'am."

The chief's meaning was crystal clear.

Griff gave a barely perceptible nod of his head before following her from the office.

Ira Pettigrew acknowledged the signal that had passed between them. If the town of Copper Creek couldn't provide a bodyguard for the widow Grayson, it would appear that Bear MacKenzie's other son had already delegated that particular chore to himself.

CHAPTER NINE

Juliet could feel Griff studying her face as she helped her sons pick up the trucks and tractors and store them in the little wooden carrying case. Though she was struggling to be cheerful, it was forced. She sensed that he could read her fear beneath the too-bright smile.

"As long as we're in town, we may as well take care of any business." He held the door as she and the boys stepped out into brilliant sunshine. "Need anything at Green's Grocery?"

Juliet shook her head. "I can't think of a thing."

"I can." Griff pointed to the Boxcar Inn. "Lunch. And once again, you won't have to cook it."

She sighed. "I guess I could have some soup."

"Oh boy." Casey clapped his hands. "Are we really going to eat on the real train?"

"Yes, we are." She managed a smile before explaining to Griff, "Every time we come to town, Casey begs me to take him and Ethan on the train. But there's never been the time or the money."

As they started toward the little restaurant, the boys danced along beside them, clearly eager to see the inside of a train.

They weren't disappointed.

The owner, Will Campbell, had worked on trains as a conductor for more than thirty years. When he retired he bought the old dining car and boxcar and converted them into a restaurant. He and his wife, Nell, proudly offered the same simple fare that had been on the train's menu for all those years.

As they were being led to their table they heard a feminine voice call, "Griff? Is that you?"

They paused to see Willow and Brady seated in a booth.

Griff handled the introductions. "Juliet Grayson, this is Willow MacKenzie and our ranch foreman, Brady Storm. These are Juliet's sons, Casey and Ethan."

"How lovely to meet you." Willow moved over to make room. "Please join us. We haven't even ordered yet."

At Griff's nod of approval, Juliet sat beside Willow, with her two sons wedged between Brady and Griff.

"What brings you two to town?" Griff asked.

"Picking up supplies," Brady explained. "And Willow said she'd come along for some things Mad wanted from Green's."

"Mad?" Juliet looked intrigued.

"My father-in-law, Maddock MacKenzie. Everyone calls him Mad."

"Is he mad at people?" little Casey asked.

"Not very often. But he is blustery."

While the adults laughed, Griff explained, "That means he can make a lot of noise. But it's good noise. Like when you and Ethan are running around shouting, but they're happy shouts."

"Oh." The little boy looked up when Nell Campbell arrived to take their orders.

After she left, Willow turned to Griff. "Whit said you were expecting some trouble when you left Wylie's."

"I was. And there was." He turned to Casey and Ethan. "How would you two like a tour of the train before our lunch comes?"

"Oh, boy." Casey's eyes lit with excitement.

The two caught Griff's hands and followed along eagerly as he led them toward the front of the dining car. As they walked away Juliet stared after them.

"Griff is really good with your sons, isn't he?"

Juliet turned to find Willow watching her and lowered her gaze. "Yes."

"I assume he didn't want them to hear what happened last night."

Juliet waited as Nell Campbell began passing around glasses of ice water. When they were alone she told Willow and Brady about the incident with Mitch.

"How horrible." Willow touched a hand to Juliet's arm. "I'm so glad Griff got there in time."

"Not half as glad as I am."

"What did Chief Pettigrew say?"

"Mitch hasn't been seen yet. The chief thinks he could come back for revenge. He doesn't want me to be alone until Mitch is caught."

"What will you do?" Willow saw Griff returning with the two boys.

"I haven't really had time to think about it yet. But I could always ask Cooper to send a couple of wranglers down from the hills to stay close."

Willow glanced across the table at Brady, whose brooding look told her he had reservations about a few wranglers keeping this young woman safe from an angry drunk seeking revenge. "We have more than enough room at our ranch for you and your boys. Why don't you stay with us?"

"But what if Mitch isn't caught? How long can I stay away from my ranch?"

Griff helped the two boys up to their seats before taking his place across from her.

Juliet looked over at him. "Willow has invited us to stay with her."

His smile was quick. "You'd love it at the MacKenzie Ranch. All the comforts of home. And, according to Mad, the best cook in Montana."

"Even if I don't have to cook, I couldn't possibly—"

"It's the perfect solution," Willow said firmly.

Griff nodded. "Why not give it a try?"

"Because..." Juliet glanced at her two boys. "I didn't bring a change of clothes."

"We have washers and dryers," Willow said gently.

"But I..." Juliet shook her head. "I'd feel like an intruder."

"I thought I'd feel that way, too." Griff chuckled. "And believe me, I had a lot more reason to think that than you do. But I've never been made to feel more welcome any place than at the MacKenzie Ranch."

"Please, Juliet." Willow lay a hand over hers. "Give us a try. If not for yourself, then for your boys."

Juliet gave her an admiring look. "You've found my weakness. I guess, for the sake of my boys..." She swallowed. "All right. Dinner. And maybe we'll stay the night."

When their lunch came they all dug in, enjoying the simple but filling fare.

And when they parted an hour later, Juliet found herself waving good-bye to Willow and Brady as their truck roared away, as though waving at old friends.

She turned to Griff. "Does Willow have that effect on everyone?"

He nodded. "She's amazing. I arrived expecting to be about as welcome as a nest of rattlers. And here I am, still living there, and feeling more and more every day as though I actually belong."

Seeing the thoughtful look in her eyes, he decided that she needed another distraction.

Spying the cute little shop down the street with the brightly-colored sign that read I's Cream, he said casually, "Who's ready for dessert?"

"I am," Casey shouted.

Ethan's eyes widened before his hand went up.

Juliet started to shake her head.

"Three against one," Griff said. "Come on." Her two sons caught her hands and danced eagerly along the sidewalk until they stepped inside the little shop that held a glass case displaying a variety of ice creams with names like Monster Maple Sugar, Chunk Chocolate, and Divine Diva Double Strawberry.

A short time later, in a courtyard beside the shop, they sat on little wooden stools set around a picnic table made from a tree stump, licking their ice cream cones.

"Mine's the best," Casey announced as he held up his cone. It had two scoops of purple ice cream topped with sprinkles

"What is it called?" Juliet asked.

"Purple People Eater. And Efan's got Blue Heaven."

The six-year-old was too busy licking his blue confection to look up.

"I think mine's better." Griff had already devoured the top layer of his chocolate ice cream, filled with nuts, cookie bits, cherries, and a dollop of whipped cream, all stuffed into an enormous waffle cone.

Juliet tentatively tasted her single scoop of Divine Diva Double Strawberry. After the first taste, she dove into it. When she saw Griff grinning at her she said, "What's so funny?"

"You. Admit it. You're loving that."

"All right. I am."

"You can't deny it's better than what you originally ordered."

She lifted her chin a fraction. "There's nothing wrong with vanilla."

"Nothing at all. But when you've got so many exotic choices, why settle for something you can have every day?"

She licked her ice cream and considered his words. "I only changed my order because you shamed me into it."

"And now you're glad I did."

She couldn't stop the smile that curved her lips. "Yes. I'm glad you shamed me into trying something new. And exotic." She looked over at her sons. "Maybe next time I'll even be brave enough to try Purple People Eater or Blue Heaven."

The two boys were grinning from ear to ear.

"Griff?"

At the sound of a deep voice Griff and Juliet looked up to see Ash and Brenna walking toward them, hand in hand.

Ash was holding the leash of a big, brown, shaggy dog.

"Hey, Ash."

"Bro."

The two slapped shoulders before Griff bent to brush a kiss over Brenna's cheek. "What brings you two love-birds to town?"

"Oh, we were just checking out the new arrivals at Orin Tamer's dealership."

Griff chuckled before turning to say, "Juliet Grayson, this is Ash MacKenzie and his wife, Brenna."

"And our dog, Sammy," Ash added.

"Hi, Ash and Brenna and Sammy." Juliet started to offer a handshake before saying, "Sorry. I think my hand is sticky from all this ice cream."

Brenna laughed. "I can't think of a better reason to have sticky fingers."

Griff pointed to the boys. "These two little wranglers are her sons, Casey and Ethan."

Spotting the boys, Sammy began wiggling all over until he was close enough to be petted. Even their ice cream couldn't compete with a happy, wriggling dog. The two boys stopped licking their ice cream long enough to run their hands over his head and back.

"He's big," Casey said.

"When I first got him, he was only this big." Brenna held her hands close together. "He was so tiny and yellow and fluffy. But now he's like a big, awkward teenager, knocking things over with that happy tail of his."

As if to prove her point, the more the boys petted him, the harder his tail wagged.

Brenna turned to her husband. "That ice cream cone looks so good. I think I have to have one, too."

"Vanilla as usual?" Ash asked her.

That brought laughter from both Griff and Juliet. Griff was quick to explain, "I had to talk Juliet into trying something exotic, instead of her usual vanilla." He turned to Brenna. "Go ahead. It's time to live life on the edge."

She laughed and said to her husband, "I'll have what Juliet's having."

"And what is it?" Ash asked.

"Divine Diva Double Strawberry," she said, taking another lick.

Ash walked inside I's Cream and returned minutes later with three giant cones: one for Brenna, one for himself, and the third for a very happy Sammy.

They sat around the tree stump table, happily devouring their desserts.

In an aside to Griff, Ash said, "Whit said you expected a little trouble last night after you left Wylie's."

"I did. And there was." He glanced over at the boys before saying, "Juliet made a report to Ira. He doesn't think she should be alone for a while. Your mother has invited us to supper. And she wants Juliet to consider staying with our family until Mitch is caught." He saw Ash was grinning and frowned. "You think that's funny?"

"No. I think you're funny."

"What's that supposed to mean?"

Ash smacked him on the shoulder. "You just said 'our family.' I guess that means you're no longer wondering whether or not you're one of us."

Griff laughed, but as the conversation swirled around him, he realized what he'd just revealed. More and more each day, as he got to know this wonderful family, he really was beginning to think of himself as a MacKenzie.

And though the rest of the family might not recognize it yet, it was a giant step for a man who'd been a loner all his life.

CHAPTER TEN

Griff turned the truck off the highway and onto the long ribbon of road that wound its way through rich grassland and rocky outcroppings, giving it the look of the Old West.

As they made a turn around a grass-covered hill, the MacKenzie Ranch came into view. The house of wood and stone rose up three stories, blending in so naturally with the mountain range in the distance that it seemed to be part of the landscape. Looming behind the house were several giant barns and outbuildings. The distant hills surrounding the area were black with cattle.

Juliet fell silent, drinking in the amazing view.

"Is this where you live?" Casey asked.

"It is. This is the MacKenzie Ranch."

"It's so big."

Griff smiled at the little boy in his rearview mirror. "That was my first thought when I saw it. You could build an entire city here, with room to spare."

"Or a whole country," Juliet said softly.

He glanced at her. "Don't let the size intimidate you."

She couldn't hold back the little laugh that escaped her lips. "Too late, cowboy. I'm already feeling over-whelmed."

"Don't be." He laid a hand over hers. "These are good people. I think you and the boys are going to be pleas-antly surprised."

She shot him a sideways glance. "Do they know how much mischief two boys can get into?"

He winked as he pulled up beside the back porch. "Willow raised two boys of her own. I'm sure she still re-members dozens of things they did."

He slid from the truck and walked around to open the passenger door. As he helped Juliet down, he could feel the slight tremors in her hand and squeezed before turn-ing to help Casey and Ethan to the ground.

Walking between them, he said, "Come on inside and meet the MacKenzies."

They walked through the giant mudroom, hearing loud voices coming from the kitchen. As they stepped inside, the voices ceased and heads turned to watch as Griff led them closer.

"I'd like all of you to meet Juliet Grayson and her sons, Ethan and Casey. Juliet, you've already met Willow and Brady."

Willow hurried over to greet them while Brady gave a nod of his head from across the room.

"This is Whit MacKenzie."

"Better known as the little brother," Whit said with a grin.

"Or, as he prefers when he's at Wylie's, the hot hunk," Brenna called from the mudroom.

"Hey, you two," Whit said to Ash and Brenna. "You must have heard that Mad's making pot roast."

"You bet." Ash kept an arm around his bride's waist as they strolled into the kitchen, leaving Sammy on the back porch contentedly gnawing on a rope. "I'd never say no to Mad's pot roast."

"Or his stew. Or his baked chicken. Or..."

Griff held up a hand. "Juliet. Boys. This is Myrna Hill."

The plump woman paused and wiped her hands on her apron before offering her hand to Juliet and then to each of her sons.

"And this is the famous Mad MacKenzie. Don't pay any attention to his name. He's a really happy cook."

"I've been reduced to cooking in my daughter-in-law's house. But at least I'm chief cook," the old man boomed. He turned away from the stove and rolled his wheelchair close to extend his hand to Juliet. Then he fixed the two boys with a look. "Which of you lads is Ethan and which is Casey?"

Casey turned to his mother with a look of surprise. "He called us lads, Mama."

"That you are," Mad said in his booming voice. "In Scotland you're lads until you become men. And to an old man like me, everyone younger is a lad. Now tell me which is which."

"I'm Casey," the younger one said proudly. "And I'm free."

"Welcome, Casey." Mad shook his hand.

"And this is my brover, Efan, and he's six."

"Do you ever let Ethan speak for himself?"

Casey shook his head. "Efan doesn't like to talk. So I do it for him."

"I see." Mad offered his hand to the older boy. "Welcome, Ethan. Six is a good age to be. I remember my sixth birthday. I rode halfway across the Highlands in a wild storm. Some day I'll tell you all about it. For now, I'd better tend my pot roast or there'll be no supper tonight."

As he turned his wheelchair and rolled toward the stove, Ethan's wide-eyed gaze followed him.

Juliet and her sons were surrounded by a crowd of joking, laughing MacKenzies, each one talking louder than the next in order to be heard above the din.

Myrna held out a tray of lemonade for the boys.

Whit passed around longnecks to anyone who reached for one.

They moved slowly across the kitchen, easing into a sitting area complete with comfortable sofas and chairs and side tables on which rested a tray of cheeses and assorted biscuits.

Willow saw the way Casey and Ethan eyed the snacks and put an arm around each of them. "Do you like cheese?"

Casey nodded. "Mama makes grilled cheese sandwiches. Griff likes them, too."

"I'll bet he does." She handed each of them a small plate. "Help yourselves."

They knelt on the floor beside the low coffee table, nibbling cheese and crackers and sipping their lemonade while the conversation flowed around them.

"How are you settling into ranch life, Juliet?"

Juliet chewed her lower lip. "I'm afraid this girl from Chicago isn't much of a rancher."

"Give yourself time." Willow patted her hand. "I grew

up here in Montana, and I wasn't much of a rancher when I married Bear."

"But you didn't need to be." Juliet blinked. "I mean, you had a husband to handle the ranching while you handled your boys."

Brady chuckled. "Don't let the lady's looks fool you. Willow can outrope, outride, and outwork most of the wranglers around here."

Juliet looked at her with new respect. "You actually work your ranch?"

Whit and Ash exchanged grins. Ash said, "She not only works it, she runs it. And with a very firm and steady hand, I might add."

"In other words," Whit deadpanned, "she not only raises the bacon, but she can butcher it, slice it up, and fry it in a pan." He broke into song. "'Cause she's a woman, W-O-M-A-N."

Everybody roared with laughter.

"Except," Mad called from the stove, "she no longer has to fry it. That's what I'm here for."

"And you do an excellent job of it, Mad." Willow blew her father-in-law a kiss.

Juliet sat back, watching and listening, and feeling all the tension of the past few days begin to slip away. There was just something about this family that had her feeling more relaxed and happy than she had in years.

While the adults continued their conversation, Ethan nibbled his cheese and walked over to stand beside Mad's wheelchair, running his hand over and over the wheel.

Seeing it, Mad paused in his work. "Are you afraid of my chair, lad?"

The boy shook his head.

"You've seen one before, then?"

Ethan nodded.

"Well then, maybe you'd like a ride, lad?"

The boy's eyes went wide before he gave a timid nod of his head.

"Here you go." With no effort at all, Mad's arms, muscled from years of propelling his chair, lifted the boy into his lap. Without any seeming break in his routine he rolled back and forth between the stove and the table, depositing a pitcher of ice water, stirring something in a pan. And all the while the boy settled himself comfortably against the old man's chest.

As the conversation swirled around her, Juliet watched her son snuggle into Mad's embrace and felt her heart nearly stop.

Seeing the look on her face, Griff leaned in to whisper, "Something wrong?"

She shook her head, afraid to trust her voice.

Seeing the direction of her gaze, Griff kept his tone low. "Don't worry. Mad may be old, but he's strong as a bull. He won't let Ethan fall."

"I'm not worried about that. Look at Ethan's face, Griff." Her lower lip trembled, and Griff could see her fighting tears. "He's smiling."

Griff shook his head. "I have to admit, I've never seen Mad have that effect on anybody. Most people, especially little kids, are afraid of his bluster. "

"Don't you see?" Moisture shimmered on her lashes. "All of Ethan's memories of his father are related to a wheelchair. Whenever I pushed Buddy along the hallway on his way to therapy, Buddy would have Ethan in his lap."

She turned away, hoping no one would see her tears. "Oh, Griff. I never thought I'd see my son smile like that again. Look at his face. He looks as though he's in the arms of an angel."

Griff tried to reconcile his image of the stern, gruff old man as an angel, but failed.

"Dinner's ready," Mad bellowed.

As the others began moving across the room toward the big table, Griff closed a hand over Juliet's. "I've heard Mad MacKenzie called many things. But this is a first." He led her toward the table. "Come on. Let's see if the food is as heavenly as the tough old bird who prepared it."

Everyone settled themselves around the wooden table, with Willow at one end and Mad at the other. Ethan sat beside the old man, while Casey chose a chair between his mother and Griff. Ash and Brenna pulled their chairs close, and though no one mentioned it, everyone was aware that the two newlyweds were holding hands under the table.

Brady sat to one side of Willow and Whit on the other. Myrna sat on the other side of Mad, closest to the long kitchen counter, in order to fetch coffee or milk during the meal.

As they passed around bowls of potatoes and crisp green beans from the garden, as well as platters of sliced roast beef and baskets of rolls fresh from the oven, they continued the conversation they'd begun over their beers.

"...one of the best cattle seasons ever." Brady held the platter while Willow helped herself. "I think this fall's roundup is going to bring the best market value in years."

"Because of the grass in the highlands?" Griff asked.

Brady nodded. "That, and the fact that spring snow-storms were minimal. We lost fewer calves this season than any spring in recent memory." He glanced toward Mad. "Don't you agree?"

Mad grinned. "It's been a rare year. No doubt about it. Plenty of rain. Plenty of sunshine. I think we'll see our profits soar."

Ash nudged Brenna. "Hear that? Maybe all this good luck is because we've merged our ranches." He turned to his grandfather. "What about it, Mad? You think Brenna's cattle are bewitched and brought their good karma with them?"

Mad gave a belly laugh. "Good cattle karma? Now I've heard everything."

He glanced at the little boy beside him. Seeing Ethan struggling to cut his meat, the old man leaned close and cut everything into bite-sized pieces. "There you are, lad."

Across the table, Juliet watched in silence and felt another tug on her heart. When she looked up, she realized Brady had asked her a question. "Oh, sorry. What were you saying?"

"I said, how about your cattle? Has your foreman given you a report on how they're doing in the hills?"

"I'm afraid not. He probably doesn't feel the need to report to me, since he knows I don't have a clue as to how things should be done."

Willow turned to her with a smile. "Don't sell yourself short, Juliet. If you do, those who work for you will, too. You don't need to know everything about ranching. In the beginning, learn a few key points. Here in Montana, weather is key. With a good season like this one, your cattle are going to get fat in spite of themselves. A good season also means you can grow more crops, and that means that you won't have to spend as much buying feed over the long winter. One good year like this can mean the difference between success and putting a ranch up for auction."

"You make it sound easy."

Willow shook her head. "Ranching's never easy. But nothing worth doing ever is. The thing about ranching that keeps us all here and working every day, without time off for vacations or sick days or holidays, is that it gives us the freedom to live the kind of life our ancestors lived for hundreds of years. And having that is worth the price we pay."

Juliet went as still as a statue. Then, very slowly, she smiled. "Thank you."

Willow raised a brow in question.

"Not only for this lovely meal." She shot Mad a quick grin. "But also for giving me a reason to stay and fight for Buddy's ranch. Until now, I wasn't sure why I was here, instead of living in some big city, where I'd feel more at home."

"And now?" Willow asked.

"You just answered the question for me. I think I want that freedom you just spoke of. Not just for myself, but for my boys. This land belonged to their ancestors. They deserve a chance to see if they're willing to work for it, too."

Griff saw the look that came into Mad's eyes. A mixture of surprise, grief, pride.

Hadn't the old man single-handedly cleared this land and made it a successful business? But what would it be worth if it couldn't be passed on to his own son? And now that son was dead.

Griff saw the way Mad looked around the table at his grandsons.

There was the old man's hope. The hope that though his son was gone now, here were three grandsons, all with different backgrounds and dreams for their future, yet they were pulling together to make his dream come true.

Griff realized that Willow hadn't just given Juliet an answer she'd desperately needed. She'd given *him* an answer, as well. He wasn't here simply because he had nowhere else to go. He stayed on, even after burying the stranger who'd been his father, because he saw his own future here, on the MacKenzie Ranch.

Maybe he wasn't the experienced rancher Ash and Whit were. At least not yet. But if grit and determination were enough to turn him into a bona fide rancher, he had no doubt he'd get there in time.

Time.

He glanced at the two little boys, alone and hurting, trusting their mother to guide them through their heartache and loss to a better place.

If he were a betting man, he'd put his money on Juliet Grayson to overcome all these troubles and show the world just how strong she truly was.

CHAPTER ELEVEN

As Myrna began collecting their plates, Ash leaned back with a sigh. "Mad, I think this was your best roast beef ever."

Mad grinned. "You say that every time, lad."

"I don't."

"Yes, you do." Whit winked at his grandfather. "You need to come up with a new compliment, bro. We've heard that one a thousand times."

Ash turned to his bride. "Do I always say that?"

"You do." Brenna nodded, before squeezing his hand. "But I'm sure your grandfather never grows tired of the compliment."

"You're right about that, lass." Mad was beaming as he turned to Myrna. "What about that special dessert you promised us?"

She paused, about to load dishes onto a serving cart. "Would you rather we eat it here, or in the great room?"

"The great room." Willow pushed away from the table. "The house is chilly tonight. I'm sure the boys would like to sit by the fire."

Everyone followed suit, getting up from the table and heading toward the door.

Mad backed his wheelchair away from the table. Before starting forward he motioned for Ethan. "Want to ride, lad?"

Ethan's smile grew, and he was lifted easily onto Mad's lap.

Seeing Casey hesitate, Mad called, "There's room for two."

With a giggle, Casey joined his brother on the old man's lap. Griff held the door while Mad wheeled through the doorway and along the wide hallway, with his two passengers wearing matching smiles of delight.

"Would you care for a tour of the house before you have dessert, lads?"

The two boys clapped their hands, and he easily propelled them along yet another hallway, where he announced each room to them.

"We call this the library. It's really the office where my son, Bear, used to conduct his business. Now it's mostly my daughter-in-law, Willow, and our foreman, Brady Storm, who conduct the business. But the rest of us sit in on many of the discussions." He wheeled along a second hallway. "This is my suite of rooms. They were added on here after my accident, so we wouldn't have to install an elevator to take me upstairs where everyone else sleeps."

The boys looked around the large, uncluttered space that offered both a cozy sitting room, with an electric fireplace and tables that held an assortment of books, and beyond that to a large, airy bedroom, with a hospital bed mounded with pillows, and beside it, another large table stacked with books. Across the room was an oversize flat-screen television. Another fireplace added cozy warmth. Like the fireplace in the sitting room, this was electric, so that it could be easily maintained by a handheld control on the bedside table.

"All right, lads. We've spent just enough time to let Myrna fill those plates with our desserts. Now it's time we get to them."

He wheeled them from the suite and down the hall until they joined the others in the great room, where a log fire was blazing on the hearth.

"Where've you been?" Myrna pointed to Mad's cup. "Your coffee's getting cold."

"I took the lads on a grand tour of the place."

The housekeeper pointed to a table set up in front of the fire. "Casey and Ethan, I put your desserts right here, so you can eat and be warm."

Casey scrambled off Mad's lap and hurried over to peer at the bowl filled with a slice of pound cake and topped with fresh strawberries and ice cream.

"Wow." He glanced over at his mother. "Did you get one of these, too?"

"I did." She looked up in time to see Ethan reluctantly climb down from Mad's lap before crossing to sit beside his brother. Even the thought of dessert didn't seem as enticing as being held in the arms of this old man.

Between bites of his gooey dessert, Casey said, "Griff's grandpa has two fires in his rooms."

"You mean fireplaces, lad." Mad winked. "Nights can

get pretty cold here in Montana. And this old body isn't as active as it once was. So I'll take all the heat I can get."

Juliet sipped strong, hot coffee before asking, "Are you still able to do any ranch chores?"

The old man shook his head. "I wish I could. The spirit's still in me. But I've become a prisoner in the house because of this—" he glowered at the chair in which he sat "—this iron chariot."

Intrigued, Juliet leaned forward. "I didn't notice any ramps when we drove up. How do you get outside?"

"One of the lads carries me." His subdued tone said much more than his words.

She arched a brow as she turned to Griff. "Didn't you say you were good with your hands?"

He nodded before a slow smile touched his mouth. "Of course. What was I thinking?"

He turned to Mad. "It wouldn't be any trouble for me to build you a ramp from the back porch. That way you'd have the freedom to go in and out without having to wait around for someone to help."

Everyone turned to the old man, waiting to see the expected explosion. Instead, his thoughtful look had them all puzzled. Now what was he plotting? They could actually see the wheels turning in his clever brain, even though, for vanity's sake, he'd resisted just such a thing for years.

"I suppose that's something you'd enjoy doing, lad?"

"I can and I will." Griff glanced at Brady. "Mind if I take one of the ranch trucks to town tomorrow?"

Brady chuckled. "You're forgetting, Griff. They're your ranch trucks, too. Take whatever you need. Garvey Fuller owns the lumber mill. He's out past town about a mile off the highway. You can't miss it. If he doesn't have the sizes you need in stock, he'll cut them for you. Just take along the dimensions you have in mind, and Garvey's your man."

"Thanks, Brady." Griff dug into his dessert and was already mentally calculating what he would do.

It would give Mad a sense of freedom that had been denied him all these years. How the old man must resent being lifted and carried about like a child.

He glanced over to see a little smile playing on Mad's lips.

Was Maddock MacKenzie already thinking about how much easier his life would be once he could escape this house without asking for help? For a strong, independent cowboy like him, this enforced idleness must seem an endless prison.

Or was the old man merely finding something other than ranch chores to keep him occupied?

No matter the reason, Griff was delighted to have a reason to use his woodworking skills.

As the sky outside the windows grew dark, and the fire burned low, the hum of conversation became punctuated with long pauses and the occasional yawn.

Ash and Brenna took their leave, stopping on the back porch long enough to hook Sammy to his leash.

Juliet looked at her two sons, lying against the big cushions Myrna had dropped on the floor in front of the fireplace. Between them sat Myrna, holding open the big book she'd brought from her room, filled with children's bedtime stories. At first, the boys had pointed to the various stories they wanted her to read. Now, after the warmth of the fire and the soft, easy murmur of Myrna's sweet voice, the two little boys were fighting a losing battle to stay awake.

Juliet turned to Willow. "If your invitation to stay the night is still on, I'm willing." She nodded toward the two limp figures on either side of Myrna, their little heads resting on her shoulders. "I don't think they can fight sleep any longer."

"And they shouldn't have to." Willow stood. "You take one and I'll take the other, and I'll show you where they can sleep."

"I'll do that." Before she could pick up Ethan, Griff was there, lifting him easily in his arms.

Juliet picked up Casey and thanked Myrna.

"They've never before had a grandmother read to them. I could see how much of a treat it was for them."

"Not nearly as satisfying for them as for me," Myrna said. "It just made my night."

Calling good night to the others, Juliet followed Griff and Willow up the stairs. Willow led them along a hallway before opening a door and switching on the light.

"This guest room has two beds, side by side, so if one of them wakes in the night, he'll have the comfort of his brother right next to him. After you've settled them in, your room is right next door." She turned to Griff. "You'll show Juliet the way?"

He nodded.

Willow hesitated. "Do you need help with your boys?"

Juliet shook her head. "You've done more than enough already. I'm used to this. It'll only take me minutes."

"All right then." Willow turned toward the door. "Good night, both of you."

Juliet hurried over to take her hand. "Thank you, Willow. You've made us feel so welcome."

"I'm glad. Because you and your boys are welcome here anytime. I'd like you to feel free to stay as long as you like."

She let herself out while Juliet returned to Casey's side and slipped off his shoes and clothes, leaving him wearing only his briefs, before tucking the blankets around him.

Grif followed her lead and removed Ethan's shoes and clothes before covering him.

Juliet leaned down to kiss both her boys, then left a light on in the bathroom to guide them if they should wake in the night.

"Come on. I'll show you your room." Griff led the way. He saw Juliet stare at her two boys for a long minute before turning away and closing the door. Then they walked along the hall to the next door. He opened it before standing aside to allow Juliet to precede him inside.

Inside, she stared around at the big bed mounded with a down comforter and pillows, and a cashmere throw tossed casually over the footstool of a nearby lounge chair. Beside the chair were a table and lamp and an array of books. Across the room was a desk and chair. On one end of the desk was a flat-screen TV.

She opened a second door to reveal a bathroom fit for a queen, with a tub and shower big enough for an army, a lovely oval sink and mirror, and all of it done in shades of white marble.

She turned to him with a look of alarm. "Oh, Griff. I don't belong here."

He merely smiled. "Neither do I. But I won't tell if you

won't." His smile grew. "I say we just kick back and enjoy all this until they discover we're frauds."

She tried to laugh, but it came out in a sigh. Before she could say more he touched a finger to her lips. Just a touch, but they both looked stunned at his boldness.

He lowered his hand and took a step back. "I'd better say good night and get out of here."

"Wait." She caught his hand and held it tightly. "Just stay a minute more. I'm feeling overwhelmed."

His smile was quick and charming. "I'm feeling overwhelmed myself. But it's not the room, it's the woman in it."

"Don't joke, Griff."

His smile disappeared. "It's no joke. And if I don't leave you right now, I just might not make it out of here."

He got as far as the door before turning to look at her. That was his downfall. In quick strides he crossed the room and grabbed her in a fierce embrace.

"I almost made it." The words were whispered against her temple as he began brushing hot, wet kisses down the side of her face until she turned her head slightly and his lips found hers. "I know you told me you don't like this." His voice was a rough growl of desperation.

"That's what I said. But right this minute I can't tell you that, Griff." She clung to him. "I need you to hold me, just for a minute."

"If I stay for a minute, it could turn into hours. I may not be able to leave at all. In fact, it's already too late. I know what touching you does to me."

And then he took the kiss deep, nearly devouring her.

Her body was crushed against him, her heartbeat wildly matching his. The feel of her ragged breath, her pounding pulse, added more fuel to the fire that raged through him.

"Wait, Griff. I need a minute..."

Her words barely penetrated the fog that seemed to have taken over his control.

Instead of doing as she asked, he backed her across the room until they were stopped by the press of the wall against her back. They barely noticed the bump of their bodies as they continued the kiss until they were nearly crawling inside each other's skin.

He was so hot he could barely catch a breath. Lifting his head, he breathed deeply before lowering his face to hers. "I could stay the night. I could—"

She lifted a hand to his mouth. "Wait. Stop. I need to think."

"I can't think. My brain..." He sucked in air, hoping to clear his mind.

"We can't do this." She put a hand to his chest.

"I know. I know." He caught her hand in his. "I'll go."

As he started to turn away she lifted herself on tiptoe to brush his mouth with hers. "I don't want you to, but I know I need to send you away."

He half-turned back to her. "I don't have to—"

"Yes. No." She breathed deeply. "Yes. Go."

His hands closed around her shoulders. "Was that no? Or go?"

She looked up at the same moment he looked down. They bumped noses, then both burst into laughter. They laughed so hard they clung together, shaking and laughing.

He pressed his forehead to hers and managed another shaky breath. "Okay. At least I know we're both crazy." He held her a little away and stared deeply into her eyes before giving a groan. "I'm going now. Just—" he backed away "—don't touch me or I won't make it."

She stayed where she was, watching as he backed across the room. Straightening his shoulders, he turned and opened the door. He stepped out and pulled it firmly shut behind him.

When he was safely out of the room he leaned against the wall and took long breaths until he was calm enough to make it to his own door.

Once inside he tore off his shirt and rolled it into a ball before tossing it across the room. He kicked off one boot, then the other, taking satisfaction in having them slam against the wall.

He stalked to the window. With his arms crossed over his bare chest he leaned against the sill and stared at the darkened sky outside, wondering if he'd ever cool off enough to sleep.

There'd been women. Too many to count. But at the moment, he couldn't remember a single one. Probably because until now, he'd never cared enough to consider them more than a distraction.

But now...

Now there was Juliet. And he wanted her more than he'd ever wanted anyone or anything in his life.

He couldn't explain why. She was angry and scared and fighting just to survive. She seemed hell-bent on attracting trouble. Add to that the fact that she had two sons with plenty of problems of their own. She could easily decide to pack up and move to a big city clear across the country, where he'd never hear from her again.

That ought to be enough to scare off any guy with half a brain.

He'd always prided himself on being a smart guy.

But he wanted her.

There was no rhyme or reason to it. He'd already made her problems his problems. He was more than ready to make her fight his fight.

And he'd brought her here, not just to keep her safe, but to give his family a chance to get to know her.

His family. How quickly they'd gone from strangers to family. And he wanted them to like this woman.

Now he knew he was a goner.

He was in over his head and slowly sinking beneath an ocean of trouble.

And all he could think about was the fact that he wanted Juliet Grayson with a hot, burning need that was becoming all-consuming.

CHAPTER TWELVE

Juliet woke with a start. One minute she was sound asleep, the next she was sitting up at the sound of a door closing. She pushed hair from her eyes and glanced at the window, where morning light streamed in.

She'd been dreaming. The dream was lost to her now, but it had been about an airplane. It had seemed so real, she could actually hear the engines drawing closer and closer.

And then suddenly she was awake, and the dream, like wisps of fog, had vanished.

It had taken her hours to fall asleep after Griff left. And no wonder, after a scene like that. Even now, just thinking about it had her cheeks growing hot.

She'd practically begged him to make love with her.

Love? How dare she call it that? She'd loved Buddy. And loved him still. It was time for a reality check. What she'd felt for Griff last night was pure lust. It was fear and loneliness. It was her hormones working overtime.

Thank heavens he'd had the common sense to leave before they ended up doing something they would have both regretted. From now on she would have to be more careful around that handsome, charming cowboy.

She slipped from bed and headed toward the shower. A short time later, while toweling herself dry, she heard another door open and close. This one seemed very near.

Draping the towel around herself, she returned to the bedroom in search of the clothes she'd discarded the previous night. They weren't on the chair where she'd dropped them. Puzzled, she turned and saw them neatly folded atop the night stand. They smelled of detergent and fabric softener.

She dressed quickly, then made up the bed before slipping quietly from her room and opening the door to the bedroom next door. Inside, the beds had been made, and there was no sign of Ethan and Casey.

Alarmed, she hurried down the stairs. Even before she reached the kitchen she heard a deep, booming voice and the higher-pitched sounds of laughter.

She walked in to find everyone already dressed and sipping orange juice or coffee.

Mad in his wheelchair was at the stove, pouring batter into a waffle iron. Perched on his knees were Ethan and Casey, watching intently as he closed the lid.

Seeing her, Casey yelled, "Hi, Mama. We're making awfuls."

"Waffles," Mad corrected.

"Oh yeah. Waffles," the little boy chirped. "I told him you make ours in the toaster."

"Those things *should* be called awfuls," the old man said with disdain. "Wait until you taste mine. You'll never eat another one of those store-bought cardboard things that pass for real food."

With a wink Griff handed her a glass of foaming orange juice.

She felt her cheeks flush as she avoided his eyes and tasted it before giving a sigh of surprise. "Oh, this is wonderful. Fresh squeezed."

Just then Willow walked into the room, wearing a look of frustration. Behind her, Brady Storm, looking equally annoyed, touched a hand to her shoulder in a show of support, which brought a weak smile to her lips.

Trailing them was the most sophisticated man Juliet had ever seen. Perfect white teeth in a tanned face that was as smooth, as polished, as the Armani suit he wore with casual elegance.

Spotting Juliet, he paused in the doorway. "Who is this? Have you added another secret family member to the MacKenzie clan?"

Willow said through clenched teeth, "Lance McMillan, this is our neighbor Juliet Grayson and her two sons, Casey and Ethan. Juliet owns the Grayson Ranch just beyond our northern border."

"Ah. Another rancher. Juliet." He took her hand and held it while he studied her before turning to smile at the others. "I see the neighborhood has improved considerably since the last time I paid a call."

He reached into his breast pocket and produced a business card. "Since you're a neighbor of the MacKenzies, I'd be happy to help you with any legal problems that might crop up. I'm especially adept at handling tax questions, and any local or federal government issues that are so vexing for ranchers."

"Thank you." She accepted the card and tucked it into the pocket of her shirt.

"Speaking of issues…" Mad shot him a dark look. "What was so important you had to fly that flashy new plane out here first thing in the morning?"

Lance's smile grew. "You like the plane?"

Mad shrugged. "I didn't see much of it as it flew over. But it's a far cry from our old Cessna."

At that moment, Juliet realized she hadn't been dreaming. She had actually heard a plane's engines just as she was waking.

"It's a Gulfstream." Lance's voice was silky. "It comes with its own pilot. I'm trying it out before committing. But I think it suits my needs."

"Your needs?" The old man frowned. "Your father never needed a jet to keep in touch with his clients."

"Those days are over. Since taking control of my father's firm, I've doubled the client list. And that's just the beginning. By this time next year, I hope to triple that number."

Willow turned to Juliet. "Lance's father, Mason, was Mad's lawyer since the two of them were boyhood friends. When our ranch started growing, it was only natural for Bear to turn to Mason, as well." She sighed as Brady held a chair and she sank down gratefully. "And dear Mason was always here when we needed him. It's something I'll never forget."

"Trust me, Willow." Lance shook his head when offered a glass of orange juice from a tray, explaining, "I have a breakfast meeting scheduled." Turning to Willow he went on smoothly, "As I've explained to you, even though my father is now retired, nothing has changed.

Despite his extended fishing trip, he took the time to look over and approve all the documents before sending them along."

"I'm relieved to hear that." Willow indicated the table. "Are you sure you and your pilot can't stay for breakfast?"

"Sorry. This is a meeting I can't miss." Lance started toward the door. Over his shoulder he called, "Thanks again for agreeing to sign these on such short notice. I know all this business can be confusing when you've lost a spouse, but it can't be helped. There's so much government red tape, it would be impossible for you to navigate without a competent lawyer to walk you through it, and I'm happy to be here for you."

He paused as though remembering his manners. Turning, he flashed a blinding smile on Juliet. "It was nice meeting you, neighbor. I hope I'll see you again. If you need any legal advice, feel free to contact me."

Minutes later, with the sound of the jet overhead, Mad announced that breakfast was ready.

Willow gave an audible sigh. "I'm sick and tired of legal documents. I hope I never have to see another."

"I'm sure this won't be the last of them, lass." Mad shot her a sympathetic look before returning his attention to the waffles.

Myrna handed Willow a glass of orange juice. "Drink. It's fresh. It will revive your spirits."

Willow managed a smile as she looked around to include not only the housekeeper, but her foreman, her father-in-law, and her children. "Thank heaven for all of you. I don't know what I'd do if I had to get through this on my own."

Juliet glanced at the housekeeper. "Speaking of thanks. I found my clothes clean and folded. Did you do that?"

Myrna smiled. "I'm up at dawn, and always looking for little chores to occupy my time. I hope I didn't wake you."

Juliet laughed. "I slept so soundly, I think a bomb could have gone off and I'd have slept through it." She crossed the room to press a kiss on the old woman's cheek. "Thank you. That was so thoughtful. I hope I can make it up to you."

Myrna's face was wreathed in smiles as she touched a hand to her cheek. "It was such a little thing. And I knew you hadn't brought a change of clothes for yourself or your sons."

Juliet glanced at her two boys, so easy in the company of Mad. The ice cream smudges were gone from Casey's shirt. The grass stains were completely erased from Ethan's pants.

"Bless you," she whispered to Myrna as she squeezed her hands.

With a smile the old woman returned her attention to the oven, removing an egg casserole along with a pan of crisp bacon.

When the waffles were brown, Mad lifted the lid and removed them to large plates before saying, "All right now. Casey, you carry the bowl of whipped cream. Ethan, you're big enough to handle that platter of fruit."

Following his directions, the two boys did as they were told while the others gathered around the big table. As they took their places, they began passing around the platters of egg and bacon and toast slathered with Myrna's homemade jellies, while Mad urged the boys to try his waffles.

Casey could barely speak around a mouthful of waffle heaped with whipped cream and strawberries, blueberries, and raspberries. "Mama, Mad's right. These don't taste anything like yours."

"If you'd like, lass, I'll give you the recipe."

Juliet laughed. "Only if you promise to come over and do the cooking, too."

"That might be a bit difficult in my condition. I doubt your kitchen has room for this contraption."

"It isn't nearly as large as this." Juliet studied the streams of light filtering through the tall windows. "Or as bright and airy. This is such a lovely room."

"It's deliberate, lass. Since I spend so much of my time here, I wanted it to be spacious enough for my wheelchair, and all the appliances and countertops to be low enough for me to work without strain."

She nodded. "This is one of the things we learned during therapy. There were building contractors who showed us renderings of their designs specifically for people in wheelchairs. Lower countertops. Barrier-free rooms without clutter that would permit the easy flow of wheelchairs and scooters." She ducked her head. "Most of them were pretty daunting."

"Because of the mess involved in the remodeling?" Willow asked.

Juliet shook her head. "Because of the terrible expense."

"Yes. I can imagine." Willow glanced across the table at her father-in-law.

Juliet squared her shoulders. "Did you have to go through extensive therapy after your accident, Mad?"

He shrugged. "The doctors ordered it. But I wasn't very cooperative."

"Not cooperative?" Willow couldn't hide her laughter. "Mad, after your first week, there wasn't a therapist left who would agree to work with you."

"Pissants." His voice dripped anger. "The whole lot of them. Weak-willed jellyfish."

"I'm sure they had a name for you, as well." Willow touched a napkin to her lips before meeting his stony gaze. "And not nearly as kind as that."

"I had a right to be angry. My whole life had just been snatched away in an instant."

Juliet nodded in agreement. "Anyone who has ever lost a limb knows what you mean, Mad. The therapists should have taken the time to probe your feelings."

Willow chuckled. "They didn't need time. Mad let everyone know exactly how he felt. They may have heard him all the way across Montana. Believe me, he didn't hold back."

Mad smiled. "Go ahead. Laugh if you want. But I'm in agreement with Juliet. I'm sure I wasn't the first angry man they had to deal with."

"Maddock MacKenzie." Willow shook her head. "'Angry' doesn't even begin to describe you back then. After your accident you were Lucifer, out to destroy the world and everyone in it. You seemed bent on making everyone in that hospital pay for being able to walk while you were confined to a bed. There were doctors and nurses who fled your room in fear for their lives."

He grinned, enjoying the mental image. "Really? Was I that strong?"

"You oozed wild-eyed fury."

"So," Juliet interjected. "You've never had physical therapy?"

"Didn't need it." He slapped a hand on the wheels of his chair and shoved away from the table. Over his shoulder he called, "I taught myself everything I needed to know to take care of my own needs. I guess you could say I'm my own therapist."

Juliet watched him roll across the room to retrieve the coffee server, waving Myrna away.

When he returned to the table, he was smiling at her boys. "Well, lads, how did you enjoy my special waffles?"

"They were the best." Casey finished a final bite of waffle, whipped cream, and berries. Before he could wipe his mouth on his sleeve, he caught sight of his mother holding up her napkin.

Looking properly chastised, he wiped his mouth with the napkin before saying, "Will you teach our mama how to make them?"

"I will indeed. As soon as I write down the recipe."

Juliet brightened. "I have a better idea. Maybe one day Griff could bring you to my place when the Romeos are having a therapy session. While you're there, you could meet some men who are learning some of the things you've already had to face. I'm sure there's a lot you could tell them. And then you could show me how to make your famous waffles."

Mad seemed about to argue. But seeing the eager, expectant looks on the faces of Casey and Ethan, he paused before saying, "Maybe I'll do just that, lass. One of these days."

Juliet knew, from the tone of his voice, that he was merely being polite.

No matter. Like him, she knew a thing or two about persistence.

* * *

"Fine breakfast, Mad." Brady pushed away from the table and started toward the mudroom. "I'm heading to the highlands. Whit, you'll take care of that broken wheel on the flatbed?"

"I'm on it." Whit turned to Ash. "You got time to lend a hand?"

"Sure thing." Ash nodded. "Brenna's heading into town for supplies. She can swing by on the way home and pick me up."

Juliet turned to Willow. "Before you head off to see to your chores, I want to thank you again for welcoming us into your home."

"You and your boys can stay as long as you'd like."

Juliet was already shaking her head. "How I wish I could just hide out here forever. I slept so well last night, knowing I was safe. But I have to get back to my place and face reality. No more hiding."

Willow gave her a gentle smile. "I understand. But remember, whenever things get to be too much, come here with your sons and take a little break."

The two women hugged before Willow stepped into the mudroom to retrieve a wide-brimmed hat and leather gloves. Minutes later she was in one of the trucks and heading across a meadow toward a distant herd.

Griff put a hand on Juliet's shoulder. "You're sure you want to go back?"

"I have to. I have a life to live, Griff." She turned to where Myrna and Mad were sharing a last cup of coffee. "Thank you both for all you did for my boys and me."

The old woman stood and hugged her.

Mad caught her hand. "Just remember. If that wrangler

Mitch returns, keep the door locked and Chief Pettigrew's number ready to dial."

"I will." She dimpled. "I was serious about having you join the Romeos. They're a grand group of men. They're not ranchers. But they're all former military men who've seen combat. You'd find that you have more in common with them than you have with some of your neighbors."

He nodded. "And I promise to give it some thought, lass." Seeing Griff holding out the keys to a truck he added, "I hope you'll come back. And bring these two with you."

He reached out and caught the two little boys in a bear hug.

Long after Casey had turned away to follow his mother and Griff to the door, Ethan was still clinging to the old man, his face buried against his neck as though breathing him in.

Juliet turned and caught sight of it, and she was forced to absorb a terrible slash of pain through her heart. When Ethan caught up with her and grabbed her hand, she took in several deep breaths to keep from weeping.

CHAPTER THIRTEEN

On the ride home, Casey chattered like a magpie, about the fancy bedroom he and his brother shared, and the size of Griff's ranch and the yummy food Mad made especially for them.

"When can we go back to Griff's house, Mama?"

She glanced at Ethan, who kept his head down, staring at the floor. "We'll try to do it again soon. And maybe we can have Griff's family to our ranch. Would you like that?"

"Yes." He gave a little fist pump that had Juliet smiling.

She turned to Griff. "You have an amazing family."

"Yeah. That's what I'm discovering."

She gave a shake of her head. "Sorry. I forgot for a moment that you're just getting to know them, too. Do you know how lucky you are to have found such good people?"

He rested his arm on the open window of the truck as

he guided it along a dirt road. "It could have turned out so differently. I don't know too many people who would welcome a secret son. Especially while they're dealing with a tragedy in the family."

"Does the police chief have any suspects in your father's murder?"

"According to Ira, everybody is a suspect."

She lifted a brow. "I don't understand."

"You've met Mad. I guess my father was just like him. A really great guy who was cursed with a hair-trigger temper. According to the things I've heard, Bear MacKenzie had as many enemies as he had friends."

They fell silent as they neared the Grayson Ranch. Griff saw Jackie Turner standing in the doorway of the barn and pulled up alongside him.

When Juliet and her sons had exited the truck, the old man touched a hand to the brim of his hat. "'Morning, Juliet. Boys."

He looked over. "Griff. I was a little concerned when I found nobody home this morning. I should have known you wouldn't leave Juliet and her boys alone."

Juliet looked alarmed. "Is something wrong, Jackie?"

"No, ma'am. Creepers. Don't go getting upset. But an airplane was here when I arrived, and several workmen were in your barn. When I asked what they were doing, they assured me that they were here at your request to fix some equipment. So I thought I'd stick around and watch until they left, just to be sure they weren't here to do any damage. They were as good as their word. Fixed that thing up in the ceiling and were on their way."

Juliet put a hand to her throat. "Oh, thank heaven. They were from Endicott Medical Supply."

"Yes, ma'am. That's what they said." Jackie returned her smile. "Now, if you don't mind, I was about to walk through your barns and finish my inventory of your equipment."

"Thank you, Jackie. When you're done, please come to the house. I'll have a fresh pot of coffee."

"I'd like that." Taking a small notebook from his shirt pocket, he turned away.

Juliet fished her cell phone from her pocket and hastily turned it on before speaking briefly into it. "Heywood? The lift is up and running. If you'd like to contact your group, they can make arrangements to begin therapy again tomorrow."

On the speaker, his tone was cranky. "What's wrong with today?"

"Nothing. Except that we can get an earlier start tomorrow."

His words held a distinct challenge. "I came over yesterday. There was an old man there who said you'd gone to town... with that marine. I tried phoning you last night and again this morning. There was no answer."

"Sorry. I was out, and forgot that I had my phone silenced. But I'm back now, and with the lift repaired, we can get back to normal. Do you want to try for tomorrow? Or is that too soon to contact all the members of your group?"

He swore. "The Romeos will come whenever I tell them to. We'll be there early tomorrow. That is, if you're not off gallivanting somewhere and we can count on you to be there."

"I'll be here." She disconnected and started toward the house, walking beside Griff and her boys. "It seems I caught Sperry in one of his moods again. I expected him to be thrilled to learn that therapy was back on track. He's been out of sorts every day it was postponed. And now, instead of being happy, he sounded like a sulky kid."

"Maybe he's bored. Without the company of his fellow Romeos, there probably isn't much to keep him busy."

"That could be." She brightened. "Still, I'm surprised that he came all the way out here yesterday, knowing the lift was still down. At least he saw Jackie, who sent him on his way." She sighed. "Tomorrow is soon enough to get back to it."

At the porch, the boys raced up the steps, eager to find their favorite toys. Juliet started to follow, until she realized that Griff remained off the porch. She turned. "Are you coming in?"

He shook his head. "Since you've got Jackie here, this seems a good time for me to head over to Garvey Fuller's mill and see about starting on some ramps around the MacKenzie Ranch."

"I'm surprised that wasn't done years ago."

"So was I." Griff shrugged. "According to Willow, Mad wasn't ready to accept his limitations then. He believed that having a ramp would tell the world he was a cripple. Who knows? Maybe because he has a woodworker in the family, it seems like a good idea to him now. I know this: It will give him freedom he will welcome."

He started to turn away when he heard Juliet say, "Griff, thanks for last night. It meant the world to me to know that the boys and I were safe. It's the first good night's sleep I've had in ages."

"I'm glad. What will you do tonight?"

She lowered her gaze. "I guess I'll call the police chief later and see if he has any news about Mitch."

"And if he doesn't?"

She looked away, avoiding his eyes. "I think it's time for me to grow up and deal with my fears."

He climbed the steps and started to reach for her before deciding against it and lowering his hand to his side. "You don't have to be here alone. Willow asked you to come back and spend the night at our place."

"No." When she realized how harsh that sounded, she tried to soften her words. "This is my problem, Griff. Not yours or your family's. I need to learn how to handle my own life."

He caught her hand and was forced to absorb a swift sexual jolt. "Look, I know this isn't my business. But if Mitch is still out there, why not accept Willow's hospitality?"

When she opened her mouth to object he said quickly, "If not for your own sake, then do it for the sake of your sons."

She lowered her head. "Now you're trying to guilt me."

He grinned and touched a finger beneath her chin, tipping up her face and forcing her to meet his gaze. "Is it working?"

She pulled her hand free and took a step back. "I can't spend my nights with you...with your family."

He caught her hesitation and decided to take the plunge. "Juliet, I know what this is about. We nearly crossed a line last night..."

She started to speak and he cut her off. "...but we didn't. And now I can feel you trying to distance yourself from me. I get it. So to put your mind at ease, I promise you I won't let that happen again. But until Mitch is caught, the danger is real. There's no reason for you to put yourself at risk because of something that happened in the heat of the moment."

Her head came up sharply. "What kind of guarantee can you give that we won't find ourselves in the…heat of the moment again, if I spend the night in the room next to yours?"

His voice held the edge of steel. "I'm fresh out of guarantees. But I give you my word that unless you say otherwise, I'll keep my distance. I may have wanted you in my bed—and still do, if you want the truth—but what I want even more is for you and your sons to be safe."

For a moment she seemed stunned by his honesty. Then, taking a deep breath, she forced herself to look him in the eye. "What happened last night wasn't just your fault. I share the blame. I …wanted you. Maybe I still do." She could feel her cheeks flaming. "But you're right. For the sake of my boys, until Mitch is caught, I need to be sensible. We're totally isolated out here. Even my wranglers are too far away to offer any help in an emergency. So, thank you for your offer, Griff. As long as your family is willing, I'll certainly sleep better if I'm surrounded by good people."

"Done." He turned away. "I'll pick you and the boys up in time for supper."

"All right. We'll be ready." She saw him pause and turn. "And this time I'll pack clean clothes for tomorrow, so Myrna doesn't have to do laundry at dawn."

"I'm sure she didn't mind." He strode to his truck and started the engine.

Juliet let herself into the house before leaning against the closed door.

What had she just agreed to?

How in the world would she find the strength to keep fighting this attraction, when she kept the object of her desire too close for comfort?

Griff unloaded the wood he'd bought at the mill, storing it neatly at the side of the house. He'd forgotten how much he missed this. He'd had a knack for woodworking since he was a teen, and had spent his summers working for a local construction firm. In the early years he'd been the crew's gofer, cleaning up the job sites, hauling away debris, running and fetching everything from water to their lunches. Later, when he was old enough to be allowed to handle the power equipment, he'd been in hog heaven.

He loved everything about woodworking and carpentry. From the smell of freshly sawed lumber to the visual symmetry when the wood was laid out just the way he'd seen it in his mind.

Though he was just beginning this latest job, he could already see how it would look when it was finished, with a long, gently sloping ramp to the back porch, and possibly another leading to the barns and outbuildings.

He began at the back porch, doing a quick sketch of the ramp he hoped to build. In no time he was laying out the boards that would form the base of the ramp. For the next few hours, as the sun climbed high overhead, he measured, sawed, hammered.

Somewhere along the way he'd shed his shirt. Each time he stopped to drain a bottle of cold water, he would pour the rest over his head. Soon his hair was plastered to his neck, and his back and arms were bronzed from the sun.

Gradually the others drifted home from their chores. Willow and Brady, down from the hills to check on the herds, paused to watch as the ramp took shape.

"Oh, Brady." Willow's smile was as bright as the sun. "I wish Mad had agreed to this years ago. Why did we give in to his foolish vanity?"

Brady slapped Griff's arm. "Because we didn't have our own home-grown handyman, that's why. But now that Mad's had a change of heart, let's just go with it."

Whit sauntered up from the barn and stopped to admire the work. "Nice job, bro."

"Thanks." Griff got to his feet and grabbed another bottle of cold water before draining it. "It's coming along."

"I think I could lend a hand tomorrow."

"Great. I'd appreciate the help."

They both looked up as Ash and Brenna drove up in a truck. Brenna stepped out and reached for a covered cake plate, while Ash trailed behind, carrying several bags.

"Hey, you come bearing gifts." Whit's grin was infectious. "I don't care what's in those bags, but I know a cake when I see one. Chocolate, I hope."

"It is. With buttercream frosting."

He wrapped an arm around his sister-in-law's shoulders. "Maybe you should let me carry that. It looks heavy."

Brenna was laughing. "If I turn this loose, you'll have it half gone before we even have supper."

"Supper." Griff looked thunderstruck. "What was I thinking? I promised to pick up Juliet and her boys."

Just then a truck pulled up and Juliet and the boys climbed down.

"Thanks, Jackie," she called to the driver.

The old man waved as he put the truck in reverse before turning and driving away.

Juliet walked up to the others, trying not to stare at Griff, who was still stripped to the waist, his body slick with sheen. "I thought, since Jackie was coming this way, I could save you that long drive."

"I'm glad you did." Griff tucked the hammer into his leather tool belt. "The truth is, I got so caught up in my work here, I forgot the time."

"Mama packed our suitcase," Casey announced proudly. "So we'll have our PJs tonight and clean clothes tomorrow."

"So this is your vacation?" Willow said with a laugh.

Casey turned to his mother. "Is this a vacation?"

"That's what it feels like." Juliet caught Willow's hand. "I'm so grateful for your hospitality."

"And we're happy for the company."

"What're you building, Griff?" Casey said as he raced over to stand beside him.

"A ramp."

"For Grandpa Mad?"

"Yeah." He grinned at the little boy's easy use of the old man's name. "Think he'll like it?"

"Yeah. When it's done, he can take me and Efan on even longer rides."

"That's the plan." Griff felt Juliet staring at him and turned to her. "Any word from Ira about Mitch?"

She gave a quick shake of her head and he let the subject go, knowing she didn't want to talk about it in front of her sons. But from the look in her eyes, he was certain something had happened.

Myrna stepped out onto the back porch. "Supper in one hour. Mad says you'd better wash up and get inside while the steaks are hot and the beer's cold."

While the others scrambled inside, Juliet remained a moment, watching as Griff collected his tools and made ready to store them in the barn for the night.

Moving along beside him, she said, "Ira told me that they've found my truck. It was abandoned on a deserted ranch outside of Copper Creek. He referred to it as the old Cleary place."

Griff shrugged. "I'm sure the others will know where it is."

Juliet lowered her voice. "There's something else."

He paused.

"Mitch called. He didn't identify himself, but I recognized his voice. He called me...a few choice names before warning me that I'd pay for the trouble I was causing him."

"Causing him?" Griff's voice was rough with anger. "What about what he'd planned on doing to you?"

"I guess that doesn't count in his mind. But he's furious that he barely evaded the state police before abandoning my truck."

"Did you call Ira?"

She nodded.

Griff stowed his tools on a shelf and hung his tool belt on a hook. Using his discarded shirt to wipe sweat from his face and chest, he realized Juliet was watching each movement with a look he couldn't quite fathom.

"Is there more?"

She shook her head and turned away.

He caught her by the arm, stilling her movement. "Is something wrong?"

"No." She avoided his eyes.

His voice lowered. "Tell me, Juliet. Did Ira have bad news?"

She gave a sound that could have been a laugh or a sigh. "No news. Good or bad. He said he had every confidence that Mitch would be caught." She sighed. "This isn't about Mitch. It's . . . you."

"What about me?"

She turned to face him, and allowed her gaze to move slowly over him, from his sweat-slick torso to the damp denims molding muscular thighs. His hair was dark and wet and falling over one eye, adding to his look of a rugged, dangerous rogue.

"You're so gorgeous, with all that sweat and muscle. And I feel . . . safe when I look at you. I can't take my eyes off you."

He went very still, his lips splitting into a wicked grin. "Wait a minute. Did you just call me gorgeous?"

"As if you don't know how sexy you look."

He slowly shook his head before reaching out to bring her close. "I hope you don't mind being kissed by a hot, sweaty cowboy. 'Cause lady, there's just no way I can resist after all those pretty words."

His arms closed around her and she was hauled against his chest.

He smelled of heat and sweat and sawdust, and she breathed him into her very soul as his mouth moved over hers. At the same time his hands moved up her sides, setting off little sparks wherever they touched. And they touched her everywhere, until her body was on fire.

She didn't know how her hands found their way around his neck, but there they were, clinging as if to a lifeline. She poured herself into the kiss, her tongue meeting his, her teeth scraping his, as she gave him everything he wanted and more.

Inside her mouth he managed to whisper, "Do you think the others will miss us if we sneak into one of the stalls?"

She laughed, but only for a moment, until he took the kiss deeper. Then her laughter turned into a soft sigh, and then a moan of pleasure as he dipped his head and took one of her erect nipples into his mouth. Despite the barrier of her shirt, it hardened instantly.

"Griff. We have to stop."

"Can't." His breathing was labored.

"Hey, Mama." Casey's high-pitched voice was a dash of ice water.

Two heads came up sharply. In the instant before the little boy stepped into the barn, they managed to move apart, though their chests were heaving.

"Grandpa Mad says to come to supper."

"Thanks, honey." Juliet knew her voice sounded as out of breath as she felt.

"Come on then." He stepped between them and took hold of his mother's hand.

Griff leaned close to whisper in her ear, "This isn't over, you know."

She lifted a finger to his mouth. Just a touch, but she heard his quick intake of breath before she started toward the door.

As she walked away she could still taste him on her lips. Could still smell him in her lungs. The smell of a man. It was something she hadn't allowed herself to savor for such a very long time.

And though she was awash in guilt, it was absolutely intoxicating.

CHAPTER FOURTEEN

By the time Griff walked into the kitchen—his hair damp from the shower, and wearing a clean shirt and denims—the family had gathered around the far side of the huge kitchen, sipping cold longnecks and discussing their favorite topic: the weather and how it was affecting their herds and crops.

Whit handed Griff a frosty bottle of beer before adding, "If this continues, roundup is going to be a challenge."

"Why?" Griff didn't really care at the moment. With Juliet smiling at him over the rim of her glass of ice water, all he could think about was that kiss in the barn. And how he wanted to get her alone and do it again.

"We'll have to hire on extra wranglers, for one thing." Brady sipped his beer. "Thanks to a gentle spring, more calves survived than ever before. The herd is nearly double what it was just a year ago. And now that we're wrangling Brenna's herds, as well, we'll have our hands full come September."

"So it's all good news." Griff tore his gaze from Juliet long enough to watch her two boys kneeling beside a low table and helping themselves to finger-sized slivers of toasted rye bread slathered with a cheese dip.

"These are really good, Grandpa Mad." Casey licked cheese from his thumb.

"I'm glad you like them, lad." Mad winked at Ethan, nibbling in silence, and the boy's face was wreathed in smiles.

Griff raised a brow at Juliet, who looked as surprised as he was.

How, he wondered, had a grumpy old man like Mad managed to charm one sad, lonely little boy?

A half hour later, at Mad's command, they gathered around the big oval table. The wonderful smells of onions and steaks on the grill, garlic potatoes steaming, and apple pies, sprinkled with cinnamon cooling on the counter, had their mouths watering.

Like the food, the conversation was soul satisfying.

"Ash and I were in town today, and Orin Tamer just got in a slew of brand-new trucks." Brenna's eyes danced with unconcealed excitement.

"And which one did my big brother pick out for you?" Whit's voice was a lazy drawl.

"Who says I'm buying my wife a truck?"

"Bro, the minute pretty little Brenna set her heart on a new truck, we all knew you were a goner."

At Whit's words, the others burst into laughter.

Ash looked properly annoyed. "Just because somebody wants something doesn't mean they always get it."

"They do if that someone is a brand-new bride married to a poor helpless lovesick cowboy who can't stop kissing her pretty little feet."

"Knock it off, Whit."

"The truth bites, doesn't it, bro?"

While the others laughed, little Casey asked innocently, "Do you let Ash kiss your feet, Brenna?"

Her eyes twinkled. "I do indeed, Casey. And do you know why?"

"So he'll buy you a truck?"

Above the laughter she said, "Well, there's that, of course. But the real reason is because it purely makes Ash so happy to kiss my dainty little feet."

Casey looked from Brenna to Ash before turning to his mother. "Did Daddy ever kiss your feet, Mama?"

Poor Juliet was mortified.

Taking pity on her Griff managed to redirect the conversation. "So, Brenna. You haven't said. What color truck do you want?"

"Black. Shiny black." She smiled. "At first I thought about a white truck, but we haul so many supplies that it would soon be black anyway." She touched a hand to Ash's shoulder. "And I doubt my husband would be happy driving a white truck."

"So you've picked out the color. When are you getting it?"

"Whenever Ash decides we need it."

Whit's smile widened. "I'm putting all my money on soon, Brenna. Very soon."

Everyone, even Ash, joined in the laughter. It was clear to all of them that he was so content with the new life he'd made with Brenna that even his younger brother's teasing couldn't dim the glow that seemed to radiate around both of them.

Griff sat back, wondering about that very thing.

Ash MacKenzie was a tough guy. No doubt about it. He'd left home after a bitter fight with his father and hadn't been seen for nearly ten years. He'd returned only after news of his father's death.

And yet here he was, reunited with Brenna, the love of his life, who had been on the verge of marrying someone else until Ash had walked back into her life.

Was love enough to change a person? Or were there other factors working in Ash's life that had brought him this much joy?

He stowed away the questions to mull when he had more time. For now, the family was thoroughly enjoying their excellent supper.

As they began passing around platters, Brady turned to Mad with a grin. "You sure know how to get a hungry cowboy's attention."

"That's 'cause I was one, for more years than I can count." Mad sat back, watching the others tuck into their steaks with enthusiasm.

"You were a cowboy, Grandpa Mad?" Casey's eyes were wide.

"That I was, lad. One of the best." Mad smiled at the memory. "Before I was old enough to shave, I was doing the work of three men. Brute strength. That's what it took in those days to tame this wilderness."

"And a healthy dose of hardheadedness," Brady added dryly.

"Aye. That, too. That was my downfall."

"You fell down?" Casey asked innocently.

"In a manner of speaking." The old man turned to him. "We had a sudden spring blizzard, trapping my herd up in the highlands. Bear warned me about attempting to try going up to the hills in such weather. I knew I'd lose all those new mothers and their calves if I didn't get food to them. So against my better judgment, I was hauling a load of feed when the rig caught an icy patch and flipped, crushing the cab and pinning me inside. I was nearly blue with cold by the time Bear found me. He returned with all his wranglers and as many tools as they could carry. It took dozens of hands and plenty of blowtorches to free me." He glanced down at his useless legs. "The doctors told me I was lucky to be alive. I'm afraid it took me a lot of years before I agreed. I thought, at first, I'd rather be dead than crippled."

"And now?" It was Griff who asked the question they all wanted answered.

"Life is a precious thing. When given few choices, we'll take almost anything over death. And now—" the old man gave them a lopsided grin "—who knows? Maybe in a few years you'll see me on TV showing folks how to cook for cowboys."

"You'd be good at it, Mad," Brady said with a laugh. "You'd probably have folks lining up to learn to rope and ride just so they could eat your cooking."

Mad joined in the laughter. "All I know is, on days like this, I'm happy I'm still here with all of you."

When dinner was over, the family prepared to have dessert in the great room.

Griff watched little Casey and Ethan draw close to Mad, who was telling Myrna to be careful loading the apple pies onto the serving cart. A serving cart he'd invented out of an old cabinet and two pairs of castors he'd found in one of the closets.

"I spent a lot of time today slicing all those apples. They were shipped from Edie Martin's orchard in Michigan. The best tart-sweet apples in the country." The old man looked around at the others for emphasis. "Only fresh apples for my pies."

"I wouldn't expect otherwise from you," Willow said with a smile.

"Exactly. So see that you treat them like gold, Myrna." He patted his knees. "Hop aboard, lads. This train's heading out."

Casey and Ethan eagerly climbed onto his lap before he turned his wheelchair toward the doorway.

The housekeeper glared at his retreating back. But Griff noticed that she did indeed handle the pies gingerly as she placed them, along with plates and forks and a large serving knife, on the rolling cart. After loading a carafe of coffee, along with cream and sugar and enough cups and saucers for everyone, she started toward the great room.

Griff stepped forward. "You go ahead, Myrna. I've got this."

She shot him a grateful smile. "Bless you, Griff." She turned. "I'll just fetch ice cream to go along with those pies."

In the great room, Casey and Ethan migrated toward the fireplace, where a log blazed. Sitting on comfortable floor cushions, they watched as Myrna served slices of pie and ice cream.

"Would you lads care to try my pie?" Mad was admiring the way the delicate pastry held up under the apple slices, topped by a mound of apple-cinnamon ice cream.

Ethan shook his head, and Casey did the same, announcing, "Efan and me just want ice cream."

"Ethan and I," Juliet corrected gently.

"You, too, Mama?"

The others grinned at Casey's innocent question.

"I believe I'll have pie with my ice cream." She decided the time wasn't right for a lesson on proper English.

Griff settled himself beside Juliet on one of the big sofas. When he stretched out his long legs, his thigh brushed hers, sending a surge of warmth through his veins.

To cover her sudden silence he said, "The medical supply company finally flew out their repairmen and spare parts, so Juliet now has her equipment up and running."

"About time." Whit dug into his pie, which was topped with a triple scoop of ice cream. "So the Romeos can get back to their therapy?"

"On top of that," Juliet said shyly, "I got a call today from the mother of a ten-year-old girl who is interested in what I may have to offer her."

"Are you a trained therapist?" Willow asked.

Juliet shook her head. "I received my training while Buddy was flying. I was about to receive my board certification when…" She paused, seeing the way her two sons were watching and listening. "I'll need to go back and be certified, but in the meantime, I'm not legally allowed to offer physical therapy. I'm merely offering a chance for the injured to get away from their wheelchairs for a little while and ride a horse."

"So it's just for fun."

Mad's tone got her to look at him. "I guess it would seem that way to some people. But riding a horse truly lifts the spirits more than anything I can think of. There's just something about sitting high in the saddle, and forgetting, for a little while, about all the things you can't do. It's therapy, but I don't need to be certified to offer it."

"Do you ride?" Willow asked her.

"I do, though not as well as someone like you who was born to it. But I want my boys to be comfortable in the saddle. It was something their father asked me to do for them."

Griff turned to Whit. "Maybe you'd like to give the boys some lessons. You're just about the best rider I've ever seen."

Mad sat up straighter, filled with pride. "And who taught you, lad?"

"You did, Mad." Whit turned to the others. "I was in the saddle even before I could walk. I used to spend all my time over at Mad's ranch, learning to ride and rope. My dad was too busy with ranch chores to have time for such things, but no matter how busy Mad was, he always had time for me."

While the others were finishing their dessert and enjoying second cups of coffee, Brenna moved to a small side table, where she'd set out some modeling clay.

As she began to work it between her hands, Casey and Ethan moved closer to watch.

"What're you doing?" Casey asked.

"I thought I'd make something for you. What would you like?"

"Can you make anything?"

She smiled. "I can try."

Casey glanced at his brother before saying, "Can you make a horse?"

She worked quickly, forming a ball of dark brown clay into one shape, and adding another smaller ball for the head. She added delicate ears, a tail, before handing it over to the two boys.

"Wow. Look, Mama." Casey ran over to show it to his mother, and then to Griff and the others.

When they'd properly remarked on it, he hurried back to kneel beside Brenna. "How'd you learn to do that?"

"I've been doing it since I was your age. My mother bought me some modeling clay, and I discovered that I loved making things."

"And now she's a famous sculptor." Ash's voice was filled with pride.

"I wouldn't say famous," Brenna said with a laugh. "But I do love sculpting."

"Can you teach us?" Casey looked at his brother, who was fingering the horse with a look of reverence.

"Why don't you show me what you can do?" She spread out the various colored lumps of clay and watched as they began to roll them in their chubby little hands.

Brenna stopped Ethan. "Look. What do you see in that shape?"

He set the round ball down on the table and she pointed. "I see a bunny rabbit. See? There's his head and one ear. Add another ear, and then a bigger ball of clay for his body, a little round tail at the end, and you'll see a bunny, too."

He did as she instructed, and soon, to his delight, the form of a rabbit began to take shape.

"Look, Casey." She pointed to the long, thin piece of clay in his hands. "I believe I see a caterpillar."

"You do?"

"Watch." She handed him a bit of green, and showed him how to add it before holding out a small chunk of blue, a little purple. She showed him how to add yellow eyes and tiny black legs.

When it was finished, he squealed with delight and hurried over to show his mother. While Juliet was oohing and ahhing over it, Griff sat back, watching her reaction with avid interest. When she sat back he wrapped an arm around her shoulders, and she reacted with surprise.

When Casey rejoined Ethan and Brenna, Mad suddenly turned his wheelchair toward the doorway. Over his shoulder he called, "Griff, would you mind giving me a hand?"

Griff was on his feet and hurrying over as the old man's chair disappeared into the kitchen. "What do you need, Mad?" He paused just inside as Mad closed the door behind him.

"Just a minute of your time, laddie."

Before Griff could ask, the old man fixed him with a look. "You've got strong feelings for Juliet."

"What makes you think—?"

Mad held up a hand. "I've got eyes. I see how you look at her. You've been devouring her like my apple pie."

Griff straightened. "I don't see that it's any of your business."

"It's my business when she's a guest under this roof. If that isn't enough, she has two little boys to think about. So if you're thinking about a quick tumble in the hay, you'd better think again, lad."

When Griff held his silence, Mad added, "I know what it is to be a man who's so befuddled by a lass, he can't think with his brain, but only with his—" he grimaced "—his *other* brain. But remember this, lad. If you truly care about a woman, you have to put what's best for her above your own desire." He paused. "That's all I'm saying. Now why don't you fetch that coffeemaker and see if anyone wants a last cup before bedtime?"

He rolled away, leaving Griff alone in the kitchen with a jumble of dark, troubled thoughts.

CHAPTER FIFTEEN

In the great room, the little table was littered with clay bunnies and worms and birds in various colors. Spurred on by Brenna's praise, Casey and Ethan had used up almost all of the lumps of clay that she'd brought.

Ethan stifled a yawn, while Casey rested his chin on his hands and watched as Brenna put the finishing touches on his clay cat by adding a long striped tail.

"There now. I think we're done for tonight." She turned to the two boys. "But if you enjoyed this, you're welcome to come over to my studio for some lessons."

"Can we, Mama?" Casey asked.

She turned to Brenna. "I'm willing, as long as it doesn't take you away from your work."

"I have plenty of time after work, and I love teaching others, especially children, the joy of creating something out of a lump of clay. Why don't you call me and we'll set up an hour or two when the boys can come?"

"Thank you, Brenna. I can see how much they've enjoyed this. And I love knowing they'd be getting lessons from a real sculptor."

Brenna turned to Ash. "And now, cowboy, if you don't take me home soon, you'll have to carry me."

He caught her hand and lifted it to his lips. "Babe, I'll carry you any time you ask."

"Oh, brother." Whit made a gagging gesture that had the others laughing. "It's time for me to get out of here, too. Before I overdose on too much of this newlyweded bliss. Brady, how about a beer at Wylie's?"

"Fine. As long as it's only one. I put in a long day, too."

"Want to join us?" Whit asked Griff, who shook his head.

Juliet walked over to where her two boys were lounging amid the floor cushions. Just minutes earlier they'd been showing off their sculptures. Now, they were struggling to keep their eyes open.

"Bedtime, boys."

Casey made a halfhearted attempt to argue. "But Mama…"

She turned to Griff, who ambled over and lifted Ethan to his shoulder. "Come on, little wrangler," he whispered. "I think you've had enough fun."

Ethan didn't argue. Instead he wrapped his arms around Griff's neck and snuggled close. From the look on Griff's face, it was clear that he was enjoying the chance to snuggle the usually timid little boy.

Juliet lifted Casey in her arms. Instead of the expected argument, he merely called, "'Night, Grandpa Mad. 'Night, everybody."

"Good night, lad," Mad called as the others waved.

* * *

Once upstairs, Griff led the way down the hallway to their room. Inside he slipped Ethan's shoes and clothes from him before glancing at Juliet, who was undressing Casey on the other bed.

"Want me to find their pajamas in their suitcase?"

She shook her head. "I think they're way too tired for that. I'll let them sleep in their briefs again."

He pulled the blanket up over the sleeping Ethan and watched as she did the same for Casey.

She moved between the two beds, pressing soft kisses to both their cheeks.

Seeing it, Griff felt a quick rush of heat before turning toward the door.

Juliet followed him out and closed the door. A few steps away she paused outside her room and turned to him with an inviting smile. "Are you tired?"

He didn't quite meet her eyes. "Yeah. It's been a long day in the hot sun. I'd better turn in."

He saw the look of confusion in her eyes and cursed himself for what he was about to do. "I forgot how much physical labor goes into building ramps. I guess I'm out of shape." He rubbed a hand over the back of his neck, and wished he could be touching her neck instead.

Closing his hand into a fist at his side to keep from reaching out to her, he took a step back. "I'll see you in the morning. 'Night."

Though it took all his willpower, he managed to turn away. But not before he saw the look of disappointment on her face.

He walked purposefully to his room and pulled open the door. Once inside he kicked the door shut and strode to the window to stare at the night sky. His hands were balled into fists. His teeth were clenched so hard they ached. But that was nothing compared to the ache wrapped around his heart.

If it hadn't been for Mad's tough-as-nails warning, he had no doubt he'd be in Juliet's room right now. In her bed. Doing all the things he'd thought about doing in the barn.

Juliet stared at the closed door of her room before crossing to slump on the edge of the bed.

All evening, during the wonderful dinner, and that amazing dessert, she'd had a fluttery feeling in the pit of her stomach, just thinking about the way Griff had kissed her in the barn.

She could hear his voice whisper, *This isn't over, you know.*

It hadn't been so much a statement as a challenge. A very tempting challenge that they would finish what they'd started when the others had given them some privacy.

And now, he'd walked away without even a good-night kiss. As though that earlier scene had never occurred.

What had happened between then and now?

Had he had time to change his mind? Had he decided that it had all been a huge mistake?

Had she said something, done something, to make him realize she wasn't worth his time?

Slowly, as though in a dream, she began to undress. In the beautiful bathroom, fit for a queen, she never even noticed her luxurious surroundings. Instead she went through the motions of getting ready for bed as though in a trance.

Once in bed she lay very still, her mind awhirl with dark thoughts.

There weren't a lot of men willing to take on a woman with two boys. Two very different boys. One who chattered like a magpie. One who never spoke a single word. But she'd thought Griff different somehow, better somehow, from all the others. She'd seen the way he got her boys to open up. Had seen the care he lavished on them. Had it all been an act to get close to her?

After the day she'd put in, she ought to fall instantly asleep. Instead, throughout the long night she tossed and turned as doubts and worries played through her mind.

There was a dangerous wrangler out there somewhere bent on revenge. And the thought of him stalking her, threatening her, had given her a feeling of being alone and afraid. But Griff had offered her a sense of security.

Maybe it was all an illusion. A false sense of security.

Maybe she was mistaking it for something quite different.

Some time in the early dawn, she came to the conclusion that Griff, by his baffling behavior, had actually done her a favor.

Last night, in the barn, after a few sizzling kisses, he'd gotten to her heart. Despite all her intentions to remain faithful to Buddy's memory, she'd been ready to open herself up to Griff and give him whatever he wanted.

How pathetic. Was she so starved for affection that she would resort to a tumble in the hay with a man she hardly knew?

What about what *she* wanted? Hadn't she come to Montana determined to work Buddy's ranch and raise his sons in the same way he'd been raised? Was her love for

Buddy so shallow that the first handsome cowboy to show her any affection had her forgetting all her good intentions?

Lesson learned, she decided.

Mitch Cord had called her the ice maiden. It was the label she had very consciously crafted, and one she intended to wear whenever she found herself alone again with Griff.

"Look, Mama." As before, Casey and Ethan were downstairs long before Juliet. They were kneeling at the long coffee table in the sitting area of the kitchen, enjoying glasses of foaming orange juice while moving their toy trucks around and around the top of the table, up and down the legs, and even across the rug underneath it. "Grandpa Mad said this was made from real oranges."

"You squeeze your own every day?" she asked.

Across the room, where he was busy at the stove, Mad nodded. "Nothing but fresh for the MacKenzie clan, lass." He shot her a level gaze. "How did you sleep?"

"Fine." She shrugged and turned away from his scrutiny.

When Griff and Whit trooped in from the barn, they paused to wash at the big sink in the mudroom. Juliet couldn't tear her gaze from Griff as he walked in, his muscles straining the sleeves rolled to the elbows.

For a long moment they simply stared at each other. Then he turned and helped himself to a cup of coffee while she sipped her orange juice.

Willow and Brady came in from the office, where they'd been going over the books. Once again, Willow was muttering her annoyance at the backlog of documents needing her attention. Her frown of concentration turned to a smile at the sight of Juliet and her sons.

"Good morning." She poured two cups of coffee and handed one to Brady before turning to Juliet and the boys. "It looks like a good day to be outdoors."

"That's good." Juliet glanced out the window at the sunlight spilling across the hills. "Because I'll be outdoors all day."

"A busy day?"

She nodded. "I'll be glad for the work. I need to be busy."

"We all do." Willow turned when Mad summoned them to the table.

Soon they were passing around platters of omelets and ham, biscuits and strawberry preserves. Myrna poured milk for the boys and topped off coffee cups around the table before taking her seat beside Mad.

Though Juliet and Griff were seated next to one another, they were careful to avoid touching. Once or twice, as their arms brushed, they quickly moved aside as though burned.

The others were too busy eating and discussing ranch chores to notice. But Mad, sharp-eyed as always, watched them without expression.

After breakfast, as Willow and Brady made plans to ride up to the hills, Juliet hurried across the room to Willow. "I want to thank you again for your warm hospitality, Willow. But I'll be heading back to my ranch now."

Willow hugged her. "You know you're welcome to spend every night here until Ira sends word that he's caught Mitch."

"I'm grateful for your offer of sanctuary. I really appreciate it. It's given me a real sense of security."

Casey and Ethan, each of them pulling a little wheeled suitcase, descended the stairs.

Seeing them, Griff plucked a set of keys from a hook on the wall. "Come on, little wranglers. I'll get you settled in the truck."

Both boys raced across the room to hug Mad and call their good-byes to everyone as they followed Griff out the door.

Juliet thanked Mad and was rewarded by a warm hug from Myrna before trailing slowly behind the others.

As soon as Juliet fastened her seat belt, Griff put the truck in gear and took off along the curving ribbon of driveway and out to the highway beyond.

"Mama said one day this week she'll let me and Efan go to Brenna's studio and make things with clay."

Griff glanced at the little boy in the rearview mirror and saw the excitement dancing in his eyes. "That should be fun. What do you think you'll make?"

Casey shrugged. "Brenna said we should let the clay tell us what it wants to be."

"Talking clay?" Griff winked at the boy in the mirror, and Casey burst into laughter.

"It doesn't talk, but it looks like something."

"I hope it doesn't look like a field of cows." Griff pointed to a hillside black with cattle. "That might take a heap of sculpting."

Both boys laughed at his joke.

For once Juliet was grateful to let the conversation flow around her, leaving her free to stare out the side window, avoiding Griff completely.

For the entire ride, she spoke not a word. Casey was too busy chattering to notice. But Griff did. Her silence was louder than any words. Whatever they'd shared in the barn had evaporated, like the morning mist that hung over the hills and disappeared as soon as the sun warmed the earth.

As he pulled up to her ranch, they spotted the rock-star bus. Heywood Sperry sat on his scooter in the doorway of the barn, scowling.

Juliet climbed out without a word before helping her boys down.

"Are you staying, Griff?" Casey called.

Griff remained behind the wheel. "No, little wrangler. I'd better get back and get to work on those ramps for Mad." He looked beyond Casey to see Juliet turn away quickly. But not before he caught the look of grim resignation in her eyes.

As he drove away he kept watching in his rearview mirror, hoping she would turn and look back.

She kept walking purposefully toward the barn and the scowling veteran, who began gesturing as she approached. She turned her back on Sperry before stepping inside the barn. And then she was out of sight.

For Griff, the drive home was endless. And the look in Juliet's eyes, like a wounded bird, weighed heavily on his mind.

CHAPTER SIXTEEN

Hearing voices, Mad rolled his wheelchair to the doorway of the mudroom to gauge the progress of the work being done on the ramp outside the door. Whit and a handful of wranglers had joined Griff, and all of them were shirtless in the blazing sun.

As always, with Whit leading the pack, there was plenty of teasing and laughter while they worked.

A truck rolled up and Ash stepped out, wearing a leather tool belt.

"Wow." Whit slapped his brother on the back. "You look like you actually know what to do with all those tools."

"That's the idea." Ash grinned good-naturedly. "I figured I couldn't let Griff and you get all the glory. So here I am." He turned to Griff. "Tell me what you want me to do, oh grand and glorious leader."

Griff chuckled. "I've got most of the boards laid out. You got a nail gun?"

Ash shook his head. "Do you happen to have a spare?"

Griff pointed to an assortment of power tools. "Over there."

Soon Ash had joined the others, and the noise level of shouts and laughter reached a fever pitch.

At midday Myrna brought out trays of ham-and-cheese sandwiches, as well as gallons of coffee and a bucket of water bottles in a nest of ice.

The men pounced on the cold drinks, causing Myrna to return with a second tub of ice and water bottles.

While the others took a much-needed break, Griff continued working. It was, he realized, the only way to keep his mind off Juliet, and the sadness he'd seen in her.

As he worked, he chewed over Mad's words. It was true that a woman like Juliet, who had already been so hurt by the loss of her husband, deserved more than a quick tumble in the hay. A mother of two sons needed to protect her reputation. It was also true that he'd been willing to go along, enjoying her company, and allowing their relationship to heat up too quickly, without giving a thought to where it might lead. But, despite what Mad thought, a quick tumble had never been his style.

So, what was his style?

He didn't really know. He hadn't thought that far ahead. Until meeting Juliet, he'd never had to worry about the future. It would take care of itself. He was just enjoying the journey along the way. And the journey had included a long list of women who had enjoyed the same things he did.

But Juliet was different. And not just because she'd

lost a man she obviously loved. She was a mother of two little boys who needed, more than anything, stability in their lives. And to his way of thinking, stability meant commitment. Not a man who was in their lives for a while, and then disappeared. They needed, and deserved, a man who would remain constant in their lives.

Was he willing to take on a lifetime with a woman and someone's else's sons?

He absorbed a quick arrow to the heart.

Someone else's son? Wasn't that what he'd been for a lifetime?

He didn't like where these thoughts were taking him.

Annoyed, he bent to his work and struggled to block out everything except the task at hand.

Griff stood back, admiring the progress they'd made on the ramps. With so much extra help, the work had moved along quickly, transforming from an image in his mind to the real thing.

The ramp at the porch level was a gentle incline, so that Mad could maneuver his wheelchair without losing control on the downward spiral. But it didn't end there. They'd already begun work on a continuation of the ramp from the house to the barn, so that a wheelchair could have a smooth run without getting mired in grass or dirt. The wooden ramp ran parallel to the driveway that led from the back porch to the barns.

Griff gathered up all the tools and carried them to the barn, storing them carefully on a shelf. Then he headed toward the house. After a day in the hot sun, he intended to take an extralong shower before driving over to pick up Juliet and the boys.

He was feeling pretty proud of himself. There had been times today when he'd managed to block out all thoughts of Juliet for an hour or more. But now, with the day's work over, her image haunted him. He couldn't wait to see her.

A short time later he descended the stairs.

Whit looked up. "I bet you're ready for an ice-cold longneck, bro."

"Sounds great. As soon as I get back with Juliet and the boys, I'll join you."

Hearing him, Willow shook her head. "Juliet phoned to say she'll be sleeping at her own ranch tonight."

Griff looked thunderstruck. "They caught Mitch?"

"No." Willow gave him a gentle smile. "I wish that were true. But Juliet said Jackie Turner has decided to lend a hand with the ranch chores. He said he prefers to sleep in the empty bunkhouse rather than drive back and forth from his daughter's ranch to Juliet's. So I guess that solves the problem of Juliet and her sons being alone and isolated, far from civilization. With Jackie in the bunkhouse, I think we'll all breathe a little easier."

"Yeah. That's great news." Griff's tone said otherwise.

"Here, bro." Whit handed him a beer. "Now we have two things to celebrate. Juliet's got a ranch foreman she can trust, and that ramp outside is just about the most professional job I've ever seen."

He touched his bottle to Griff's, and the two drank. The beer tasted bitter in Griff's mouth.

Over dinner, Ash and Whit, relieved to have the hard work of the day behind them, were louder and funnier than usual. Though their barbs and jokes were usually directed at one another, they were their own best audience, laughing like loons.

Griff made a halfhearted attempt to follow along, but at some point he simply tuned them out and ate the rest of his meal in silence.

When dinner was over, Myrna held up a tray of freshly baked chocolate chip cookies. "I baked extra, thinking Casey and Ethan would be here. Will I serve them in the great room?"

Willow nodded. "I'd like that. And I'm sure the others are ready to kick back and relax."

As they shoved away from the table, Griff paused at the doorway to the mudroom. "I think I'll pass on dessert tonight, Myrna. I'd like to get back to work."

"Now?" Willow couldn't hide her surprise. "It'll be dark soon, Griff. You've put in a full day already. Why not wait until morning?"

He tried to smile, but there was a dangerous light in his eyes that said more than words. A light that reminded the entire family of Bear, when he was in one of his dark moods. "This can't wait. I need to do it now." Almost as an afterthought he added, "Thanks for the great dinner, Mad. Good night, everyone. I'll see you all in the morning."

As he strode out, an awkward silence settled over the group.

Griff paused to wipe sweat from his eyes and studied the line of sturdy boards he'd added since supper time. His accomplishments should have given him a sense of satisfaction. Instead, he found himself cursing the darkness that had come sneaking up on him. Like it or not, he would have to quit for the night.

With a muttered curse he began collecting his tools. He turned and nearly collided with Mad, who had rolled his wheelchair along the section of ramp already completed.

Griff dropped a hammer and let loose with a string of rich, ripe oaths. "You startled me. I didn't hear you coming."

"Obviously." The old man fixed him with a look. "Something wrong?"

"Nothing." Griff picked up the tool and started away.

"Hold on, lad." Mad's words weren't so much an invitation as a command.

Griff turned back, his eyes narrowed. "You got something to say?"

"Maybe I do." Mad took a moment, collecting his thoughts. "I'd know a thing or two about temper. The MacKenzies have been cursed with it for generations. So your temper doesn't concern me as much as the why of it."

"Can't a man be mad for no reason?"

Mad shook his head. "Not in this family. With the MacKenzies there's no gray. There's only black and white. There's only happy and mad. And you're mad enough to be out here working like a dog when any other man would be sound asleep after the kind of crazy day you've put in. So I'll ask you again, lad. Why?"

Griff avoided the old man's eyes. "What does it matter?"

"Sometimes it helps to talk."

"There's nothing to talk about. Like you said. I'm cursed with a temper. Let it go." He swung away and hauled the heavy tools to the barn.

By the time he headed to the house, Mad was nowhere to be seen.

It was just as well, he thought. He wasn't in a mood to share his thoughts with anyone.

Thoughts as dark, as gloomy, as the black, starless night.

Thoughts that he couldn't seem to sort out.

Thoughts that were driving him stark raving mad.

For the rest of the week Griff worked tirelessly on the ramp, often returning to it after supper, until darkness would drive him indoors for a few hours to sleep before waking at dawn to start again.

For every day that Griff grew more and more moody, Mad grew more and more lighthearted as he eagerly watched the progress.

Ash and Whit and the wranglers joined in whenever their chores permitted, studying the crude blueprints Griff had drawn for himself. By the end of the week, a series of ramps linked the house with the barns, freeing Mad to roll happily about the ranch yard, paying visits to places he'd been prohibited from reaching for years.

Once the ramps were completely connected, he moved easily from place to place, feeling like a kid on Christmas morning. Sharing his joy, the family trailed behind Mad's wheelchair, admiring the finished product.

"Oh, Griff. Just look at what you've accomplished." Willow placed a kiss on Griff's cheek. "You have to feel so proud."

Griff ducked his head. "Yeah. Thanks."

"Great job, Griff." Brady shook his hand.

"You do good work, bro." Both Ash and Whit slapped him on the back and punched his shoulder.

He turned away, as though embarrassed by all the fuss.

Later, after supper, they lifted a toast to Griff, who reluctantly joined them in the great room and downed his beer in quick swallows before heading up to bed, saying he needed to get some sleep.

When he was gone, Willow turned to her sons. "Do either of you know what's wrong with Griff? I would have thought by now he'd have resolved whatever was bothering him."

They shook their heads.

She turned to her father-in-law. "Mad? Any ideas?"

"I may have one or two." His eyes twinkled. "But I'd like to be certain before I say." He polished off his beer before saying, "I believe I'm ready for bed, too. I'll say goodnight, now. I'll see you all in the morning."

"'Morning, lad." Mad had parked his wheelchair beside the table and was sipping fresh orange juice when Griff stepped into the kitchen. "Looks like you and I are the only ones up so far."

Breakfast was already warming on the stove. Steam arose from a skillet of fried potatoes and onions, and another skillet of scrambled eggs. Bacon sizzled, and coffee perfumed the air.

While Griff poured himself a cup of coffee, Mad watched him. "Now that your big project is complete, what've you got on schedule for today?"

Griff shrugged his shoulders. He'd spent the night wondering the same thing. "Is there something you need?"

Mad smiled. "As a matter of fact, there is." He paused a moment. "I was hoping you might fly me to the Grayson Ranch today."

Griff's frown was back. He fixed the old man with an angry stare. "Why?"

"Do I need a reason?" The old man looked like the cat that swallowed the canary.

"Yeah." Griff's tone was abrupt. "What's this about, Mad?"

"Juliet invited me to see for myself how her horse therapy is working. And since I can now get myself to the plane and back, and since your schedule seems to be free, I think it's the perfect time to accept her invitation."

Griff turned away, wondering at the way his heart rate speeded up at the mention of Juliet. Not that it mattered. He hadn't heard a single word from her since they parted. Apparently, she hadn't missed him any more than he'd missed her.

"Sure. Why not?" He turned back. "When would you like to leave?"

"Right after breakfast."

Griff tossed the last of his coffee down the drain. "Fine. I'll go check out the Cessna now. Don't hold breakfast for me. I'm not hungry."

CHAPTER SEVENTEEN

As the little Cessna soared across the lush hills, black with cattle, and crossed over to Grayson territory, Mad gave a sudden sigh of disgust. "Old Frank Grayson must be turning over in his grave."

Griff pulled himself back from his thoughts. "Yeah. It's shocking to see the difference between the properties."

Mad shook his head. "It's as if someone drew a line right down the middle of the land. On one side, thick grass and herds of cattle, and on the other, barren soil and vacant hillsides." He pointed to a dilapidated range shack. "How can Jackie Turner bear to see how far it's fallen?"

"I'm sure it bothers him, Mad. But how much can one man do?"

"I'll tell you what I'd do." The old man stared at the land below. "For openers, I'd get rid of any wrangler unwilling to go the extra mile for me. I'd offer a bonus to anyone who offered to repair a range shack and live in it for at least six months while tending my herd." As they circled the ranch house and barns, he added, "And I'd offer an extra bonus to anyone willing to start repairing all this." He waved a hand. "Look at the condition of this place."

He pointed to the tricked-out bus, looking conspicuously out of place beside a rusted old truck. "What's that?"

"It belongs to Heywood Sperry. According to my pal, Jimmy, Sperry's family is loaded."

"What's he doing in a place like Copper Creek?"

Griff shrugged. "That's a good question. He seems to spend most of his time making those around him miserable."

There wasn't time to say more as the plane began its descent and came in for a smooth landing along the strip of asphalt.

Even before Griff stepped out of the plane, Casey and Ethan were running up to greet him.

"Griff. I knew it was you. I told Mama it was you." Casey gave Griff a fierce hug before turning to his brother. "Didn't I, Efan?"

The older boy nodded and shyly stepped close enough for Griff to haul him up into his arms for a hug.

For a moment he held both boys close, wondering at the feeling of joy that poured through him.

Just then the copilot door opened. When Ethan spotted Mad, he raced around to throw his arms around the old man's waist.

"Well now, laddie, that's the warmest greeting I've had in a long time. I've missed you, too."

Griff removed the wheelchair from the rear seat and helped Mad into it. Before he could begin to push it forward, Mad patted his lap. "Come on, lads. Hitch a ride."

They needed no coaxing. They hopped up on his lap and gave whoops of delight as Griff wheeled them toward the barn.

The strip of asphalt ended at the entrance to the barn. Once there they paused to allow their eyes to adjust from bright sunlight to the dimmer light inside the big building.

What they saw had them staring in surprise.

In the center of the barn Stan Novak—his shaved head gleaming in the glow of overhead lights, his rail-thin body no bigger than the size of a teenage boy—sat in the saddle of a swaybacked mare that moved in a plodding circle while Juliet issued softly spoken commands.

"You're doing great, Stan. Now slow your mount. Bring her to a halt. Good. Now turn her to the left."

The man followed her commands before shooting her a wide, gap-toothed grin. "How'm I doing, Juliet?"

"Just fine, Stan. You have Princess completely under control."

She turned to a heavily tattooed veteran who looked like a linebacker. "How about it, Hank? Are you ready to follow Stan?"

Hank Wheeler gave a quick shake of his head. "Not today, Juliet. I'm just not ready."

"You're never ready." Heywood Sperry's angry bark got everyone's attention. As usual, he wore a muscle shirt to show off his toned upper body. His face was marred by a scowl.

"Mama." Casey shouted from his perch on Mad's lap. "Look who's here with Griff. It's Grandpa Mad."

Jimmy Gable shouted out, "Hey, Griff. I was hoping I'd get to see you again."

Griff managed a smile and a wave to his old marine buddy.

Juliet's icy look in Griff's direction turned into a blazing smile when she spotted Mad. She hurried over. "You came."

"You invited me, remember? I figured it was time to take you up on your invitation."

"Oh, Mad, I'm so glad to see you." She clasped his hand. "Will you ride when I've finished with the others?"

He shrugged. "Maybe. For now, I'll just watch."

"What're they doing here?" Sperry's frown deepened. "I thought you were offering this service for veterans."

Jimmy Gable's voice cut in. "I told you. Griff and I served in the marines together. He's my old captain."

"He's not mine." Sperry's voice was a growl of anger. "Come on, Juliet. We're paying customers, and you're wasting our time."

Ignoring him, Juliet said to the entire group, "You know Griff Warren. Now I'd like you all to welcome Griff's grandfather, Mad MacKenzie."

"Hey, Mad," the voices rang out. "Welcome to the club."

Mad smiled and nodded.

Sperry's voice rose above the others. "Just 'cause he's in a wheelchair doesn't mean he's part of the Romeos."

"Just ignore the crabcake," Jimmy said with a laugh. The others laughed with him.

"All right, Stan. Time for your dismount." Juliet guided the machine to the man on horseback, lifting him easily from the saddle to his waiting wheelchair.

Then she turned to a young man whose face was as round as a basketball, his stomach protruding over the waist of his faded denims. "Okay, Billy Joe. It's your turn to get in the saddle."

He began alternately shaking and sweating. Without warning he broke down in tears.

Juliet put an arm around his shoulders and leaned down to say, "It's all right, Billy Joe. You know you never have to do anything you're not comfortable doing. But you haven't tried since you came back this week." She knelt in front of him. "Did you forget to take your antianxiety medicine again?"

He wiped his eyes with a rag before nodding.

"How long this time?"

He blew his nose. "I don't know. Maybe a week or more."

"You know what happens when you don't take your prescriptions, Billy Joe."

"Yeah." He looked away. "I get scared."

"But when you take them, you're not so afraid."

"But I get spacey when I take all that medicine."

"Which would you rather be? Scared all the time, or a little spaced-out?"

He shrugged. "I guess spacey isn't so bad."

"That's right. So tonight, before you go to bed, be sure you take your medicine. And Billy Joe, you need to have a talk with your doctor. Okay? It isn't safe to discontinue strong medicines in the middle of treatment. Promise you'll talk to your doctor? He may even be able to find something that doesn't have so many side effects."

He sniffed and nodded.

She patted his shoulder affectionately before turning to Jimmy Gable. "You ready, Jimmy?"

"Sure thing." He grinned and waited while she adjusted the lift. When he was comfortably settled in the saddle, he waved to Griff. "Hey, look at me. I'm a cowboy."

Following Juliet's instructions, he began putting the mare through her paces, having her walk in a circle, halt, turn, and walk in the opposite direction. When he'd become comfortable in the saddle, Juliet led the mare out into the sunshine and turned horse and rider into a corral. Soon the mare was moving along at a swift pace, with Jimmy smiling from ear to ear.

Half an hour later, his smile began to falter.

"You're feeling tired, aren't you, Jimmy?"

At Juliet's words, he nodded. "I guess this body isn't used to all that movement."

"No it isn't. Remember. You have to build up your muscles gradually. After all, you're using body parts that aren't routinely used. So you need to take it easy, and let me know when you're tired before you reach a point where you could start to experience pain."

Jimmy grinned. "Feeling pain isn't so bad. At least I'm feeling something."

A short time later he returned to the barn. The lift delivered him back to his wheelchair and he couldn't hide his sigh of relief.

From his position to one side Sperry made a sound of derision. "Crybabies. The whole pack of you."

"I didn't see you stick it out for half an hour, Sperry." Jimmy glanced at his companions, who nodded their agreement.

"That's 'cause we've been out of commission for so long. My muscles atrophied."

"Like your brain," Stan Novak shouted.

"Good one, Stan," Billie Joe said through his tears.

"All right, gentlemen." Juliet smiled at the circle of men. "I know this week has been a tough one, coming back after the equipment was down for so long. But I think you're all showing amazing improvement." She clasped each man's hand. When she clasped Sperry's, he clamped his other hand over hers, holding on when she tried to step away.

"That's enough, Heywood." With an effort she removed her hand and turned to the others. "I hope to see you all again on Monday. For now, have a safe trip back to town, and enjoy a relaxing weekend."

As they rolled past her, each of them had something to say to her.

"Thanks, Juliet. You're the best," Stan Novak said.

"I'm sorry I didn't take my meds, Juliet. But I'll do better next week," Billy Joe whispered.

"I know you will, Billy Joe."

"Thanks for all the time you give us, Juliet." Jimmy Gable rolled past, then waved at Griff. "Will I see you in town this weekend?"

"I'll try to get there, Jimmy, but I can't promise," Griff called.

Not to be outdone by the others, Heywood Sperry hung back, allowing the others to roll toward the bus while he caught both of Juliet's hands in his. "Next week I go first. Remember, I'm the leader of this pack."

"If you go first one day, you have to go last the next, Heywood. That's the rule. As for being the leader, these men are all capable of leading themselves."

His tone sharpened to a low note of barely controlled fury. "I've warned you before, Juliet. Don't ever contradict me. Understand? I started this group, and I can disband them just like that." He snapped his fingers before turning his electric scooter away and moving toward the waiting bus.

Like the others, he rolled onto the rear platform of the bus and pushed the button for the hydraulic lift that transported the passengers inside.

Minutes later, when the bus rolled away in a cloud of dust, Mad cleared his throat. "How do you manage to stay so calm with all those hotheads?"

Juliet smiled at him. "When Buddy was in the VA hospital, most of his companions were in various stages of grief and anger. Most of the anger is directed at themselves, because they can't do what they once did." She arched a brow. "Didn't you ever experience those feelings, Mad?"

He winked. "You bet. And still do. But you're that amazing thing we hear about, lass, but rarely see. Grace under pressure. You're the calm amidst the storm. You were grand to watch."

They looked up as a truck came to a stop outside the barn. A woman, clearly frazzled and out of breath, stepped down and approached Juliet. "I hope I'm not too late."

"Too late?" Juliet shot her a puzzled frown.

"I phoned you a week ago, asking if you'd allow my daughter to try riding under your care."

"Oh, yes." Juliet glanced toward the passenger side of the truck and could see the pale, frightened face of a young girl.

She sighed. "You didn't call back for an appointment. My group is finished, but there's always time for one more, especially since you've come so far. Do you need help getting her in here?"

Before the mother could reply, Griff was crossing to the truck. "I'll take care of it."

From the back he removed a wheelchair. Setting it down, he opened the passenger door. While her mother watched, he gently lifted the girl to her chair.

"Thank you," the mother whispered as she walked along beside her daughter, while Griff easily pushed the chair into the barn. "This is Sarah. She's ten."

"Ten and a half," Sarah corrected.

"Of course. I forgot. Ten and a half. And I'm Rose Benning."

"Welcome Sarah and Rose. I'm Juliet, and these are my sons, Casey and Ethan, and my neighbors, Griff Warren and Mad MacKenzie."

"MacKenzie?" Rose paused. "Was your son Bear MacKenzie?"

"Yes, ma'am." Mad braced himself for what he knew was coming.

"I'm so sorry for your loss."

"Thank you." He always felt himself bristling under these offers of sympathy from kind strangers.

He motioned toward Griff, hoping to deflect the attention. "Griff here is Bear's son and my grandson."

"I thought you called him Warren—"

Before she could ask more, the old man said, "Different names, but all one family."

"I...see." She turned to Juliet. "If this isn't a good time..."

"The time is perfect." Juliet explained about the lift, and what it did, before Rose cut her off.

"I'm used to carrying my daughter, and lifting her. I don't mind getting her into the saddle."

"I'd prefer to use the lift." Juliet showed the girl how it worked, and how it would feel as it moved her from the wheelchair to the saddle. "Would you like to try it?"

When Sarah nodded, Juliet began the process, while Rose watched from the sidelines with a worried frown.

Once in the saddle, the girl held onto the saddle horn with both hands. Juliet kept hold of the reins and began walking Princess in a circle. Gradually, as the mare kept up a steady pace, the girl's demeanor changed so completely, it was as if a switch had been turned on. From the mare's back, Sarah waved to her mother before giving a joyful laugh. "Look at me, Mom. I'm riding a horse again."

"Yes, you are. You look good up there, honey."

"I feel good, too."

They circled the ring a number of times before Juliet brought Princess to a halt. "Do you want to go again, or would you like to take a break?"

Reluctantly, the girl said, "Maybe I'd better get down now. But can I do this again another day?"

"You can come as often as you like," Juliet assured her.

By the time the lift had returned her to her wheelchair, Sarah's smile was as bright as the sun. To her mother she whispered, "You know what it felt like?"

"What?" her mother asked.

"While I was in the saddle, I felt like all the other girls in my class. The ones who can walk."

Griff rolled her wheelchair to the truck and lifted her inside before stowing her wheelchair in the back.

When Rose got behind the wheel, mother and daughter waved and called their good-byes. As they drove away, both had tears in their eyes.

Juliet turned to Mad. "Okay. It's your turn."

He shook his head. "Lass, you have to be exhausted. You've been doing this all day now."

"You came all this way. You can't leave without at least giving the lift a try." She took his hand. "Are you willing?"

He nodded. "I guess, now that I've seen a little girl use it, I'd look like a coward if I didn't at least try."

"Everybody's afraid of something." Juliet adjusted the lift for size and weight, before fitting it to Mad.

Within minutes he was out of his wheelchair and in the saddle.

"How did that feel?"

He was grinning. "No effort at all. And no time to be afraid. I feel like one of those time-travel characters. One minute I'm wheelchair bound, the next I'm back in the saddle where I used to spend most of my time."

"Good." She handed him the reins. "I'm sure an old cowboy like you doesn't need me to lead your mount through her paces."

As Princess began a slow circle, his face was wreathed in smiles.

Griff looked up at him. "How does it feel, Mad?"

The old man shook his head in wonder. "Now I know why Sarah changed so drastically. I'm not earthbound. I'm myself again. My old self. I'm a cowboy, lad. Back in the saddle, and free as the breeze."

As he continued circling, he glanced over to see the way both Casey and Ethan were clinging to Griff's hand.

And he saw something else. The way both Juliet and Griff were struggling not to stare at one another. But though they were making a valiant effort, they couldn't quite succeed. Every once in a while Juliet would dart a quick glance at her sons, clinging tightly to Griff's hands, and then at the man himself. And when she would turn away, Griff would chance a quick glance her way, with a look of pain that was so shocking, even from this distance, it was obvious what he was feeling.

Maybe he'd been wrong, Mad thought. Maybe what Griff was feeling wasn't mere lust. From what he could see, the feelings between these two appeared to be something much deeper.

Maybe he'd meddled in something that had been none of his business.

It wouldn't be the first time. And now, having rushed in like a fool where angels fear to tread, he knew he had no choice but to clean up the mess he'd made of things.

CHAPTER EIGHTEEN

After he was once again settled into his wheelchair, Mad caught Juliet's hand. "Now, finally, lass, I understand what brings people all this way just to ride a horse. 'Tis such a simple thing, but it lifts the spirits. I'd forgotten how it feels to be in the saddle, with that powerful animal beneath me, carrying me across a field." His eyes crinkled with the memory. "The little girl, Sarah, said she felt like the other girls. The ones who can walk." His tone softened. "I felt that way, too. Like the old Maddock MacKenzie who'd often ridden horseback clear across this land, from sunup to sundown, feeling like a king in his very own kingdom." He gave a joyous laugh. "King of the world. That's how I felt."

Juliet's smile matched his. "I've seen it change so many lives, Mad. I know it's a little thing, to offer someone a chance to be in the saddle. But just to be free of your wheelchair, for even a little while, is transforming."

"It is that." He turned to the two little boys, who stood watching and listening. "This work your mama's doing is important work, lads. Do you know that?"

At their look of surprise, Juliet laughed. "All they know is that my work causes them to spend too many hours here in the barn. If they had their way, they'd be in the house, playing with their trucks. But I refuse to let them stay alone, so far from me. So they're stuck out here until my work is finished."

Griff looked around. "Why not set aside a play area out here for them?"

Juliet shrugged, as though the idea hadn't occurred to her.

He walked around before pointing to a corner of the barn that was far enough from the work area that it wouldn't interfere with the men or the work Juliet did. He paced it off in one direction, then another, before looking at her. "It wouldn't take much for me to build them a raised box right here in the barn where they could set up their trucks and cows and some farm buildings. Their own miniature ranch." He turned to Casey and Ethan. "Would you boys like that?"

Their eyes went wide. "Can he, Mama? Please," Casey pleaded.

"I'm sure Griff has better things to do with his time than build a place for you two to play."

"It won't take much time at all." Instead of talking to Juliet, he directed his words toward her sons. "If you boys say yes, I'll start on it tomorrow."

"Yes. Yes." Casey was jumping up and down, while Ethan was content to nod his head.

"Done." He turned to Mad. "I'm thinking we've kept

Juliet and the boys out here long enough. You ready to get home?"

Mad was grinning. "I was hoping to give Juliet a lesson on making my famous waffles, or at least a chance to taste her grilled cheese sandwiches. After all, Casey said she makes the best in the world. But I guess I'll just have to wait for another time."

Juliet was quick to accept his challenge. "If you come back tomorrow before noon, I promise I'll make my famous grilled cheese sandwiches. And if there's time, you can teach me how to make your waffles."

Mad turned to Griff. "How about it, lad? Are you up to flying me back tomorrow?"

"Why not? While you're enjoying lunch, I'll get busy on that play table."

He stepped up behind Mad's wheelchair and began pushing it toward the barn door.

"Wait." Mad held up a hand and called to the two boys, "Ready to ride, lads?"

They hopped up on his lap. Griff pushed them across the concrete floor of the barn and onto the strip of asphalt, halting only when they got to the plane.

After exchanging good-byes, Griff lifted Mad into the plane and stowed his wheelchair behind the seat. As he circled the plane to step into the pilot seat, he saw Juliet herding her sons some distance away, where they stood watching. Without a word he climbed inside.

Minutes later the little plane was airborne. Griff circled once, and tipped the wings while Mad waved to the figures on the ground. Then they headed toward home.

It wasn't lost on Mad that Juliet and Griff had barely

exchanged half a dozen words in all the time they'd been together.

Mad adjusted his sunglasses and sat back, feeling tired. But it was a good tired. He felt like a man who'd climbed a mountain and was now resting at the pinnacle, observing the beauty of the scene below him. "It pains me to admit something to you, lad."

Griff glanced over.

"I thought Buddy's widow was turning his family ranch into a spa. Now that I've experienced what she's offering, I see how wrong I was. What she's offering to those men, and that little girl—" he grinned "—and even to me, is hope. Hope for something better than just a seat on the sidelines, watching the world go by."

"You thinking about resuming your work on the ranch, Mad?"

At his question, the old man grew silent. Finally, after long moments, he nodded. "Not as a working cowboy, mind you. But I'm thinking that with your ramps and that mechanical lift Juliet has in her barn, I could enjoy a good deal of freedom."

"You're thinking of getting one of those lifts?"

Mad shrugged. "Who knows? I may look into it."

Griff made a gentle turn toward the distant hills. "I have to admit, I'm surprised."

"No more than I am, lad. This isn't what I expected when I left home today."

"What did you expect?"

Another shrug. "I'll tell you. I thought I'd get some kind of mumbo-jumbo, feel-good lecture about how those of us confined to wheelchairs have to learn to settle for whatever we can get." His voice lowered as he sorted through his thoughts. "I got all those lectures after my accident. And I was grateful that my son and daughter-in-law were able to take me in and make a place for me in their lives. But even in my chair, I'm me. And the me I know is an old cowboy on horseback, riding across my land, directing my wranglers, herding my cattle."

He fell silent for a long time before saying, "That's how I met my Maddy."

"Your wife?" Griff turned his head and studied his grandfather. "I've never heard you mention her name before."

"That's because even after all these years, it hurts too much." Mad stared at the land far below. "Juliet reminds me of her. When we met she was this little thing who looked so small and fragile, I thought she might break if I so much as touched her. But I was wrong, lad. There was nothing fragile about Madeline Gordon. Her parents, like mine, came over from Scotland. She was a nurse, but there were no hospitals here, so far from civilization. She traveled from town to town by horseback, tending the sick everywhere she went."

"Sounds like a hard life for a woman."

"Aye. And what a woman. I met her in a fierce snow-storm. I was up in the hills, tending my small herd, when spring turned into winter overnight, and the land was buried in a several feet of snow. 'Twas so high I sought refuge in a cave. By the time I'd found it I was starving and half frozen. I set about starting a fire, and then hunting for game. When I returned to the cave with a deer, Maddy was sitting by the fire, wrapped in my only blanket, with her clothes spread out around the floor of the cave, dripping water and ice, and her horse tethered in a corner of the cave, munching the grass I'd put there for my own mount."

"Where did she come from?" Griff asked.

"Some far-flung ranch miles from the nearest settlement. She'd smelled my fire, and said it saved her life. We spent the next five days in that tiny space, talking late into the night, sleeping side by side next to the fire without ever touching, and by the time the snow had melted enough to let us return to our lives outside that cave, I knew I had to see her again." He chuckled. "She'd warned me about her father. A fierce bear of a man who believed in his heart that no man would ever be good enough for his only daughter, who was the light of his life. But I rode for three days and nights to reach his ranch, only to learn that Maddy was off delivering a baby, miles from there. So I spent the next two days with the old man, trying to convince him that I was good enough for his angel."

"I guess you did a good job of it."

"You're wrong there, lad." Mad chuckled at the memory. "When he asked me how I'd met his daughter, I told the truth. That I'd spent five days and nights in a cave with her. By the time Maddy got home, her father was in a terrible rage and declared me and Maddy unfit to be part of his family. When she told him that we hadn't done anything wrong, he ordered her to prove it by sending me away. And she did. I wasn't permitted to see her again for a year. If, he declared, at the end of that time we still wanted to wed, he would consider it."

"So you survived the year apart?"

"Barely. I was in a terrible fit of temper after a year without the girl of my dreams. But when I rode up, old

Grant Gordon declared that I hadn't done enough penance. He wanted us to wait another year."

"What did you do, Mad?"

He chuckled. "I witnessed the most amazing sight. Tiny little Maddy standing up to her giant of a father and telling him that if he thought so little of her that he believed she couldn't make her own choice of a mate, he no longer had a right to order her about like a child. And then she surprised us both by saying she was leaving with me, and that if he hoped to ever meet his grandchildren, he would have to accept me as the man she'd set her cap for. She left that very minute, with nothing but the clothes on her back. We rode into the nearest town and found a preacher. The next day we were home on my poor, miserable ranch, which she promptly turned into a home."

"Did her father ever accept you?"

Mad nodded. "About a month after we left, he rode up in a wagon, loaded with furniture and clothing that had belonged to his wife. He looked around, said it was obvious that I needed his help, and he moved into a shed on the property. He worked alongside me until the day he died. But he lived long enough to see your father born. 'Twas he who chose the name Murdock for his only grandson, since it was a family name in both our clans. But 'twas also he who chose the nickname Bear, which stuck. Never again was your father called anything but Bear. And I'll tell you, lad, Maddy's father died a happy man." He paused before adding, "I often think how different my life would have been if Maddy had listened to her father. I'd have never known the happiness that stays with me to this day. Know this, Griff. When you meet the lass of your heart, don't let anyone or anything come between you. Not even the wisdom of an old man who thinks he knows what's right for everyone."

As the MacKenzie Ranch came into view, Griff shifted his attention to bringing the little aircraft down for a smooth landing.

But later, as he lay alone in his bed, Mad's words come back to him.

He found himself smiling in the darkness.

That sly old man.

And then, his heart lighter than it had been for days, knowing he had the perfect excuse to see Juliet again, he began planning the play table he would build for Casey and Ethan.

If he worked it right, it could end up taking him days. And maybe, just maybe, he could atone for all the pain he'd caused her.

Alone in Bear's office, Willow sat writing checks and sorting through the various papers that littered the desktop.

Thankfully, Bear had loved his paperwork. He'd kept meticulous books. But that didn't make the job easier in Willow's eyes. She would rather do the most odious jobs around the ranch than have to tackle the dreaded paperwork.

It wasn't that she didn't understand it. She was a smart woman, and she knew about taxes, insurance, repairs necessary for the various pieces of equipment, as well as the maintenance needed on the house, barns, and outbuildings. Not a year went by without the need for a new roof, a new motor, a new tractor or cattle-hauler. But the very act of keeping ledgers irritated her.

Give her a horse and a rope, and turn her loose on the range, and she felt young and free as a girl.

Lock her up in Bear's office and order her to justify the figures in the ledgers, and she was as jumpy as a cat in a rainstorm.

She'd tried to persuade Brady to take over this necessary drudgery, but he'd argued that it wasn't his place to know the details of her financial empire. That had been the exclusive territory of Bear, and now it was hers. Period. No arguing.

Dear Brady. Though he was, first and foremost a cowboy, content with the hundreds of chores necessary to the operation of a ranch of this size, he was also the kindest man she'd ever met. He and Bear had bonded as young men, and they had shared a mutual affection and respect. Without Brady Storm's steady hand directing the wranglers, many of whom were seasonal workers who came and went on a whim, she would have been lost. And now, it was Brady's calm, reasonable demeanor that kept her going when the paperwork, the legal maze, and the million and one irritating questions surfaced, causing her to lose her confidence. On those rare occasions when she felt alone and vulnerable and was reduced to tears, it was Brady who offered her the comfort of his wise words and strong arms. He'd been sworn to secrecy, so that her family members would never know the depth of her fear or her overwhelming despair.

Her accountants in Helena were honest and efficient. They were more than up to the challenge of preparing tax statements and end-of-the-year worksheets. But they had only the figures that she gave them. The daily tallies were her responsibility. And though she hated the work, she did it because it was necessary to the operation of the ranch.

She studied the latest bank drafts until her eyes felt too heavy. She stowed them for another day, then cleared away the rest of the paperwork and strode out of the office.

Once upstairs, she felt the familiar ache of loss as she climbed into the big bed she'd shared with her beloved Bear.

Despite the tumultuous feelings that pulled and tugged, she was asleep within minutes. And in her dreams, she was riding across a meadow, and watching a man astride a big bay stallion coming toward her.

In her dream there was no paperwork. No drudgery. There was a feeling of complete and utter joy as she urged her mount into a gallop before being enveloped in a warm, loving embrace.

CHAPTER NINETEEN

Griff bounded into the mudroom and eased off his dung-caked boots before rolling his sleeves.

Seeing him, Whit shot him a quizzical look. "Did you already muck the stalls?"

"Yeah. I figured I'd get an early start."

"Early? It's barely dawn."

"It is?" Griff was grinning. "I guess I was awake earlier than I thought."

Whit turned back toward the kitchen. "If you've done the barn chores, I guess that gives me time for another cup of coffee."

Griff washed up and followed him, helping himself to a tall orange juice before turning to Mad. "Ready for another day at Juliet's?"

Mad shook his head. "Sorry, lad. You'll have to go without me."

At Griff's arched brow the old man explained. "I promised Brady I'd go to town with him today."

"What about Juliet's grilled cheese sandwiches?"

Mad shrugged. "You'll just have to eat my share. Tell her I'll try to get back to her ranch next week."

"Okay." Griff downed the orange juice in one long swallow. "Your loss." He turned away, missing the devilish smile on his grandfather's face.

Griff was unloading the lumber from the rear of the planc when Casey and Ethan came bounding up to greet him.

"Hey, Griff." Casey peeked inside the plane. "Where's Grandpa Mad?"

"He couldn't come today. But he said he'll try to come with me one day next week." Griff looked around. "Where's your mom?"

"Talking to Mr. Turner."

The two boys watched as Griff hauled the lumber into the barn, then returned for more. When all of it had been unloaded, he strapped on his tool belt and got to work.

Casey pointed. "Why are you putting those together like that?"

"These boards will be the base. The bottom. Everything else will rest on these."

"What're those?"

"Those boards will form the top."

"That doesn't look like a table."

"Not yet. But it will when I finish."

"And then me and Efan can play with our trucks?"

He grinned at the boy's grammar, before deciding that he'd leave any correction up to Casey's mother. "That's right."

"Hear that, Efan? We'll have our very own play table and we can bring all our trucks out here."

A happy smile played on Ethan's lips. It was, Griff thought, such a pleasure to see this silent, often sad little boy looking happy for a change. For the next hour he sawed wood, nailed it, and pieced it together until the play table began to take shape.

At the sound of voices he looked up. Juliet and Jackie Turner stepped into the barn.

Juliet's voice was accusing. "There you are. Casey and Ethan, I told you it was all right to say hello to Griff, and then you were supposed to return to the house."

"But Griff's making our table. We need to be here to help him."

"That's fine, as long as you tell me where you are and what you're doing. But you never came back, and I had to come looking for you."

Casey ducked his head. "Sorry."

Griff got to his feet. "I'm sorry, too. I thought you knew they were with me."

"Contrary to what you've been told, I don't have eyes in the back of my head."

Casey's eyes went wide. "You don't?"

Seeing the grin on Griff's face, Juliet turned away. "You can stay out here with Griff for another hour. Then I'll expect you to come in for lunch."

To her retreating back Casey called, "Can we bring Griff?"

"Fine. It's the least I can do to repay him for all this work."

The tone of her voice didn't match the words. Griff realized they were back where they'd started. She was annoyed that he was here, and whatever he did to make it up to her wasn't going to be enough.

Jackie remained after Juliet had gone.

Griff shook his hand. "How are things going, Jackie?"

"Better'n they were, but not nearly good enough yet."

"Well, however much you can do to help, I'm sure Juliet's grateful just to have someone ease the burden."

The older man watched as the two little boys began chasing one another around the barn. "I don't know how she does it. Since I've started here, I've never seen that young woman stop. She does the work of three, and still this place keeps beating her back. Solve one problem, two more crop up."

Griff raised a brow. "What's wrong now?"

"What isn't?" Jackie pointed. "That house is falling down around her. The roof leaks. The plumbing's stopped up. The lights flicker on and off. This barn roof is practically bare. The bunkhouse where I'm staying has cracks in the wall big enough for critters to climb through. The range shacks are barely habitable."

After listening to the litany of complaints, Griff repeated some of the things Mad had said he would do if he were in charge.

Jackie listened politely, digesting everything before scratching his head. "I like the way Mad thinks." He nodded. "A couple of those suggestions just might be a starting point." He offered a handshake. "Thanks, son. I appreciate you relaying that to me." He turned away. "Now I'd better start tackling that mountain of work."

A short time later, as Griff finished up the base of the table, Juliet stepped into the barn.

Her tone was gentler, as though she'd had a talk with

herself and decided to call a truce. "Lunch is ready. I made grilled cheese sandwiches. And Griff, you're welcome to join us. I made plenty."

He set aside his tool belt and trailed the two little boys to the house where he bent to the sink and washed before stepping into the kitchen.

Remembering Jackie's words, he took the time to look around, seeing the dark stain along one wall, indicating a leak in the roof, and noting the fact that Juliet had to unplug the coffeemaker before plugging in the can opener.

With so many problems, it would be hard to know where to begin. But it occurred to him that an overloaded electrical system could spell serious trouble in the form of a fire. He made a mental note to contact Brady for the name of a good electrician in town.

As he took a seat at the table, he heard the approach of the bus, signaling the arrival of the Romeos.

Juliet looked out the window and gave a hiss of annoyance before turning to Griff and her sons. "The men are here, so I guess you'll have to eat lunch without me." She pointed to the stove. "The sandwiches are staying warm under that lid. There's fresh coffee in that pot, and milk in the fridge. I cut up some fresh peaches for dessert. The plate of peaches is over there." She nodded toward the counter before starting toward the door.

"What about your lunch?" Griff asked.

"I'll eat something later." She was already out the door and bounding down the steps.

He moved about the kitchen, setting the food on the table, fetching milk for the boys. As they ate their lunch, he teased and joked and kept Casey and Ethan in high spirits. The same couldn't be said for his own spirits. He'd come here today with high hopes of making amends for his earlier behavior. Now it looked as though the only thing he'd accomplish this day would be creating a play space for the boys. At least, he thought, it wasn't a total waste.

Griff stepped into the barn, trailed by Casey and Ethan, carrying an armload of cars and trucks, in anticipation of the soon-to-be-completed play table.

Spotting them, Jimmy Gable's eyes widened. "Hey, Captain. I didn't know you were here. Where've you been hiding?"

Griff high-fived him. "Having lunch with the boys up at the house. How're you doing, Jimmy?"

"Good. Juliet says I'm her favorite cowboy."

Heywood Sperry's voice was rough with sarcasm. "She says that to everybody, you stupid jerk."

Jimmy swiveled his head, hoping to inject some humor. "Hey. Only my brothers are allowed to call me stupid."

"Probably 'cause they're all brain-dead."

"That's enough, Sperry." Hank Wheeler, astride Princess, reined in his horse to stare daggers at the man on the electric scooter. "Jimmy's never done anything to you. Why do you have to go out of your way to act like such a creep?"

"That's not acting," Billy Joe Harris shouted from across the width of the barn. "That's all Sperry knows how to be. A mean-mouthed, insulting creep."

"You shut that mouth," Sperry shouted back, "or I'll go over there and shut it for good."

"You better bring a posse," Stan Novak snarled. "'Cause you lay a hand on Billy Joe, you'll answer to me."

"I'm real scared," Heywood said through clenched teeth.

Juliet held up a hand.

In the silence that followed, she said, "Hank, you did so well today, I think you deserve a round of applause." She turned to the others.

All but Sperry joined in clapping their hands for the tattooed vet, who was grinning like the Cheshire Cat. Minutes later he was back in his wheelchair, while Billy Joe took a turn on the mare.

Griff returned his attention to putting the final trim on the play table, allowing the voices of the Romeos to recede into the background. While he worked, he marveled at the way Juliet could handle a group of such diverse men, all with hair-trigger tempers.

Shortly after the bus bearing the Romeos had left in a cloud of dust, Griff looked up at the sound of Jackie Turner speaking to Juliet.

"I just talked to Cooper up in the hills. He and a couple of his wranglers will stay there with the herd, while the others take a break and head to town. He says they're getting antsy for a little night life after all that time in the highlands. I agree that a weekend in town will do them good, if you have no objections."

Juliet touched a hand to his sleeve. "I trust your judgment, Jackie."

"All right. If you need anything at all, you call me." He turned away. "I'll be at my daughter's for the weekend, and I'll see you Monday morning, unless you need me sooner."

She nodded before heading up to the house.

As Jackie climbed into his truck, Griff hurried over. Through the open window he said, "You're not staying on?"

The old man shook his head. "I promised my daughter I'd be home for the weekend, to spend some time with my grandchildren." He stuck out his hand. "Thanks again for passing along Mad's suggestions. I told Cooper about them, and he said as soon as the wranglers return on Monday morning, he'll talk to them about maybe earning a little extra if they're willing to do some repairs on the range shack."

"That's a start. Thanks, Jackie."

As the old man drove away, Griff pulled out his cell phone and called the police chief.

"Ira? Griff Warren. I'm out at Juliet Grayson's place and wondering if you've had any leads on Mitch."

The chief's voice boomed over the phone. "He's called twice in the past week, leaving menacing messages on Juliet's phone. Fortunately, she was too busy to pick up, and he left them on her cell, and she was able to play them back for me."

Griff's eyes narrowed. "Are you able to trace where they're coming from?"

"Not yet. I've got the state police giving me a hand, but so far, no luck."

"So basically, he could be anywhere." Griff listened to more before saying with a sigh, "Okay, Chief. Thanks."

He looked inside the barn in time to see Casey and Ethan happily moving their cars and trucks around the table, loading miniature cows inside a metal cattle hauler, lost in the joy of make-believe.

He walked to the house and knocked on the door.

When Juliet opened it, she stared at him, then looked beyond him to the barn. "Where are the boys?"

"I left them playing." With a jolt of sudden knowledge he said, "I just checked with the chief, and he said you've had more menacing calls from Mitch."

Except for the sudden narrowing of her eyes, she said nothing.

"Now I know why you're worried about the boys being left alone. Don't worry, I'll be heading back to the barn to stay with them. But I'd like you and the boys to fly back to the MacKenzie Ranch with me for the weekend."

She was already shaking her head. "I'm not running away again."

"It's not running away."

"What would you call it?" She fixed him with a cool look.

"I'd call it seeing to the safety of yourself and your sons."

"We'll be fine." Before he could argue further she took in a deep breath. "There are way too many things that need to be done here. I can't keep running away and hoping this ranch will take care of itself." She waved a hand. "Look around you. It needs a caretaker. It needs me." Her voice lowered. "And I need this ranch. I need to be here."

As she started to close the door he caught hold of it. "Fine then. I'll just stay here, too."

"You can't."

"Why not?"

"You're not welcome." She shot him a look. "And you know why."

"I deserve that. And a whole lot more. But I'm staying. And you needn't worry. I'll keep my distance and sleep in the barn."

He released his hold on the door and swung away, giving her no chance to argue.

"Fine. Sleep in the barn if you insist. When supper's ready, I'll send some out with the boys." She clung to the door like a lifeline, struggling to contain her fear. "Now, if you don't mind, send them in for their baths."

He continued walking without saying a word.

Before stepping into the barn he removed his cell phone from his pocket and punched in a number. When he heard Mad's voice he said, "Don't hold supper for me tonight."

"Why, laddie? You planning a romantic dinner at the Grayson place?"

Griff gave a dry laugh. "Some romance. From the sound of things, I'll probably be eating crow."

"Then why are you staying?"

"Because Jackie Turner left to spend the weekend with his daughter and her kids. Because Mitch Cord has been leaving threatening messages on Juliet's phone. And after checking with Ira Pettigrew, I learned he's no closer to finding this creep."

"And that means that Juliet and the boys are in danger."

"Right." Griff's tone was bleak.

"Why not bring Juliet and her boys here?"

"I tried that. She's adamant about staying home. She's dug in her heels this time."

"All right, laddie. You do what you think's best."

"I'm staying the weekend. And in case you're wondering, I'll be sleeping in the barn."

He could hear the old man chuckling as he disconnected.

It didn't do anything to improve his mood.

CHAPTER TWENTY

Griff turned the other horses out into a pasture before mucking the stalls, spreading fresh straw, and filling the troughs with feed and water. Only Princess, who had spent the day working, was allowed to remain. While she happily chomped her oats, he hosed down the cement floor of the barn.

As the last of the sunlight faded, he sat on a bench outside the barn and oiled his tools. He wiped his forehead, wishing for a cold beer, and wondered, for the hundredth time, why he was doing all this.

He could be back at his ranch now, enjoying a long-neck and a good meal while laughing at Whit's jokes and teasing the lovesick newlyweds.

Lovesick.

An apt description, he thought. There were Ash and Brenna, joined at the hip, unable to start a single sentence without the other one finishing it. Looking at one another like wolves about to devour prey. It was blindingly clear to anyone who saw them that they were wildly in love.

And then there was this strange situation between him and Juliet. How could it possibly be anything even remotely like love? She could barely stand the sight of him. And he was feeling so miserable, he wasn't even sure why he was staying, except that he needed to keep her and her boys safe.

That didn't make it love.

Worrying about someone's safety wasn't the same thing as loving them. It was just his marine training kicking in. He had a sense that there was danger somewhere out there, and he needed to do whatever he could to minimize it.

Once Mitch Cord was caught, he could get back to his life.

He swore as he began storing the cleaned, oiled tools and his tool belt in the back of his truck. He looked up to see Casey standing on the porch, calling his name. When he drew close enough he could see the little boy, dressed in clean pajamas, his slicked-back blond hair still wet from his bath.

"Mama says you should come in for supper."

"Thanks, Casey." He climbed the steps and rolled his sleeves before washing up.

When he walked into the kitchen, Juliet had her back to him as she stirred something on the stove. The wonderful aroma coming from the oven had his mouth watering.

"Anything I can do to help?"

Without turning she motioned with the spoon. "Everything's ready. If you'd like something cold, it's in the fridge."

He opened the refrigerator and couldn't believe the sight that greeted him. A gallon of milk, a pitcher of lemonade, and a six-pack of long necks.

He whispered a prayer of thanks before twisting off the cap and taking a long, deep drink of ice-cold beer before turning to the boys. "Lemonade or milk?"

"The lemonade's for Mama. She said we have to drink milk."

"Smart move." He filled two glasses with milk and deposited them in front of Casey and Ethan. He filled a tall glass with lemonade and set it beside Juliet's plate before picking up the longneck and leaning against the counter as he drank his fill.

Juliet lifted a roasting pan from the oven. While she placed a roasted chicken on a platter, along with potatoes, carrots, and snap peas from the garden, she called, "If you'd like, you can carve this up while I get the rolls."

Griff picked up a sharp knife and soon had their plates heaped with slabs of roast chicken and all the trimmings.

Juliet passed around the rolls, hot from the oven, before taking her seat. Griff sat at the opposite end of the table and helped Casey cut up his food before giving a taste.

"Now this was worth waiting for." He winked at the boys. "Your mama sure can cook."

"And you sure do like to eat, don't you, Griff?"

"I sure do." He grinned at Casey before taking another bite. Then he turned to Juliet. "I thought you were going to send my supper out to the barn."

"Too much work." She buttered a roll and looked everywhere but directly at him. "And I'm fresh out of energy."

"I can see why. You're a mom, a rancher, a therapist. It would be nice if you could get some help with those Romeos."

She nodded while she nibbled her roll. "They're a handful."

Casey tugged on Griff's hand. "Is our play table done?"

"It is. I added whatever trucks and farm animals you had in the barn. You can bring the rest out tomorrow."

"Oh, boy." Casey turned to his brother. "Did you hear that, Efan? It'll be just like our ranch."

Ethan's smile was enough to light up the room.

Casey shot a pleading look at his mother. "Can we go see it after supper?"

Juliet shook her head. "You'll see it in the morning."

"But I want to see it now. Please."

Sensing her weariness, Griff lay a hand over Casey's. "If you two went out to the barn now, you'd get your nice, clean PJs all dirty. Not to mention your feet. The play table and all your trucks will still be there in the morning, just waiting for the two of you."

Casey stabbed at a carrot. "Okay. Besides, Mama said she was going to read to us before we sleep."

Pleased that he'd managed to direct Casey's attention away from the barn, Griff grinned. "What's your favorite story?"

"The one Myrna read to us. About a little cub that gets lost in the woods."

"Why is that your favorite?"

"'Cause he's scared, but he's so brave." Casey studied Griff. "Were you ever scared when you were a marine?"

"Plenty of times."

"But you're big." The boy stared in consternation at his mother. "You said the little cub was scared 'cause he's little and lost. Can big people be scared and lost, too?"

"It can happen to anybody," she explained patiently.

"I thought…" He paused and tried again. "I thought when I got big I'd never have to be scared again." He turned to Griff. "So, when you're scared, do you hide in a tree and wait for somebody to find you?"

"I haven't tried that. What would I do if nobody ever came looking for me?"

Casey's eyes got big as he mulled that over. "What do you do when you're scared, Griff?"

"I think about all the people depending on me, and then I face down my fears and do whatever I have to."

"Even if you'll get hurt?"

Griff nodded. "Getting hurt is part of life. We fall down, and we hurt, and then we get up and try again. And again. And again."

"Even if you're hurting?"

"Even then."

The little boy pointed to the thin white scar below Griff's ear. "Did that hurt you a lot?"

Juliet was quick to say, "Casey, it isn't polite to ask about someone's wounds."

"It's all right." Griff turned to Casey. "It hurt. A lot. But I got up and fought back."

"Did a bad man hurt you?"

Griff nodded. "A very bad man, who wanted to hurt my friends, too."

"But you stopped him?"

Griff gave him a gentle smile. "I stopped him."

"Good." Casey made a little fist pump before glancing

down at his empty plate. "Thanks, Mama. Can me and Efan go play in the other room?"

She was too tired to correct his grammar. "Yes, you may."

When the two boys were gone Griff carried the dishes to the sink and began to wash them while Juliet sat sipping her lemonade.

In a low voice so her boys wouldn't overhear, she said, "Jimmy Gable told the Romeos about your wound and said it almost cost you your life. He told us you saved your entire company. He's so proud to know you."

Griff flushed. "Jimmy's a good guy. But our war experiences are old news."

Juliet fell silent, lost in thought.

When she finally pushed away from the table and picked up a towel, Griff took it from her hands. "You've done enough for one day. Go read to your boys. I'll clean up here and then head to the barn."

Too tired to argue, she merely nodded. "Thanks. Good night."

"'Night."

Half an hour later he let himself out the back door and walked to the barn. The evening had grown dark as midnight. He looked up to see storm clouds roiling across the sky, completely obliterating the moon and stars.

From the sting of the wind, it promised to be a full-blown thunderstorm.

As if on cue a clap of thunder echoed across the heavens, followed by a blinding flash of lightning.

While he spread a saddle blanket over a fresh mound of hay in an empty stall, he heard the first patter of raindrops on the tin roof. Minutes later it had turned to a drenching downpour, drumming an ear-splitting tattoo above him.

Griff kicked off his boots and slipped off his shirt before settling himself in his makeshift bed. As he leaned back on his elbows, he found himself wishing he'd thought to bring along a second longneck. Or maybe a fresh pot of coffee.

It was going to be a long night. He only hoped the steady beat of rain on the roof would soon lull him into sleep.

Griff awoke with a start to find the hay beneath him, and the saddle blanket, soaked. He looked up to see a steady river of rainwater falling from a hole in the roof to the railing of the stall. From there it was snaking its way across the rail to fall in puddles beneath him.

With a few well-chosen curses, he snatched up his wet shirt and boots and beat a hasty retreat from the stall.

He turned in time to see a dark-clad figure looming up in the doorway of the barn.

Juliet, sheltered by a tattered old rain slicker held over her head, looked like a ghostly apparition. When she caught sight of him facing her, she let out a gasp.

"Oh, Griff. I'm so sorry."

He dropped his boots to grab hold of her arm. "What in hell are you doing out here in this?"

"I...couldn't sleep. All I could think was that you were out here under this leaky old roof, while the boys and I are snug and dry in the house."

"You're a little late." He pointed to the river of water running from the stall across the barn floor before disappearing down the drain in the floor.

She studied the rainwater glistening in his dark hair. "Come on inside. I'll get you a towel and some dry things."

"Thanks. I'll take you up on it."

He picked up his boots and took hold of one side of the slicker. Keeping his strides short enough for her to match, they raced through the downpour to the house.

Inside he tossed aside his wet things in the sink while she hung the slicker on a hook by the door.

They turned, and nearly collided before stepping quickly apart.

Juliet hurried away and returned with a fluffy bath towel and moth-eaten terry robe that had seen better days.

"This was in one of the storage bins. Probably belonged to Buddy's father. I doubt it will fit, but it'll give you some cover while I toss your things in the dryer."

"Thanks." He slipped on the robe. "No need for you to dry my stuff. I can handle it."

She pointed. "The dryer's in that corner. I'll make some coffee."

As soon as she walked away he shucked his jeans and toweled his hair dry before tossing everything in the dryer.

Barefoot, wearing a robe that barely covered his thighs, he stepped into the kitchen.

She turned and couldn't help laughing. "Sorry. But you look like one of those cartoon characters whose clothes have shrunk."

"Yeah." He looked down at himself and grinned. "Just how tall was Buddy's father?"

"Judging by the way that robe fits you, I'd say he was

about half your size. And now, to add insult to injury, you have to sleep on that lumpy sofa in the other room."

He chuckled. "Not that it matters. I'll take the sofa over that lake in the barn." He studied the way she looked in a pair of boxer shorts and cami. "Of course, I could always bunk upstairs."

She turned and caught the gleam of humor in his eyes. And something else.

"Sorry. The boys have no room left in their bed."

"Darn. Well, I suppose I could make the supreme sacrifice and bunk with their mother."

"Nice try, cowboy. Their mother sleeps alone."

"What a waste."

She filled two cups with steaming coffee and carried them to the table.

As she bent to set his in front of him he leaned close. "You smell good."

She nearly bobbled the cup. "I'm sure, after a few hours in the barn, anything would smell good."

She quickly moved to sit at the opposite end of the table. Keeping herself as straight and tall as possible she fixed him with a look. "I want you to know how much I appreciate everything you do for us. The play table. Spending the night in the worst possible conditions when you could be asleep in that beautiful MacKenzie Ranch house."

"I don't mind. Really."

"I know you don't, and that only complicates matters." She looked away. "Having you here is a problem, Griff."

"Sorry. The last thing I want to do is add to your problems."

She shook her head. "I've told you how I feel."

He nodded. "You're still in love with your husband."

"Exactly. And I need to feel that I'm remaining... loyal to him."

"I understand guilt. I've been dealing with my own."

"You?"

"You may not have noticed, but Mad feels very protective of you and your boys. He gave me a lecture about how the mother of two boys deserves better than a tumble in the hay."

Her eyes widened. "He did?"

"Yeah. And ever since his blistering comments, I've been doing my best to keep my distance."

"I see."

The storm raging outside seemed to have stalled directly over the house. There was a giant clap of thunder that had them both jolting. Lightning strikes set off a display of fireworks outside the window.

Juliet was up and pacing. "That sounded like it hit something."

Griff strode to the window and glanced toward the barns. "I don't see any flames. I think maybe we got lucky."

There was another boomer, and Juliet stiffened, wrapping her arms about herself.

"Hey." Griff stepped up behind her and wrapped his arms around her to soothe. "It'll soon blow over."

"I know. I hate that I'm such a coward."

"You?" He turned her to face him, rubbing his hands over her shoulders, down her back. "You're the bravest woman I know." He looked down at her, dressed in her skimpy night clothes, his gaze trailing from her high, firm breasts peeking through the cami, to her bare toes. "And the sexiest."

"Griff…"

He hadn't planned it. It just happened. One minute he was offering comfort, the next he was seeking it.

He lowered his face. His mouth covered hers in a kiss so hot, so hungry, he saw stars. And wondered whether it was the storm outside, or the storm within.

"I want you to know I didn't mean for this to happen," he muttered inside her mouth. "Not that I'm complaining…"

"I know." A sigh rose up from deep inside her. "I've tried so hard, but…" She twined her arms around his neck and offered her lips to him.

That was all the invitation he needed. He took her mouth with a fierce hunger that had them both gasping. And then they were lost as, with soft sighs and whispered words, they wrapped around one another, desperate for more, hungry for all they could have.

With his mouth on hers, he absorbed the shock of the rolling thunder that shook the walls. At first, he thought it was her kiss that had rocked him. Then, as he realized the storm had intensified, he could feel the entire house shudder.

"Griff…"

"Shh." He took her mouth again.

She returned his kisses with an urgency that had him gripping her hips, pulling her closer.

"Griff…"

Before she could say more, there was the sound of hurried footsteps on the creaking stairs, and two little boys, rubbing their eyes and looking absolutely terrified, threw themselves against the two of them.

"Mama, Efan and me are scared."

Hearts pounding, chests heaving, Juliet and Griff stepped apart just as her two sons jumped between them.

And though their pulsebeats throbbed in their temples and their lungs were starved for air, they found themselves comforting two trembling little boys as though nothing mattered as much as their well-being. But while they soothed and comforted, they kept glancing over the boys' heads to stare at one another with looks of absolute hunger.

While Juliet led the two little guys toward the table, keeping her arms firmly around them, Griff stepped back to watch and listen. And found himself marveling at the ease with which she slipped from the role of temptress to that of loving, caring mother.

It was, he realized, one more reason why he loved her.

Love.

The very thought of it filled him with the most amazing feeling.

Right now, though he wanted her desperately, he knew he could put aside his needs for those of Juliet and her sons.

And he knew something else, as well.

When the time was right, he would make love with her. It was no longer a matter of if, but when. He would show her, in every way possible, just how deeply he felt.

For now, he could be as patient as she needed him to be. Not an easy trait for a MacKenzie. But he was willing to learn patience, just as he was willing to learn how to be a MacKenzie.

CHAPTER TWENTY-ONE

Casey looked over at Griff, who was dressed in a tattered robe. "Why are you wearing that?"

He managed a quick grin. "My clothes got soaked out in the barn. It seems I chose a bed right under a hole in the roof."

"Why?"

"I forgot to look up."

Casey giggled. "Will you sleep on the sofa again?"

"Looks like I don't have a choice." He shared a knowing look with Juliet, whose cheeks were still bright pink. Maybe, if they were lucky, they could hurry the two boys back up to bed and finish what had been so abruptly interrupted.

The little boy turned to his mother. "Will you come upstairs now and sleep in our bed?"

"You and Ethan have each other. Isn't that enough?"

"Me and Efan are scared of the storm."

Her heart still racing, Juliet took in several deep drafts of air and ruffled her son's hair. "I'm not sure there's room for me, but I could sit on the edge of the mattress and tell you both some stories."

Griff interrupted. "You need your sleep. Why don't I sleep on the floor of their room? That way they won't be crowded in bed, and I'm sure it'll offer as much comfort as that old sofa."

Surprised and touched that he would give up his privacy for the comfort of her sons, Juliet gave it a moment's thought. "If you're serious, there's an old bedroll up in the attic. I'm sure it was used on hunting trips. At least it would soften that hard floor a bit."

Griff nodded. "Show me where and I'll get it."

They finished their coffee and turned out the lights before climbing the stairs to the second floor.

Juliet pointed to a trapdoor in the ceiling. "This is a pull-down stairway that leads to the attic. I'll get a flashlight."

She disappeared inside her room and returned with the light switched on. Griff took it from her and climbed the stairs to the attic above. When he located the bedroll he hefted it over his shoulder and climbed down before turning off the flashlight. Then he folded up the stairs and closed the trapdoor.

In the boys' bedroom he unrolled the thick sleeping blanket on the floor beside the bed, while Juliet located a pillow.

While her sons scrambled into bed, Griff tested the makeshift bed. "Much softer than the hay out in the barn. Drier, too. And none of the lumps of that old sofa downstairs." He sat up. "You two going to be okay in here if that storm keeps thrashing about outside?"

Two little heads nodded.

Casey said, "As long as you stay here with us all night."

Griff winked at Juliet, sealing the deal. Though he may have thought about slipping away later and finding her, he had to let that idea go.

"Okay then. Would you like a story while you fall asleep?"

"Oh, boy." Casey let out a whoop while Ethan grinned from ear to ear.

Griff shot Juliet a lopsided grin. "Say good night to your mom."

"'Night, Mama," Casey chirped.

Ethan waved a hand.

"Good night, boys." She blew all of them kisses, directing one toward Griff, before turning out the light and closing the door.

As she was walking away she heard Griff's deep voice. "Keep in mind that I don't have Myrna's bedtime story book. But I'll do my best. Once upon a time there were two little boys. Their names were..." After a slight pause she heard, "You two get to name them."

"Casey and Efan," came the excited response.

"Right. There were two little boys named Casey and Ethan, and one day..."

With a smile, Juliet stepped into her bedroom and closed the door. After climbing into bed she lay wide awake, wondering why she was feeling suddenly left out.

One minute she'd been swept away by Griff's kisses, wanting the same thing he wanted. The next, she'd had to put aside her own feelings and deal with the very real fears of her sons.

What was even more amazing to her was that Griff had been able to put aside his needs, as well, to deal with theirs.

She could hear giggling in the next room, and realized that while her two boys were having the time of their lives, she was alone in her bed, hoping the storm would soon end.

She wished, more than anything, she could go next door and climb into bed with her boys. Not just to be closer to Griff, but because it sounded as though they were having fun.

Despite their fun, however, she realized something else. Her boys weren't the only ones feeling safe and secure.

Just having Griff here with them had changed everything.

What an amazing guardian angel had come into their lives.

While the storm raged outside, rattling the windows, she fell into a deep, dreamless sleep.

Juliet showered and dressed before pausing to peer into her sons' room. The bed was empty. On the floor, tucked up in the bedroll, Ethan and Casey lay on either side of Griff, their breathing soft and easy. Griff lay between them, one arm around each of them.

The sight of it had unexpected tears springing to Juliet's eyes. She turned away and rushed headlong down the stairs to keep from blubbering like a baby.

While coffee brewed she struggled to calm the intense emotion swirling inside.

What had triggered those tears? Was it just the knowledge that Ethan and Casey trusted Griff enough to climb into his bedroll? Or was there more going on here?

She didn't know too many men who would sacrifice their own comfort for someone else, when there was nothing to gain except stiff, aching muscles. Yet here was Griff, giving up his home, his bed, to see to their safety.

Her heart swelled.

Before she could sort through her jumbled thoughts, she could hear the sound of laughter, and footsteps, and running water. A short time later Griff and the two boys, freshly showered and dressed, walked down the stairs.

"Good morning." Juliet kept her back to them as she cracked eggs and fed bread into the toaster. "There's orange juice and coffee."

"'Morning." At Griff's deep voice she glanced over her shoulder to see Casey and Ethan wearing identical smiles. "How did everyone sleep?"

"Good," Casey answered for all of them. "Me and Efan got scared of the funder and Griff said we could sleep next to him."

"That had to be a tight squeeze in one small bedroll."

Griff winked at the two boys. "We made room."

He casually crossed the room and poured a cup of coffee before leaning against the counter beside Juliet. "How did you sleep?"

"Like a baby."

"Good. With all you do, you deserve to sleep."

As he remained beside her, she felt herself blushing. It occurred to her that what she really wanted to do, more than anything, was to turn into his arms and hug him fiercely.

When the toast popped up she was grateful for the distraction. "Here." She handed him a platter of toast and scrambled eggs.

Minutes later they gathered around the table and dug into their breakfast. While they ate, Casey related every minute of their fun evening with Griff.

"He told us stories about two brave little wranglers named Casey and Efan. They had superpowers. They could brand calves, rope stray cows, ride bulls clear across the pasture, and even fly planes and drive tractors. And all before they were four. Isn't that right, Efan?"

His older brother grinned, showing a mouthful of toast and eggs.

"Those are some stories," Juliet said with a straight face. "What about the storm? Did you hear it?"

"Not after we got in Griff's bedroll. I guess it blew away while we felled asleep."

Juliet glanced at Griff, who winked and seemed to be thoroughly enjoying his breakfast as much as he was enjoying Casey's narrative. She sat back, sipping coffee and feeling an odd sense of peace and contentment she hadn't felt in years.

Casey sat on the floor of the mudroom and struggled into his sneakers. "Can me and Efan go to the barn now and play with our trucks?"

While Griff began clearing the table he turned to Juliet. "You go along with them. I'll clean up here and join you."

She was shaking her head. "Griff, you've done enough."

"Go on." He stacked the dishes in the sink. "This won't take more than a few minutes."

She hesitated only a moment before trailing her sons to the barn.

Griff was humming as he washed the dishes. He ought to be feeling stiff and sore after a night on the floor. But in truth, he was feeling happier than he had in days. He was glad now that he'd insisted on staying the night. Just by being here, he had turned a corner in his relationship with Juliet.

Relationship? Did they actually have such a thing?

That had him grinning. He never knew from one day to the next just what their relationship was, but at least for today, it seemed on steadier ground.

He couldn't understand all of her fears, but he knew this much: She'd left behind the only life she'd ever known to start a new life with a man she'd loved. And when that life had been cut short by a tragic accident, she'd been left to pick up the pieces while sorting out what she would do going forward. Not an easy job for anyone. But for a woman with two little boys who were totally dependent on her, it must seem an insurmountable task. Yet here she was, not only coping with a painful loss, but rebuilding her own life and planning for a future for her two sons.

No wonder he couldn't walk away. He was in love with Wonder Woman.

He grinned at the image that conjured in his mind.

Yeah. Wonder Woman. And he was a mere mortal, caught up in her superpowers.

When he heard Juliet's frantic shouts, Griff dropped the dishtowel and raced out the door. His heart contracted at the thought that one of the boys had been hurt.

In the barn he stared around at a scene of complete destruction.

The electronic lift was hanging at an odd angle from the ceiling. The play table was tipped over, the toys strewn about in a sea of mud. Princess's stall was missing a door. The floor around it was spattered with blood. The mare huddled in a corner of the barn, blood streaming from a cut on her leg.

Juliet turned to Griff with a look of shock. "I've never seen so much damage from a storm. And from the look of all this blood, Princess must have cut herself on the door."

He crossed to the mare and examined the wound to her leg. "Phone Jackie and ask him to call for a vet. This looks deep."

He walked over to where the two boys were trying to right the table. "I'll do that."

He took note of the broken legs and left it where it lay. "I'll repair those legs later today. As for the rest of this, we'll clean up the mess, and then it'll be good as new."

Casey pointed to the far wall, where words had been scrawled in what appeared to be red spray paint. "What does that say, Griff?"

Griff read the words before picking up Casey and catching Ethan's hand, turning abruptly toward the door. Seeing Juliet talking on her cell phone to Jackie, he caught her by the arm and dragged her along with him.

She shot him a look of complete surprise. "What are you doing?"

His tone was curt. "Take Casey and Ethan up to the house. And stay there with them."

She pocketed her phone. "There's no need. Jackie's on his way. I told him about the storm damage."

"This isn't from the storm. I'm calling Chief Petti-grew." He pulled his cell phone from his pocket and dialed.

As he did, Juliet started back into the barn. Before he could stop her, he heard the deep voice of the police chief and was forced to concentrate on the reason for his call.

"It's Griff Warren, Chief. You'd better get out to the Grayson Ranch right away."

As he started after Juliet, he saw her stop and gasp, and realized he was too late to keep her from reading the hateful words sprayed on the wall in bright red letters.

Ice maiden or whore?
Ask the Marine who spent the night with her.

CHAPTER TWENTY-TWO

Jackie Turner and Chief Ira Pettigrew drove up the long dirt driveway within minutes of one another.

Griff had suggested that Juliet remain in the house with her boys until after the police chief had time to examine the crime scene. That way, the chief could talk openly, without having to worry about having two little boys overhear things that could frighten them.

Griff stood in the open doorway of the barn as the two men exited their vehicles. His hands were clenched tightly at his sides in impotent rage.

"'Morning, son," Jackie called. "Princess hurt herself during the storm?"

Chief Pettigrew looked from Jackie to Griff. "You called me out here for an accident with a horse?"

"This was no accident—it was deliberate." Griff's voice lowered with barely controlled anger. "At first glance, we thought the destruction in the barn had been the result of the storm. But then we saw that." He pointed to the spray-painted message of hate on the wall.

Both men reacted in the same manner, with a huff of outrage, and a sudden narrowing of their eyes.

"I thought it best if Juliet kept the boys away from this."

The chief nodded. Jackie crossed to the mare and bent to examine the wound. When he looked up he was frowning. He took his phone from his shirt pocket. "If you don't mind, I'd like to have Doc Pickering take a look at Princess."

The chief agreed. "I'd appreciate Doc's opinion on this." He walked around the barn, noting the missing door of the mare's stall. "She may have kicked this during the height of the storm. Or she may have kicked it after being cut."

"There's a third alternative," Griff said quietly. "Someone in a fit of rage may have ripped it off its hinges before taking out his fury on a helpless animal."

The chief's look was grim as he considered Griff's words. Then he removed his phone and took several pictures of the message scrawled on the wall before moving around the barn, snapping shots of the destruction.

When he came to the play table, he paused. "I don't recall seeing this in here last time I stopped by."

Griff shook his head. "It's new. I built it yesterday for Casey and Ethan, so they could play with their cars and trucks whenever their mother gets busy with clients."

Ira Pettigrew examined the workmanship. "You do good work, Griff."

"Thanks."

The chief shook his head. "Although I guess someone

doesn't appreciate it. I see a couple of the legs have been broken off."

"It was overturned when we found it. I started to turn it upright before I realized I was at a crime scene. After that, I left everything untouched."

The chief looked around. "See anything else that's been damaged?"

Griff pointed to the lift. "Juliet had to wait weeks to have that repaired. Now it's damaged again, and who knows how long it will take to get a repair crew back out here."

Ira gave a hiss of disgust. "This was no random attack. The items destroyed are necessary to her work or her boys. Juliet's most patient mare. The electronic lift. A new play space for the boys. The words of that note. All point to a very personal attack."

His voice lowered. "I'll wait to hear Doc Pickering's verdict on the mare, but I'm betting all my money on that wound having been a deliberate attack, too."

A short time later a battered truck wheezed up the driveway, emitting a trail of smoke and noise. A tall young man with a blond beard and sun-streaked hair in a ponytail stepped out and ambled into the barn, calling a greeting to Jackie and Ira.

"Hey, Teddy." Jackie hurried forward to grasp the young man's hand. "Ted Pickering, I'd like you to meet Griff Warren."

"Bear MacKenzie's other son?"

Griff nodded and offered a handshake. "That's right. Nice to meet you, Dr. Pickering."

"You're the image of your father."

Griff nodded. "I've heard that a time or two."

The veterinarian looked around. "Where's our wounded mare?"

Jackie jerked a shoulder toward the doorway. "I put her out in the corral. Figured you'd want to examine her in good light."

"Great." The young veterinarian nodded toward Griff and Ira before following Jackie to the corral.

Ira continued moving around the interior of the barn, snapping shots of things that caught his eye, and pausing to examine things that might prove to be clues.

When Dr. Pickering returned, his demeanor had changed from sunny to irate. "I can't say for certain, Chief, but my guess is the mare was struck by a sharp instrument." His voice betrayed his deep-seated anger. "Why would anyone want to harm an animal?"

"The same reason he wrote that message," Ira said through gritted teeth.

The vet looked absolutely stunned as he read the words painted on the wall.

He turned to Jackie. "I'd like to ask permission of the owner to take the mare back with me so I can keep an eye on that wound. I wouldn't want it to get infected."

Jackie nodded. "I'll take you up to the house and introduce you to Juliet Grayson."

"Right. Buddy's widow." The doctor shook his head. "I'm sure she's had enough to deal with. A shame she has to handle this, too."

A short time later the veterinarian drove away with Princess loaded into a horse trailer hooked to the back of his truck.

When the dust settled, the chief turned to Griff with a look of grim resignation. "I've asked the state police to assist in stepping up the hunt for Mitch Cord. I've forwarded all the pictures I took. One of their crime units will be out here to check for clues and take whatever prints they find. In the meantime, I'll have to ask Juliet and her boys to stay clear of the barn until later today, when the state boys have finished their work here." He sighed. "What all this says to me is that Mitch Cord's anger is now way out of control. This is a very dangerous situation."

Griff and Jackie exchanged knowing looks, aware of the cloud of danger that hung over Juliet and her little boys.

"Thank you, Chief Pettigrew." Juliet stood on the back porch while Casey and Ethan sat at the kitchen table, distracted by an unexpected snack of sliced peaches over ice cream. "I appreciate everything you've done for me."

Ira watched as the state crime unit wrapped up their investigation and signaled that they were leaving. Then he turned back to Juliet. "I know I don't have to remind you to take extra precautions until we find the son of a—" he paused "—until Mitch is safely behind bars."

She gave a long, deep sigh. "I will."

Jackie's voice was stern. "I'll be close by in the bunkhouse, Chief." He turned to Juliet. "And I won't be going home to my daughter's until Mitch is caught."

"That's good news." The chief turned to Juliet. "I know this isn't easy, ma'am. But it won't last forever."

She held up a hand. "What worries me is that Mitch Cord seems to be very good at staying out of sight. Nobody has even caught a glimpse of him so far. What makes you think this time is different?"

"Because these are the acts of a desperate man. And often, when a man gets desperate, he gets careless. When he does, we'll be ready for him."

.She crossed her arms over her chest, and it was obvious that she was mulling the chief's words.

To ease her concern, Griff said, "Until he's caught, I'm staying, too."

She turned to him with a shake of her head. "You have a life, Griff. And a family. You can't just walk away from your own obligations to babysit me."

He winked. "Maybe I like babysitting." At her frown he merely grinned. "Okay. Maybe there's another solution." He turned to Ira. "Chief, is there a firm in town that offers round-the-clock security?"

Ira gave him a look that said he must be crazy to even ask such a question. "You're talking about Copper Creek, son. The closest thing we have to a security firm is me. And I'm responsible for all the citizens, which means I can't spend all my time protecting just one, even if I'd like to."

Jackie chuckled. "You might find bodyguards and security companies in some big city like New York, but you're not going to find something like that here in Montana. And especially not here in the middle of nowhere. In Copper Creek, we all look out for each other. We pride ourselves on taking care of our own."

Griff turned to Juliet. "I guess you have your answer. It's Jackie and me, or a big-city security firm, which would have to be imported since it doesn't exist around these parts."

Juliet stood tapping a foot on the wooden step. Finally she said softly, "I'll admit that I'm terrified. But since I need to keep working if I intend to keep my ranch from foreclosure, I guess I'll take whatever help I can get and try to stay on course with my life."

Griff arched a brow and turned to the old man. "Looks like she's decided to trust her safety to you and me, Jackie. We're officially the Juliet Grayson security detail."

"Creepers. I'm right proud to be on board, son." Jackie clapped a hand on his shoulder as they exchanged smiles and handshakes.

They kept the jokes flowing as they trailed the police chief to his truck. Once they reached it, the jokes faded away, and they talked quietly about the seriousness of the situation looming before them.

Ira's voice was pure ice. "See that one of you is with that little lady at all times until Mitch is found. The level of anger and violence in that barn has me really concerned for her safety."

Griff nodded. "I'll try to keep things light for the sake of her boys. But I think Juliet knows this is deadly serious."

Jackie glanced toward his truck. "I intend to have a rifle at the ready while I'm handling chores. I'll alert Cooper and the wranglers to do the same. And at night, I'll have my weapon right beside the bed. Keep in mind, son, if you need me, I'll be up to the house in a minute flat."

The chief turned on the ignition and put his truck in gear. Through the open window he called, "Don't take any chances. If you spot Mitch, call me right away. The state police have assured me they can have a copter here within half an hour."

Griff met the chief's dark gaze. "It only takes a second to fire a gun. If a man's determined, he can find more than enough time to commit a crime and get clean away in half an hour."

The chief nodded. "That's why it's so critical that the two of you keep that little lady and her two boys in your sight all the time until Mitch Cord is behind bars."

CHAPTER TWENTY-THREE

After getting Ira's permission from the state police to clean up the mess in the barn, Griff finished painting over the last of the red letters, running the long-handled roller vertically and then horizontally, until there was no trace of red bleeding through the fresh layer of paint.

It wouldn't do for two little boys to see something this hideous on their barn. Even if they didn't understand the words, they would have plenty of questions about what the words were and what they meant.

What sort of sick mind would do such a thing to a woman like Juliet?

A woman like Juliet. Griff stood back, allowing those words to play through his mind.

She'd been through so much. And yet, for all her pain, she spent her days trying to help others who were suffering.

What kind of creep would call her a whore?

It came to him instantly. An out-of-control angry man. A man who wanted her for himself. A man who might have fantasized that he could persuade or take her by force, and now had to come to grips with the fact that he could never have her, because too many people had rallied around her to keep her safe.

When Griff's cell phone rang he plucked it from his shirt pocket and studied the caller identification before greeting his grandfather. "Hey, Mad. Sorry I haven't called today. I've been distracted. Something happened here last night."

As quickly as possible he described what had occurred, and answered the old man's rapid-fire questions.

"Yeah. Ira's been here.... No. There's been no sign of Mitch yet. But I think with the state police assisting, it shouldn't be too long before he's in custody.... I won't be coming home. I told Ira I'd be staying here until this is put to rest.... Don't you worry. We're not alone. Jackie will be staying in the bunkhouse. He's up in the hills right now, conferring with Cooper and the wranglers on the best way for everyone to pull together and keep Juliet safe."

He paused to listen before saying, "That would be great, Mad. I know Juliet would appreciate anything you can do." He listened again before adding, "You know I'll keep you and the family up on the latest as it happens."

When he rang off he turned with a thoughtful look. Content that he'd completely obliterated any trace of the hateful words, he made his way to the house.

The bus rolled up the driveway at its usual time. Seeing it, Juliet raced down the steps of the house, trailed by her two sons, to alert the men on the bus of the change in plans before they began the difficult and time-consuming task of disembarking.

Through the open driver's window she shouted, "Heywood, I told you not to come today. Weren't you listening?"

Instead of responding he threw the switch that lowered the hydraulic platform, and when it reached ground level, Jimmy Gable rolled his wheelchair free.

"Hey, Juliet. Hey, Casey and Ethan." His face was wreathed in smiles before he looked beyond them to call, "Hey, Captain. Nice to see you here."

"You, too, Jimmy." Griff walked closer. "I'm surprised to see you, though."

"Why is that?" Jimmy moved his chair aside as the platform lowered, depositing Hank Wheeler.

"The lift suffered some damage in last night's storm." Griff shot a warning look at Juliet, alerting her that he had decided a white lie was simpler than explaining the truth.

"Hey, that's really awful. And after just getting it repaired." Jimmy shook his head. "I wish I'd known sooner. I had a chance to win a big jackpot at today's poker play-off over at Wylie's."

As the platform deposited Billy Joe Harris, Juliet gave a hiss of annoyance. "I phoned Heywood and told him not to come."

Just then the platform returned to the back of the bus, where Heywood positioned his scooter and waited his turn to be lowered to the ground.

"Why'd you drag us out here, Sperry?" Hank Wheeler demanded.

Heywood grinned. "You got something better to do?"

"I don't know about Hank." Jimmy showed a rare flash of anger. "But you knew I wanted to be in that poker tournament today."

"Shut up, you freakin' crybaby." Sperry shook his fist in Jimmy's face before grabbing the front of his shirt and pulling him close. Through gritted teeth he said, "When you asked to join the Romeos, I told you who was leader. I spelled out the rules of the game. You do what I tell you or else."

Juliet crossed her arms over her chest. "What we do here isn't just a game. And what kind of leader would bring these men all this way, knowing the lift was out of commission?"

"The Supreme Commander, that's who." He looked her up and down before giving her a lazy smile. "Maybe I just felt like taking a long, scenic drive in the country. And now, I'm enjoying the scenery here even more." He turned to Griff. "I hope you're on your way home, cowboy."

Griff leaned against the side of the bus. "Who says I'm leaving? Maybe I'm already home."

He watched Sperry's smile dissolve into a snarl of anger which he turned on Juliet. "Okay, so your precious lift is out of commission. That doesn't mean we can't do some other stuff. When I was in the VA hospital, they used to massage my back and arms. I wouldn't mind having you try a little of that."

Juliet was already shaking her head. "I've made it clear that I'm not a certified therapist." She turned in a semicircle, speaking to all of the men. "If you want that kind of hands-on therapy, you'll have to head to the nearest VA hospital."

"Which, for me, is thousands of miles away." Jimmy Gable checked his watch before looking up. "If we leave right now, I can still make that poker tournament."

Sperry turned his electric scooter toward the barn. "Let's just see how much damage that lift suffered in the storm."

Juliet was about to stop him, but his scooter lurched forward so quickly he was inside the barn before she could say a word.

Once there, he looked around with a frown. "It doesn't look that bad to me."

She pressed the button that normally activated the lift, and the machine remained silent and unmoving. "Does that answer your question? It's completely out of commission, and it won't be operating again until the company can send new parts and a repairman to install them."

As she started past him he caught her hand. Annoyed, she looked down at their joined hands, and then into his eyes, glinting with his own weird brand of dark humor. "All right, Heywood. You've had your fun for today. And you've satisfied your curiosity about the lift. Now it's time to take the men back to town. Please don't bring them back until I tell you I'm ready to help them."

"Sure thing, *Mrs.* Grayson," he said, leering at her, "especially since you said the magic word. *Please.*"

She pulled her hand free and stormed out of the barn, with Heywood Sperry gleefully grinning and rolling along behind her.

Once outside he rolled onto the platform and used the hydraulic lift to return to the front of the bus. One by one the other members of the Romeos followed suit.

Jimmy Gable saluted Griff and flashed the return of his

good humor before rolling onto the platform. As he ascended he called, "Today's jackpot is three hundred. Want a piece of the action?"

"No thanks, Jimmy." Griff waved a hand. "It's all yours. I hope you win."

"Have no doubt about that." He winked. "Ask anyone in Copper Creek. I'm the luckiest poker player around these parts."

The men called and waved as the bus, with Sperry at the wheel, turned around and headed toward town.

When they were gone Juliet huffed out a breath. "Why is Heywood so annoyingly contrary? I specifically told him the lift was down, and I didn't want him to bring the men out here today."

"Some people thrive on being negative. I think Sperry's one of them. You could see that he enjoyed spoiling Jimmy's day."

"But why? How can a person enjoy making other people miserable?"

Griff shrugged. "Maybe now that his life has been altered by war, he wants to punish everyone else. Or maybe he just wants to be the center of attention. He knows the Romeos will grumble on the way back to town about the waste of time, and all the while Sperry's day has just gone exactly the way he wanted it, because he was the one calling the shots, whether they liked it or not. I think Sperry is all about being in control."

Juliet pressed her hands to her temples. "I'm sick and tired of thinking about that nasty man."

As she turned away, Griff caught her by the shoulder. Knowing her boys were close, he kept his tone soft. "Try not to think about anything. Just get through the day, and let the authorities do their job. Who knows? Maybe you'll hear from Chief Pettigrew before the day is over, telling you they've found Mitch. And then things can settle down to normal."

She let out a long, deep sigh. "I don't even know what normal is. It's been too long since anything in my life has gone right."

He pointed to her two sons. "Look at them. Casey and Ethan are just fine. And that's all because of you."

Her frown dissolved into a smile. "They really are special, aren't they?" She squeezed his hand before turning toward the barn. "I guess I'd better get to my chores."

"I'll give you a hand."

While Casey and Ethan happily moved their cars and trucks around the floor of the barn, Griff and Juliet stayed busy, mucking stalls and hauling feed and water to the horses. But every so often Griff paused to wipe sweat from the back of his neck. And when he did, he took a moment to enjoy the vision of the small blonde in faded denims and T-shirt who, even while handling a pitchfork, never failed to take his breath away.

By midafternoon they both looked up at the sound of a truck's engine coming near.

As they stepped to the doorway of the barn they saw a convoy of trucks, all bearing the MacKenzie logo on their doors. Whit and Ash helped Mad out of the first truck and lifted him into his wheelchair. From a second truck Willow and Brenna stepped out, carrying an array of foil-covered pans. The third and fourth trucks held Brady and half a dozen wranglers, who busied themselves removing an assortment of tools.

Mad rolled up to the barn's entrance. "How are you holding up, lass?"

Juliet smiled. "I'm fine, Mad. And even better now that I see all of you." She looked beyond him to smile at everyone. "I wasn't aware that I was throwing a party."

"Not a party, lass." Mad held out his arms as the two little boys came running toward him. Lifting them to his lap he hugged them before saying, "We're here to work." He stared around. "It doesn't look so bad in here."

"You should have seen it before Griff tackled the cleanup."

She and Griff exchanged smiles. The gesture wasn't lost on those watching.

"Well." His tone unusually gruff, Mad turned his wheelchair toward the house. "I hope you don't mind, but I'm about to take over your kitchen, lass."

She gave a mock shudder. "Having seen the kitchen at your ranch, I can't imagine how you'll manage to get any work done here. I'm afraid it's in sad need of repair."

"Not to worry, lass. I could cook over a campfire or on a hot plate, if need be. I'll be just fine." He turned to his grandsons. "I'll need your help getting up that porch."

"That's why we're here." Ash began pushing his wheelchair, while Whit walked alongside. As always, Casey and Ethan sat on Mad's lap, thoroughly enjoying the ride.

At the porch the little boys stood by while the two men easily lifted their grandfather and carried him up the steps and into the mudroom. They paused while Griff hauled the wheelchair into the house.

Once Mad was settled, he again lifted the two little boys to his lap before looking around with interest. "This looks just like my ranch, before Maddy decided it needed to be updated. I believe that was back in the fifties."

That had everyone chuckling.

"Be careful of the appliances," Griff cautioned. "If you use too many at one time, you'll blow a fuse. It's something I was hoping to take care of soon."

"You were, were you?" The old man gave him a long, appraising look before dismissing all of them. "Go on with you, now. The wee lads and I have work to do. And so do you."

"We're working with you, Grandpa Mad?" Casey asked.

"Indeed. The two of you will run and fetch while I... work my magic."

As Griff stepped out the door, he turned to Whit and Ash. "What do you make of the look in Mad's eyes?"

Ash chuckled. "The old man's up to something."

Whit nodded. "Either we'll enjoy the feast of a lifetime tonight, or he'll end up blowing up the whole house by ignoring your warning about overloading the circuits."

Griff took a deep breath. "Let's hope for the feast. I've got enough on my hands right now without having to clean up after an explosion."

CHAPTER TWENTY-FOUR

There was no time to worry about Mad's intentions. A truck from Garvey Fuller's mill arrived with a load of lumber. It was quickly unloaded and stacked next to the barn.

After conferring with Juliet and Jackie, Brady sent his work crews out in different directions with orders to get their specific jobs done quickly and efficiently. Jackie took charge of the wranglers who would go with him to the hills to join forces with Juliet's crew.

"No matter where you go," Brady said sternly, "remember to keep an eye out for Mitch Cord. He could be anywhere on the property."

A second crew was dispatched to the house, where they began tearing out the sagging porch, while others climbed to the roof to inspect the shingles. Brady and his crew crawled over the barn, repairing the holes in the roof while testing any beams for decay or rot.

An electrical crew drove up and disappeared inside the house.

A plumber and his assistant arrived, conferred with Brady, and then walked into the house. Minutes later he, too, disappeared inside.

Juliet stood in the doorway of the barn, looking slightly dazed at the sight of all the activity going on around her. She turned to Willow. "I feel so terrible that I can't pay all these kind people."

Willow smiled. "Have they asked for payment?"

"Not a word. But look at them." Juliet sighed. "So many people, and so many supplies." She turned to study the mountain of lumber, and shingles, and boxes of nails and screws and mysterious fittings. "I could never even begin to afford all this."

Willow touched a hand to her arm. "Since this is Mad's project, why don't you let him worry about it?"

"Mad is doing all this?" Juliet looked as though she might cry. "Why?"

"Maybe he has a soft spot for pretty young widows." Willow caught her hand. "Come on. Let's go for a ride."

"In your truck?"

Willow laughed. "On your horses."

"What about my sons?"

Willow touched a finger to her lips. "Shh. Don't give them another thought. Mad insisted that they'll be with him and Brenna the entire day. I believe, besides getting a few cooking lessons, Casey and Ethan will be sculpting with Brenna."

"Oh, Willow." Juliet reined in her mount at the top of the hill, and stared at the land spread out below. "This is the first time I've ever had the chance to see it all from this vantage point."

Willow drew her mare to a halt. "Drink it in." She waved an arm. "Now you can see why men are seduced by all this land."

Juliet's voice grew hushed, as though she were in some great cathedral. "This is what Buddy wanted for his sons. What he wanted for all of us." She felt tears threaten and blinked furiously. "He should be here instead of me."

Willow caught her hand. "I know how you feel."

The young woman's head came up sharply, and she met Willow's direct gaze. "Yes, you do. You're probably the only one here who really understands exactly what I'm going through. I'm so sorry about your loss."

They sat for long minutes, holding hands and staring at the beauty around them.

"Let's walk a bit." Willow slid from the saddle and Juliet did the same.

Holding the reins, they led their horses through the tall grass, lifting their faces to the sun.

At length Willow broke the silence. "At first, I thought as you did, that Bear should have been the one to live on here. This is his land. His slice of paradise. He worked his entire life carving out this ranch, these herds, for his sons. But slowly I'm coming to terms with the fact that everything happens in its own time. You and I are here because we were fortunate to love men who loved this land. Even though they can't be here with us any longer, we can carry on their legacy. We do it through our careful management of the things they built here. And we do it through their sons. Our sons. And because of that, this is no longer just theirs, but it's now ours as well. Our land and our legacy."

As her words sank in, Juliet looked around again, seeing it all in a new light. Though her lashes were still damp with tears, she could feel a lightness around her heart.

"Ever since coming here, I've thought of this as Buddy's land. Buddy's ranch. And yes, his legacy. I've never thought of it as mine, to do with as I please."

"Nobody would blame you if you sold it and returned to the city."

"That's what people expect, isn't it?" Juliet turned to Willow. "They think the city girl will either give up or mismanage the old Grayson place."

"Are they right?" Willow smiled. "Or would you like to prove them wrong?"

Slowly Juliet nodded. "I want to succeed here. Not to prove anybody wrong, but because this is where I want to be. I want to raise my boys here. I want them to love this land the way the Grayson family has loved it for generations. But I also want it to be mine, and not just the old Grayson place."

Willow gathered her close and hugged her fiercely. "Then do it. Make it yours. Take your life in your hands and make it the success you know it can be."

Juliet stepped back and took a long, deep breath. "I have a long way to go before I become as comfortable in my role as you are."

Willow laughed, a soft, girlish sound. "I see I have you as fooled as everyone else. Here's the naked, painful truth. Every day now, I wake up wondering if I can live up to the MacKenzie legacy. And every night, as I fall into bed, I realize I'm another step closer to my goal. But it isn't easy. Because every day of my life, I miss Bear with an ache around my heart that never leaves me."

Juliet's eyes rounded. "Thank you for your honesty."

"Thank you for listening. There's something special about sharing the truth with someone who has experienced something so similar. And your loss isn't quite as fresh as mine." She pulled herself into the saddle and turned to Juliet. "Tell me. Does it get easier?"

Juliet mounted before saying softly, "I'd like to say it does, but I'm still hurting, and still trying to find my way through this maze." She glanced shyly at Willow. "Can I ask you something personal?"

Willow nodded. "Ask away."

"Do you think you could ever love again? Or would you feel guilty?"

Willow fell silent before finally saying, "I haven't really thought about it. My loss is so fresh. But I do think I'd have to work through a great deal of guilt if I found myself attracted to another man."

Juliet's words were little more than a whisper. "Yes. That damnable guilt. As though somehow, by allowing myself to love another man, I'll be betraying the first man I ever loved."

"Exactly." Tears welled up in Willow's eyes. "And yet, I know Bear would be the first one to tell me that I had a right—in fact, I had a direct order from him—to have a future with someone I loved, if that person was deserving of my love and loved me back."

The two women sat, silent and teary-eyed, sharing the moment.

"Come on," Willow called at last. "I'll race you back to the barn."

With their hair streaming out behind them, and their laughter carried on the breeze, they urged their horses into a run.

The entire ranch was swarming with workmen. The house, the barns, and even the bunkhouse roof and walls were being patched, mended, repaired. The mountain of wood and supplies had dwindled to a small pile, while several stake trucks sat idling, heaped with debris.

Juliet and Willow turned their horses into the corral before pausing at the doorway of the barn.

Inside, Brady was walking around staring upward while men with hoses poured water over the newly repaired roof. Satisfied that they'd patched every leak, he called for them to turn off the faucets.

Seeing the two women, he walked over and tipped his hat. "The barn's in good shape now, Juliet. We'll be checking out the roof on your house in about an hour."

She shook her head in wonder. "I can't believe how much work you've done already."

"It doesn't take long with a crew this size." He smiled at Willow, his gaze sweeping over her face with a long, lingering look. "Did you have a good ride?"

"A really good ride." She glanced at Juliet. "And a good visit, too."

He stared after them as the two women linked arms and started toward the house.

The sun was sinking low on the horizon when Brady moved between the house, the barn, and bunkhouse, to call the workmen together for supper.

Ash and Griff had set long planks across wooden

horses set up under a giant cottonwood tree, while Whit hauled covered roasting pans from the house to a buffet table set up next to the porch.

When everything was ready, they carried Mad down the newly made steps of the bigger, wider porch and out into the grass where his wheelchair had been parked.

Everyone lined up to fill their plates before taking seats at the makeshift tables.

"Great roast beef, Mad," one of the wranglers shouted.

"Try the lasagna," another called.

"The fried chicken. It's the best," Whit said between mouthfuls.

"Thanks, lads. I did my best." Mad was beaming as the compliments continued to flow.

Casey and Ethan, seated on either side of him, regaled their mother with a recitation of the entire afternoon.

"First, Auntie Brenna set up our studio in the parlor," Casey said.

"Auntie Brenna?" Juliet shot a look at Ash and his wife, seated in the shade of the tree while they tasted each other's food.

"Uh-huh. Auntie Brenna said when she was growing up in Copper Creek, she called everybody in town auntie or uncle. It's a sign of 'spect."

"Do you know what that means, lad?" Mad asked.

The little boy shrugged. "I guess she held up signs whenever she saw specks of dust on them."

Mad nearly choked on his food as he struggled to hold back the laughter.

"So, Auntie Brenna made you a studio?" Juliet asked.

The little boy nodded. "And me and Efan made so

many things out of clay, Auntie Brenna said we were both genies."

"Let me guess." Ash winked at Juliet before turning to Casey. "Could she have called you a genius?"

"Yes. Bof of us. Genies." While the others laughed, Casey seemed not to notice. "And then Grandpa Mad let me stir the gravy," he said solemnly. "And Efan and me got the first taste of his famous chocolate cake."

"Do you remember why it's famous, lad?" Mad asked.

The little boy nodded. "'Cause years ago it won a blue ribbon at a county fairy."

"Fair, lad." Though Mad tried to correct him, it was too late. Everyone was laughing too hard to hear him.

"So," Whit asked with a straight face. "Did the county fairy turn the blue ribbon pink?"

Casey turned to Mad. "Could she do that?"

Mad shrugged his shoulders and, while the others continued laughing, gave up trying to explain.

"I bet the county fairy wishes she could be here to taste Mad's famous fried chicken." Whit winked at Juliet, who was sipping lemonade and grinning from ear to ear. It was clear that she was having a wonderful time.

Seeing her so relaxed, Griff leaned close to whisper, "Now this is what living with the MacKenzies is all about."

She touched a hand to his shoulder. "You're so lucky to have found them. I can't remember the last time I've had such a fantastic day."

"When you consider how it started this morning, that's quite a turnaround."

She nodded.

And as the teasing and laughter continued swirling

around her, she found herself marveling at how far this day had come.

She'd been so stunned by that message painted on the wall of her barn. And so desperately afraid that she would find danger at every turn. Yet here she was, at the end of a day that had seen her buildings repaired, savoring a wonderful meal and enjoying the company of this amazing family. And all because of her connection to Griff.

Connection. Now wasn't that the perfect word?

Though they were very different, she felt somehow connected to him.

She glanced at him. Did he feel it, too?

He chose that very moment to turn to her, and she felt the oddest sensation deep inside.

As though his heart had touched hers.

She gave him a happy, relaxed smile, and he returned it with one of his own.

Across the table, Mad studied the two people, seeing the love in their eyes. He wondered if they even knew yet what they were feeling.

Probably not. Love was funny that way. One minute you were feeling all alone in the universe. The next you were wondering how you could have ever survived without that special someone.

He chuckled. They'd know soon enough. Love had a way of sneaking up and, without any warning, shooting an arrow straight through the heart.

"What so funny, Grandpa Mad?"

At Casey's question he merely grinned. "Life, lad. This crazy life we lead is the funniest, grandest thing in the whole world."

CHAPTER TWENTY-FIVE

It was late by the time the last truck drove out of the yard and moved along the gravel drive toward the distant highway.

Juliet's wranglers formed a convoy of trucks to return to the hills and the herd, while Jackie Turner bid good night and took himself off to the newly remodeled bunkhouse, after enjoying three helpings of everything. The MacKenzie wranglers left in a second convoy, led by Brady.

Long after they'd gone, Mad insisted on staying to help with the cleanup. While his grandsons removed all trace of litter from the yard, the women joined Mad in the kitchen, washing roasting pans and every pot and pan Juliet owned before returning them to their proper shelves in the cupboards.

Juliet turned to Willow. "I'm so glad you thought to bring plastic and paper, or I'd have run out of dishes."

"Don't thank me." Willow nodded toward Mad, seated at the table regaling Casey and Ethan with stories of his childhood. "This was his party from beginning to end."

Juliet surprised the old man by walking up behind him and throwing her arms around his neck. Bending close she pressed a kiss to his cheek. "How can I ever thank you for today, Mad? You can't imagine what all this means to me."

He patted her hand. "I'd know a little about feeling helpless in the face of trouble. One of the best things about being my age is, I don't have to ask permission when I want to do something for somebody. I just do what I want, and ask forgiveness later."

She knelt down beside his wheelchair. "There's nothing to forgive. This was the kindest, sweetest thing anyone's ever done for me."

"I'm glad, lass." He glanced across the room at Griff, who was watching Juliet just as he had throughout the entire day. It was plain his grandson couldn't keep his eyes off her.

Taking pity on him, Mad managed a fake yawn. "And now, if you don't mind, I'm ready to leave." He turned to Ash, who had agreed to fly him home in the Cessna, parked behind the barn. "Get me to my chariot, lads. This old body is ready for bed."

There were hugs all around as everyone bid good night to Juliet, Griff, Casey, and Ethan.

As his grandsons were wheeling him out the door, Mad winked at Casey and Ethan, whose eyes were practically closing. "Bid your mother good night, lads, and get yourselves off to bed." He winked. "And that's an order."

"Goodnight, Grandpa Mad," Casey called.

Ethan waved as Mad was carried out the door.

Both boys ran upstairs to peer out their bedroom window as Mad was settled into the plane. And as it lifted into the air, the boys waved until it was just a speck in the sky.

Juliet and Griff climbed the stairs and watched as Casey and Ethan turned from the window.

"Need some help getting into your pajamas?" Griff asked.

Without hesitation both boys threw themselves into his arms.

With a soft chuckle he muttered, "I guess I got my answer. Come on, little wranglers. You've put in a long, satisfying day."

With his help, both boys were out of their clothes and into their pajamas in minutes.

Before Juliet could suggest brushing their teeth, they were in the bed and their eyes were closing. As she turned out the light, she called, "Good night, boys."

In reply she heard the soft, even breathing that told her they were already fast asleep.

"Look at all this." After coming downstairs, Juliet danced out onto the new porch and lifted her arms wide before twirling around to admire the structure which was now the width of the house, with a lovely wide railing around three sides, and wide steps with their own safety railing to grab. "Isn't this amazing? It's exactly as I'd always pictured it, if and when I could afford to have it done."

"It looks perfect here. And smells perfect, too." Griff inhaled the smell of new wood. "I'm glad you like it. Once we got started, I realized we'd jumped into all this without even asking you what you thought."

"What I thought?" She laughed. "Oh, Griff. I thought I was in some kind of dream. All those workmen swarming over the place, and all of them doing the dozens of things I'd always wished I could pay to have done. I honestly believed I'd never live long enough to see it all come true."

He gave a shake of his head. "Mad's quite a guy."

"Isn't he?" She stared at the slowly darkening sky. "But it isn't just Mad. It's your whole family. Willow. Brenna and Ash. Whit." Her voice lowered. Softened. "You. Giving up your own comfort to see to mine."

"I'd give up my life for you."

He said it so softly she turned, eyes wide, to simply stare at him.

"Griff…"

He touched a finger to her lips. "Don't say a word. Just let me hold you."

She moved into his arms and lifted a hand to brush a lock of hair from his forehead. And then, framing his face with her hands, she stood on tiptoe to brush his mouth with hers.

He went very still, absorbing the quick rush of heat, the sexual thrill that poured through his system.

Her voice was a whisper on the breeze. "Are you going to kiss me back?"

"Not yet."

"Why?"

"I need to know how you're really feeling, Juliet. You've admitted there's lingering guilt about betraying Buddy's memory. I don't ever want to add to that guilt."

When she said nothing, he stepped back.

She caught his hand. "Wait. I need to explain. There *is* guilt. Maybe there always will be. I'm living on Buddy's ranch. I'm the mother of his sons. I want them to know something of their father as they grow up. Those memories of my first love will always be with me. But Willow and I had a lovely, long talk during our ride today. And she made me realize that I'm not alone in these feelings. Maybe every woman who has ever loved and lost someone dear has to deal with this. But even while I grieve my loss, I realize that I have to move on. And when I'm with you I feel—" she took in a long, deep breath "—I feel alive again. I feel brand-new. As though I've walked into this glorious adventure, and I can't wait to see what tomorrow brings with you."

She became suddenly shy, as she realized how much she'd revealed.

She released her grasp on his hand and took a step back, breaking contact. "I'll understand if you feel put off by the fact that I will always love Buddy."

"Is that what you think?"

She raised an eyebrow. "Then what's wrong? Why are you looking at me like that?"

"I'm trying to give you time. I'm afraid if I move too quickly, I'll scare you away again."

She shook her head. "I don't scare easily, Griff."

"I've noticed. But this time you'd better mean it. Because once I touch you, I won't be able to stop. I'll just devour you right here."

She gave a jittery laugh. "Maybe we'd better go inside first."

"Too late." He shook his head. "I'm already in way too deep."

"Oh." She stepped closer and brushed his mouth with hers.

This time his arms tightened around her, gathering her firmly against him, and she was aware of his arousal. And just as suddenly, aware of her own.

"Oh." She whispered it again, softly, before his mouth crushed hers.

The kiss spun on and on as he backed her roughly against the door.

"Griff, Jackie might be outside..."

Reaching around her, he managed to open the door enough to back her into the mudroom.

Then his hands were on her, moving over her, touching, kneading. Hers moved around his waist, then up his back, and still it wasn't satisfying enough for either of them. Desperate for more, they changed the angle of the kiss as her fingers dug into the back of his head. His hands were at her shoulders, then down her back before clutching frantically at her hips.

"All these clothes..." In one quick motion he tore at her shirt, ripping the buttons as he managed to free it from the waistband of her jeans.

He reached around her, freeing the hook of her bra. It drifted to the floor.

"Juliet." His hands were on her, and then his mouth.

She gave a moan of pleasure at the feel of those rough fingertips moving over her, as he began to satisfy his need to touch, to taste. To feast.

Suddenly he reached for the snaps at her waist at the same moment she reached for his. After much fumbling they managed to free themselves of the last of their clothes.

He drew in a ragged breath. "If this is just a dream..."

She touched a finger to his lips. "If it is, don't wake me. I want you so badly, Griff."

He lifted her in his arms and started across the kitchen. In his ear she whispered, "My room..."

"Too far." He knew he'd never make it up the stairs.

He tried for the parlor, but even that was too far. The minute she wrapped her arms around his neck, he knew he was done.

In the hallway he lowered her to her feet and kissed her, then kissed her again.

Trembling with need, she wrapped herself around him. He lifted her off her feet and backed her against the wall.

"Don't move." Sweat beaded his forehead. "If I can just take a minute, I'll get you to the sofa."

"Griff." She framed his face with her hands and covered his mouth with soft, butterfly kisses. "I don't need the sofa."

"That's good." He returned her kiss, then for good measure kissed her again, slowly, lazily, drawing out all the sweet flavor of her mouth. "'Cause we're never going to make it."

His breathing was ragged; his heartbeat thundering. If a bomb had gone off, he wouldn't have been able to tear himself away from her. She was all he could taste. All he could focus on. All he wanted and needed.

Because they were both trembling, they dropped to their knees on the floor. His hands were rough as he gathered her into his arms, damp flesh to damp flesh.

It would be so easy to simply take her, fast and furious, and end this almost unbearable hunger. But he wanted, more than anything, to make this first time with her as perfect, as pleasurable, as possible. Her admission of guilt had him wanting to take even more care with her.

And so he forced himself to slow the pace. His kisses

gentled, as his lips glided over her face, her neck, the hollow of her throat.

Her little hum of pleasure told him that she was grateful for the chance to breathe. But with each kiss, each gentle touch of his hands up her leg, over her gently rounded hip, her breathing began to speed up.

When his thumbs encountered the swell of her breasts, he felt her body tense, her heart rate accelerate.

When she wound her arms around his neck and pressed her mouth to his, he sensed the change in her and thrilled to it. This was no longer a surrender to passion. This was an all-consuming hunger that matched his. He could read it in her eyes. Taste it on her lips. Hot. Hungry. Desperate.

This was what he'd wanted. Just this.

His touch was no longer gentle, but demanding. His kisses no longer persuasive, but insistent.

Heat rose up between them, clouding their vision, as he ran hot, wet kisses down the column of her throat to her breast and took one erect nipple into his mouth.

She sighed his name, but the word ended abruptly when he moved to the other breast to nibble, to suckle. To feast.

Her hands fisted in his hair. On a moan of pleasure she offered him everything. And he took. With a greed that startled them both. With tongue and teeth and fingertips he drove her up and over the first peak until her eyes glazed with pleasure. He gave her no time to recover before taking her up again.

"Griff." His name was little more than a frantic whisper.

"I wanted to wait. I wanted to make this perfect."

She covered his mouth with hers. "It is perfect, Griff. You're perfect."

He'd wanted to go slowly, but the need was too great. Though he struggled to hold back, he could feel his body so hot with desire, he would surely burn to ash if he didn't soon find relief.

He moved over her and felt her body straining toward him, eager for release. He saw her eyes widen as he entered her. Though he'd wanted to be gentle, the sudden change in her gave him no chance to be in control.

With a soft moan she drew him in, and the beast inside him fought to be free. When she wrapped herself around him, gripping him as tightly as he was gripping her, he knew he'd lost himself completely.

They came together in a fierce, all-consuming storm and began moving, lungs straining, hearts hammering.

He called her name as he felt himself climbing with her to the very center of the universe. And then there were no words as they took each other up and over with a driving, desperate need that had the world exploding in color behind their eyes.

It felt in that final shattering moment, as if they'd left the entire world far behind, to enter another universe.

It was the most amazing journey of their lives.

They lay, still joined, their bodies slick, breathing ragged, heartbeats erratic.

Griff touched his big hand to her cheek and studied her face. "I'm sorry. I never meant to be so rough. You okay?"

She was quiet for so long, he felt his heart stop.

At long last she said, "I'm fine."

"I got out of control. Sorry."

She managed a laugh. "I'm not."

At his raised brow she brushed her mouth over his. "I'm not sorry, Griff. And you weren't rough. You were...amazing."

He felt his heart begin to beat again. "You mean it? You're not having regrets?"

"Griff." She leaned up on one elbow to stare down into his eyes. "We agreed to be honest. So here's the truth. I feel..." She sighed. "I feel...like I've just climbed Mount Everest, or walked on the moon. I feel amazing." She wrapped her arms around his neck and kissed him long and slow and deep before pausing for a breath. "I feel...delicious. I feel...so lucky to have found you."

"I'm the lucky one," he muttered against her lips.

With a lazy, satisfied grin he lay back, loving the feel of her small, slender body draped across his chest. He could stay this way forever.

She traced a fingertip over the scar that ran from below his ear to just above his heart. "This could have killed you."

"It came close."

"Want to talk about it?"

He shook his head. "We all have scars. Some, like mine, are visible. Most, like yours, like Ethan's, are well hidden. But they're still there, reminding us of what we've been through and survived."

"We *are* survivors, aren't we?" She snuggled close, her fingers playing with the hair on his chest.

His deep voice warmed with laughter. "If you keep that up, we may have to go for seconds."

She lifted her head and simply smiled, a woman's little cat smile.

It was all the invitation he needed.

He scrambled to his feet and scooped her up into his arms. "Your choice. Your bed or the lumpy sofa."

"My...bed."

He was halfway up the stairs before she got the words out.

CHAPTER TWENTY-SIX

W hen did Ethan stop talking?"

Griff and Juliet lay among the bed linens in a tangle of arms and legs, deliciously sated, sharing bits and pieces of their personal history.

All through the night they'd made love, learning so many new and fascinating things about each other. Every time they came together it was fresh and wonderful. At times they'd taken a wild ride through a storm of passion. At other times, they'd felt as lazy, as comfortable, as old lovers who'd been together forever. But always they were joyous, almost feverish in their discovery of such rare and simple treasures.

"When his father died." She fell silent, going back to that dark time in her life. "We didn't know a soul in Tampa, so Ethan spent every day at the VA hospital with me. He was three, just the age Casey is now. I was going on pure adrenaline, expecting another baby, caring for

Buddy, and trying to carve some time each day for Ethan. Despite his tender age, he went everywhere with us. He sat next to his father's hospital bed, and more often in it, tucked up beside Buddy, listening to doctors and nurses who came and went. He traveled in his father's wheelchair to therapy, and to burn treatments. The three of us were inseparable. And then, suddenly we were alone."

She sat up, wrapping her arms around her drawn-up knees. "At first, I was so caught up in my own grief, I wasn't aware of how profound Ethan's grief was. Then, when I noticed that Ethan wasn't speaking at all, I contacted a specialist. We had just started weekly sessions when Casey was born, and I had to let everything go to tend to him. When I finally reconnected with the doctor, she suggested that I relax and allow Ethan to proceed at his own pace."

She glanced at Griff. "He's six now, and ready for school. Well…" She shrugged. "I'm told that way out here, so far from town, he will probably be home- and e-schooled, but still, he'll need to communicate with a teacher online and in the occasional group sessions, and I just don't know how he'll handle it."

Griff took her hand in his, amazed as always that such a small, delicate hand could do so much hard work. "He's a really bright kid. He may not talk, but he knows everything that's going on around him. He seems happy and relaxed. Especially now that he's connected with Mad. Maybe you ought to take the expert's advice and just wait and see."

She sighed. "I don't know that I have any choice. He'll talk when he's ready. I just hope it's soon. He's missing out on so much."

"Speaking of missing out..." He drew her close and covered her mouth with his. "We have a lot of time to make up."

She laughed and pushed against his chest. "Glutton."

"I am. And it's all your fault, woman. You made me wait, and want, and imagine, but the real thing is so much better than my imagination."

They were both grinning as he drew her down into his arms. And then there were no words as they came together in a storm of passion.

It was still dark outside the windows when Juliet started to slip out of bed.

Griff closed a hand around her wrist, stopping her. "Where are you going?"

"I can't sleep." She chuckled. "Too excited, I guess. I feel like a kid on Christmas morning."

"Yeah. I know what you mean. Me, too." He brushed a kiss over her mouth. "Maybe I'll start the chores. That way I'll have them done early and we can take the boys to see my family."

My family. Just saying the words made his heart lighter.

"Oh, that would be fun." She got to her feet. "I think I'll start breakfast. I know I can't make Mad's waffles, but maybe I'll make those awfuls Casey told him about."

He drew her close and kissed the tip of her nose. "I'd be happy to taste your awfuls, ma'am."

As Juliet walked off to shower, he looked around for his clothes before remembering that he'd left them in a heap downstairs. Comfortable in his nakedness, he ambled down the stairs and dressed before heading for the barn and a round of predawn chores.

* * *

Griff turned Juliet's horses into the pasture while he mucked out the stalls. Afterward he filled troughs with feed and water.

He was whistling as he hosed down the barn floor and watched the filthy water swirling down the drain.

He looked up to see the rock-star bus pulling up outside, with Heywood Sperry at the wheel. Except for Sperry, the bus appeared empty.

Puzzled, he walked to the open doorway just as the hydraulic platform descended, with Sperry seated on his scooter.

At the sight of Griff, sleeves rolled to the elbows, a pitchfork in his hand, Sperry's jaw dropped. "What in hell are you doing here this early?"

"I could ask you the same. Where are the rest of the Romeos?"

"Don't know and don't care." Sperry looked him up and down, then beyond him, seeing the wagon filled with wet straw and dung, the hose still spewing water down the drain, and the truth dawned. "You spent the night again?"

"Again?" Griff's brows shot up. "You keeping score, Heywood?"

"I'll leave that up to you. Guys like you probably sit at Wylie's every weekend to boast about how many women you scored." Sperry pushed a button on his scooter, turning toward the house.

With a shake of his head, Griff took his time storing the pitchfork on a hook along the wall and turning off the hose. By the time he'd ambled up to the house, he could hear Sperry's voice, thick with fury.

"I can't believe a woman like you would accept charity."

Juliet stood on the porch, drying her hands on a dishtowel. "You may call it charity, but I call it generosity. I've never met such welcoming, kindhearted people as the MacKenzie family. They brought all the wranglers they could spare, just to help out a neighbor."

As Griff climbed the steps she reached out a hand to his. "And just look at this porch." Her tone softened. "Griff did most of the work himself. I can't believe how talented he is."

Sperry's eyes glittered with a strange light. "Oh, I can believe it. He was just boasting about his many . . . talents. But then, since he's already treating your barn chores like his own, I guess he didn't need to brag about spending the night."

Juliet was frowning as she turned to look at Griff.

Instead of engaging in an argument with Sperry, he merely squeezed her hand and winked. "How're those awfuls coming?"

That brought an unexpected smile to her lips as she followed suit and resolved to ignore Sperry's insulting insinuations. "They're coming along just fine. And you'd better get inside and grab a shower. I heard the boys upstairs. They'll be down soon and ready for breakfast."

"I'm ready now. I've worked up a powerful appetite." He brushed a kiss to her cheek before turning away. At the door he called, "See you, Heywood."

"Not likely." Sperry's voice changed from furious to triumphant as he said to Juliet, "I drove out here to tell you that I'm disbanding the Romeos."

"Disbanding? Why?"

"Why not? I can't stand being around them. And they've made it plain they can't stand me, either." He paused before saying, "Sorry you'll have to lose all that money they've been paying you for the privilege of riding your old nag and playing cowboy." A sly smile crossed his face. "Of course, if you'd like me to reconsider, I might give it some thought. For a price."

"'Morning, Mama." Casey danced out on the porch and sidled up beside Juliet, with Ethan trailing close behind. "Griff's here. He's upstairs taking a shower and said he'll be down to eat breakfast with us. Isn't that great?"

"Yes, it is." Juliet took a moment to hug each of her boys before turning back to Heywood.

His tone was shrill. "Are you ready to hear the cost of getting the Romeos back?" There was a long pause, and, like a kid who knew he was throwing a tantrum, he looked at her with an air of expectancy to gauge her reaction.

Instead of taking the bait, Juliet said, in her sweetest voice, "I have no choice but to respect your decision to disband the group, since you were the one to form it in the first place. I do hope you'll let them know that I encourage all of them to continue their therapy, if not here, then somewhere else."

Gathering her sons close, she herded them inside.

As the screen door closed, Sperry shouted a stream of obscenities before turning his scooter toward the bus. Minutes later the vehicle roared off in a cloud of dust.

"That mean man is mad at you, Mama," Casey whispered.

Juliet merely smiled. "That man is mad at the whole world, honey."

* * *

"Well, look at this." Mad peered out the window and turned to Willow. "Griff's home. And he's brought Juliet and her sons."

"Oh, how grand." Willow stepped out the door to greet them as the truck came to a halt at the porch. Mad followed her out, grateful once again for the ramp that made it possible to move about without waiting around for someone to help.

As the two boys skipped down from the backseat, Mad opened his arms. "Welcome back, lads."

They flew into his arms and settled themselves on his lap, ready for a ride up the ramp. They weren't disappointed when Griff caught hold of the back of the chair and started pushing.

"Juliet." Willow embraced her and kept an arm around her shoulders as they walked inside. "I'm so happy to see you."

"We should have called to let you know we were coming."

"Why, for heaven's sake? Don't ever feel that you have to ask permission before coming by to visit. You and your boys are family to us. And family never needs an appointment."

Juliet felt a little thrill at her words. Did these people have any idea how precious their warm acceptance meant to her and her boys?

As they stepped into the kitchen Juliet breathed in the wonderful fragrance that perfumed the air. "Do I smell bread baking?"

"You do." Myrna hurried over to hug her. "Mad and I are trying a new recipe for cheese bread."

"It smells heavenly."

"Good. Now let's hope it tastes heavenly, too." She turned to press a kiss to Casey's cheek, and then Ethan's.

"Will you read some stories to us later, Grandma Myrna?" Casey asked.

At the little boy's easy use of the nickname she'd asked him to call her, the old woman gave a sigh. "Of course I will."

Both boys snuggled on Mad's lap as he wheeled around the room, showing them all the foods that were in various stages of preparation for a huge ranch lunch.

Gradually the others began drifting in from the barns and surrounding fields. Whit and Brady, back from a night in the hills and badly in need of shaves, looked ruggedly handsome. Both men shook hands with Griff before hugging Juliet and the boys. Then they gratefully accepted ice-cold longnecks from Myrna.

"You always know just what a guy needs, Myrna." Whit said and took a long pull of beer.

"I grew up on a ranch. I saw days when my daddy could drink a beer before breakfast, after he'd been up in the hills with a herd for weeks at a time."

When Ash and Brenna walked in arm in arm, wearing identical smiles, Whit couldn't resist teasing. "You two always look like the cat that swallowed the canary. What've you been up to, besides the usual romantic goo we'd rather not hear about in any detail?"

"We went to town this morning," Ash said over everyone's chuckles.

"Any particular reason?" Whit nudged Brady, and the two men shared knowing grins.

"Naw." Ash accepted a tall glass of ice water from

Myrna before adding, "We stopped by Orin Tamer's dealership."

"You don't say?" Whit's smile grew. "So, which truck did you buy for your bride?"

"A four-door, black, all-wheel-drive monster that can climb hills, get me through a blizzard, with room for family in the backseat." Brenna said it all so quickly the entire family roared with laughter.

Mad managed to say to his grandson, "Just looking, were you, lad?"

Ash grinned good-naturedly. "Yeah. But since Orin happened to have only one like it in stock, and it was exactly what Bren's been wanting, I figured I'd better snap it up before somebody else did."

"Very wise, lad." Mad winked at Whit. "But then, that's what happens when a man loses his heart to a beautiful woman. He starts out wanting to do all the chores around her place. The next thing he knows, he can't wait to buy her things."

Whit's tone was dry, but his eyes were dancing with laughter. "Like a diamond to seal the bargain if she's a typical woman. But if she's a rancher, nothing says 'I love you' like a big old monster truck."

Willow kissed Brenna's cheek. "I knew you'd bring Ash around to your way of thinking."

"Hey." Ash dropped an arm around his wife. "It was my idea."

Willow and Myrna couldn't help laughing before Willow said drily, "You're even better than I thought, Brenna. Not only did you get the truck of your dreams, but the man of your dreams believes it was all his idea."

The family continued teasing Ash and Brenna as they

gathered around the table. Myrna and Mad passed around a giant bowl of fresh garden lettuce and tomatoes, thick slices of meat loaf, and a huge pan of bubbly macaroni and cheese, along with cheese bread hot from the oven.

Griff and Juliet chose seats on one side of the table, with Casey beside his mother and Ethan beside Griff. Before they started to eat, both Juliet and Griff took the time to cut up the boys' food.

"Oh, Mad." Juliet looked up after her first bite of meat loaf. "This is wonderful."

"Thanks, lass. Would you like my recipe?"

She nodded. "I'd love it." She turned to Griff, putting a hand on his. "Do you like meat loaf?"

"I never did before." He closed his other hand over hers and met her smile with one of his own. "But that was before tasting this. If you can duplicate Mad's recipe, meat loaf will be on the top of my list."

Across the table Mad watched the two of them, noting a new softness in Griff's eyes. Even his voice had taken on a softness that hadn't been there before.

So much of the tension had disappeared from Juliet's face. She seemed more relaxed and happy than at any time since he'd met her.

He bit back the smile that split his lips. By heaven, his grandson was a changed man. And all because of the woman and her two little boys who'd looked so lost and confused when he'd first met them.

Juliet was changed, too.

These two had just found that powerful potion that had the ability to change the world.

Love.

And the grand thing about it was, neither of them seemed aware of it yet. They were too busy feeling to sort through what had just happened to transform them both.

But they'd figure it out in time. And when they did...

He sat back, sipping strong, hot coffee and grinning like an old fool.

CHAPTER TWENTY-SEVEN

After lunch, while the men moved across the room to talk over ranch chores, the women remained in the work area of the kitchen to help Myrna with the cleanup.

"When do you get your truck, Brenna?" Juliet said as she began loading dishes in the dishwasher.

"A couple of days. Orin said he'd call when the paperwork is ready." Brenna continued wiping down the table before glancing at Juliet. "When will you bring Casey and Ethan to my studio for some playtime?"

Juliet shrugged. "I've been so busy, there hasn't been time to even think about it. But I'll try to come by with them in the next week."

"They've already discovered that they love playing with clay." Willow carried a stack of serving dishes to the counter, where Myrna transferred the leftovers to plastic bags.

"And who knows?" Brenna paused. "Maybe one of them will show a real talent for it."

"Another sculptor in the family." The thought of it had Willow smiling.

When Juliet's cell phone rang, she slipped it out of her pocket to look at the caller ID before announcing, "It's Chief Pettigrew."

At once the room went silent as everyone gathered around her.

"Yes, Chief?" She turned on the speaker so they could all hear.

"Good news, Juliet. The state police just contacted me. They've picked up Mitch Cord. They tracked his cell phone to Midland, a little town about a hundred miles north of here. He was spotted in a bar in the town. When the state police checked, the bartender recognized some of the wranglers Mitch had been with as a crew from the Stedler Ranch, just outside the town. Apparently he'd been working there. He was arrested without incident."

There were high fives all around as Juliet said, "Oh, that's the best news ever. Thank you, Chief Pettigrew."

"You're welcome. It always makes my day sweeter when I'm able to report good news. I'll be talking to you in the next day or so when the authorities bring him back to town for arraignment."

As she rang off, Juliet's eyes filled with tears.

Seeing them, Griff gathered her close. "Hey. It's finally over, Juliet. Now you can start to breathe again."

"I know." She savored the comfort of his arms before pushing a little away. She wiped her tears before accepting congratulations from the others.

Casey and Ethan were caught up in the spirit of the

moment, even though they didn't really understand what had just happened.

"Are you crying, Mama?" Casey asked.

"Yes." She sniffed and hugged him, and then his brother, before straightening. "But these are happy tears."

Willow hugged her fiercely. "Such wonderful news, Juliet. It's been a long time coming, but now you can relax and just let go of all your fears."

At her words, Juliet was beaming. "I've had to deal with so much bad news, that I'd started to believe I'd never again hear anything else. But now..." She shook her head, trying to take it all in. "I guess it'll take me a while to adjust my thinking."

"Enjoy it, lass." Mad rolled close and reached out his hand to hers. "You'll be heading home with a light heart indeed."

"Home." Her smile grew as she turned to Griff. "I can't wait to go home and tell Jackie and the wranglers the good news. It will ease everyone's tension."

Griff caught her hand. "Let's do it now."

With hugs all around, they said their good-byes and headed out to the truck. As they drove away, waving to the MacKenzie family, who'd gathered on the porch to see them off, Juliet turned to Griff with a dazzling smile. "Mad was right. My heart feels lighter than it ever has. I feel as if the weight of the world has been lifted from my shoulders."

He reached over to squeeze her hand.

Keeping their fingers linked, he lowered the window and let the fresh summer breeze fill the cab of their truck.

It was, he decided, a very good day to be alive.

* * *

Jackie Turner was delighted with Juliet's news. He phoned Cooper in the highlands, letting him know the wranglers could relax their guard.

Later he knocked on the kitchen door. When Juliet answered, he whipped off his wide-brimmed hat before stepping inside.

"I conveyed your news to Cooper and the wranglers. And I thought, since Mitch is in custody, I'd spend the night at my daughter's place, then come back in the morning. I've been missing my grandchildren. In the past year I got used to seeing them nearly every day."

Juliet touched a hand to the old man's arm. "Of course you need to go home. I'm sorry you had to sacrifice seeing your grandchildren because of me, Jackie. And I do thank you so much. Please take the rest of the day off and go home early. I'll see you tomorrow."

He gave her a broad smile. "I believe I'll do just that. If I leave now, I can help my grandkids with their chores, and maybe take them to town for supper at the Boxcar Inn."

"They'll love it." She smiled. "And so will your daughter, when she learns she won't have to cook tonight."

He chuckled. "I'll see you tomorrow, Juliet."

She watched as his pickup moved down the lane. Then she began searching through her cupboards for the bottle of champagne she'd tucked away ages ago. This was the perfect night to open it.

Though Casey and Ethan didn't completely understand the reason for the celebration, they were enjoying every minute of it, from the juicy steaks on the grill to the special brownies their mother baked, served with dollops of chocolate chip ice cream and tall glasses of milk.

"Is it your birthday, Mama?" Casey licked every crumb from his plate.

"No. Just a very happy day."

Seated at a picnic table in the shade of the big cottonwood, the little boys were delighted to be basking in the glow that surrounded their mother and Griff. All afternoon the two adults had been whispering, their faces wreathed in wide, joyful smiles.

After dinner the family took a walk around the yard, with Griff and Juliet holding hands while the two boys raced ahead of them, chasing after fireflies.

Juliet stopped to watch her two sons. "Look at them, Griff. Laughing and playing like normal kids."

"Why not? They *are* two normal kids."

She turned to look at him. "That's just it. For the longest time they weren't allowed to be normal. Ethan spent so much time at a hospital, he thought that was what all kids did. And neither boy knew what the word *home* meant. But now, they're here where they belong. The danger is gone, and they can just live like everyone else."

Griff kissed the tip of her nose. "Nobody lives like anybody else."

She pulled back. "What's that supposed to mean?"

He caught her hand and began to walk again. "What's normal? A kid who has no father? A kid who spends months, even years, in a hospital? A kid who goes off to military school because he's troubled?"

She stopped and tugged on his hand. "I never thought about it before. I guess you're right. We all have baggage."

"Exactly. And we all have to figure things out." He put an arm around her shoulders. "Fortunately for you and me, we don't have to figure out the whole world's problems tonight." He paused to brush a quick kiss to her temple. "In fact, I have some very special plans for tonight that won't require a whole lot of thinking."

"You do?" She looked over at him. "What exactly do you have in mind?"

"After two little boys fall asleep, I'm going to spend the entire night showing their mother just how special she is."

Her smile grew. "I can't wait."

"Neither can I." He turned her into his arms and kissed her.

As Griff and Juliet stepped apart, he muttered, "That was just a sample. I'll save the rest for later."

"Promise?"

His smile was slow and lazy. "Oh yeah. Count on it."

"One more story, Griff. Please."

Casey and Ethan, hair slick from their bath, dressed in fresh pajamas, lay in the big bed they shared.

For over an hour they'd laughed at the silly stories Griff made up.

Now, though Casey begged for one more, Griff could see their little eyes growing heavy. "I think I'd better save the rest of my stories for tomorrow night."

"Will you be here?"

"I will if it's all right with you. Do you want me to be here?"

Two heads nodded at the same moment.

"Well then, you bet I'll be here."

"Okay. 'Night, Griff." Casey looked toward the doorway just as his mother stepped in. "Griff tells the best stories."

"I heard that last one as I was coming up the stairs." She leaned close. "Umm, you both smell so good." She kissed Ethan, and then Casey. "Good night, my sweet boys."

"'Night, Mama."

By the time she turned out the light, both boys were drifting into dreamland.

Juliet poured the last of the champagne into two stem glasses and stepped out to the back porch to offer one to Griff.

He touched the rim of his glass to hers. "Here's to happily-ever-after."

She flushed. "I never believed in it before."

"And now?"

She met his steady gaze. "I'm ready to believe."

They leaned on the rail and sipped while watching the path of a shooting star.

"Quick." Griff nudged her shoulder. "Make a wish."

"It's already come true." She sighed as she studied the canopy of diamonds in a midnight sky. "I think the stars are bigger here in Montana."

"Maybe because we're closer to heaven."

She laughed. "You made that up."

"Didn't Casey tell you? I'm good at making up stories."

"You're good with my boys. It isn't forced. It's just so easy and natural with you, Griff."

"They're easy to be with."

"Have you ever been around little kids?"

He shook his head. "But then, I've never had a brother before, and now I have two. Why should it be any different with kids?"

"Some men would consider two boys a lot of work."

"I'm not some men, Juliet. I'm just me. And I consider myself lucky to have found you and Casey and Ethan."

"I think we're the lucky ones."

"Okay then." He took the glass from her hand and set it beside his on the railing before gathering her close. "We're lucky to have each other. Now, let's stop talking and head upstairs to your room."

Against his mouth she whispered, "You don't want to go for the lumpy sofa?"

"For what I have in mind, we'd better choose the bed." He kept his arm around her as he led her inside and closed the door.

Once inside he lifted her easily in his arms and started up the stairs. Laughing, she wrapped her arms around his neck and pressed her lips to his throat.

He gave a low moan of pleasure. "Now see, that's why I decided to go for the bed. You've got my blood so hot, it just might take me hours to show you all the things I'm thinking about doing."

"If you run out of ideas, I might have a few of my own, cowboy."

He carried her through the doorway of her room and nudged the door shut before lowering her to the bed. Against her mouth he said, "If we're lucky, we might not get any sleep at all tonight."

"I'm game if you—"

He cut off her words with a kiss so hot, she could feel her toes curling. And then he kissed her again for good measure. And all the while his big, work-worn hands were weaving a magic all their own, until the two of them were lost in a lover's paradise.

CHAPTER TWENTY-EIGHT

You fixed it."

Casey and Ethan stepped into the barn where Griff and Jackie had been working since breakfast.

The two boys danced around the play table that was even better than before. Besides replacing the broken legs, Griff had added several buckets of fresh sand and had carved it into mountains, roads, even a tunnel they could drive their little toy trucks through.

"I left your trucks, cars, and ranch animals in the box for you two to unload."

The two little boys eagerly began setting out their toys and running them up and down the hills and valleys.

At the sound of an overloud truck engine, everyone looked up to see the young veterinarian, Dr. Ted Pickering, just stepping out of his vehicle before circling around to the horse trailer hooked to the back.

When he led Princess down a ramp, they gathered around.

"She's healed?" Jackie asked.

"Good as new." Dr. Pickering walked her around in the sunlight, proving that she could walk without a limp.

He bent to the wound, which was now barely visible. "I was worried about infection, but she's a tough old mare." He looked over at the foreman. "Want her in a stall, or out there?"

Jackie nodded toward a fenced pasture, where several horses were busy nibbling grass. "Might as well turn her loose with the others. She probably missed them as much as they missed her."

A short time later Princess was walking across a field of wildflowers toward a cluster of horses.

The young veterinarian pointed to the house. "Is Mrs. Grayson home? I'd like to give her my report."

Griff nodded. "She's fixing lunch. Come on. I'll go with you." He turned to the two little boys. "Want to come along?"

"Can we stay and play?" Casey asked.

Griff turned to Jackie. "Do you mind?"

The old man shook his head. "I've still got plenty of chores to see to here in the barn. They can stay with me as long as they like."

"Okay." Griff turned and walked with the veterinarian. When he glanced back, the two boys were lost in make-believe.

In the kitchen, Juliet greeted the doctor and offered him a glass of lemonade.

"I've never refused a tall, cool drink on a warm summer day," he said with a grin. As he sipped he gave Juliet a report on Princess. "It was a deep puncture wound. A slight trace of infection, but a simple application of antibiotic did the trick. It's healed nicely, and she doesn't seem to have any aftereffect from it."

"I'm so relieved." Juliet handed Griff a frosty glass. When their hands brushed, she looked up at him and felt the heat rise to her cheeks. After the night they'd spent, she wondered that he could still make her blush. Maybe, she thought, he would always have this effect on her.

Forcing her attention back to the doctor, she said, "What do I owe you?"

He dug into his pocket and handed her a computer printout. "There's no rush, Mrs. Grayson."

"But there is. When we called you, you hurried over without question. I think it's only right that I should return the favor. If you'll wait a minute, I'll pay you right now."

Minutes later she returned with a check.

He slipped it into his pocket and handed her his empty glass. "Thanks, Mrs. Grayson."

"Call me Juliet."

"And I'm Ted. It's a pleasure doing business with you."

He turned and shook Griff's hand before heading for the door.

Before he could walk out with Ted, Griff's phone rang. He pulled it from his pocket and saw the caller. "Hey, Jimmy."

"Griff." The word was little more than a croak.

"Jimmy? What's wrong with your voice?"

"Listen, Captain. You're in danger. All of you need to—"

The phone went dead.

Juliet was busy at the sink, setting the empty glasses down. She glanced over her shoulder. "Who was that?"

"Jimmy Gable." Griff dialed Jimmy's number.

Outside, he heard the roar of an engine and found himself smiling at the thought of the ancient truck the young vet drove.

When there was no response on the other end of the phone, Griff felt a growing sense of unease. "The phone didn't even ring. The line's just dead."

Juliet chuckled. "That's what happens when you don't pay your bill. Maybe he missed a payment."

"Well, that could be it. But I don't like the way he sounded. There could be something wrong."

Griff stared at it a moment, then dialed the police chief. When he heard Ira's voice he told him what Jimmy had said before adding, "It may not be anything, but I don't have a good feeling about this. I wonder if you could look in on my friend. If he isn't in his room over at Ken and Karen's bed-and-breakfast, he's usually at Wylie's playing cards. I didn't like the sound of his voice, Chief. His words were barely above a whisper, but he seemed to be warning me about danger."

"Danger? Did he say what kind?"

"No. He just said there was danger and we should all— And then the line went dead."

"I'm sure you misunderstood. You said he was whispering."

"I know what I heard."

"Okay, I'll check it out, Griff. But while I have you on the line, I need to talk to you about something else. I'm still holding Mitch for attempted assault on Juliet

Grayson, but the state police have cleared him of any damage done to Juliet's barn. He has witnesses to prove he was drinking in a bar over a hundred miles away that night, with no way to make it to Juliet's and back."

"Hold on a moment, Ira." Griff motioned for Juliet to come closer, so she could hear the conversation.

Switching it to speaker, he said, "Could Mitch have done the damage to Juliet's barn earlier?"

"If you recall, there was a storm that night. Mitch was helping a rancher secure his herd in a corral. Then he went with some of the wranglers to a bar in Midland. That's more than an hour away from Copper Creek. He was with them until the bar closed, and they all went back to the bunkhouse together."

Griff felt a quick rush of frustration. "If it wasn't Mitch, then who did it?"

Ira's voice sounded thoughtful. "That's the question we all want answered. The state police are questioning whether little boys may have scrawled that message."

Juliet shot Griff an incredulous look.

Griff voiced their mutual thoughts. "Are they suggesting it was her sons? They're three and six, barely old enough to spell anything, let alone words like the ones in that message. Why would the state police even suggest such a thing?"

Ira chose his words carefully. "After checking my photos of the words on the barn wall, it was determined that they were written by someone no more than three or four feet tall. And that's the height of a child."

Griff glanced at Juliet while he turned the chief's words over and over in his mind.

Three or four feet. The height of a child. Or...

He swore as the thought suddenly formed in his mind. "Or someone in a wheelchair."

Juliet's hand flew to her mouth.

"A wheelchair? Are you accusing someone in particular?" The chief's tone was guarded.

"I hope I'm wrong, Ira, but there's a guy in town. A guy in a wheelchair who seems to be mad at the whole world. A guy named Heywood Sperry. I hate to suggest that a fellow veteran could be behind this, but you might want to find out where he was on the night this went down."

"I'll get right on it. As soon as I check on your friend Gable."

"As far as I know, they're both staying at the bed-and-breakfast."

"That should make things easier. Don't worry. I'm on it."

When the line went dead, Griff turned to Juliet. "I hope I'm wrong. But Sperry seems to spend a lot of energy worrying about the time I'm here with you. Has he ever expressed any interest in you?"

"As in...romantic interest?"

Griff nodded.

She gave a quick shake of her head. "His behavior is so frustrating, it's about as far from romantic as anything I could think of." She paused before asking, "What about your friend, Jimmy?"

"You think he could have left that message?" Griff immediately shook his head. "He's one of the sweetest guys I know. But I am worried about him. His voice, that strange message..." He shrugged. "I'll see what Ira has to say after he checks things out."

They both looked up as Casey slammed into the room, sobbing as though his heart was breaking.

"What's happened?" Juliet stooped down and gathered him into her arms. "Did you fall, honey?"

"No." He pushed free of her arms and turned to Griff, tugging frantically on his leg. "You have to go after Efan."

"Go after him? Where is he?"

"I don't know." The tears started falling faster. "That mean man came and hurt Jackie. He hurt him really bad. Jackie fell down. He's lying in the barn all bloody. Then the mean man tried to grab me, but Efan pulled me away, so the mean man caught Efan instead."

Griff and Juliet exchanged puzzled looks before Griff shouted, "Stay here with Casey."

Pulling his cell phone out of his pocket, he raced out of the house and ran the entire distance to the barn, with Juliet and Casey doing their best to keep up with him despite his warning to stay in the house.

Jackie Turner lay near one of the stalls, as still as death, in an ever-widening pool of blood. Beside him was a bloody shovel.

Griff knelt beside him and felt for a pulse. Relieved that the foreman was still alive, he leaned close. "Jackie, who did this?"

"That crazy guy...calls himself boss...Romeos."

"Heywood Sperry?"

"That's...him."

Griff was already speaking into his cell phone. "Ira. I'm in Juliet's barn. Heywood Sperry viciously attacked Jackie Turner with a shovel. He's bleeding from the head. We need a medevac copter out here right away."

He motioned for Juliet to grab the saddle blanket tossed over the stall railing. The old man's teeth were chattering, a sure sign that he was in shock.

As Juliet wrapped it around him, Jackie clutched Griff's arm. "He's got Ethan."

"God in heaven." Into his phone Griff said, "Sperry kidnapped Juliet's son, Ethan." He listened to the chief's staccato words, then repeated them to Jackie. "The chief wants to know how he got here. What's he driving?"

"His bus."

In the back of his mind Griff recalled the roar of an engine, mistaking it for Dr. Pickering's noisy truck.

He conveyed the message to the police chief. "He shouldn't be too hard to find. You won't see too many rock-star buses out on these roads."

He rang off, then stepped out of the barn to phone Mad. As quickly as possible he explained the situation, then returned to kneel beside Jackie.

"Hang on, now. The medics are on their way by helicopter."

He turned to Juliet. "Until they get here, we need clean towels and several blankets."

She nodded, grateful for something to do.

As soon as she was gone he gathered little Casey into his arms. The boy wrapped his chubby arms around Griff's neck and sobbed against his chest.

"That mean man's going to hurt Efan the way he hurt Jackie."

"No, he isn't." He held the little boy close, wishing he knew how to ease his fears. Hell, he couldn't even ease his own.

By the time Juliet returned with the supplies, Griff's

shirtfront was soaked with the little boy's tears. Thinking quickly, he said, "Now Casey, I need you to be very brave." He wrapped a clean towel around Jackie's head and said to the little boy, "You need to hold this towel just like this. Can you do that?"

Casey nodded solemnly.

"Good boy."

He turned to Juliet. "The medevac will be landing soon to take Jackie to the hospital. My family is on the way, too."

When his cell phone rang, Griff answered on the first ring. "Yes?"

"Ira Pettigrew here. We found your friend Jimmy Gable."

Hearing the solemn tone of the police chief, Griff's heart nearly stopped. "And?"

"He'd been badly beaten. Dr. Mullin wants him flown from the Copper Creek Clinic to a hospital in Helena where they have better facilities."

"Was he able to speak?"

"Barely. He was too injured for us to ask him any questions. But the bloody baseball bat used against him was lying beside him."

"Just like Jackie Turner," Griff mused aloud.

"Exactly." The chief's voice lowered. "The state police experts are on their way here to examine Sperry's room. They'll go over it for any clue as to what this is all about. In the meantime, they're sending up helicopters as well as a convoy of land vehicles."

"I've contacted my family. They're taking up the Cessna, and they'll have as many wranglers as they can spare out looking."

"Good. Now I want you and Juliet to stay there."

Griff gave a hiss of frustration. "I need to be out looking for this madman."

"I know. That's a natural enough inclination. But for now, until we hear from him, we need Juliet where we can find her. When someone snatches a kid, they want your attention."

"He has that."

"Exactly. Next, we hope he'll call Juliet to tell her what he's really after. Until then, stay at the house with her where we can reach the two of you. And Griff"—the police chief's voice trembled with a rare emotion—"you try to keep that little woman calm."

As he rang off, Griff realized he'd just been given the hardest task of all.

CHAPTER TWENTY-NINE

Ash." At the MacKenzie ranch, Mad was shouting orders to the entire household. "Get the plane ready."

"Ready for what?"

As quickly as he could, Mad recounted what Griff had told him.

After their initial shock, the MacKenzie family did what they always did. They rallied around Mad as their leader.

"Ash and I will fly to Juliet's ranch. The rest of you should break up into teams and take the ranch trucks. We'll meet at Juliet's place to decide where to go from there. But on the way, be on the lookout for a big, flashy bus driven by one of the veterans in that group that calls itself the Romeos."

Myrna was wringing her hands. "Why would anyone snatch Juliet's son?"

"A pervert. A sicko. A madman." Mad's voice was low

with fury. "Whatever he is, we're going to find him and bring that lad home to his mother."

Willow wrapped an arm around Myrna's trembling shoulders. "Come on. You'll ride with Brenna and me."

Whit and Brady were already on the phone to their wranglers in the hills, alerting them to the danger and asking them to report any sightings of the bus.

Rifles and ammunition were loaded into trucks, along with binoculars and phone chargers, jackets, and even cold weather gear, in the event the hunt dragged on into the hills.

Mad rolled his wheelchair along the ramp toward the distant barn that housed the Cessna. Once again he felt a wave of gratitude for Griff, who had made his mobility possible.

When he reached the plane, Ash nodded. "It's fueled. I did a preflight check. I'll help you up, Mad." He lifted his grandfather to the passenger seat and stowed his wheelchair behind the seat.

Once in the pilot side he turned to the old man. "Okay, Mad. Buckle up. We're ready to roll."

As soon as they were airborne, they looked down to see the convoy of trucks just leaving the ranch and fanning out, one taking the main highway, another following the back roads. As they flew up over the hills they saw the long line of wranglers on horseback, also fanning out to travel the little-known dips and ridges of the highlands.

Seeing the tight set of Mad's mouth, Ash reached over to touch a hand to his. "We'll find him, Mad."

The old man's words were spoken in a halting voice, revealing the depth of emotion. "He's such a wee thing.

And with his father dead at such a young age, he's already been given a heavy load to carry."

The two men fell silent as they studied the desolate land below. There were so many places in this vast wilderness where a man desperate to hide could be swallowed up, never to be heard from again.

The truck bearing Willow, Myrna, and Brenna arrived at the Grayson Ranch first. The three women found Griff, Juliet, and Casey standing beside a helicopter, where a doctor and nurse were preparing Jackie Turner before takeoff. His head had been professionally swathed in dressings, and an intravenous drip already inserted into his arm.

While they watched, the copter began its ascent, its blades flattening the grass and sending the trees into a crazy dance.

Willow gathered Juliet into her arms. "How are you holding up?"

"Oh, Willow." Juliet struggled against the tears that threatened, knowing if she started to cry, she might never stop. For Casey's sake she needed to be strong. "I'm terrified."

"Of course you are. But for a little while longer you need to be strong, not only for yourself, but for your boys."

Juliet pushed herself free of Willow's embrace and shook her head. "I can't stay here and do nothing. I just can't." She hugged her arms about herself, pacing like a caged tiger. "Ethan's out there somewhere, in the clutches of a madman. I need to go after him."

Griff gathered her close. His words were muffled

against a tangle of hair at her temple. "I know how you feel. It's killing me to wait here. But the chief wanted us to stay. Not just for Casey, but for Ethan, as well. When they find him, the authorities need to know how to reach you."

She was already shaking her head. "They can reach me by cell phone. I can't stay here."

Little Casey latched onto his mother's leg. "Don't leave, Mama. If you go, I want to go wif you."

Myrna stepped forward and gently picked him up. Against his temple she murmured, "I'd really like you to stay here with me. You can help me fix all of your brother's favorite foods, so that when he gets home, we'll have a lovely surprise for him. Will you help me?"

Casey sniffed, considering. "Can we make Grandpa Mad's waffles?"

"If you think Ethan would like them."

"He loves them."

"Then that's what we'll make." She turned to Griff and Juliet. "Time for you to go."

To Willow and Brenna she said the same. "Go now. Casey and I will be just fine here. But be sure you check in with us from time to time."

Juliet kissed her cheek. "Thank you, Myrna. You'll never know—"

The old woman touched a finger to her lips to silence her. "I do know. Now go."

As Griff and Juliet settled into one truck, and Brenna and Willow settled into another, Myrna carried Casey across the yard and climbed the steps to the porch. There she set him down. Still holding hands, they waved as the trucks circled around and headed toward the back country. Then the old woman and the little boy made their way inside. And though she continued murmuring words meant to soothe, Myrna's lips were trembling, and her hands were none too steady.

"Griff." Ira Pettigrew's voice boomed over Griff's cell phone. Even without pressing the speaker, Juliet, seated in the passenger side, could hear every word. "Are you and Juliet still at her ranch?"

"We couldn't stay there and do nothing. We're on the road just south of the Grayson Ranch in the direction of Bald Mountain."

"I understand. I guess if it were my boy, I'd do the same." He cleared his throat. "Now listen. The state boys are going to monitor all our calls. Punch in the following number." He enunciated each number clearly as Griff added it to his cell phone. "Each time any of us has information, it will be immediately transmitted to all of us, so that they know where we are and what we've found."

"Thanks, chief. I'll pass this along to Brenna and Willow. They're following us."

"Do it now, so I don't have to pass along information twice."

He rang off while Griff called Brenna's cell phone.

A minute later the chief called back, and this time his voice was heard by everyone who had been included in the state monitoring program. "The state boys are sending me an electronic grid of the territory they'll be covering as they do the flyover. I suggest you concentrate on that stretch of hills leading to Bald Mountain. I'll get there as soon as I can. But keep an eye out. That's some pretty bleak landscape."

Ira's voice rang with authority. "I know I don't have to tell you that we're dealing with a crazy here. And not only crazy, but desperate enough to snatch a kid. The state boys think he intends to use the boy as a bargaining chip, either with us or possibly with the mother. I'm inclined to agree with them. Does the boy's mother have a history with this guy?"

Griff handed his phone to Juliet. She spoke cautiously, knowing everyone was hearing her words. "I don't remember Heywood Sperry, but he claimed to have seen me almost daily at the VA hospital in Tampa, where I spent months with Buddy and Ethan. I had so many other things going on at that time. A critically wounded husband struggling to stay alive. A three-year-old who never left my side, and a difficult pregnancy that required what little strength I had left." She paused. "But Sperry once boasted to the Romeos that he'd seen me every day. How is it that he remembers me, and I would have sworn I'd never laid eyes on him until he showed up here in Copper Creek?"

"For all the reasons you just mentioned. You had way too much going on." The chief sighed. "This information is being passed along to the state boys. They're the ones who will piece it all together. But I know this: We need to find this guy as quickly as humanly possible, before he has a chance to slow down and think about hurting his next victim."

As he rang off, Griff's hands tightened on the wheel. Juliet spoke not a word. But everyone knew the truth of what he'd said. They had to find Heywood Sperry. Had to. Before he had a chance to vent his fury on a helpless little boy.

As the silence settled around him, Griff's eyes behind the mirrored sunglasses narrowed with a sudden flash of fury. Ethan had to be safe. If Sperry hurt that fragile little boy, he would move heaven and earth to find him and make him pay.

"What's that?" Juliet pointed to the fire burning in a low ridge just off to their right.

"Could be a brush fire." Griff hit the brake as he caught sight of just what was burning. He was out the door and sprinting down the ravine, tugging aside the mass of tree limbs and vines.

Cupping his hands to his mouth he shouted, "It's the bus."

As the others rushed over he pressed the number he'd been given to the communications center, transmitting the news to everyone. "We've found the bus."

"Where?" Chief Pettigrew demanded.

When Griff gave them the location, one of the state officers said, "We flew over that exact area."

"You'd have never spotted it from the air without that fire." Griff sounded out of breath. "It was hidden beneath a camouflage of tree branches and brush. The fire's fresh. He can't be too far from here."

"Any sign of Sperry or the boy inside?"

Griff peered through the windows. "It's empty." He studied the ground. "But there are tire tracks in the earth. Deep. They appear to be a heavy-duty truck. Sperry must have planned this ahead of time. Hold on. I'll have to put you on hold while I try to force open the bus door."

He handed his cell phone to Juliet and gave a mighty

kick of his booted foot against the jammed door. Then he and Juliet rushed inside while Willow and Brenna remained outside.

Griff gave a muttered exclamation and motioned for Juliet to retreat. "You'd better get a team here, Chief. I nearly stepped on a syringe and a small vial." After a moment's silence he said, "Valium. That's how he's managing to control Ethan while he drives."

The chief's voice came over his phone. "Any sign of blood, Griff?"

A very long silence before Griff said, "None that I can see. I guess we'll be grateful for small favors." He watched as the flames began to spread. "I've got to get out of here before it blows. Whatever evidence is in here will be destroyed." He leaped clear and climbed to the top of the ravine to rejoin the women.

"Hold on, Griff. The team is mapping exactly where you are." The chief swore. "Okay. They're on it. They'll be there in minutes."

As he waited to hear more, Griff reached for Juliet, who stepped into his arms and clung to his strength.

"Oh, Griff. We were too late."

Hearing the sound of tears in her voice he said softly, "I know what this is doing to you. And I wish we could have been here sooner. But know this—Ethan's a strong little boy."

"Strong?" She pushed away to look into his eyes. "How can you say that?"

"Listen to me, Juliet. When Sperry grabbed Casey, Ethan had the presence of mind to pull his little brother away, leaving himself open to becoming the target instead. That makes him a hero in my mind. And I'm not going to let him do such a brave and wonderful thing in vain. He's going to survive this. I know it."

"Oh, Griff. I pray you're right." She could barely get the words out over the pain in her heart. "I couldn't bear it if anything happened to him."

He turned to Willow and Brenna, hugging each one in turn. Then he led the way back to their trucks. Into his phone he said, "We're going to keep climbing, Chief. It's the only way he could be headed."

Even as they started away they could hear the drone of a state police helicopter approaching the spot where the bus had been abandoned.

And though Griff had offered Juliet all the comfort he could muster, the fear continued to grow in his mind that a madman like Sperry could fly into one of his famous rages, and little Ethan would be the one to pay the price.

CHAPTER THIRTY

Juliet scanned the road ahead of them in the fading light. "Do you think he's still ahead of us?"

"I'm sure of it." Griff brought the truck to a halt and stepped down to study the ground.

Brenna brought her truck to a rolling stop behind him, and she and Willow joined Griff and Juliet, who were studying the clearly visible tracks.

Willow glanced at Griff. "He doesn't seem to care if we know where he's going."

"He likes being in command. He's setting this up so we have no choice but to follow."

Brenna held a hand to shade her eyes as she stared at the trail heading upward. "What happens when we get to wherever he wants us to be?"

Griff turned back toward his truck. "Then we pray."

* * *

Chief Ira Pettigrew was highly agitated. Whenever that happened his words became a volley of staccato phrases aimed like bullets at the listener.

"Griff." His voice boomed over the cell phone. "Put me on speaker so Juliet can hear."

"She can hear you, Chief. I think all of Montana can." Despite his attempt at levity to ease the tension, Griff pushed the speaker button on his phone.

"The state police have been searching the room Heywood Sperry was renting at Karen and Kevin Becket's bed-and-breakfast. They found an entire album filled with pictures of you."

"Pictures of me?" The chief's words caught her by such surprise, she felt as if she'd just slammed into a brick wall and all the air had left her lungs. "I never posed for pictures. And especially for Heywood Sperry. I've told you, Chief, I didn't even remember the man when he came to my ranch with the offer of bringing a busload of veterans for therapy."

"Well, ma'am, he knew you. There are images of you pushing Buddy and your little boy in a wheelchair, apparently while Buddy was in the hospital. Pictures of you sitting at Buddy's bedside and feeding him. Pictures of you cradling your boy in your arms in a hospital chair beside Buddy's bed. And pictures of you assisting the hospital therapists, massaging Buddy's arms and back. There are hundreds of them. What the state police experts are saying is that it proves one thing—this guy is obsessed with you."

She pressed her hands to her temples, rubbing at the vicious pain that throbbed. "I didn't know. How could I? I never noticed him."

"There's more. The state police have been running a background check. Heywood Sperry was a munitions specialist in the Army. Served in Afghanistan until he encountered an IED on the road to Kabul that tore him up real good. Lost both legs and suffered severe head trauma. That's when he became a patient at the Veterans Affairs hospital in Tampa, at the same time as Buddy. He was there not only because of his physical problems but his serious mental disabilities, as well. His room was directly across the hall from Buddy's. Which means he could have been observing you for months without your knowledge."

"But why? There were hundreds of women there. Wives. Daughters. Mothers. Nurses. Doctors. I'm sure many of them were single. Why did he have to become fixated on me?"

"We may never know, ma'am. But this much we know—he had a reason for grabbing Ethan."

Something in his tone had Griff and Juliet turning to stare at one another.

"What does that mean, Chief?" Griff was watching Juliet's composure beginning to slip with every word the police chief spoke.

"Juliet, Sperry left a note on his computer. In it he gives you the chance to save your son. Of course, at the time he thought he was stealing the younger one – Casey. At any rate, his note says that when he reaches his destination, wherever that may be, he'll let Casey go if you agree to take his place."

There wasn't even a moment's hesitation in her response. "Of course I'll take Ethan's place, Chief. Oh, yes. I pray it's soon. I'll do that in a heartbeat."

"Hold on now. It may not be that simple. There are conditions. He expects you to come alone. No police. And especially no Griff. He expresses an extreme hatred for Griff Warren." The police chief paused. "Does he have good reason?"

Griff and Juliet spoke in unison.

"No."

"Yes."

Ira's voice sharpened. "Okay. You first, Juliet."

"Obviously he's jealous that Griff has . . . come into my life. But I can reassure him that, if he promises to release Ethan, Griff will no longer be a threat to him."

Ira said, "Now your take on this, Griff."

"Juliet's right about the jealousy. I was too blind to notice how deeply he resented me, because he seemed to resent everybody. But there's no way I'm going to stand back and allow Juliet to become his hostage, even for the sake of Ethan. There has to be a way to keep both of them from him, Ira."

The chief's voice softened somewhat, though he was still obviously agitated. "I agree, Griff. And believe me, we're all working on it. We have sharpshooters, but they have to be in position, and we don't yet know where this will end."

"This road leads to just one thing—the top of Bald Mountain. If you climb high enough, and cross down on the other side, you'll find yourself in wilderness. So I think it's safe to say that he's planning on crossing the mountain range and disappearing into the back country with his hostage."

"The state police agree. They have helicopters in the area. They're trying to stay behind the hills, to keep from spooking him. But we're tracking him every step of the way."

"How about the rest of my family?" Griff asked.

"Mad and Ash are in the family plane. We've given them coordinates. But, like the police, they're trying to remain invisible. Whit and Brady circled around you and have been driving that area for the past hour, along with a convoy of police vehicles, hoping to spot Sperry's truck."

Juliet's voice was eerily calm. "Now that I know where he's headed, I need to get there as quickly as possible, to spare poor Ethan any more agony."

"I understand what you're going through, Juliet. But remember that this man has already committed a string of serious crimes. He no longer has anything to lose. A man like that is a powder keg just waiting to explode."

"He has my son, Chief Pettigrew. I'll risk anything to save Ethan."

Ira could be heard sighing before he said, "All right, everyone. Mrs. Grayson is heading up Bald Mountain. If and when we hear from Heywood Sperry, we coordinate our plans and let her know what we want her to do." His tone softened a bit. "Keep your eyes and the lines of communication open. And hope that this madman stops soon. But when he does, no matter what he says, Juliet, you're not to allow yourself to become his hostage, even in exchange for your son's life. With this guy's hair-trigger temper, it could end up being a disaster for both of you."

"Hurry, Griff." Juliet was beyond listening. She had but one thought playing through her mind. Ethan was somewhere up ahead. She would do whatever it took to save him.

* * *

Mad was the first to spot the truck from the air. "There."

He pointed, and Ash studied the dark, custom-fitted truck with the oversized tires and a hydraulic lift in the rear. His communication system was tuned to the state police frequency. "Sperry's near the top of Bald Mountain. Not off in the brush as expected, but following the road."

A police expert's voice responded. "It all seems to fit. He torched the bus so we'd spot it. And now he's following the road up the mountain so we can follow. He didn't leave that note on his computer by accident. He knew we'd search his room and find it, along with the album. This is all part of a plan."

Ira Pettigrew's voice came over the frequency. "And just what is the plan?"

"He wants Mrs. Grayson to meet up with him. He wants her to offer to take her son's place."

"But why?" Ira sounded more puzzled than angry. "What's his endgame?"

"When I have the answer to that, Chief, I'll let you know," came the police expert's voice from headquarters. "The truth is, he may have no plan other than to run away with the object of his obsession."

Griff and Juliet had been following the conversation between the chief and the state police experts. Griff turned to Juliet. "You need to know that you're the one he wants, and you have been from the beginning. He's using Ethan to get to you."

She nodded. "Nothing matters right now except getting Ethan away from him."

"Listen to me, Juliet. You can't do that at the cost of your own life."

She shot him a look of complete disbelief. "Aren't you listening? I don't care about my own safety. I care only about saving my son."

"It's what we all want." He reached over and found her hands, twisted together in her lap, as cold as ice. "But if we're careful, we can get Ethan back without risking your safety."

"I won't listen to you, Griff." She was shaking her head. "I refuse to take the chance that Ethan could be hurt while we're being 'careful.'"

Griff spotted the truck on the side of the road up ahead. Into his phone he said, "Heywood Sperry is directly ahead of us. Can you see his truck?"

"We have him," came the reply from the command post. "Our helicopters are already dropping six sharpshooters up ahead. They should be within range in four to six minutes." The voice lowered. "Mrs. Grayson, you need to do exactly as told from this point on. Understood?"

"I understand."

"If he offers your son in exchange for you, insist that he release the boy, at least halfway, before you start forward. That will give our sharpshooters the opportunity for a clear shot, without danger to you or your son. Agreed?"

Juliet's voice was calm. "Yes."

"We want to prevent bloodshed. I would ask that the rest of you remain far back and as invisible as possible, to minimize the chance of being hit by stray gunfire. I don't want any dead heroes. Is that understood?"

Griff couldn't dispel the sudden knowledge that this

was all wrong. Everything had been too carefully chore-ographed. He'd been in enough military situations to know that in the heat of battle, nothing ever went as planned. Least of all the perceived strategy of the enemy.

In this case, Heywood Sperry was not only the enemy, but a fellow veteran who had faced the same wartime situations, and knew precisely what the other side was thinking and what they were planning.

Sperry had to know that the state police would bring in skilled marksmen. He had to know that Juliet would be willing to sacrifice herself for her son. He had to know...

Suddenly, it was all becoming clear to Griff.

"Chief—" Before Griff could state his feelings, there was a great, shuddering explosion beneath them and the truck in which they were riding was flying through the air. It tumbled end over end before coming to a sudden wrenching stop.

Even before the dust settled, the passenger door was yanked open and a knife flashed, cutting neatly through the seat belt holding Juliet. Through a shower of stars Griff reached out to steady her and found only air. She was no longer beside him.

He shook his head to clear it and could see, through the shattered windshield, Heywood Sperry on his scooter, dragging Juliet by the wrist. When he finally stopped, some distance away, she was kneeling in the grass, bleed-ing from the forehead, looking dazed and barely con-scious. Beside her, clinging fiercely to her was Ethan.

Griff managed to force his door open and jumped out of the truck before racing across the distance that sepa-rated them.

"I told you not to come." Sperry's voice was calm and

collected. He actually smiled. "I knew, of course, that you'd be here." He could have been talking about the weather as he continued in that same cool voice. "And that's exactly the way I planned it. Because now, marine, you get to watch the woman we both love die right in front of your eyes."

"You don't have to do this, Heywood." Griff's eyes were hot and fierce, studying the man as he looked for any way to free Juliet and Ethan. "I know how much you'd enjoy killing me. Let me take their place and I promise you I won't fight you."

"Aw. Isn't that touching? Sorry. I don't have any use for you. Now Jules..." Sperry gave a mad, high-pitched laugh. "I can think of a lot of uses I could have made of you."

"Jules?" She stared at him in horror. "No one but Buddy ever called me that."

"Yeah. That's what he told me. Just before he died." There was wild laughter as Sperry added, "Oh. Did I ever mention the fact that I was the one who pulled his plug? I figured he'd outlived his usefulness to me and to you, Jules."

Out of the corner of his eye Griff saw Whit and Brady crawling in the grass from the opposite direction. Behind them were half a dozen sharpshooters beginning to fan out.

Thinking quickly to hold Sperry's attention, Griff said, "We're alone up here, Sperry."

That had Sperry throwing back his head and roaring with laughter.

"You think that's funny?"

"Don't try to con a con, marine. I know the drill. While

you keep me talking, all those rifles are getting into position. But they don't scare me."

"All right. You're not afraid of the consequences. Why not tell me what this is about?"

"It's about a woman who was everything I'd ever wanted, wasting her time on a man who didn't appreciate her."

Juliet sucked in a breath on the pain his words caused. "Don't you dare talk about Buddy like that in front of his son. My husband was a hero."

"Some hero. Oh, sure. I heard his story from the medical people. He stayed with his plane rather than risk having it hit a playground full of kids." He snorted his disapproval. "And then what happened? After all you did for that man, massaging his arms and back, spoon-feeding him, working with the therapists hour after hour, while you cared for his kid and even carried another inside you, what did he do?" His face contorted with rage. "The damned fool died without a fight. You wasted all that time and energy and love on a guy who died, and all that time, you never even once noticed the guy in the next room who was willing to live for you. The guy who really loved you." He lifted her hand and stared at it. "And when I came to your ranch and offered to give you money to do for me what you did for him, you took my money, but you still never noticed me. And then, the lowest blow of all, you let this marine into your house. Into your bed. Into your heart." He continued holding her hand so tightly she cried out. "Oh, does that hurt? I guess I finally figured out how to get your attention. I killed your husband. I killed your foreman. And I killed MacKenzie's best friend. And now I have your son. And guess what? You'll remember my name now, won't you?"

"Is that all you want, Heywood?" Despite the pain and terror that gripped her, Juliet managed to lower her voice. Soften it. "Someone to care about you?"

His eyes narrowed. "I wanted you to look at me the way you looked at your husband all those long days and weeks and months in the VA hospital."

"I can do that, Heywood. But first, you have to let Ethan go."

He shook his head. "Don't try to fool me with that act. You're too late." His voice rose to a shout. "I'm not stupid. I know there are a dozen or more cops watching my every move. I know that you've got sharpshooters getting ready to take me out. You know what I have to say to that? Welcome, all of you. I'm ready to let you end my misery."

He released Juliet's hand while he leaned down to draw Ethan closer.

With a smile he spoke in a loud, clear voice. "Go ahead. See? I'm not holding them. You've got a clear shot. Put me out of my misery."

Griff watched as the shadowy figures stood and took careful aim.

All the hairs on the back of his neck bristled, and he struggled to figure out what was wrong with the picture in front of him.

Sperry, happily begging to be shot. Sperry, damaged veteran, wounded munitions expert.

Munitions.

He studied the front of Sperry's shirt. The slight bulge beneath it that could be concealing explosives.

"Stop!" Even though he knew it was too late, Griff was shouting at the top of his lungs, "Sperry's wired to blow and kill them all."

At the same instant that he saw the flash of gunfire, he leapt across the distance separating him from Juliet and Ethan and flung them aside before falling on top of them, shielding them with his body as a terrible explosion ripped through the clearing, lighting up the sky.

The scene erupted in chaos as the police and the MacKenzie family raced forward from all directions, shouting, swearing, forming a tearful circle around the charred earth and what was left of Heywood Sperry.

The impact of the explosion had left Griff dazed and disoriented. His shirt and one boot had been blown away, revealing a body bearing dozens of bloody wounds. A body lying as still as death.

Beneath him, shielded from flying debris, Ethan and Juliet crawled free. Seeing Griff's still, bloodied body, Ethan flung himself against Griff, burying his face in Griff's neck, sobbing as though his heart had been broken.

Ash pushed Mad across the clearing, pausing beside Griff and Ethan. The old man tried to lift the boy into his arms, but Ethan evaded his touch and clung to Griff.

The little boy's words were torn from a throat raw with tears. "Please, Griff. Don't die, Griff. Please don't die."

As the medics moved in, Griff stirred, hearing a voice from so far away, he wondered if he were merely dreaming.

It came again, louder. A little boy's voice that he'd never heard. And yet, even with his eyes closed, he recognized it as Ethan's.

"You can't die, Griff. Please."

Griff roused himself enough to whisper, "I...won't die, Ethan." He tasted his own blood and swallowed before managing, "I have...too much to live for."

Around them, nobody spoke. Nobody moved.

Despite the destruction, Juliet and the MacKenzie family knew in their hearts that they'd just witnessed a miracle.

CHAPTER THIRTY-ONE

Griff lay on the examining table in the Copper Creek Clinic while Dr. Dan Mullin and his assistant, Kate Kelly, treated the dozen or more burns caused by the explosion.

"Looks like you enjoy living dangerously," Dr. Mullin muttered.

"I may have, once upon a time. Now, I think I've had enough of it." Griff looked at Juliet, who was seated on the other side of the bed, clinging tightly to his hand. Her other arm was around Ethan's shoulders.

The little boy and his mother had been examined by the doctor and pronounced fit. Even the sedative administered by Heywood Sperry had now worn off, leaving no side effects in little Ethan's system.

The boy kept his gaze locked on Griff, as though afraid to look away for fear his hero might disappear.

Juliet, too, was watching the examination with fearful eyes.

When Dr. Mullin stepped aside, the door to the examining room burst open and the entire MacKenzie family surged forward, surrounding the bed.

Myrna released Casey's hand, and he flew across the room and into his mother's arms. After kissing her, he turned to his brother and wrapped his arms around Ethan's neck. "Myrna said you were safe, Efan. Were you scared?"

Ethan nodded.

"But you saved me from that mean man. How'd you know what to do, Efan?"

"I didn't. But Daddy told me I had to be the man of the family and always take care of the baby Mama had growing inside her. And that baby was you, Casey. So I knew I had to do something to save you."

Casey's jaw had dropped at his first words. "Efan. You're talking."

Ethan smiled for the first time. "I guess I am."

"How come?"

Ethan shrugged. "I don't know. The words just started when I thought the mean man killed Griff. You should have seen Griff, Casey. He was a hero just like Daddy, and I was afraid he'd die like Daddy did." He turned to look at the man in the bed before ducking his head.

Hearing him, Griff reached out and closed a hand over Ethan's shoulder. "There's only one hero in this room, Ethan. And that's you. You saved Casey and ended up being taken prisoner in his place. And that's just about the bravest thing anyone can do."

"I was scared," he said softly.

"We were all scared. But you kept your head, Ethan. You did the right thing. And that's what counts."

"So, lad." Mad wiped a tear from his eye before leaning close to squeeze Griff's arm. "The doc says you won't have to be flown to the hospital in Billings."

"Actually," the doctor remarked as he removed his gloves, "what I said was that Griff refused to be flown to Billings. There's a difference."

"Of course there is." Mad was grinning. "Despite the name, he's a MacKenzie. A little explosion isn't going to scare him."

"It had me scared." Ash stood at the foot of the bed with his arm around his wife's waist.

Brenna nodded. "When I heard those explosives going off, I was terrified."

"We all were." Whit glanced at his mother, who had dropped into a chair beside the bed. Before he could go to her, Brady was there, offering her a glass of water, his hand on her shoulder for comfort.

She accepted it with a smile of gratitude, and closed her hand over his.

Mad patted Griff's arm. "Will you be coming home tonight?"

"That's up to the doctor."

Dr. Mullin studied Griff's face before saying, "I'd prefer you have a night here. I'd like to keep an eye on some of those deeper burns, to watch for any sign of infection."

Griff nodded. "That's it, then. I'll come home tomorrow."

The others began settling into chairs and lounges, ready to stand guard over their own.

Seeing what they intended, the doctor shook his head. "You can't all stay through the night. This is a medical clinic. There are sick people here who need their rest. Kate will see you out now."

His assistant opened the door and stood waiting, giving them no chance to refuse. Grumbling loudly, the MacKenzie family got to their feet and began to say their good-byes.

After all but Juliet and her boys had left, Dr. Mullin turned to her with a smile. "If you'd like to stay the night, I can have Kate bring in another bed for your sons, and a lounge chair for you."

Surprised, she started to protest. "But you said—"

"That was for Griff's benefit, Mrs. Grayson. The MacKenzie clan can be overwhelming until you learn to take them in small doses. But I have a feeling that you and your boys would be the perfect medicine for Griff." He paused. "Shall I get that bed and lounge?"

She smiled and nodded. "Yes, please."

When all was in place, she watched as her two boys climbed into the bed and soon fell into an exhausted sleep. Then she stretched out on the lounge positioned directly beside Griff's bed. As she drew up a blanket, his hand found hers.

With a deep sigh of contentment, she absorbed the warmth of him, the strength of him, before drifting into sleep.

"They're coming." Whit hurried inside the ranch house to give the heads-up to Myrna and Mad, who had been cooking all day.

In honor of this happy homecoming celebration, Myrna had baked a four-layer vanilla torte, with whipped cream and strawberries between each layer, while Mad prepared a slow-cooked pot roast with all the trimmings. There were creamy mashed potatoes, garden peas, and a salad of greens and vine-ripened tomatoes, freshly picked and tossed with his homemade sour-cream ranch dressing.

The family gathered on the back porch as the truck driven by Juliet, and bearing Griff and her boys, rolled to a stop. The minute they stepped out, they were surrounded by MacKenzies with hugs and kisses and high fives.

Mad's wheelchair rolled down the ramp, and the old man held out his arms. Ethan and Casey launched themselves close for hugs before snuggling onto his lap for a ride to the house.

Even before everyone was inside, the police chief drove up. As he stepped out of his vehicle he called, "I hope I'm in time for supper."

"Perfect timing, Ira," Mad called as he shook the chief's hand.

When they stepped inside the kitchen, Griff breathed deeply before hugging Myrna. "This place has a smell like no other. I can't quite place it."

The old woman beamed. "Maybe it smells like home."

His smile was quick. "Yeah. That's what it is."

While Whit and Ash passed around cold longnecks, Myrna held out a tray of lemonade for Casey and Ethan.

Ash turned to Griff. "How are the burns healing?"

Griff shrugged. "Doc seems happy, so I guess they're fine."

Mad's head came up sharply. "Are you in pain, son?"

Griff was quick to shake his head. "Not enough to complain. Just enough to be uncomfortable."

The chief cleared his throat. "What you did up there on Bald Mountain was amazing, Griff. If you hadn't acted so quickly..." He took a sip of ice-cold lemonade. "Someone should have realized what that creep was planning."

"Someone did," Whit said. "And just in the nick of time."

The chief nodded. "That's just the point. All those experts, and not one of them thought about the fact that Heywood Sperry had cleverly planned his own death. He just wanted to add to our misery by having one of us pull the trigger that would end three lives in such a spectacular fashion. It would have had the rest of us reliving the horror of it for a lifetime."

Just hearing those words had Griff touching Juliet's arm, as if to assure himself that she was really here with him. "I had a sense that something wasn't right. That something was missing. And then I realized what it was. Sperry's anger. Always before, he hated everybody and everything. But there, he seemed almost euphoric about the fact that he had this captive audience. I added that to the fact that his specialty in the military was munitions, and I just knew he'd decided to put on a really big show."

Ira Pettigrew shook his head. "We'd have played right into his hands if you hadn't spoiled his carefully laid plans, Griff."

The group fell silent as they contemplated the enormity of what had happened.

When at last Myrna called them to supper, the family crossed the room, circling the table. Mad rolled his wheelchair to the far end and invited Casey and Ethan to sit on either side of him. Willow sat at the other end, with

Brady on her right and Whit on her left. Ash and Brenna, arms around each other, sat side by side, while the chief took a seat on the other side of Ash. Griff took Juliet's hand and led her to a chair across from Brenna before taking the seat beside her.

Throughout the long meal, while the others raved about the pot roast, the creamy potatoes, the garden vegetables, Griff ate in silence. When at long last Myrna began slicing the torte and topping each slice with vanilla ice cream, Ethan and Casey were the first to dive in.

"Cake, Griff?" Myrna said as she paused beside his chair.

"No, thanks, Myrna. I'll just enjoy my coffee."

"Juliet?" She held out a plate, but Juliet shook her head. "Not tonight, Myrna. But thank you."

With a raised eyebrow, the old woman circled the table, passing out dessert, and then refilling coffee cups.

Mad looked over at Griff. "You're quiet, lad."

Griff shrugged. "I guess it's all catching up with me."

"You're hurting?"

He shook his head.

"Having a flashback to a battle?" Ash asked.

Griff considered that before saying, "Maybe that's it. I never thought I'd be grateful for three tours of Afghanistan. But without it, I never would have been able to think like Sperry."

"All of us are grateful, too, lad." Mad watched as the family gathered around him. "There's an old Scottish saying: 'Every road we've taken leads us to where we need to be now.'" He paused to swallow down the lump in his throat. As always, when emotion took over, his burr thickened. "I hope you understand. 'Twas no accident that brought you to this place. You needed to be here, Griff Warren, with your family. Just as your family needed you to be here at this moment in time."

To keep the tone from growing too somber, it was Whit who deadpanned, "At least this time he didn't quote dear old Robbie Burns, his favorite poet."

"You'll not speak ill of Robbie," the old man said. Then, when he realized that his grandson was baiting him, he turned to the little boys beside him. "Remind me to tell you sometime about Robert Burns, Scotland's favorite son, lads."

Whit winked at the others. "Ah. Another generation about to be lectured on the beauty of poetry, especially that of the Ploughman Poet himself."

"It's glad I am to know that at least a little of those lectures have sunk into that fuzzy brain of yours, Whit MacKenzie. Now, lads"—Mad turned to the two little boys—"climb onto my lap and we'll go in the great room and sit by the fire while I tell you a bit about Scotland, and our beloved Robbie Burns."

"Maybe you could save that for another night, Mad." Griff was up and standing stiffly behind Juliet's chair. "I think it's time I got Juliet and the boys home."

Mad looked from Griff, who looked fierce enough to fight a dozen Heywood Sperrys, to Juliet, who appeared confused by this sudden turn. "If you say so, lad."

The two boys hopped off Mad's lap and walked over to stand on either side of their mother.

With her sons beside her, Juliet moved slowly around the table, hugging everyone and offering thanks for the lovely meal. Then she and Ethan and Casey trailed Griff out the door.

He held out his hand. "I know you drove here, but I'm feeling strong enough to drive now."

Without a word she handed him her keys and helped the boys into the back before settling herself in the passenger's seat.

On the long drive home, while Juliet kept up a running conversation with Ethan and Casey, Griff drove in silence. Finally, as the headlights swept the house, he pulled up to the back porch before turning off the ignition.

Juliet leaned back a moment, drinking in the view. "I really feared that I'd never see this place again."

"Yeah. I know what you mean." Griff's voice was hushed.

"It's funny. For the longest time this ranch didn't feel like home. I was here to keep a promise to Buddy. But now . . ." She shook her head, trying to take it all in. "Now it's really mine. Oh, I'm still not a rancher. But I deserve to be here." She turned to Griff. "Does that make any sense?"

"It makes perfect sense to me." He climbed out and circled around to help her and the boys down from the truck.

Keeping her hand in his, he walked with her up the wide porch steps, and stood aside as she opened the back door.

"Casey and Ethan, you can go upstairs and get ready for bed, and I'll be up in a few minutes to tuck you in."

The boys ran ahead, eager for their own beds after a night at the clinic.

"Would you like coffee?" Without waiting for Griff's reply, she plugged in the coffeemaker and set out two mugs.

Turning, she saw him staring out the window at the darkened sky. "You're quiet tonight."

"I've got a lot on my mind."

She walked up beside him. "Anything you'd like to share?"

He gave a quick shake of his head. "You've been through so much."

"So have you."

He turned then, and the look in his eyes had her heart dropping to her toes. "What's wrong, Griff?" she said.

He caught her hand. "Let's go upstairs and tuck in the boys."

She dug in her heels. "They can wait. Talk to me."

He shook his head and climbed the stairs, with Juliet trailing slowly behind.

In the bedroom, Ethan and Casey wore matching pajamas while sitting in the middle of the bed, jabbering.

When they caught sight of their mother and Griff, Casey said, "Efan told me that mean man said our daddy was a coward for dying."

Juliet gave a gasp of outrage.

Griff settled himself on the edge of the mattress. "That mean man was sick. His words were lies. You boys can both be proud of your daddy. He gave his life to save girls and boys just like the two of you. Your daddy really wanted to live and watch his boys grow up on his family ranch. And now that I've been here, I can see why. You're both very special. And so is your mama."

Ethan ducked his head.

Casey, never shy, said, "Efan told me you were a hero, too. And that you love our mama. Do you?"

For the first time in hours, Griff smiled. "I do, Casey. I

love her very much. As much, in fact, as I love the two of you."

"You do?" Ethan's head came up and he stared at Griff with a mixture of surprise and delight.

"I do." He caught their hands and lowered his voice. "I'm thinking of asking her to marry me. But I need to talk to you first." He turned to Ethan. "You said your daddy told you to be the man of the family. And to take care of your mama and baby brother."

"I'm not a baby," Casey protested loudly.

Griff chuckled. "I know that. But at the time, you weren't even born yet, so he thought of you as a baby." He turned back to Ethan. "So, I think, before I ask your mama to marry me, I should ask your permission. Now, I understand that you already have a daddy in heaven. But if it's all right with you, once we got married, I'd like to ask you and Casey to become my sons."

"Your real sons? Not just pretend?" Casey's eyes were wide.

"Real sons. We'd go to court and petition that I would be your father here on earth, and you would be my sons."

"Oh boy." Casey's face was wreathed in smiles as he turned to his brother. "Say yes, Efan. Ple-e-e-e-ease?"

Ethan looked from Griff to Juliet and back again before solemnly asking, "If you marry us, will Grandpa Mad be our real grandpa?"

Griff swallowed the grin that tugged at the corner of his mouth. "Definitely. I think it's safe to say he already is. But then it would be legal."

"Is legal important?"

At his solemn question, Griff nodded. "It is. You see,

I never had a legal daddy until it was too late. So I want everything between us to be legal."

The little boy's head nodded. "Okay. Mama, will you marry Griff?"

"Wait." Laughing, Griff stood and lifted Juliet to his place on the edge of the bed between Ethan and Casey, before getting down on one knee before her. "Juliet, I love you with all my heart and soul, and when I thought I was about to lose you, I knew my life would never be the same again. Now that you're safe, and Ethan's safe, will you do me the honor of becoming my wife?"

"Say yes, Mama," Casey prompted in a loud whisper.

She was laughing through her tears as she took Griff's face in her hands and stared into his eyes. "I was so afraid when we came upstairs. Afraid of what might be going through your mind. And my heart was so heavy, I thought I'd surely die if you were having second thoughts. And now..." She placed his hand over her heart. "Listen."

Both Casey and Ethan placed their chubby hands over Griff's.

"How does it sound?" little Casey asked.

"Like the best sound I've ever heard." Griff said solemnly.

"But you haven't said yes yet, Mama." The little boy was frowning with impatience.

"Yes." She glanced over to see both boys clapping and then jumping up and down in the middle of the bed. "Yes. Yes. Yes."

And then all she saw were Griff's eyes, shining with love, as he lifted her into his big, strong arms and swung her around and around before setting her on her feet and kissing her until she saw stars.

Casey was cheering.

Ethan was shouting her name.

And oh, she thought as she clung to this wonderful, brave man, and heard the joy in her sons' voices, weren't these just the best sounds in the whole world?

EPILOGUE

In the tiny town of Copper Creek, millionaire rancher Bear MacKenzie and his family were the local rock stars. This day, all eyes were on Bear's other son, Griff Warren, who was about to wed Buddy Grayson's widow, Juliet.

It wasn't clear which of that duo garnered more gossip: the pretty Juliet, who had heroically offered herself as hostage to free her little son from the clutches of a madman; or Griff, who had risked his life to save them both.

Dr. Mullin's assistant, Kate, proclaimed them the most glamorous couple since Ash MacKenzie had won his lost love, Brenna Crane. For a town that held outsiders at arm's length, it was quite a compliment that both Juliet and Griff had been warmly embraced by everyone. And this day, everyone was converging on the Grayson Ranch for the big event. Of course, one of the reasons for the size of the crowd, though no one would ever admit it, was to see this strange new ranch that was rumored to be more New Age health center than working ranch.

Griff stepped into the kitchen, where the air was perfumed with the most amazing, mouth-watering scents. It was a beehive of activity. Everyone, it seemed, had something to do.

Everyone but the potential groom.

A convoy of trucks from the MacKenzie Ranch had arrived at the Grayson Ranch earlier that morning in a cloud of dust. The leader of the pack was Mad, in his new, custom-fitted truck with a hydraulic lift. As the lift descended, a proud Mad pressed the button on his brandnew electric scooter and rolled up a ramp to the back porch of Juliet's house.

Griff, Juliet, and the two boys had stood waiting to cheer him on. Juliet hurried over to welcome him with a kiss. "Look at you."

"Looks like you've already mastered this new toy." Griff leaned close to hug his grandfather.

"Piece of cake." The old man opened his arms to the two little boys who danced across the porch and onto his lap. After hugs and kisses he said, "There's no time to waste, lads. We're here to start cooking."

Myrna had stepped from the second truck, carrying armloads of pots and pans and deep-covered dishes containing mysterious treasures.

Willow and Brenna whisked Juliet upstairs to prepare for the big day.

Ash, Whit and Brady ambled up from the barn. Ash dropped an arm around Griff's shoulders. "Come on, bro. The house is no place for a prospective groom."

Ash and Whit led Griff toward the barn. There were so many people milling about the yard, they had to stop every two steps to accept congratulations and make small talk. Most of the talk centered on the changes Juliet had planned for the Grayson Ranch. It would still operate as a cattle ranch, but now she would be welcoming wounded veterans and others who were handicapped in some way, not only for therapy, but to be employed as wranglers. The new name, Hope Ranch, signified the official change of direction.

Griff paused to talk quietly with Jackie Turner, who was there with his daughter and grandkids. Though he still bore the scars from his attack, the doctors in Billings had assured the old man that there seemed to be no ill effects.

"Creepers," he declared. "I can't wait to come back and be foreman of the new Hope Ranch."

"Captain."

Hearing his name, Griff turned to find Jimmy Gable seated beside a group of pretty young ladies who couldn't seem to do enough for the smiling veteran.

"Jimmy." Griff enveloped his marine buddy in a great bear hug. "So glad you're strong enough to attend my wedding."

"I wouldn't miss it." Jimmy's smile was as bright as the day's sunshine.

"Think you're strong enough to rejoin the Romeos?"

Jimmy shook his head. "Right after your wedding, I'm flying home."

"I thought you couldn't wait to get away from their smothering."

"Yeah." The young veteran chuckled. "I thought so,

too. But during my rehab I realized I actually missed all that smothering."

Griff glanced at the pretty women surrounding his friend. "This isn't enough?"

Jimmy winked. "Hey, they're great. But they're not family. I'm sure you know what I mean, Captain."

Griff nodded. "Yeah. Of course, I'm still learning about being part of a family."

He slapped Jimmy on the back, then continued to wade through the crowd until he reached the makeshift bar where Wylie and Nonie Claxton had taken charge of serving.

"Hey, cowboy." Nonie sidled over and planted a big kiss on Griff's mouth. With a laugh she said loudly, "I figure that's the last chance I have before you get yourself hitched." She gave a mock sigh. "Another MacKenzie bites the dust." She looped an arm through Whit's. "Looks like it's just you and me now, honey."

He leaned over and kissed her cheek. "Suits me just fine. This was all part of my evil plan. I've eliminated another of my competition."

While the others roared with laughter, Nonie went about serving the cold longnecks favored by most of the cowboys.

When Mad's electric scooter rolled up, the brothers looked surprised.

"Aren't you supposed to be cooking?" Ash asked.

"Got it under control. And my latest invention, a screen that fits over the steam tables so the guests can see the food, but flying insects can't land, is going to be the hit of the day."

His grandsons rolled their eyes.

"And since the women have ordered the wee lads upstairs for showers and fancy clothes," he added, "I have plenty of time to be with all of you." He turned to include Brady Storm, who had just joined them.

Mad eyed the beer in his grandson's hand. "No need for that swill today, lad." With a mysterious smile he said, "Follow me."

With Brady and his three grandsons trailing behind, he led the way along a new ramp that led to the fenced pasture. As the mares and their yearlings frolicked across the meadow, he produced a bottle of good scotch whiskey and five crystal tumblers. "Today," he said with that twinkle in his eye, "we drink the good stuff."

Brady poured and passed around the tumblers.

Mad lifted his in a toast. "To you, Griff. Our family is richer for having you with us."

With murmured words of approval they touched glasses and drank.

"To Juliet," Griff managed over the lump in his throat. "She and those two boys have given me something I never dreamed I'd have."

They touched glasses and drank.

"To Bear," Brady said solemnly.

Glasses clinked as they toasted and drank.

"Aye, lad. I feel my son here with us." Mad fought the tears that sprang unbidden to his eyes. "And I know that soon the authorities will unmask his cowardly killer." He drained his glass.

When he looked up, Griff handed him an empty tumbler and started away.

"Hey," Whit called. "Where're you going?"

When he didn't bother to answer, Whit looked around at the circle of men.

Ash put a hand on his younger brother's arm. "It doesn't take a genius, bro. All that talk about Pop has him needing to make sure Juliet and the boys are okay. It's probably part of the marine code."

"Or maybe," Brady said with a grin, "it's imprinted in his DNA. He is, after all, a MacKenzie."

"Oh, don't you both look perfect." Juliet knelt down and smoothed Casey's cowlick, then straightened Ethan's string tie, as Willow, Brenna, and Myrna looked on.

Both boys were dressed in brand-new denims and crisp white shirts with string ties, looking for all the world like an artist's rendering of Western cherubs.

Willow touched a hand to Juliet's arm. "Their mother looks just as perfect."

"Thank you." Juliet studied her reflection in the tall looking glass. Instead of a gown, she'd chosen a simple, ankle-length slim skirt of denim, with a pretty white silk peplum top, and her mother's pearl necklace and earrings. On her feet were cowboy boots. "Some of our guests will probably think this is too casual. But I wore a white gown once, and this time I wanted to wear something that would honor this ranch, this beautiful setting."

"You honor us all," Myrna said softly.

"And you've all been so warm and welcoming." Juliet drew her boys front and center. "Casey, Ethan, and I wanted to give you these gifts, before the ceremony."

The two boys stood holding their hands behind their backs, wearing the biggest smiles in the world.

Juliet embraced Brenna. "I never had a sister before. It's a wonderful feeling. And so, to my new sister..."

Casey and Ethan handed Brenna a small wrapped box.

She opened it to find a framed clay sculpture.

"It's you," Casey announced to everyone's laughter.

"I can see that it's me. I believe I have two very talented students." Brenna knelt down to kiss both boys.

Juliet hugged Willow. "Thank you for always being there when I needed you. It's nice to know I have a mother I can always call on."

Casey and Ethan handed Willow a slightly larger wrapped box.

She opened it to reveal a toy figurine of a woman on horseback holding a lasso.

"Mama says if we promise to work hard, you'll teach us to ride and rope as good as you."

"Oh, you sweethearts. I'd love to teach you both." She hauled them into her arms and kissed them.

Juliet turned to Myrna, wrapped her arms around her shoulders, and drew her close to press a kiss on her cheek. "So far I've gained a sister and a mother. With you, I've gained the very best grandmother in the world."

Casey and Ethan handed her a pretty wrapped box. Inside she lifted out a crude drawing of a woman holding two little boys on her lap while reading a book.

Casey proudly announced, "Efan drawed most of it, but I drawed the book 'cause I love the way you read to us."

"I've never received a nicer gift in my life." Myrna kissed both boys before lifting a finger to wipe the tear that squeezed from the corner of her eye.

Griff strode through the kitchen without a pause and took the stairs two at a time until he came to the closed bedroom door. Without bothering to knock he shoved it open.

And simply stared.

Willow, Brenna, and Myrna were gathered around Juliet. Seeing the fierce look on Griff's face, they began to close the circle, hoping to hide the bride from his view.

"It's all right." Juliet touched Willow's arm before holding out a hand to Griff. "The question is, are you all right?"

He caught her hand. Squeezed. "I'm fine now."

She studied the look on his face. "What happened?"

He shook his head as if to clear it. "Guy talk. Toasts. A mention of Bear, and I suddenly had this powerful need to see for myself that you and the boys were okay."

Her smile was serene. "I guess you'll always be our fierce guardian." She turned to the others. "I think Griff needs a moment alone with us."

Taking their cue, the three women stepped from the room, blowing kisses to Griff, Juliet, and the boys before closing the door.

Finally alone, Griff drew in a deep breath.

"Nerves, cowboy?"

He shook his head. "Not the kind you mean. But all that talk of Bear...my father..." He stopped, and finally found his smile. "But you're all here, and we're all fine."

"Yes, we are." Juliet touched a finger to his lips. "Thanks to you." She caught his hand. "Hey, cowboy. Ready to get married?"

He lifted Casey in his arms and caught hold of Ethan's hand. "The more important question is, are you boys ready to become my family?"

With shouts and cheers, they were beaming as they stepped out of the room and walked down the stairs and out into the fresh air, where an entire town was waiting and watching.

Griff took a moment to drink it all in. Summer had faded into glorious, golden days of autumn in Montana. Vast fields of wheat were being harvested and stored in barns and sheds for the coming winter. Sagebrush-covered foothills ascended up the sides of mountain ranges that were already capped with snow. Glacial lakes called to hot, tired cowboys bringing their herds down from the high country.

As they walked toward the big golden cottonwood where the minister stood waiting, they paused along the way so that Juliet could hug Jackie Turner. Griff paused beside Jimmy Gable's wheelchair and shook the veteran's hand. The young man's smile was as radiant as the sun.

They smiled and nodded at Dr. Dan Mullin and his assistant, Kate, and at Will and Nell Campbell, owners of the Boxcar Inn, and Karen and Kevin Becket, who ran the bed-and-breakfast in town, and accepted congratulations from Mason McMillan, long-time lawyer for Bear MacKenzie, and from his handsome, smooth-talking son, Lance.

Griff gave a thumbs-up to Whit and to Ash and Brenna, who would serve as witnesses, and to Willow and Brady, to Myrna, and to Mad, seated in his shiny new scooter.

And then they were standing in front of the preacher, speaking their vows. Griff looked at the two little boys and the woman who had suddenly become his whole world. His family. And he thought of all the crazy turns his life had taken.

If his mother hadn't lost her heart to a cowboy all those years ago, and decided, on her deathbed, to let Bear MacKenzie know he had a son, none of this would have been possible. If Juliet hadn't promised Buddy she would raise his sons on his family's ranch, they would have never met. And now ...

As the ceremony ended, he knelt down to gather the two little boys into a tight embrace. Lifting them both in his arms he kissed his new bride. Against her mouth he whispered, "Do you know what this means, to a man who's never had a family? Because of you and Ethan and Casey, I have a brand-new life."

He glanced at Mad and saw the old man's tears. And then suddenly Mad's words came to him. *Every road we've taken leads us to where we need to be now.*

As those words washed over him he knew, finally, a sense of complete peace.

CASEY'S AWFUL WAFFLES

INGREDIENTS:

- 2 cups all-purpose flour
- 1 teaspoon salt
- 4 teaspoons baking powder
- 2 tablespoons white sugar
- 2 eggs
- 1½ cups warm milk
- ⅓ cup butter, melted
- 1 teaspoon vanilla extract

DIRECTIONS:

1. In a large bowl, mix together flour, salt, baking powder, and sugar; set aside. Preheat a waffle iron to desired temperature.
2. In a separate bowl, beat the eggs. Stir in the milk, butter, and vanilla. Pour the milk mixture into the flour mixture; beat until blended.
3. Ladle the batter into the preheated waffle iron. Cook the waffles until golden and crisp.

Top with whipped cream and fresh strawberries, or the fruit of your choice.

Serve immediately.

While tending his cattle up in the hills, cowboy Whit MacKenzie is surprised to find a gorgeous woman riding out an approaching storm in his tent. It's clear she's hiding something, but Whit will do anything to protect her—even risk his own heart...

Please see the next page
for a preview of

*THE LEGACY OF
COPPER CREEK.*

CHAPTER ONE

MacKenzie Ranch—Today (Early Spring)

Whit MacKenzie pushed the last of the hay from the flatbed truck before parking at the mouth of Stone Canyon, where he'd left his horse tethered. Satisfied that the cattle milling about in the snow had enough food to keep them alive for the duration of the blizzard that had come roaring in across the mountains, he mounted old Red, his favorite roan gelding, and headed toward the range shack in the distance.

The cabin was one of several spread out along the farthest perimeters of the sprawling, thousand-plus acres that made up the MacKenzie Ranch. These cabins had been built in remote locations to accommodate the wranglers who tended the giant herds of cattle that summered in the high country. Equipped with a wood-burning fireplace and a generous supply of logs, and enough canned food to last a month or more, it was the perfect shelter from the unexpected spring snowstorm that had already dumped eight feet of snow and didn't look as though it would end anytime soon. Besides the snow that blanketed these hills, there was the wind, howling like a monster, creating giant drifts that slowed horse and rider's pace to a crawl. Whit found himself wishing he'd brought along a snowmobile instead of old Red as he faced into the blizzard, pulling the brim of his hat low before hunching deeper into his parka.

He'd spent all of his life here in Montana. Whether the temperature soared to a hundred or dipped to twenty below zero, Whit MacKenzie knew no fear of the elements. Snow in April or September, and wildflowers popping up before spring had a chance to melt the frost, were as natural as breathing.

Despite his parka and wide-brimmed hat, he couldn't ignore the bone-chilling cold and the snow lashing his face like shrapnel. The thought of a warm shelter and the bottle of good scotch he would splash liberally in his coffee as soon as he settled in, had him smiling. After nearly twenty hours of never-ending work, his body was desperate for sleep. He couldn't wait to slip out of his frozen clothes and into one of those thick blankets that covered the bunk beds.

Some cowboys couldn't bear the isolation of the hills, preferring instead to share a longneck and a bowl of gut-burning chili at Wylie's Saloon with the rest of the wranglers from neighboring ranches. That, and the promise of a quick tumble with one of the hot chicks who waited patiently in town for the weekend rush, was all they needed to get them through another week of endless chores.

For a loner like Whit, the thought of time away from his big, loud family was as necessary as food. As tempting as one of his grandfather's steaks cooked to perfection on the new grill he'd had installed in the ranch's giant kitchen. Without question, Whit loved his family. His mother, Willow, and grandfather, Mad. His brother Ash and Ash's wife, Brenna; and the half brother, Griff, he'd never met until this past year; and Griff's new bride, Juliet, and her two little boys, Ethan and Casey. Ever since the murder of their father, Bear MacKenzie, the family had drawn even closer. But maybe because of their closeness, he cherished his alone time more than ever.

In the lean-to that abutted the cabin, he unsaddled old Red and toweled him down before filling troughs with feed and water. Grabbing up his rifle and saddle bags, he trudged around to the door of the range shack and leaned a shoulder to it. Just as he did, he caught the unexpected whiff of wood smoke.

Inside he dropped the saddle bags and rifle on the floor before turning to secure the door.

"Move a muscle, you're dead."

He felt the press of something hard between his shoulder blades at the same instant he heard the whispered words.

"What the hell...?"

"I said don't move."

It was too late. On his lips was a snarl of rage as he turned to face his attacker. The beam of light from a flashlight momentarily blinded him. He lashed out with a fist, sending the flashlight clattering to the floor. "You'd better not miss on your first shot, because there won't be a second..."

Now that the blinding light had been deflected, the words died in his throat. The weapon was a broom handle. And the one holding it was a female, wrapped in a blanket, thick blonde hair tumbling over her shoulders and down her back in a riot of tangled curls. Her eyes, more green than blue, were wide with absolute terror.

His blood was too hot to cool, despite what he saw. In one smooth motion he knocked the broom aside, then pulled away the blanket, to assure himself she wasn't hiding a weapon underneath.

Too late, he realized his mistake. There was no weapon, and no way she could be hiding anything. Beneath the blanket he saw only the tiniest bikini briefs and a nude lace bra. And an expanse of pale firm flesh that had his throat going dry as dust.

Her eyes blazed, and he would have sworn he could feel daggers aimed straight at his heart.

Her words were pure ice. "Okay. You've looked long enough. You make one move toward me, cowboy, I'll rip your head from your shoulders and feed it to the wolves."

It was the sexiest voice he'd ever heard. Low, sultry, breathless. Sheer bravado? he wondered. Or calm, cool anger?

In his whole life, Whit had never backed away from a fight. And though the MacKenzie temper already had him by the throat, the look of her, like a cat poised to pounce, had laughter bubbling up instead of the expected anger.

"You and what army, honey?"

She tossed her head, sending that wild mane flying. "I'm not your honey. And if you think I'm just going to stand here and let some lecherous drifter—"

His hand shot out, gripping her wrist so firmly her head jerked back and her eyes went wide with undisguised terror.

"I warned you..." Her words died in her throat when he dragged her close.

"I heard you." His voice was little more than a growl. "Now *I'm* warning *you*. I'm tired. And I'm mad as hell. You're trespassing on my land. This is my range shack. You have one minute to explain why I shouldn't throw you outside in that blizzard and let the wolves have a tasty little meal tonight."

When he released her, she rubbed her sore wrist while backing away. "First I need my clothes..."

"Don't bother on my account."

With a half grin of appreciation, he watched as she turned away and snatched at a makeshift clothesline strung across the upper bunk, retrieving a pair of denims and a plaid shirt.

Whit couldn't help admiring the air of dignity about her as she slipped into the jeans and covered herself with the shirt, buttoning it clear to her throat before turning to face him.

He picked up the discarded flashlight and set it on the small kitchen counter, and noted the way she put the distance of the room between them, while her gaze darted to his rifle on the floor, then back to his face.

"Don't even think about it," he warned.

She stood, ramrod straight, her head high, her chin lifted like a prizefighter.

He watched her through narrowed eyes. "I didn't see a vehicle outside. And the only horse in the lean-to is mine. How'd you get up here?"

"I...walked."

"From where?"

"A friend's ranch."

"This friend have a name?"

"It's none of your business."

"Okay. We're done." He tossed his parka over the back of a wooden chair and, carrying his rifle with him, stormed across the room.

Turning his back on her he sat on the edge of the lower bunk and eased off his boots with a long, deep sigh, grateful that she already had a fire burning on the hearth.

She was so startled, she started toward him, then froze. "What are you doing?"

He never even looked up. "Making myself comfortable... in *my* cabin."

"But you can't..." She paused and tried again. "Look, I know you said this was your place and..."

"It *is* my place. And I'm in for the night."

"Can't you just go back to your ranch?"

He did look up then, his eyes reflecting the weariness he was feeling. "In case you haven't noticed, there's a blizzard raging out there."

"Are you calling a little storm a blizzard?" She stalked to the door and pulled it open. A wild gust of wind snatched it from her hand and sent it slamming against the wall. Within seconds snow billowed inward, dusting the floor at her feet.

With a look of disbelief she stared at the alien landscape outside. Everything was buried beneath mountains of snow. With great effort she forced the door shut and set the lock before turning to face him.

"I'm sorry. I didn't realize..." She took in a breath. "I know I should leave, but I don't see how I can."

Whit shrugged. "Looks like we're stuck with each other until it's safe to travel."

He crossed to the small kitchen counter and dumped bottled water into a coffeemaker, along with a measure of ground coffee from a package, before setting it on a grate over the fire. Soon the little cabin was filled with the wonderful aroma of brewed coffee.

"Want some?"

At her nod, Whit filled two cups and opened the bottle of scotch, pouring a liberal amount into his coffee. "Want a splash of this?"

She shook her head.

"Suit yourself." He handed her the cup and leaned against the small wooden table as he took a long, satisfying drink.

As the warmth snaked through his veins, he looked up to see her watching him.

Though he was far from feeling human, he managed a smile. "My name's Whit. Whit MacKenzie."

"Cara Walton."

"We'll talk in the morning, Cara Walton. I'm afraid if I don't crawl into that bunk right now, I'll be asleep on my feet."

He drained his coffee and set the empty mug in the sink before crossing to the bunk beds.

The blankets on the lower bunk were mussed, indicating that his uninvited guest had been sleeping there. No matter. He didn't have the energy left to climb to the top bunk.

There was no energy left for modesty, either.

Without a thought about the woman, he shucked his wet denims and plaid shirt, tossing them over the back of a chair to dry. "Sorry, Goldilocks. I'm reclaiming my bed. You'll have to make do up there." He nodded toward the upper bunk.

Rolling beneath the covers he set the rifle beside him, closed his eyes, and fell into an exhausted sleep.

Cara stood across the room, reeling from the assault on her senses. First there had been the sudden appearance of this stranger in the dark of night and their terrifying scuffle.

What were the odds that somebody would stumble on this cabin in the middle of nowhere? Not just somebody, but the owner. Wasn't this just her luck? And why should she be surprised? Nothing had ever gone right in her life. Everything that other people took for granted seemed just out of her reach. And in the past year, when she'd thought things were turning around, even the simplest things had been turned upside down. All her dreams, all her plans, snatched from her grasp. Add to that the fact that everybody who mattered to her was gone, she was feeling scared and extremely vulnerable, and she was feeling overwhelmed.

She'd thought this little cabin in the middle of nowhere might turn out to be her sanctuary, at least until she could sort out her future. And now this cowboy showed up just in time to send her packing yet again. And not just any cowboy, but one who'd casually undressed in front of her, displaying that perfectly sculpted body. For a moment she'd actually thought he was going to make a move on her. When he'd turned instead to the bed, she'd felt a wild sense of relief, until she realized that he'd meant it to be an insult. Proof that to him, she didn't even exist. A nobody. She was just an inconvenience that he had already dismissed.

She bit her lip as she watched and listened to the man

in the bunk. *Her* bunk, she thought with a rush of annoyance. She couldn't believe he was actually asleep. One minute he'd come rushing in like a tornado, and the next he was out like a light. But at least that fact gave her time to think. To plot her next move.

She'd heard the wind howling outside the cabin, of course. But she'd been so sound asleep, she'd never bothered to get up and check on the weather. Who would have predicted a blizzard in early April? Judging by the amount of snow she'd spotted out the door, it could be up to the roof by morning.

That little trick of Mother Nature's would require a change of plans. She couldn't just slip away while the cowboy slept. That meant that she might be forced to spend a day or more in these tight quarters with an arrogant, hot-tempered, gorgeous cowboy.

She finished her coffee and set the mug in the sink before turning toward the bunks. First things first. She would sleep while he was sleeping, so she would be fresh in the morning, and better able to stay one step ahead of him.

As she switched off the flashlight and climbed the rustic ladder to the upper bunk, she gave a grim smile. Wasn't it just her luck to be trapped in the wilderness with the most gorgeous man she'd ever seen, and be forced to find a way to keep him as far away as possible?

At least that part shouldn't be too hard.

After all, how much would it take to outsmart some backwoods, muscle-bound, hunky cowboy?

Fall in Love with Forever Romance

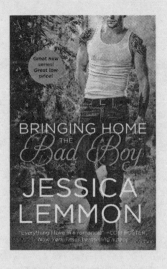

BRINGING HOME THE BAD BOY
by Jessica Lemmon

The boys are back in town! Welcome to Evergreen Cove and the first book in Jessica Lemmon's Second Chance series, sure to appeal to fans of Jaci Burton. These bad boys will leave you weak in the knees and begging for more.

HOT AND BOTHERED
by Kate Meader

Just when you thought it couldn't get any hotter! Best friends Tad and Jules have vowed not to ruin their perfect friendship with romance, but fate has other plans...Fans of Jill Shalvis won't be able to resist the attraction of Kate Meader's Hot in the Kitchen series.

Fall in Love with Forever Romance

FOR KEEPS
by Rachel Lacey

Merry Atwater would do anything to save her dog rescue—even work with the stubborn and sexy TJ Jameson. But can he turn their sparks into something more? Fans of Jill Shalvis and Kristan Higgins will fall in love with the next book in the Love to the Rescue series!

BLIND FAITH
by Rebecca Zanetti

The third book in *New York Times* bestseller Rebecca Zanetti's sexy romantic suspense series features a ruthless, genetically engineered soldier with an expiration date who's determined to save himself and his brothers. But there's only one person who can help them: the very woman who broke his heart years ago...

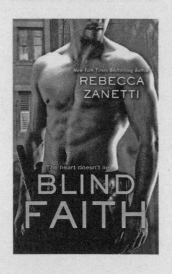

Fall in Love with Forever Romance

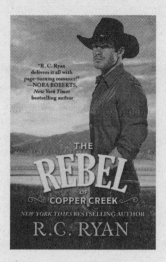

THE REBEL OF COPPER CREEK
by R. C. Ryan

Fans of *New York Times* best-selling authors Linda Lael Miller and Diana Palmer will love this second book in R. C. Ryan's western trilogy about a young widow whose hands are full until she meets a sexy and rebellious cowboy. If there's anything she's learned, it's that love only leads to heartbreak, but can she resist him?

NEVER SURRENDER
TO A SCOUNDREL
by Lily Dalton

Fans of *New York Times* best-sellers Sabrina Jeffries, Nicole Jordan, and Jillian Hunter will want to check out the newest from Lily Dalton, a novel about a lady who has engaged in a reckless indiscretion leaving her with two choices: ruin her family with the scandal of the season, or marry the notorious scoundrel mistaken as her lover.

Find out more about Forever Romance!

Visit us at
www.hachettebookgroup.com/publishing_forever.aspx

Find us on Facebook
http://www.facebook.com/ForeverRomance

Follow us on Twitter
http://twitter.com/ForeverRomance

NEW AND UPCOMING TITLES

Each month we feature our new titles
and reader favorites.

CONTESTS AND GIVEAWAYS

We give away galleys, autographed copies,
and all kinds of exclusive items.

AUTHOR INFO

You'll find bios, articles, and links to personal websites
for all your favorite authors—and so much more.

GET SOCIAL

Connect with your favorite authors, editors, and
other Forever fans, and share what's important to you.

THE BUZZ

Sign up for our monthly romance newsletter,
and be the first to read all about it.

VISIT US ONLINE AT

WWW.HACHETTEBOOKGROUP.COM

FEATURES:

**OPENBOOK BROWSE AND
SEARCH EXCERPTS**
•
AUDIOBOOK EXCERPTS AND PODCASTS
•
AUTHOR ARTICLES AND INTERVIEWS
•
**BESTSELLER AND PUBLISHING
GROUP NEWS**
•
SIGN UP FOR E-NEWSLETTERS
•
**AUTHOR APPEARANCES AND TOUR
INFORMATION**
•
SOCIAL MEDIA FEEDS AND WIDGETS
•
DOWNLOAD FREE APPS